Tropical Sins

Tropical Sins

by

Dana S. Cohen

Kingston Publishers Limited
1A NORWOOD AVENUE, KINGSTON 5, JAMAICA (W.I.)

Published by Kingston Publishers Limited
1a Norwood Avenue, Kingston 5, Jamaica
ISBN 976-625-037-5

Cover design by Ronnie Nasralla Promotions
Typeset by Expertype Graphix Ltd.
Printed by Stephensons Litho Press Ltd.

To my maternal grandmother, Anne Black – because she believed.

To MSG – for making all my dreams come true.

Acknowledgements

The process of writing *Tropical Sins* was a major force in my life for over five years. So many people were helpful in the research that it would be impossible to thank each and every one. However, there were a few people without whose help and support this book would never have become a reality.

My deepest thanks and appreciation to Cindy Doyle MacRae whose support, friendship and editorial advice were invaluable.

Thanks to Richard and Shiel Todd for sharing their love of blue marlin fishing. The experience was unforgettable.

Special thanks to Gordon and Diane Arnold, The Hon. Don Brice, Sandra Grant, Tinoa Rodgers, Liz McAdam, Jennifer Laing, Benni Blitzblau, Maxine Williams and the Hon. Hugh Hart for their unwavering support. The late Custos Val Parnell was very helpful and provided me with fascinating information on pimento.

I must also extend a personal thanks to the staff at the Jamaica Information Service, particularly the Regional Services Department and Library staff. Without their assistance in research, *Tropical Sins* would not have had the same depth and degree of authenticity.

A mention must be made of the Sandals Resorts, particularly the assistance of David Roper who was always available for my infinite questions. My appreciation to the staff at Trident Hotel and Villas who were always hospitable during my many weekend sojourns while working on the book.

My gratitude to my family who supported me emotionally through the many drafts and frustrations that the writing process involves.

Thanks to Dana Stewart of International Voyager Media who was so helpful in translating the manuscript through three computer languages. And Samantha Hughes, whose extraordinary patience and generosity were greatly appreciated.

And to Kim Robinson-Walcott – thanks for your time, helpful suggestions and patience in the editing of this manuscript.

Most of all – to the people of the island of Jamaica – for your warmth, wicked ways, days filled with sunshine and nights filled with tropical sins.

Chapter 1

The weather was magnificent. The sky was a baby blue canopy gently caressing New York on its first spring day. Jacqui took a deep breath, enjoying the hint of freshness in the air. The city had been cleansed, the grey squalor that had permeated everything had disappeared.

Overnight, Manhattan had been transformed from a vulgar old woman of winter to the smiling fresh ingenue of spring. The newspaper hawker at the busy East Side corner watched Jacqui, one of the bright spots of his morning, as she walked down the block towards him.

"Extra! Extra! Read all about it! King Does it Again!" he shouted hoarsely as he had done every morning for the past thirty-four years from the exact same spot. He watched Jacqui pause to sniff the yellow daffodils and pink tulips in the white plastic buckets on the sidewalk outside the Korean market. The sun picked up the reddish highlights of her hair, accentuating her natural elegance.

Handing him a dollar, she quickly scanned the headlines before she looked up at him and smiled. He hesitated as he passed her the change, wishing he was thirty years younger.

"How about going dancing tonight?" he asked with a twinkle in his eyes.

"Sure. Pick me up at eight," she said, winking playfully at him.

Jacqui crossed 54th Street to the Third Avenue Coffee Shop. The smell of frying bacon and fresh coffee overwhelmed her senses. The shop had been in the same place since the end of World War Two. Its linoleum floors were peeling, there were plastic flowers on the counter and vintage Coca Cola signs on the walls, but the coffee was great, the food fresh, and Gus, the owner, was a character.

Taking the first seat at the counter, next to the window with the half-drawn blind, Jacqui took a quick glance at the diner's patrons. Sitting next to her was a leonine-haired man wearing an immaculately tailored pin-striped suit, reading the *Wall Street Journal*. He vaguely resembled a man who had been investigated by the Security Exchange Commission for insider trading. In the booth behind were two bums, who looked like they had spent the night sleeping on a subway grate in Grand Central Station. On her right, there were several very chic New York ladies, two construction workers and a Madonna lookalike who was sitting next to a woman with a beehive hairstyle, wrapped in a bright pink hair net.

Moving down the counter, Gus was pouring coffee, picking up money and shouting orders. Several years before, threatened with huge rent increases, he had nearly been forced to close the diner. When Gus told Jacqui about the impending closure, she went into action, convincing her editor, Josh Travers, that *Elegant Travel* should do a story on the Classic American Diner. The Third Avenue Coffee Shop got a rave review and Gus suddenly became an overnight celebrity.

"Good morning, Gus," said Jacqui as he poured her a steamy mug of coffee. "How's business?"

"Not too bad. Lunch is picking up," he said, looking around at the crowded diner, the bells of his 1922 cash register ringing constantly in the background. "Where are you off to next?" he asked.

"I don't know yet, but today's the day I find out."

"Don't forget to send me a postcard," he said as he eyed the wall above the counter. "I want to keep my collection going." Behind Gus, taped to the wall, there were at least two dozen postcards from all over the world. Most of them were from Jacqui on her many trips as a writer for *Elegant Travel* magazine.

"This time I want a framed picture of the cover," he added, moving swiftly down the counter to take another order.

* * *

Geoff Roth, president of GRI Advertising, sat in his offices on 59th Street, overlooking Madison Avenue. The glass desk top held a set of black ivory pencil holders and a matching ashtray. Straightening his Italian silk tie, he pulled a Marlboro cigarette out of a fresh pack and lit it with his Cartier lighter. Taking a deep draw, he relished the first burning sting of the nicotine as it hit his lungs.

He licked his lips and took a sip of coffee. His main client, Martin S. King, also known simply as The King, had made the headlines once again with his daring takeover of another Atlantic City casino. He was not only a genius in the real estate market but he had a shrewd sense of timing for the stock market. He and the media had an ongoing love affair as America watched one of the sons of the streets of New York rise to become one of the richest men in the United States.

Despite his wealth and trappings of power, the resorts and casinos bearing his name that were the most sumptuous in the world, Marty King was a simple man. He never missed bringing the challah, the Sabbath bread, home for every Friday evening meal or forgot his humble beginnings on the Grand Concourse as the son of an immigrant labourer who still spoke more Yiddish than English. Having Marty King as a client ensured Geoff's own imminent rise to power.

Glancing at the other headlines, he read with interest

that there had been a dramatic rise in cocaine transshipments through Jamaica. The United States Drug Enforcement Agency was working with the Jamaican government to stop the steady flow of drugs from the island. There was no comment from either side about the reported rise in illegal weapons but it was feared that this was linked to the increased violence of the Jamaican posses, operating in more than a dozen cities in the United States.

Geoff watched his cigarette burn into one long ash before he made his plans. Consulting his electronic diary, he buzzed his secretary. Without a good morning or a glance in her direction, he began to fire instructions.

"Fax this article to my contact in Jamaica. Cancel my noon appointment at the Plaza. Reschedule that for tomorrow. Call the King Casino in Atlantic City and confirm my attendance at this evening's function," said Geoff.

"Yes, sir," said the secretary meekly, anxious to retain her job longer than the last month's two secretaries.

"I want you to make a reservation for me to Grand Cayman for tomorrow night, returning the next day through Miami," continued Geoff. "I'm leaving for Washington right now. Call Congressman Ogilvy's office and tell him I'm on my way. Did the list of *Elegant Travel's* quarterly stories come in?" He glanced up, his cold hard grey eyes registering no emotion.

"Yes, it did," she responded, handing him a piece of paper. "Chile, Egypt and Jamaica."

After she left the office, he opened the bottom drawer of his desk with a special key and extracted two folders. He locked them in his briefcase, carefully relocking the drawer. Without a backward glance, he grabbed the jacket of his one-thousand-dollar custom-made suit and left his office.

* * *

4

Gary Gordon, a visitor to New York but by no means a stranger, walked by Gus's diner. Slowing down, his eyes took in a luscious pair of legs in the window. The Venetian blind shielded the face, but what little he saw froze him in his steps.

He watched Jacqui slip her right leg into a red heel, accentuating her toned calves. In what seemed a moment of excruciating slowness, she finally put on the other shoe, running a slender manicured hand with long supple fingers along her leg. That action sent a momentary fire-burst through his body.

Jostled out of his trance by a passing pedestrian, Gary moved on with the memory of those long shapely legs burning in his mind. "No time for any fun or games today," he warned himself as he moved towards Lexington Avenue with a distinct swagger in his walk.

* * *

Jacqui pushed through the herd of humanity crowding the sidewalks, entering the Citicorp Building from Third Avenue. She squeezed herself into the elevator between a short fat woman in tennis shoes and a six-foot hunk who reeked of Aramis, and silently ascended to the *Elegant Travel* offices on the twenty-seventh floor. She slipped into her office quietly.

Taking her notebook, Jacqui walked down the soft mauve and grey halls sparsely adorned with strategically placed tropical plants.

The corridors were lined with pictures from *Elegant Travel* magazine covers. She paused at the cover picture of the Royal Mile in Edinburgh where she had covered the International Jazz Festival.

Jacqui knew that her meeting with Josh Travers, her managing editor and mentor, would be like jumping out of a plane without a parachute. He scrutinized everything carefully before he made his decisions, but then expected his writers to plunge right in. Plunge she would, wherever he would send her. She only hoped he would not penalize her for her past mistakes.

"Jacqui, I'm glad you are back. Josh is driving me crazy this morning," said Pat Huxley, Josh Travers's personal assistant. In his usual style, Josh had dumped his entire briefcase on her desk, confident it would somehow be sorted out. Receipts, dry cleaning bills, notes on assignments, minutes on meetings were all on pieces of paper of various descriptions, including matchbook covers and cocktail napkins. Jacqui was convinced that Pat was responsible for Josh's day-to-day functioning.

"I'm trying to make arrangements for Chile, but the whole country is on strike. Airlines, phones, pilots, hotels, teachers, police and I don't know who else. Is there anyone left? I'm trying to book a ticket for Josh. It starts in Ireland, then there's France, Israel, Miami, Nassau, Mexico, to name a few stops," said Pat.

"How long is the trip?" asked Jacqui.

"Thirteen days," said Pat, shaking her head. "I don't know how he does it." At that moment, Josh's door flew open, framing a pale man holding a stack of files. Heaving them on Pat's desk in one fluid motion, he beckoned Jacqui into his office.

"We have a lot of ground to cover this morning because you are leaving first thing tomorrow," he said as he seated himself away from the three-window panorama of the East River. "I'm sending Matthew to Chile. He did an excellent job on the winter review of ski resorts out west." He began to unbutton the cuffs of his shirt. "I just pray the Chileans stop striking long enough so he can get the story. Now Jacqui – you are heading south as well. Not to Egypt; I know that you have an itch to get back to North Africa after your review of Morocco, but I have something that requires a sensitive touch, a very delicate assignment."

Jacqui shifted uncomfortably in her chair, remembering that the last 'sensitive' assignment she had received had had her freezing to death in Montreal in the middle of winter.

"You're going to a place where no matter how late you are you will still be on time. And if you are very, very lucky you may even see time stand still," Josh said mysteriously as he reclined in his chair.

He watched as Jacqui sat there impassively. No emotion showed on her face, but her brown eyes tinged with yellow gave her away. He knew she was anxious, especially after the King Casino scandal when the magazine was accused of taking bribes. If it hadn't been for his intervention with Fiona Geller, the editor in chief, Jacqui would have been fired. Fiona knew as well as he did that Jacqui had built a loyal following of readers and so agreed to a suspension. The best he could do was get her a temporary job while she waited out the time like a prison sentence.

"Pack your bikini and suntan oil. You're going to Jamaica," said Josh, watching her whole face light up. He understood only too well how easily Jacqui could be manipulated. "You remember that last year we ran a cruise/island supplement," he continued. "It featured popular ports of call in the Caribbean with sidebars on selected hotels. Elizabeth Hartley, our correspondent out of Miami, covered Jamaica and the Cayman Islands. She gave one of the hotels, The Falls at Ocho Rios, a poor review, especially in terms of management." He handed her a file.

'The Falls boasts nicely furnished rooms and beautiful facilities,' Jacqui read, 'but don't expect too much from the service. The management is shoddy at best. Fall for The Falls? Think twice.'

"Quite a commentary," she responded, knowing that by tomorrow morning she would have memorized everything inside.

"It gets very messy," said Josh as he rolled up his sleeves. "Fiona got a very strongly worded letter from Tropical Properties, the parent company for The Falls, demanding a retraction and a full apology. A lawsuit has been threatened. I just received a letter from Heart, Myerson and Patterson, a law firm in Kingston, with a thinly veiled threat to sue us into the next century if the magazine doesn't print a retraction. I hate bowing to blackmail but the magazine has received the most responses discrediting one of our reviews in our history.

"We've been steadily losing our market share for the past two quarters to *Condé Nast Traveller* and *Travel and Leisure* magazine. *Elegant Travel's* credibility with our readers and advertisers demands another review. I should add, not just another review – but an unbiased and credible story."

"How are we going to do that?" asked Jacqui.

"We will do Jamaica as a cover story with sidebars on three different types of resorts – villas, cottages and all-inclusive properties. You are scheduled to stay at The Falls first – before they discover your affiliation with the magazine, then Pimento Hill Golf and Yacht Club and the Blue Marlin Inn," said Josh, pulling off his tie. Jacqui knew that in the course of any discussion with Josh he always managed to do a slow striptease.

"When you're at The Falls, I want you to keep your association with the magazine quiet. I don't want the management to know they are being reviewed. We'll prepay your bill through your personal account. They usually look for a couple so sending you down on your own immediately may be our best shot at objectivity. Trevor Berry, the editor of the *West Indian* magazine, will be meeting you at the airport and making your inland arrangements. It's our correspondent magazine in the Caribbean," he added, handing Jacqui her ticket. "A great deal rests on this story. We can't afford to lose any more market share, or a lawsuit."

"How long is the assignment and what are you looking for?" asked Jacqui, growing excited. It was the break she had been praying for.

"First of all, plan on being away at least three weeks. Next – this isn't purely a holiday atmosphere like some of the smaller islands. Jamaica is more than a beach. It's a pretty complicated little country. Nothing is what it appears to be. There is a soul to the island. It has a character all its own and I want you find it.

"Cover the resorts, but I don't want to make it too obvious that we are responding to public pressure. I want an overview of the country so take time to stop in the villages, watch the sports, listen to the music, whatever it takes. Discover the individual magic that makes this place so special. Touch the island life – taste the spicy food, smell the pungent odours and feel the balmy nights."

Josh had an onion theory about writing. Peel back each layer and notice the changes, then write about the differences. He gave this pep talk to each of his contributing editors to help them establish the mood and tone of the story.

"I've gotten some positive feedback on the story you wrote about Texas just before your suspension. I ran it last month," he said, hoping to give her some confidence. Jacqui was a rare talent as long as she could be properly directed. He had sent her to Montreal to calm an irate hotelier and not only did she charm him, but she came back with a survey on the best hot chocolate that became the number one story that year. He needed her and the enormous following she had built.

"Just one other piece of news, I guess," Josh added, catching Jacqui's eye. "I thought you wouldn't mind the irony. I got a call from Geoff Roth. It seems that the King Organization wants to increase their print advertising with the magazine next year."

"I don't believe it," said Jacqui, the colour draining from her face.

"Your old friend has also persuaded the Desert Palm Resort in California to offer a publicity contract to the winner of the Jamaica Open Golf tournament that will be held at Pimento Hill in Montego Bay," said Josh. "So I'm afraid that Geoff Roth may be at Pimento Hill when you're there. I hate to be telling you this, but I think you should know for your own good. I saved you once, but I don't think I could do it a second time."

He continued talking but Jacqui was lost in thought. The bitter memory of her suspension from *Elegant Travel* because the King Organization had threatened to pull all their advertising filled her with a sense of dread and anxiety. Marty King was not too happy about paying bribes to reporters for positive stories and told Fiona Geller, the editor in chief, in very explicit terms. Though she denied any wrongdoing it was difficult to explain how fifty thousand dollars had miraculously appeared and disappeared from her bank account.

Every time she thought about Geoff, she felt anger and regret. It had been six weeks of madness – a luxury she couldn't afford. It had nearly cost her a career she loved and her professional integrity. By the time she realized that she was just one of the stepping stones on his rise to the position of power and influence that he sorely craved, Geoff was already on to his next victim, chosen as carefully as he had chosen her. She swore it would be the last time she would mistake personality for character.

"Jacqui, are you listening?" asked Josh, shifting a stack of files on his desk.

"To every word," said Jacqui with a smile she didn't feel

as she shook her head, her chestnut hair touching her neck.

"You have a lot to do before you leave tomorrow. I want you to bring back the best September issue we've ever done. Try not to involve the magazine in any more controversy, if you please," said Josh, his attention already on other matters.

As Jacqui stood to leave, Josh called her back. "By the way, Jamaica has a way of reviving the spirit and soothing the soul. Maybe it can work its magic on you," he said, in a rare moment of kindness.

Chapter 2

Gary Gordon woke at five a.m.. He watched the rain trickle down the window of his tenth floor suite at the Algonquin Hotel in Manhattan. He was tired, but he couldn't sleep. The phone rang once, startling him. Reaching over, he turned on the bedside lamp.

"Gordon, where have you been? I've been looking for you for days. You should be up and out of bed," said Ainsley Gunther, one of Gary's oldest friends.

"Ainsley, wha' 'appen?" said Gary, wide awake.

"Truth be told I'm as busy as hell and up to my neck in problems," said Ainsley. "Nothing that can't be handled."

"Isn't it your birthday soon?" asked Gary.

"Tomorrow. One month to the day after yours, remember? I've enjoyed this month thinking that you're in your forties while I'm still in my thirties," he said, laughing. "By the way, my call to you at this ungodly hour isn't to get birthday wishes out of you. When are you coming home?"

"Tomorrow. Is there a problem?" asked Gary.

"I wouldn't call it a problem but it's a matter that requires your immediate attention," said Ainsley. Gary immediately picked up the inflection in his friend's voice.

"I'll be there this afternoon," said Gary.

"I'll leave a message for you," said Ainsley. "By the way, has the Algonquin changed much? Is Tony still in the Blue Room?"

"He's still here and the hotel is even more beautiful since the restoration. He's plagued me with reminiscences of our visit twenty years ago," said Gary.

"I recall that they kindly asked us not to return," said Ainsley, laughing.

"They kindly asked us not to return together," Gary retorted. "See you soon." He hung up the phone, swung his muscular legs onto the plush carpet and reached for his briefcase, extracting his black book. He dialled a number, and waited for a moment before identifying himself and making his request. When he put down the phone, he ran his hand through his curly hair, realizing he needed a haircut, and plodded to the shower.

* * *

"Freddy, please don't get upset. I don't want your blood pressure going up," said Jacqui as she tried to shake the excess rain off her umbrella and raincoat. "I know I am a little late, but we can still make the flight, can't we?" she asked innocently.

"I don't know what you call a little late, but whatever you call it, you picked a hell of a day for it," Freddy said gruffly as he inched his way through the snarled traffic, the windshield wipers ineffective against the pounding rain. The radio news was full of reports of flooded highways and accidents from the city, the island, New Jersey, Westchester and Connecticut.

They hit a bottleneck on the Grand Central which delayed them for some minutes before the traffic began to inch along; then, as they approached the airport, they plodded through a sea of yellow cabs and limousines. When they finally reached the departure gate, Jacqui jumped out of the limo in her bright yellow raincoat and brought her fingers to her lips, letting out a piercing whistle.

A porter dressed from head to toe in blue rubber moved towards her. Just as he reached her side, a yellow cab pulled into the space behind Freddy's limousine, splashing her with cold, muddy water. Muttering angrily, she caught a glimpse of a tall man running from the cab, carrying a royal blue leather garment bag over his shoulder.

She tried to wipe the mud from her raincoat as she followed the porter to the x-ray check-in area. He pushed her bags to the front of the line, ahead of a woman laden with gold jewellery and accompanied by several large boxes, a barrel and a baby. She tipped the porter, noticing a tall, broad-shouldered man standing at the counter. As she leaned forward to push her luggage on the scale, his fresh, clean masculine scent captivated her. Her eyes took in the fine cut of the sports coat that moulded his body, outlining his rippling muscles, as he moved from side to side impatiently.

"I'm terribly sorry, sir," Jacqui overheard the ticket agent tell the man. "There are no available seats in first class or any other section on the flight. I can give you a first-class seat on the next flight." Her long red manicured nails tapped on the console. "That is the best I can do. You don't have a reservation."

"I see," said Gary. "I was assured that there would be a seat on this flight."

"No sir. I've checked twice," said the ticket agent.

"Thank you for your help. You've been most courteous," he said graciously, moving across the hall to the pay phone.

Jacqui followed his movements, taking in his deep golden colour and rugged features. As he dialled, he suddenly glanced up and caught Jacqui's eye. She was captured in a pool of emerald. Amused at the source of her fascination, the woman behind tapped her gently to indicate it was her turn.

Jacqui presented her tickets and documents to the agent and was promptly handed back her boarding pass. "The

14

flight leaves in twelve minutes from Gate 26. That's about a half a mile. If you want to make the flight, you had better run like you're trying out for the Olympics," said the ticket agent.

"Twelve minutes," said Jacqui, setting her watch. "Please tell them not to leave without me. I'll make it."

After passing through security, she pulled the belt of her stained yellow raincoat and strapped her purse around her shoulder. Her brisk pace turned into a marathon run. She jumped over suitcases, banged into an elderly man and pushed through a group of travelling nuns. She passed Gate 18 with less than five minutes left. Sweat was pouring down her face and her breath was coming in short spurts. It took all her reserve energy to sprint the last few gates.

"Jamaica," she said breathlessly, showing her boarding pass at the gate, praying she hadn't missed the flight. Her stub was pulled and she was quickly motioned through the passageway as the duty-free liquor was being delivered. For once the forced dry air of the plane felt good on her sweaty face. She had run for a lot of flights in her career, but this was a very close call.

After she was directed to a first-class seat, she took off her raincoat, stowed it in the overhead compartment and sat down, trying to catch her breath. The baggage compartments were being sealed and the flight attendants were making all the necessary preflight arrangements.

Just before the passenger door was sealed, a senior airline executive boarded the plane. He spoke briefly to the flight attendant and they both looked in Jacqui's direction before approaching her.

"Miss Devron, I am afraid there is a problem. You were erroneously assigned this seat," explained the airline official. "If you would be so kind as to collect your things and follow me."

"I'm sorry, but I have to be on this flight," said Jacqui,

wondering why they didn't pick on someone else.

"Please, Miss Devron. We are terribly sorry about the inconvenience, but this is a priority seat and your reservation was made only yesterday. I must ask that you gather your things. We can't delay this flight any longer."

Jacqui was furious and she felt her cheeks redden with embarrassment. With several pairs of eyes on her, she flipped open the overhead compartment and grabbed her raincoat, following the airline official off the plane.

Gary watched Jacqui walk down the ramp. His eyes flicked slowly down her body, taking in her thick brunette hair tinged with red highlights, the bedroom eyes and long elegant neck. Her red cotton shirt and miniskirt clung suggestively to her body and her long lean legs seemed to go on forever. That was his weakness. She had the look he liked – totally put together without even trying. He moved his gaze back to her face. Her intense brown eyes, tinged with yellow, were narrowed in anger as her very essence hit him with a bolt of pure sensuality.

"Enjoy your flight," said Jacqui coldly, stopping right in front of him. "You'll be sitting in my seat."

"I'm sorry if you were inconvenienced," said Gary amiably, reaching down to pick up his royal blue garment bag. "I'm sure the airline will make up for any difficulties." He wondered if she was one of those typical American tourists who invaded the island by the hundreds each week looking for fun in the sun.

"Well, thanks for making this a great morning. Where do I send my cleaning bill to?" she asked, holding up her raincoat.

Gary pursed his lips to suppress a smile, but he couldn't hide the laughter in his emerald eyes as he boarded the plane.

"Why do attractive men think their shit doesn't stink," she fumed silently, her huge brown eyes narrowing with rage as she followed the airline executive. "Who does that man think he is?" she asked.

The steward nodded his head in agreement, wondering who was the man who could force the largest U.S. airline with the best record for ontime performance to delay the flight.

* * *

Two hours later Jacqui was on another flight with a host of bleary-eyed honeymoon couples who looked dazed and half drunk. It was only when the doors were sealed and the plane taxied down the runway that Jacqui settled back in her seat. She watched the New York skyline fade from view as the green Atlantic swelled ahead of her.

Opening her bag, her fingers touched on the worn, cracked binding of *The Drifters* by James A. Michener. She took it out and read the inscription from her father that brought back memories of her fourteenth birthday, when a blizzard had buried the flat plains of Ohio under ten feet of snow for a month.

'To my daughter Jacqui – Fly high and proud. May your spirits soar with the eagles. Your loving father – Jace Devron.' Tears filled her eyes for a moment. It had been a perfect gift. She had read until her eyes burned and she could recite passages by heart. For months, she dreamed of nothing else but the sun-drenched beaches of Torremolinos, drinking red wine and watching exotic flamenco dancers.

From her first eventful meeting with Josh Travers seven years ago, she had visited more countries than she had ever dreamed possible. Travelling had become her way of life, filling her with an intoxicating sense of freedom and purpose. When she was suspended, Jacqui had felt as if she was a bird whose wings had been clipped.

The cover story on Jamaica was the most important

assignment of her career. She had to prove she was a credible journalist and confirm Josh's unwavering faith in her. This was her chance to redeem her reputation.

The sea changed from a vivid green to a pale blue as Kingston swelled into view, nestled by rugged mountains that gently encompassed her sprawling mass. The island emerged from the sea with a magnificence she had seldom seen anywhere in the world.

As she walked down the ramp, a blast of heat overwhelmed her. She felt as if her body had been put in a microwave on high. It was so humid that Jacqui felt as if she would melt right there on the tarmac, her hair instantly drawing up into a profusion of bouncy curls.

The Jamaica Military Band, dressed in their velvet and brocade uniforms dating back to the Crimean War, stood on the tarmac playing the National Anthem. Wondering if they had to meet each plane, Jacqui pitied them as they sweltered in their long-sleeved jackets. There was a red carpet rolled out and a full honour guard with a long line of people standing around waiting.

After waiting an eternity to get through the immigration line because there were only two lines open to serve four arriving flights, she entered the large customs hall. The fans did little to help as the sweltering heat reduced her into one wet rag. When eventually the bags from her flight were unloaded, incredibly hers were among the first to come off, but it took another half an hour on the customs line. When she finally made it to the front, the customs officer acted as if he was doing her the greatest favour in the world. Poking around in her bag, he asked if she had any apples or fresh meat before stamping her card, motioning her through. She was stopped one more time before she was finally ushered out into the burning sun.

A human wall of dark faces confronted her as she stood in the blinding hot sun, trying to adjust her eyes. Digging into her bag for her sunglasses, she somehow heard her name being called over the din. Approaching her was a slender man, solidly built, with finely sculpted features and bittersweet chocolate colouring.

"Welcome," said Trevor, putting out his hand with a warmth and friendliness that immediately put her at ease. "Josh described you perfectly. I must say, I had a hell of a time arranging the military band for your arrival."

She looked shocked for a moment, until Trevor's breaking laughter forced him to reveal the truth. "The president of Venezuela just arrived on an official state visit," said Trevor, smiling. "The prime minister, leader of the opposition, cabinet and dignitary corps are all on hand to welcome him," he added as he ushered her into his Volkswagen.

They drove along the Palisadoes Road with the Blue Mountains shrouded by clouds in the distance. There were three sailboats in the harbour, their spinnakers billowing in the wind, creating a kaleidoscope of colour against the crystal-clear blue sky.

"You must come by and see our operations at the *West Indian* while you're in Kingston," said Trevor. "We don't have the circulation of *Elegant Travel*, but we have a loyal following, especially among cricket fans.

"There is an international conference taking place in town and there isn't a hotel room to be had. I've arranged for you to stay at a friend's flat. His name is Ainsley Gunther, and he's out of town for a few days. You'll just be there overnight and tomorrow you're off to The Falls at Ocho Rios. How I envy you and a few days of pampering."

They rounded a gentle bend in the harbour road, driving past a sign that read, "Undertakers love Overtakers." Jacqui was startled by the poverty as they skirted the downtown area, but she put all her preconceived notions aside when they passed through New Kingston, once the site of

19

Knutsford Park race track. It was urban living, Caribbean style, with modern office buildings set on wide palm-lined avenues dotted with irregular stalls and push carts loaded with food and merchandise at every corner. The parade of goats, speeding minibuses and loud motorcycles with masses of people added to the confusion.

Passing through town, they climbed steadily through mountains with beautiful residences edging the side of the road. The air was instantly cooler and the lush tropical greenery carpeted the hillsides. Trevor pulled up at a small townhouse complex. Taking her bags, he ushered Jacqui through a lovely courtyard, crowded with exotic plants. A pleasantly plump woman with skin the colour of coffee opened the door to greet them.

"Welcome to Jamaica," she said, introducing herself as Rubie. "I'm 'ere fe tek care of ebery likkle t'ing," she said, patting her generous chest.

"Thank you," said Jacqui. "I look forward to my stay."

"I'm sure you'll be comfortable here," said Trevor. "I need to ask you something. Why is there such a need for secrecy when you review The Falls? Tropical Properties is usually very generous in providing accommodation to the press. I know the general manager of the property, Robert Davids, personally."

"Tropical Properties has threatened to sue *Elegant Travel* about a review they wrote last year. Josh thought it would be more credible if the management didn't know they were being reviewed. You know, they may go the extra mile to ensure my stay is a pleasant one if they know that I'm associated with the magazine. That's the reason for the secrecy," explained Jacqui.

"Who am I to argue with Josh," said Trevor. "If he says that's how we play it, then that's how we'll play it. I don't guarantee it will be a secret for long, though. This is a small island. Josh knows that. He was an English teacher in Port

Kingston, one of the worst parts of the downtown ghetto. He was a young idealistic peace corps volunteer who was very active in community affairs. Some of the old people still talk about him. He started home delivery of food for the indigent," said Trevor.

Jacqui was surprised at the revelation, wondering why Josh had never told her he lived in Jamaica and more importantly, why he hadn't covered such a sensitive assignment himself.

"You'll be pretty busy while you're here," said Trevor. "While you are at The Falls, try to catch the polo match at Chukka Cove. Next week is the Jamaica Open Golf Tournament at Pimento Hill. I'll be there covering it for the *West Indian* magazine. It is one of the highlights of the season because it attracts the best golfers from the PGA and the LPA tours."

"After that ?" asked Jacqui, smiling.

"Josh was right. He said you really like to get down to business," laughed Trevor. "You have a reservation at the Blue Marlin Inn in Port Antonio. It's less developed than the rest of the island, but it is the most beautiful part. And I don't know if you're too tired, but there's a party at the Yacht Club tonight for the regatta. I'm on the entertainment committee. If you like, I could have a friend pick you up."

"I would love to," said Jacqui.

"His name is PJ Burrowes and he is quite a character," said Trevor. "Don't tell him anything you don't want blasted all over town. He is quite a well known newspaper columnist on the island."

"Trevor, thanks for everything. I really appreciate all your help," she said, seeing him to the door.

Afterwards, she looked around the ground floor, instantly taken with the house. The dining room held a lignum vitae table with handsome armless cream chairs resting on a coconut parquet floor that was polished to a high sheen.

The living room was warm and inviting with beautiful Jamaican paintings on the walls. There was a masculine air to the room, with an entire wall devoted to plaques and trophies. She crossed the room to inspect them. Ainsley Gunther was an accomplished man. There were trophies for deep sea fishing and marksmanship honours in every category.

She found a copy of the *West Indian* magazine on the coffee table. Settling on the couch, she read an article about a test match in Australia. She tossed the magazine away, wondering how two teams could play for three days, score a century and then call the match a draw. After playing in the hot sun for so long, someone had to win so the loser could buy the first round of drinks.

Picking up the newspaper that was on the coffee table, she saw the lead story was about a suspected drug boat eluding the authorities:

The Coast Guard led a four-hour chase of an unidentified boat early yesterday morning. The Police Information Centre stated that radar picked up the signal from the unauthorized vessel at Don Christopher's Cove at approximately 3:00 a.m. The vessel successfully evaded the Coast Guard patrol and slipped into international waters at dawn.

There was more about the rise in cocaine transshipments and an appeal from the prime minister to each and every member of society to aid the government in their efforts against crime.

She put the paper down, noticing a basket of newspapers tied together next to the couch. Judging from the number of papers, it seemed as if Ainsley had been gone nearly a week. Taking out the last few days' newspapers, she tore at the rubber bands that had melted onto the newsprint in the heat. As she spread the newspapers over the coffee table, she saw that the headlines defied the illusion that Jamaica was a peaceful little tropical paradise.

Just yesterday a gun battle had taken place in Trench Town and the police had seized a huge collection of semi-automatic weapons and rifles. Two police officers had been shot while off duty.

"Josh was right. This place is more intricate than most of us suspect," thought Jacqui, putting the papers aside to inspect the rest of the townhouse.

Chapter 3

With the power of a gale force hurricane wind, PJ breezed into the house. He helped himself from Ainsley's bar, nibbled at the cheese in the refrigerator and thoroughly beguiled Jacqui with his charm. He had a freckled reddish-brown complexion and short kinky titian hair and was in his early forties.

"I must thank Ainsley for leaving such wonderful things in his bar," said PJ, opening a can of cashews. "Ainsley and I are old friends from boarding school, so I can exhibit this kind of unspeakable behaviour. Trevor tells me you are on a working holiday of sorts. Where will you be?"

"I'm going to Ocho Rios tomorrow," said Jacqui.

"Fabulous. The polo match between St. Ann and Kingston is on Saturday and I'm determined that Kingston will at last emerge victorious," said PJ with a gleam in his eyes. "I'll make a deal with you. If you promise to be Kingston's biggest fan I'll buy you the best fish dinner in Port Royal."

"I'll boo St. Ann and root for Kingston," said Jacqui.

They drove along the Palisadoes Road in PJ's little MG convertible. Jacqui's hair was flying in the wind, mingling with the sea mist that surrounded them on the narrow strip of marshy road. The intoxicating feeling of freedom overwhelmed her as she watched the breeze rustle the coconut palms.

"Port Royal hasn't changed in a hundred years," PJ said, as they entered the town through the old stone gate.

Everything from the street layout to the buildings was frozen in time. The ruins screamed out their story of pirates, looting and legends of buried treasure.

When they neared the fishing pier, PJ pulled up to a restaurant called Cherry's, parking by the curb. Several tables and rickety-looking chairs had been placed on the sidewalk and onto the road. A large Red Stripe delivery truck was honking furiously, trying to force its way down the narrow street. After slamming his door, the driver backed down the road, honking the horn again as he hurled out a string of curses.

They took a seat at one of the rickety tables, balanced by PJ with a matchbook as he called for two Red Stripe beers.

"On weekends, there is always a group that goes out to the cays, tiny islands off the coast. There's Rackham's Cay, named after the famous scoundrel. Every twelve hours it disappears, leaving only a trace of lighter blue water surrounding its sand. Lime Cay is quite large for a cay and has trees for shade. Maiden Cay is about the size of a handkerchief."

After several minutes a waiter came to take their order, moving so slowly that Jacqui thought he might be half dead. Moments later, a brown-skinned woman with an ample bust and multicoloured hair curlers in rows on her head appeared out of the small cookhouse. Spotting PJ, she came over to greet him.

"How come yuh stey 'way so long?" demanded Cherry.

"I've been coming to eat here since I was a boy," he explained to Jacqui. "I just ate here last week."

After an interminable wait, a bamboo plate of fried pink-tailed snapper with the oil still sizzling on it and another plate of fried bammy, made from cassava, were set unceremoniously on the plain table. They each received half a paper napkin. They ate the piping hot fish with their fingers, smothering it in vinegar and hot peppers. Reggae music blared from a well packed rum bar on the adjacent street to a captive audience. PJ motioned to one little boy, who eagerly brought Jacqui a water coconut.

After dinner PJ lit a cigarette while Jacqui went to the outdoor water pipe to rinse her hands. Shaking the water off, she returned to the table. An engine backfired in the distance. For a split second she thought it was the roar of a cannon.

"What was Port Royal really like in the pirate days?" she asked, noticing that the sky had turned into a deep shade of amethyst.

"The buccaneers were the law and favours were bought with plundered jewels," said PJ, smiling. "It was the haven of every cutthroat pirate who was lucky enough not to walk the plank. It was the richest and most sinful city in the world at that time. Sir Henry Morgan was the wildest blackbeard to sail the Caribbean seas. He pillaged and plundered his way from Panama to Cartagena, terrorizing trading ships and looking for buxom wenches to warm his bed. But after he became governor, he put the fear of God and the hangman's rope in everyone.

"At the height of its immorality and decadence, an earthquake in 1692 came and swallowed up half the city and most of its wealth. The fishermen say that there's a church down there and you can hear the bell toll to remind us of the lost souls," he said, as he paid Cherry with several crisp bills.

They drove back towards town, passing the airport before pulling off the Palisadoes Road. PJ followed a windy road to the Royal Jamaica Yacht Club, nestled in a protected cove on Kingston Harbour. There were over a hundred boats of all sizes including three hundred-foot yachts, sailboats of every make, racing boats and motor boats. They walked past the club room, filled with trophies and a roster of the yacht club presidents dating back to the

26

1880s. The game room held ping pong and billiard tables and there was a lively game of darts being played in one corner.

The large bar, which opened onto the pool deck, was packed with partygoers. Jacqui felt her tiredness evaporate when she heard the music. Following PJ to the bar, they were greeted by Trevor who introduced her to his wife Maxine, a small, dark woman with short hair. She caught the undercurrent of the look that passed between PJ and Maxine and tried not to notice when they both excused themselves to walk to the pool deck.

Handing Jacqui a rum and Pepsi, Trevor began pointing out some of the boats while he introduced her to a few people.

"Well, look who's here," he said as he pointed out a sleek Boston whaler with half a dozen scantily clad young ladies scampering off it. "Let me fill you in. That is quite a group getting off *Rum King*. Each one of those ladies is a former Miss Jamaica beauty queen. The gentleman with the grey patch in his hair is Charles Whittingham. He owns Island Builders, a local construction firm. Give Charles a chance to scope the party. He'll be by for an introduction, though I do think you are a bit too old for him."

"Thanks a lot ," said Jacqui, sipping her drink.

"The tall man with him is Allistair Brody, a lawyer," Trevor continued. "If you saw him in town, you wouldn't recognize him. He usually wears a velvet waistcoat with a gold pocket watch and carries a walking stick. It doesn't matter how hot it is."

"Who's that?" asked Jacqui, as she saw an obese balding man with a pasty oatmeal complexion making a painful and awkward attempt to get off the boat. His features were buried behind layers of fat, while his middle appeared to have the diameter of a tyre for an eighteen-wheel truck and his ankles seemed the size of ten-pound bell weights.

"Derrick Bloomfield, he's a special adviser to the prime minister and the member of Parliament for Port Kingston," said Trevor. "He's put on a hundred pounds since his last girlfriend left him. The young lady he's talking to is a former beauty queen with the IQ of a nail in the heel of my shoe and a body with a thousand miles of good road."

Jacqui watched as the beauty wrapped the snivelling man around her finger. "He's what we call pussy-whipped," said Trevor.

Jacqui felt an arm encircle her waist from behind. Taken aback, she was introduced to Charles.

"I'm delighted," he said with a leering smile on his face, as he held Jacqui's hand. Although the gesture was presumably meant to beguile her, she was left with a cold feeling and wished he would leave. There was something about him that she found disturbing. Jacqui didn't know if it was his ill-fitting shirt or the unruly patch of grey in the dark hair that framed his light brown skin, making him seem more unattractive than he really was.

"I look forward to learning more about Miss Devron. Will you be here for the Jamaica Open?" he asked.

"I may be. I am not quite sure of my plans," she said offhandedly.

"Do try to make it. I have a lovely villa there called Dreamscape. You must come."

She glanced toward *Rum King*, and saw a man leap off the yacht, distractedly waving his hand trying to get Charles's attention. Alerting Charles, she couldn't help but notice that there was something very odd about the man's hand.

Catching a glimpse of the dock, she wandered down, admiring the sleek and graceful boats. They rocked gently, the soft sound of bells echoing in the wind as the buoys moved with the tide. As she turned around to walk back to the party, the music and lights of the club were abruptly cut off .

"Oh shit," she murmured, stopping where she was, afraid to take another step in the darkness.

"It's not that bad. It's just the B-6 generator at Old Harbour kicking out," said a voice from a sailboat in front of her. A lantern lit up, illuminating a white-haired, bearded gentleman at the helm. "It will be over in less than an hour. Why don't you come up for a drink?" he asked, holding up the lantern while he extended his hand.

"Don't mind if I do," said Jacqui, climbing onto the boat. "I'm Jacqui. Jacqui Devron," she said.

"I'm Donald Francis. Let me freshen up your drink. Rum and Pepsi?"

Jacqui nodded her head. "How did you do in the race today?" she asked, settling herself down on one of the deck cushions as she accepted the drink.

"We really won, but with the handicap, it worked out to be third. Do you sail?" he asked.

"Not as much as I would like to. I live in New York so the opportunity doesn't present itself too often," she said.

"Is this your first trip to Jamaica?" he asked, ruffling his full white beard with his tanned calloused hand.

"First trip, first day," responded Jacqui.

"Ah, the first time is always so special – a milestone," said Donald. "I hope you enjoy your stay. Let me know if you want to come sailing," he offered.

"Are you a Jamaican?" asked Jacqui.

"Born and bred," said Donald. "I grew up surrounded by water. I'm descended from a long line of shippers. My great-grandfather used to collect salt at Pigeon Island to send it to England. Lately, I've been sailing quite a lot. It's how I ease my troubles."

"What troubles do you have, an affair of the heart?" asked Jacqui gently.

"No, unfortunately not this time," said Donald. "This is

the kind of trouble I don't think you would understand."

"Try me," said Jacqui. "I just might."

"Almost two tons of ganja were found on one of my ships in Miami. It was confiscated and held on a fifty-million-dollar bond in Miami. I have the most modern integrated electronic surveillance system, but somehow they still got through it. I know who is behind it, but I just can't prove it. Not yet, anyway," said Donald. "The funny thing about all this is that now everyone thinks I must be very rich if I can think about posting the bond. It certainly has improved my social life."

"I'm sorry this all happened, but I'm glad to hear it improved your social life. I wish I had the same luck!" Jacqui laughed bitterly.

"You sound like a lady who has known a bit of trouble," said Donald.

"Too much," sighed Jacqui, breathing in the salty air.

"What happened?" he asked, taking a sip of his drink.

"I made a mistake in judgement which nearly cost me my job. I thought I was a good judge of character but I learned the hard way I wasn't," said Jacqui, finding herself telling Donald about her involvement with Geoff. It seemed easier to talk to a stranger under the anonymity of the electric blue sky than she had found with anyone else.

"Jacqui, my new friend, I have a few years on you. I can only tell you that my heart has been broken a dozen times and time heals all wounds," he said softly.

"My dad used to tell me that when I was little," said Jacqui. "He is a pretty terrific guy. You would probably like him."

"I'm sure I would," said Donald.

The lights came on as suddenly as they had gone off and seconds later the music tripped back in. "I really must be getting back. PJ will probably be wondering what happened to me. Many thanks for the drink," she said, wishing she could spend more time with Donald.

"The pleasure was all mine. Hope to see you again."

"I may just take you up on that sailing invitation," said Jacqui, jumping off the boat onto the dock.

She returned to the party, finding PJ at the bar with Maxine, looking much happier.

"How did you fare during the power cut?" he asked.

She noticed a smear of lipstick on his collar.

"Just fine,"she responded.

"We have one more stop to make before I take you back home," said PJ.

Jacqui went to say goodbye to Trevor who wished her a pleasant stay at The Falls.

"I'll expect to hear from you next week," he said. "If you have any problems, call me at the office. Good luck with your match, PJ. Don't be too hard on Gary Gordon."

"How about GG not being too hard on me," said PJ as he led Jacqui to the car.

Instead of taking the main route, PJ detoured through downtown Kingston, past the historic buildings and the redeveloped waterfront with its cluster of high-rises. They went past Harbour Street, King and Queen, Duke and Princess, where commercial buildings were sandwiched in between gingerbread wooden houses built at the turn of the century.

PJ pulled down Water Lane. The alleyway was so narrow it barely accommodated his car. They took another turn onto Barry Street before turning down another side street. The smell of rotting garbage nearly made Jacqui gag. Surrounding her, irregular zinc fences bordered small areas which served as yards for several families. At the nearest corner, a fire burned in a can, the only light on a burnt-out dark street, devoid of street lights. Half a dozen youth hung around, their dark skins glistening in the firelight with a sheen of sweat. Jacqui caught sight of one of the youth's eyes. They were blank, the loss of hope etched in his hardened features.

"This is a stark reminder that poverty is endemic to the way of life here. In places like Rema, Tivoli and Trench Town, the posses as they are known in the States and yardies as they are called in England have their roots," explained PJ. "Behind these ghetto walls is a sizzling cauldron ready to explode at any moment. Each group of streets is ruled by a different gang with loyalties to one of the two political parties, the Jamaica Labour Party and the People's National Party. "

"Where are we now?" asked Jacqui, as they passed through a deserted street, the hollow shells of burnt-out buildings reminiscent of a war zone.

"We're in the West Bank. Tel Aviv lies just on the other side and Beirut is around the corner," said PJ. "They say if a Tel Aviv dog wanders past the border into the West Bank, it will be shot. There are other areas like Little Havana, Russia, Mexico and even Angola.

"The problem is that cocaine transshipments are increasing in record numbers, and bringing more guns into the hands of the posses. You see – the drug trade is so well placed, so intricate that it touches everyone, directly or indirectly, at every level of the society."

"Isn't the government trying to do something about it?" asked Jacqui.

"Sure, but whichever the party in power, the resources to both effectively wage war against drugs and finance development are woefully inadequate. Corruption is rife in the system. For instance, the average policeman makes what would be considered a subsistence wage in any First World country. Most of the police stations don't have vehicles, modern communication equipment or even weapons," said PJ as he pulled onto a well lit main road, and sped towards Stony Hill.

Jacqui breathed a sigh of relief. She was shocked by the contrast of the horrendous poverty and the neatly manicured green hills. She wanted to close her eyes and wipe away the ugliness, but the vision of the young man with the hopeless blank eyes on the ghetto street corner haunted her.

* * *

Gary parked his BMW behind the Yacht Club. He glanced across the dark panorama. The power cut couldn't have come at a better time. He slipped unnoticed past the party, walking silently to the channel that offered boats shelter during the tropical storms. He made his way along the dock to *Tropical I*, his fifty-foot Bertram.

He checked the boat and its contents, started the engine from the upper deck and quickly cast off. He stayed within the five miles per hour speed limit until he passed the second channel marker with its blinking fluorescent red light. Once out on the open harbour, Gary picked up speed, feeling the thrust of the engine as it responded to the touch of his finger.

The lights flickered on, igniting the hills of Kingston in a jewelled splendour. The harbour of San Francisco and the gentle cliffs of Sardinia didn't hold the same magic for him. He recognized Coopers Hill, Red Hills, Stony Hill, Jack's Hill, and followed the snake road of Skyline Drive to where the army camp at Newcastle was just a tiny glimmer on the foothills of the Blue Mountains.

Through the black of night, Gary crossed the harbour, passing the downtown waterfront district. He slowed as he neared Port Bustamante, the industrial shipping centre. At berth five, he cut his engine and tied up the boat securely. He looked around for a moment in indecision, not wanting to do what he had to do. Then, with the ease of a practised athlete, Gary swung himself onto the high dock, and found himself staring at the barrel of a rifle aimed directly at his chest.

"Good night,"said Gary pleasantly, his heart pounding in his ears. "I'm here to see Crime."

"Why yuh wan' fe see 'im?" asked the man, holding the weapon level.

"Me have some business wid him," said Gary. "Come nuh, man. Me know him good."

"Why dem call him Crime?" the man asked, pointing the gun at Gary's head.

"Because Crime nevah pay," said Gary, forcing a laugh. "Tell him is de green-eyed devil a come fe call. "

"Me 'ear bout yuh. Me nevah know it wuz yuh," the man said as he lowered his gun. "Crime, someone 'ere fe see yuh."

"A wha' go on," said a short man with a pock-marked face coming out from a small hut with a zinc roof. "Long time me nuh see yuh. Me nevah know yuh is de devil."

"A strange t'ing but me is de devil," said Gary. "Me have de stuff fe yuh."

"Where?" asked Crime.

"In de boat," said Gary.

"How yuh package it?"

"In sealed tins of ackee," said Gary. "No dog cyaan sniff t'rough dat."

"Ah true," said Crime. "Yuh jus' lef' it wid me. Me a go tek care of it. Jus' pay me de money. "

"Wha' 'bout de boat?" asked Gary, reluctant to part with it.

"Nuh worry yuself. By tomorrow morning, it a be back a de dock with jus' a few gallons less of gas. Me promise me nah lick it up."

"How yuh goin' get it out?" asked Gary.

"Me have me customs man ready and waiting," said Crime. "Me know dis business good," he smiled, gesturing towards the most current model of a BMW convertible.

Gary walked away, passing through the bonded area, his entire body drenched in perspiration. He reached the gate and unlatched the handle. When he pulled to open it the gate swung out at him, knocking him against the fence. He felt the bile rise in his throat as the ground turned to putty under his feet. A slight earth tremor occurred, and passed in less than a minute, but left Gary with an ominous feeling of things to come. The dogs which had been eerily silent started to howl as the sea kicked up angrily.

* * *

The Moby Dick rum bar was a small smoky hole in the wall with a few tables and rickety seats. A dim light cast shadows on the rum bottles on the shelves. The back part of the bar had raw cement walls with a zinc roof leading out to an alley. The ever-present stench of urine wafted inside.

Sputo walked inside, nodding to Clock, the bartender, who had earned his nickname because one arm was shorter than the other. He moved to a corner table where three men sat waiting for him.

He greeted the men, awkwardly helping himself to some brandy from a bottle on the table. He grunted as the fiery liquid slid down his throat, warming his belly.

"I declare de executive committee of de Storm and Thunder posse h'open," said Sputo.

"Why yuh g'wan wid yuh foolishness," said Whiskey. He was a large man with enormous hands that could crack a coconut with one blow. "Why yuh call dis meeting an' mek me come a town. Yuh know me hate it."

"We haffi move de boat," said Sputo.

"Me nuh like dis ya last-minute business,"said Whiskey, showing his displeasure as he bolted down his third white rum and milk.

"Him right," said Jack, his right-hand man. "Everyt'ing tie up in Don Christopher's cove. Me nuh wan' fe move."

"Yuh bumboklaat. Yuh so fuckin' stupid. Yuh nah read de paper?" said Sputo, the whites of his eyes showing in rage. "Yuh wan' fe sit inna General Penitentiary? Anyway, is jus' fe dis week. Me nuh like dis United Nations monkey business an' de boss nuh like it neider."

The group was silent. When the Lord of Trench Town and leader of the Storm and Thunder posse spoke like that, everyone listened. He was the only man who was able to keep the escalating ghetto war from getting out of control, but more importantly he was their vital link to the never-ending supply of arms. He directly controlled the level of street violence in downtown Kingston.

"Me a hear yuh," said Niney, a slim tall black man with heavy-set cheeks. "Me no like dis government business eider. Right now, t'ings cool in Treasure Beach. Me have every likkle t'ing under control." The dim light picked up the glint from his gold teeth.

"Wha' 'bout de guns?" asked Jack. "Me tired fe 'ear dem soon come. Me wan' dem now. Warwicka Posse get some new automatics – criss, pretty likkle t'ing dem. Me a hear from one of de brothers," he said, boasting his knowledge to the other men.

"Me sey dem soon come," said Sputo with a look that suggested he would kill them where they sat and then go out and buy a new suit and cry at their funerals. "No more talk of dis foolishness or yuh nah live to regret it." A deadly silence settled around the group.

"Yuh right, boss," said Whiskey, breaking the uncomfortable silence and raising his glass in a toast. "Storm and Thunder, a we rule t'ings. Clock, get more ice. De lord wan' anudder drink."

Chapter 4

Tall coconut palms shaded the entrance to The Falls at Ocho Rios and the dancing fountains glistened in the sun as Jacqui walked by the four-column entrance to the lobby. Giving her name at the front desk, she glanced around at the elegant open reception area, decorated in vibrant tropical prints.

Jacqui was exhausted. The morning had been spent researching the history of the island at the National Library, followed by a long drive through Mount Diablo, the mountain pass to the island's north coast. The check-in took a long time as a group from Italy was checking out and they were running all around the lobby, in and out of the gift shop with their last-minute purchases. Lloyd, the recreation coordinator, accompanied her to her room, giving her a tour of the property along the way.

"All meals, drinks, water sports, entertainment and riding are included in one price. You'll never have to sign a bill or take out your wallet the entire time you're here."

"That sounds perfect," said Jacqui, smiling as Lloyd led the way. They passed the miniature falls that cascaded on the far side of the lobby behind the tour desks. He pointed out Ivories Piano Bar behind the Sunset Lounge where afternoon tea was served. There was a movie room with a full schedule from nine a.m. until the early hours of the morning. Scandals, the bright neon-lighted disco, was off the main dining room and the seaside dining terrace overlooked the pier.

Leading her past the beach bar and grill, he walked her along the beach toward the pool with the swim-up bar and the outdoor entertainment area. Several hundred yards offshore from the white-sand beach was a small island with a single palm tree. There were a few small cabanas on the western tip and a canoe tied up to the dock.

"That's where we hold our weekly island party with a seafood picnic that can satisfy anyone," said Lloyd.

Her ground-floor room, decorated in baby pink with apple green highlights, had been designed with the comfort of the guest in mind. There was a large bathroom and oversized dressing room, and a king-sized bed. The sliding glass doors opened onto a patio that held two Queen Anne bamboo chairs and a hammock.

"Please let us know if you need anything. Orientation is in the Sunset Lounge at sundown," said Lloyd.

She unpacked, settling into the comfortable room, before slipping into her magenta and black bikini. Packing her beach bag with a towel and book, she walked through the garden to the long beach, where the sun against the aqua blue water beckoned her. The beach bar was crowded with guests, their bodies slick with oil, shining in the bright sunlight.

Ordering a fruit punch, she spied a Japanese man walking on the beach wearing plaid shorts, a sunvisor with Datsun printed on it and black socks with open-toe sandals. Round glasses set off his round face as he alternately took pictures with each of the two cameras dangling around his neck.

After taking a swim to the raft in the warm satin water, Jacqui settled down on a lounge chair. She picked up her book, trying to get involved with the story, but the sun lulled her and the gentle breeze seduced her to sleep.

* * *

Gary walked by the beach on his way to the stables, wearing jodhpurs, worn riding boots and a tobacco-coloured polo shirt. He wanted to squeeze in an hour of practice on Soon Come before the polo match the next day. PJ was getting too good to allow him the luxury of an easy win. He stopped when he saw Jacqui sleeping in the sun, her face covered by a hat and sunglasses. Gary took in the high-cut bikini that moulded her body.

When he returned over an hour later, he saw that she hadn't moved an inch and her skin had taken on a pinkish glow. Signalling one of the beach boys, he told him to put an umbrella over Jacqui. Watching him put up the umbrella, Gary saw her turn in her sleep, pulling her leg up as she rubbed her ankle against her calf. Controlling the urge to walk over and touch her, Gary moved away, knowing he had sighted that week's prey.

* * *

The Sunset Lounge was decorated with small tables, wicker chairs and hanging bird cages. Plants and wooden carvings gave a feeling of intimacy. The lounge was filled with guests enjoying cocktails. Brian Foster, the resident manager, was giving a lively orientation to the new arrivals. Just listening to his descriptions of the boat cruises, shopping in Ocho Rios and rafting on the White River, peppered with his natural enthusiasm for life, infected everyone. People who might never have spoken to each other were suddenly very relaxed and joking.

Ordering a drink at the bar, Jacqui was admiring the sunset when she saw the Japanese man and a petite woman walk into the bar, pointing excitedly at the doctor bird that played on the railing. They ordered cocktails and sat down in a set of comfortable chairs next to Jacqui.

"I'm Sushimashi Tai Kaishai and this is my wife Nikko,"

the man said. "She speaks no English."

"I'm Jacqui. Your name is Sushimanashi?" she blurted, fumbling over his name. "I'm sorry."

"No worry. My American friends call me Al," he said good-naturedly.

They were joined by a middle-aged couple who introduced themselves as Johnny and Frances Brenner from Iowa, on their fifth visit to The Falls. Jacqui sipped her drink slowly, watching the last rays of sunlight melt into the sea, leaving lingering shades of breathless pink and coral in the sky. Her eyes rested on the silhouette of a man standing on the pool deck whose classic broad shoulders and sinewy physique were outlined in the dusk. Even with his back to her, she could see that he had an impatient stance. Though he was standing still, in conversation with another man, his toned muscles rippled through the thin fabric of his trousers and cotton shirt.

It was the first time since Geoff Roth that a man had piqued her interest. She wondered who he was.

* * *

Gary was in deep discussion with Robert Davids, the general manager. They had been close friends ever since they shared a room at boarding school at Munro in Jamaica and later in England. Their bond of loyalty was something very deep and treasured.

"Where have you been today?" asked Gary. "I thought we were supposed to get in a few hours of practice. You know that PJ has been practising for weeks."

"I wish I could lead the life of leisure that you do," said Robert with a grunt. "I have a hotel to run and spent the most god-awful day at the annual hotel industry meeting."

"Should I ask how it went?" Gary smiled.

"You know – the usual trickery, backstabbing, petty

40

competition, social climbing and political intrigue that seem to govern not only the association but everything else these days," said Robert.

"Better you than me," said Gary. "You always have so much patience for this nonsense." His voice lowered. "Robert, I need a favour."

"Don't tell me. You bought another horse. That's all I need," said Robert.

"No, it has to do with the boat," said Gary.

"Your Welcraft is here," said Robert, confused.

"I don't mean the Welcraft. I'm talking about the Bertram. I need to put it in a safe place," said Gary.

"I don't have the room here," said Robert flatly. "I don't care how much you beg me, but I'm not letting that sea-going monster near my dock. Why don't you just charter it out and forget about it for a while. I'll arrange it. I'll do anything to keep it away from my hotel and save our friendship."

"Fine," said Gary. "That sounds just fine."

"Your mother called twice," said Robert.

"Thanks for telling me," said Gary, checking his watch. "I haven't called her since I got back from New York. She'll be having her dinner so I'll call her later."

* * *

When Gary turned, Jacqui nearly spilled her drink on Al Tai Kaishai. It was the same arrogant creep who had stolen her airplane seat. What was he doing here? she wondered, studying his chiselled profile. He hadn't acted like a tourist. She sensed something so powerful about him that she couldn't stop looking at him. He was obviously a man who was comfortable in his own skin, very much at ease with who he was. It was evident in the magnetic aura of confidence that clung to him like a veil.

A tall exotic-looking woman wearing white harem pants floated across the lounge, leaving in her wake a trail of perfume so overpowering that Al sneezed. Her café au lait complexion and long full head of sumptuous dark hair that fell on her bare shoulders had every man in the room watching her.

Jacqui watched her walk over to the two men and put a protective arm on Gary, awkwardly interrupting the conversation. With what seemed to be only half an ear on her comments, he let his eyes wander around the lounge, catching Jacqui's gaze. She saw his eyes flicker with recognition – he seemed to have remembered her from the airport. He nodded his head slightly and smiled at Jacqui. She returned his smile with a look that, if it could kill, would have put Gary six feet under without roses. His smile broadened as he returned his attention to his conversation.

All through the five-course dinner, the limbo dancing and pyrotechnics display and a solitary walk on the beach, Jacqui could not push away the image of the arrogant green-eyed man. Even later in her room, as she slipped down into the soft sheets, his strong chiselled face and mocking smile flashed through her mind.

* * *

Jacqui walked to the beach after breakfast. She lay on the sand, enjoying the warming rays of the sun. When it became too hot, she doused herself in the crystal blue water. It felt like silk against her skin. The goat races were starting on the beach and Jacqui moved to a stool at the bar to watch. Each participant was given a goat on a rope and the first one to run across the finish line with his goat won. Al was the first to join up as Jacqui and Nikko cheered him from the sidelines. He fell in the sand, his glasses flying off into the water, but he was undaunted. By the third race he had gotten the hang of it and won, jumping up and down and hugging the goat.

Nikko asked Al something in Japanese to which he shrugged his shoulders. "Nikko want to know what we do today?" he said.

"Tell Nikko we are going to the polo game and you should bring a lot of film," said Jacqui.

After lunch at the beach grill, Jacqui went back to her room to shower, slipping on a pair of white jeans and a fuchsia t-shirt with front pocket. From her experience at the World Cup Polo Championship in Palm Beach several years before, she knew a match of polo could be sweltering as well as exhilarating.

She met the Tai Kaishais in the lobby and they hired a taxi driven by Ibo, a Rastafarian with long dreadlocks. Al, Nikko and Jacqui all piled into his Lada car and drove through the crowded main street of Ocho Rios, sharing the road with donkey carts and Mercedes Benzes. Jacqui felt as if she were riding backwards on a camel, feeling every pothole and stone in the road. The car seemed to have no shocks, suspension or anything else vaguely resembling twentieth-century automotive engineering.

Ibo drove like a fighter pilot on a life and death mission, overtaking car after car on the narrow road that was lined by an ancient stone wall. He explained that Ladas were Russian cars that the government had received in exchange for bauxite.

"Dem call the Lada 'Lord 'a mercy'," said Ibo in a low voice that belied his six-foot frame.

Nikko laughed when she heard the translation. They drove through fields of sugar cane, barely moving in the hot air. Chukka Cove was set by the sea, fringed by the polo field of velvet green. Arriving at the field, Ibo deposited them at the club house, an old wooden structure with a large open viewing area facing the field.

The bar was already packed with locals and visitors awaiting the final championship match. They wandered into the clubhouse, looking at the trophies and plaques of championship matches. Draped around the high ceiling of the main room were the flags of Barbados, the Dominican Republic, the United States, Britain and Argentina. In one corner of the room there was a case filled with medals, trophies and a silver tankard with the inscription "Most Outstanding Polo Player of the Year." Jacqui noted that the name Gary Gordon was listed four times.

The players began to slowly canter onto the field, their polo mallets in hand, taking practice swings at the ball. Jacqui spotted PJ at the far end of the field, and could almost feel the crackle of tension that hung like the still hot air in the stands at Chukka Cove.

At a corner table in the Players' Lounge, with an excellent view of the fields, an older woman sat, elegant and sophisticated with long white hair twisted in a loose bun at the back of her head. She looked as if the scenery had been created just for her. Scanning the field with her binoculars, she put them down in a graceful movement when a man greeted her.

"Hello, Countess. Hope you're feeling better," he said.

"Fine, thank you," she responded, inquiring about his family.

Jacqui was watching her, trying to figure out a way to talk to her, when the woman caught her staring. Walking over to the table, Jacqui was struck by her bewitching hazel eyes.

"Good afternoon. I was wondering if I could look at your programme?" asked Jacqui.

"Certainly," she said, motioning Jacqui to sit down. "You're on holiday from the States?" she inquired as Jacqui passed her back the programme.

"New York. My name is Jacqui Devron," responded

Jacqui, looking at the woman's hands. Instead of beautifully manicured nails, they were ragged and chipped, but the fingers were warm and sensitive, the freckles mingled with age spots. They were the kind of hands that could instantly soothe a child's fevered brow or paint a masterpiece filled with vibrant colours. Catching Jacqui staring at her hands, the Countess pulled away.

"You're a painter," said Jacqui, gently touching her hand.

"How did you know?" asked the lady, amazed.

"There's a sensitivity to your hands," she said, hoping she hadn't offended the woman.

"One other person once said that to me years ago. My life changed forever the moment I first heard those words," she said, her eyes getting glassy for a moment, as she reached out to touch Jacqui's hand. A friendship had bonded instantly.

"You must have loved him very much," said Jacqui sympathetically.

"He was my first love. He introduced me to the world of art and the things we do when we are young. It was a far cry from my sheltered childhood in Jamaica as the youngest of eight children, and the only daughter. But the war came and with it the devastating events and experiences that altered so many lives and changed so many destinies," said the Countess, lost in her own thoughts.

"I apologize for going on like that. Why did you let me do it?" she asked, smiling at Jacqui.

"I am so interested. I am an only child," said Jacqui. "I can't imagine growing up in such a big family."

"They spoilt me to death. It was Felix, my second oldest brother, who dubbed me the Countess, but my real name is Julia Henry. I guess the name has stuck."

"Did your brothers play polo?" Jacqui asked.

"Every one of them," the Countess responded, laughing.

The bell indicating the first chukka sounded, accompanied by the thundering of hoofs on the field. Jacqui immediately recognized the emerald-eyed man who wore the captain's insignia on his red shirt, representing St. Ann. He galloped toward the ball, his polo mallet suspended in mid-air, before he executed an offside neck shot that landed neatly at his number one position, who tapped it in, scoring a goal for St. Ann.

"If you really want to see polo being played, watch Gary Gordon. He has a six handicap which puts him among the top players in the world. Prince Charles who played against him only has a four," said the Countess, without taking her eyes off the field.

'So that's Gary Gordon. PJ didn't have to worry that I might cheer for St. Ann,' she thought, fuming. Yet, despite her anger, she felt a surge of sensual excitement creep over her as she watched Gary gallop across the field, his lean body melting into the sinewy lines of the horse, creating the illusion they were one.

"Do you understand how the game is played?" the Countess asked.

"I've seen it played a few times at Palm Beach but I'm vague about the rules," Jacqui admitted

"A chukka is like a quarter or a period of play," Julia explained. "There are usually four, but there can be six. Each chukka lasts seven minutes." There was a single warning bell at seven minutes and thirty seconds later two bells clanged, indicating the end of the first chukka.

Ninety seconds later, the players were back on the field with fresh mounts, the bell sounding for the second chukka. Jacqui watched PJ for a moment but her eyes were pulled to Gary, who seemed to hold a captivating grip on his players, inspiring them to win.

"Are they using handicaps today?" she asked.

"No, today is a scratch game. Since handicaps are

determined for the team by the individual skills of the players, the scoring would have been skewed in favour of Kingston," explained Julia. "Handicaps range on a scale of negative two to ten, except in Argentina. There they rate their handicaps from zero to ten, but their zeros are usually better than most threes."

The score was six for St. Ann and five to Kingston at the end of the second chukka. Taking a five-minute break, the players changed their mounts and reviewed their strategy. Borrowing Julia's binoculars, Jacqui watched PJ gallop forward to take command of the field, sweat pouring down his freckled face. He hit an over-the-neck shot, pushing in a goal for Kingston to even the score. The shouts roared from the field as well as the crowd.

"G'wan boy, take it away," was heard. PJ shouted instructions to his players, preparing them for St. Ann's onslaught. Surveying the field from his mount, Gary glanced around at his teammates, gave a signal and galloped down the field. "It's mine, it's mine," shouted PJ, moving in on Gary's right flank.

Executing brilliant polo strategy, Gary drove an under-the-neck shot upfield. It landed inches away from the mallet of number two, Mary Lodge, a female player with a three handicap. As she tapped it into the goal, the crowd was up on their feet, cheering.

"Perfect shot," said Julia, her face glowing with excitement. "Not too long, not too short."

Jacqui watched the St. Ann team gallop to their captain's side, earth flying in their wake, as the sweat dripped down their backs. Kingston tried valiantly to even the score during the fourth chukka, but with little success. The final score was ten for St. Ann and six for Kingston. Shouting exuberantly, the St. Ann team, led by Mary Lodge, carried Gary off the field.

Amid the jokes and light-hearted laughter, the players

took their horses off the field, placing the reins in the hands of excited stable boys. The crowd swelled around them, like a swarm of bees to honey, as they moved to the Players' Lounge for many well deserved cold beers.

"Hey! Foreign girl!" called PJ, waving at her across the crowd as she followed Julia into the clubhouse.

Surrounded by teammates and admirers, Gary picked up a bottle of beer and gulped it down, slamming his empty bottle on the bar with a flourish. "Next round is on PJ," he shouted in a raw sensual voice that brought cheers of approval from the large crowd that had gathered.

"To Jamaica's, if not the world's, best polo player," shouted someone in the crowd.

"Here's to breaking a losing streak," Gary said, raising another bottle to the crowd.

"Move over, Gordon," said PJ playfully as he pushed his way to the bar, picking up a beer bottle. "A good match," he said, holding his bottle aloft. "You played hard. You played well – even if you had an unfair advantage. And just for letting you guys win, the next round is on you," said PJ, smiling as the crowd applauded.

Julia and Jacqui both reached for bottles of Red Stripe from a passing tray, laughing at a comment they had heard from one of the players. There was an exuberance to the gathering that made Jacqui feel as if not one single soul there had a worry or a care in the world. It was as if their entire reason for living was to have a good time at that moment. The music, upbeat and pulsating, was synchronized with the mood. PJ joined them for a moment, first kissing the Countess and then Jacqui.

"Hello, Countess. Hello, Jacqui. I hope you both enjoyed the game, despite my performance."

"You played brilliantly," said the Countess.

"You always say that, even when Gary manages to make me look like a bumbling fool. You're my most faithful fan. I don't think you've ever missed a match."

From the bar, Gary watched Jacqui talking to the Countess and PJ. He took a step forward, but was blocked by three adoring young fans, each one of them a potential beauty queen. In the middle of his sentence, PJ was grabbed away by a group of friends. In a roar that sounded like an Indian war cry, Gary was picked up by three of his players and deposited next to PJ. They were surrounded by a human circle, as more bottles of beer instantly appeared and everyone took their turns dousing them with the cold liquid.

Al stood a few feet from the Countess, snapping pictures, trying to comprehend what was going on. Nikko tugged his sleeve and he shrugged his shoulders.

"Nikko wants to know what they are doing?" he said.

"They are celebrating the joy of victory and humility of defeat," said the Countess. "That means they are wasting an awful lot of good beer."

"Strange custom," commented Al, turning to explain it to Nikko who looked strangely from the Countess to the men who were pouring beer over PJ and Gary. "Do we have to do it too?" asked Al.

"No, not at all," said Jacqui, as the Countess joined in with the laughter, her hazel eyes lighting up.

The sun began its slow dramatic descent across the sky and Julia touched Jacqui's hand, squeezing it gently.

"I must be leaving. I'm having dinner guests this evening," said the Countess. "I'm so glad to have met you."

"And I you," returned Jacqui. "I'll be at The Falls until next week. I hope to see you again."

"I'm sure our paths will cross. Enjoy your stay in Ocho Rios. An old friend once told me this and I will share it with you. In this complex island, rich with intrigue and sin, remember it is only with the heart that one can see rightly. What is essential is invisible to the eye."

"*Le Petit Prince*," said Jacqui with surprise, as the Countess kissed both her cheeks.

* * *

Jacqui wandered into Ivories Piano Bar after dinner. It had a warm intimate atmosphere with a circular mahogany bar, and a white grand piano in the centre of the room with stools set around its broad base. There were small discrete conversational areas separated by huge potted palms.

Two oil paintings hung on the wall. One was of a young mother and child walking on the beach, with the colours of the water perfectly captured. The second one was much larger: a watercolour of The Falls. Looking in the corner, Jacqui saw it was signed C and she wondered if it was the Countess.

A young man was playing the piano, starting off with "Summertime" from Porgy and Bess. She heard the moving melody and when she looked up, she found she was staring at Gary Gordon, who was leaning against the wooden door frame, watching her. They exchanged a long glance before Gary walked in, a distinct swagger in his gait.

"Good evening, Dulcey," said Gary to the pianist. "Johnny and Frances, I didn't know you were back?" He introduced himself to Al, who looked him up and down, and Jacqui couldn't tell who was more shocked when he greeted Nikko Tai Kaishai in Japanese. When he reached Jacqui, he merely put out his hand. "Gary," he said.

"Jacqui," she responded, taking it, surprised at his cool gentle touch.

The exotic-looking woman that Jacqui had noticed the evening before walked into Ivories, and saw Gary talking to Jacqui. Immediately, she moved towards him.

"I've been looking for you," she said with a smile that was so phony that Jacqui wanted to be sick.

"Here I am," said Gary, dropping Jacqui's hand as he introduced her to everyone as Trina Doyan. Jacqui watched as she charmed the men with one look, and took absolutely no notice of the women. Nikko flashed a look at Jacqui and despite the language barrier Jacqui knew they had read each other's minds.

Dulcey had an amazing repertoire and had everyone clapping their hands, begging for an encore. "I would love to, but I need a short break. Mr. Gary, why don't you give these old keys a whirl?"

"I don't think so," said Gary.

"Come on," said Dulcey. "When I get back we can do one of our famous numbers together."

"Oh, Gary, you must. Play one of those Noel Coward tunes your mother likes so much," insisted Trina, her diamond and emerald bracelet flashing in the light.

Gary sat down on the bench that Dulcey had vacated and played a warm-up tune before breaking into "I'll See You Again" by Noel Coward. Jacqui watched his long graceful fingers on the ivory keys as she listened to him sing.

" 'I'll see you again, / Whenever spring breaks through again.' " He smiled at Jacqui, who felt as if she was the only one in the room, so compelling was his presence.

Suddenly Jacqui felt something cold running down her leg. When she looked up, she saw that Trina had spilled her drink on her. "So sorry, Jill," she said, smiling apologetically, as she handed Jacqui a single napkin.

"The name is Jacqui," she said, picking up her own napkin, trying to wipe away the mess.

"So sorry, Jacqui," said Trina, slowly sauntering over to the bar to get some more napkins. "How clumsy of me."

"Never mind," said Jacqui, standing up. "I think I'll say good night now."

"Don't go yet. The party is just starting," said Gary, rising from the piano bench.

"That's all right," said Jacqui. "Thanks for a lovely evening."

She made her way back to her room, instantly peeling

off her dress the moment she stepped inside. 'What a little bitch,' thought Jacqui, running the dress under cold water, hoping it wouldn't stain. She put on her short silk robe, and was preparing for bed when there was a knock at the door.

"Who is there?" she asked.

"Bar service," said a male voice.

"I didn't order anything," said Jacqui, moving to the door.

"It was ordered for you," said the voice.

Opening the door, she found Gary Gordon standing there with two fluted champagne glasses in one hand and a bottle in the other.

"Hi," he said, holding up the bottle.

"I didn't order a drink," she said.

"I know, but you left so abruptly that I didn't have a chance to apologize and ask you to join me for a drink, so I brought it to you," he said, grinning arrogantly. "Aren't you going to invite me in?" he asked.

"I don't think so," she said.

"Well then, take these," he said, shoving the glasses and bottle into her hands, as he suddenly took a step inside. Without warning, he grabbed her shoulders, pulling her against his firm chest. He moved his hands down her body with deliberate slowness, watching her startled expression. It didn't last more than a few seconds, but it inflamed her senses, sending her body reeling. Before she could move or utter a response, he backed away, brushing his finger against her lips.

"I just wanted to see what you felt like," he said, smiling into her eyes before he closed the door.

Jacqui leaned against the door, still holding the champagne and glasses. Warning signals went off in her head, telling her to stay away from Gary, but there was excitement and bewilderment mingled with the danger that enticed her.

Chapter 5

The warm Caribbean breeze felt like a lover's embrace as Jacqui walked along the beach at The Falls, admiring the collage of blue towels matching the sea. She ambled over to the pier, noting the kayaks, canoes and sunfishes that were available for the guests.

She was looking with envy at a sixteen-foot Boston Whaler with "The Falls III " painted in gold and blue letters on its side when Gary walked out onto the dock. He smiled at her, putting his hand out.

"We're almost ready to go. I'm just doing a last-minute check on the engine."

"Go where?" asked Jacqui, tilting her head in defiance.

"The Sans Souci. Are you ready?" he asked.

"I am not going anywhere with you," said Jacqui, turning to leave.

"Please don't be like that," said Gary. He reached out to touch her but dropped his hand before his fingers grazed against her skin.

"Be like what?" she asked. "You stole my seat. Not took but stole. Do you think you should toss people off their flights because it suits *your* travel plans?"

"I didn't know it was yours. I am truly sorry. Let me make it up to you. I'll introduce you to Charlie. He's a one-hundred-year-old turtle that lives in a cave under his bar," said Gary charmingly.

"I am not getting in a boat with you. You might throw me overboard out at sea," said Jacqui, smiling in spite of herself.

"Humour me, please. Ease my conscience about the mishap at Kennedy Airport. Come take a ride with me?" he asked in such a beguiling manner that Jacqui dropped her guard. Sensing this, he quickly ushered her onto the Boston Whaler, barely giving her time to protest.

Gary manoeuvred the boat slowly from the dock, then pulled the throttle back full speed once they passed through the reef. Jacqui braced her feet on the floor, holding on to the deck for dear life. She was sure that Gary was driving like a maniac just to get a rise out of her.

"The sun is really bright this morning. Take my hat," said Gary, handing her his baseball cap.

"No thanks," she said, gripping the deck, praying she wouldn't get sick. He would probably enjoy that too much.

He slowed down when the peach-coloured Sans Souci Hotel came into view. After docking the boat, he extended his hand to help Jacqui out, leading her past the inviting mineral pool where water aerobics was being taught, up a stone flight of stairs to the hotel. Gary picked up a package for Robert Davids and then took her on a tour of the public rooms. He smiled when he saw her delight at the lounge decorated with miniature hot air balloons. They had delicious fruit punches served in chilled glasses in Charlie's Bar and watched him emerge from his cave to eat lobster and lettuce for breakfast.

"Not too long ago, the owners of this hotel thought it was time that Charlie had a mate," Gary told her. "They brought in a lovely young lady turtle from Cayman, but Charlie made her life miserable. That's when they found out Charlie was a girl."

"Are you trying to tell me that it took one hundred years to figure out Charlie was a female?" asked Jacqui incredulously.

"Yes it did," Gary laughed – then added, "But I knew

you were one from the moment I laid eyes on you." He was looking at her in a way that left her feeling flushed, and she was relieved when he indicated that it was time to leave.

Gary took a more leisurely ride back to The Falls, pointing out beautiful villas nestled in blue coves. As the hotel came into sight, Gary showed her a cove that was almost hidden by the overgrowth.

"That's Whispering Waters," said Gary. "It's a beautiful little cove surrounded by two cliffs. It's difficult to get to unless you walk behind the hotel."

"Is it deep?" asked Jacqui, noticing the indigo-turquoise colour of the water.

"There's very deep water on the outskirts of the reef. It really is two reefs that run parallel to each other with only a small opening to get through, so it's treacherous to navigate," said Gary.

He pulled the boat to the dock at The Falls with ease. He headed for the beach bar and Jacqui followed him slowly, still feeling wary of him. He ordered two ice-cold beers. The Tai Kaishais joined them, their noses already peeling. Al had been taking pictures of a hermit crab that had washed up on the beach. Nikko began jumping up and down excitedly when a Bob Marley song was played on the public address system. She mouthed the words in English.

"Gary san, I have a question to pose to you," said Al.

"Shoot," said Gary, settling back on the stool, placing his baseball cap on Jacqui's head.

"In two days Nikko's birthday. I want her to have a birthday she will always remember. You see, she promise to have baby this year if she have birthday party with reggae music and dancing. She think I forget her birthday. In Japan, it would be tomorrow but Nikko not fully understand international date line. She think it yesterday, not today, like tomorrow," said Al, thinking he made perfect sense.

"You want to have a birthday party for her?" asked

Gary, trying to comprehend Al's story.

"Yes, for the baby," responded Al.

"I'll talk to Robert Davids and Brian and see what they can do. I'm sure they can rustle up a cake," said Gary.

"What about the reggae music?" asked Al, looking concerned.

"Plenty of it," replied Gary, smiling.

They all had lunch together at a table shaded by a colourful umbrella near the beach grill. The fresh fruit salads and vegetables tasted as nature intended and were delicious. Gary kept a running dialogue of Japanese and English so Nikko and Jacqui could ask each other questions. He was as smooth and charming as a seasoned statesman.

The liquor and sun took their toll on Jacqui and she felt her head begin to pound and her vision blur. She put on her sunglasses, trying to keep attentive, but the pain only intensified.

"Please excuse me," she said, standing up. "I need to go back to my room."

"Are you all right?" asked Gary, concerned.

"Fine, just a headache," she answered, waving her hand as he rose, but the pain suddenly moved to her eyes.

"I'll walk you back." He was leaving no room for argument as he excused himself. "I told you to wear my hat," he said, escorting Jacqui to her room. Not wanting to, she leaned against him, the pain severe and sudden. She handed Gary her key without a word.

"Take a cool shower," he said as he moved around the room, drawing the drapes and turning on the air conditioner. "You have a spot of sunstroke. Take two aspirins, rest and drink plenty of water, and you'll be fine this evening." His fingers touched her forehead. "See you later."

Jacqui took a cold shower, letting the water run through her hair, trying to dull the throbbing pain in her head.

Forcing two aspirin down, she wrapped her wet hair in a towel, pulled on an oversized t-shirt, and dropped into bed. Her ears were ringing as she surrendered to a troubled sleep.

* * *

Gary quietly let himself into Jacqui's room with her key, balancing the tray with one hand. He glanced at the sleeping figure. Hearing her groan, he put the tray on the dresser, and cautiously approached her. In her sleep, she was tugging at the towel she had wrapped around her hair. Gently removing it, he found himself sitting by her side, stroking her hair.

* * *

It was late afternoon when she awoke. Putting her hands on her head, she felt for her towel, and spied it neatly folded on the chair. Her eyes moved to the dresser and she slowly dropped her hands. A pitcher of chilled coconut water along with a single rose and her room key lay on the tray.

Getting out of bed shakily, she poured herself a glass of coconut water and looked at the strange colour of the rose. It was a hybrid between pink and red. "Hope you're feeling better. Sunset Bar – 7:00," read the note attached to the flower. Turning the note over she saw the PS, "You are beautiful when you sleep."

A smile played across her lips. She felt a tinge of excitement and anticipation that she had forgotten existed.

* * *

Gary paused at the entrance of the Sunset Bar, catching the last rays of the startling sunset. He saw Jacqui, waiting by the rail, talking to two single men who had just arrived. Her tan blended with the green silk of her open-back top that clung to her breasts like a bee to a honeysuckle. A sudden shaft of desire ran through his body.

"I see that you are feeling better," he said as he joined her, slowly tracing his hand from her neck to her shoulder, as he casually greeted the two new arrivals.

"I am," said Jacqui, pulling back, startled at his intimacy. "You were really very kind."

"Nonsense," said Gary, lightly dismissing her thanks with a wave of his hand. "What are you drinking?" he asked.

"I don't know, I don't want a pina colada or yellow bird. I want something that goes down easy and smooth," she said .

"I know just the thing," he said, leading her to the bar. "Roy, I want you to make me two of your finest Tropical Sins."

"No problem, boss," said the efficient bartender. He carefully measured the mixture of rums and fruit juices that matched the colour of a Jamaican sunset. He served it in tall glasses which he placed before them with a flourish.

"Mr. G, that is an Original Tropical Sin. You know no one else in the world can make them like I can," he said proudly, waiting for Jacqui to take a sip.

"I know that, Roy. You're the best," Gary said.

She tasted the drink, letting it slowly roll along her tongue before she swallowed, licking her lips. "It's absolutely delicious," said Jacqui, smiling at him.

"My t'anks, mi lady," said Roy, filling three more complicated drink orders without missing a beat.

"Outside of missing your flight coming to Jamaica, how are you enjoying your stay?" Gary asked.

"It's been really nice so far. I like The Falls a lot. There seems to be a lot to do, but I don't feel pressured to do

58

anything," said Jacqui. "The island has a lot of character, unlike some places I've been to. Were you born here?" she asked.

"Born and growed," he answered.

"This is my first trip to Jamaica, but I've been fascinated by the island ever since I can remember. I guess everyone is. Tell me, what is so unique about this island?"

"Such a simple question with so many complex answers," he said, sensing her deep and probing mind. He had been right. She wasn't the typical tourist seeking a fantasy escape.

"If you really want to know about things that are unique, I'll try to tell you a few interesting little bits of trivia," he continued easily. "For instance, did you know that there are more miles of road per square mile than anywhere else in the world? And the one I like is that there are more churches in Jamaica for its size than anywhere else in the world."

"I'm impressed," said Jacqui, smiling.

"I think one of Jamaica's most interesting features is that it is the only place in the world where they actually plan to lose fifty percent of the coconut crop to thieves." Gary's rich laughter blended with Jacqui's.

When three stars stood out against the electric blue sky, he led her to the pool terrace. "I'm a semi-permanent resident here. Since one of my best friends runs the hotel, I'm allowed a few small but cherished privileges," he said, directing Jacqui to a covered trellis by the pool. "I thought after this afternoon you might enjoy a quiet dinner away from the crowd."

In the corner was one table, beautifully set with English bone china, silver and crystal. The whole scene was illuminated by a glass hurricane lantern.

"Oh!" exclaimed Jacqui, taken by the romantic setting. "This is really beautiful."

He escorted her to the table, making sure she was

comfortable before taking his own chair. The wine steward appeared out of nowhere, to take their order.

"Good evening, miss, good evening, Mr. Gary," he said. "So pleased you could dine with us this evening. It is a fine evening, don't you think? Have you decided on dinner? I can recommend the filet or the grilled snapper."

"Two filets mignons," said Gary, looking to Jacqui for approval. She nodded. "Do you prefer red or white wine?" he asked.

"Red, please," responded Jacqui quickly.

"Mr. James, I recall you once told me that when Jamaica gained independence from England in 1962 you were so moved that you put away a case of wine. What happened to that wine?" asked Gary.

"Lord, Mr. Gary," said Mr. James, breaking into a broad smile. "You remember everything. True, your grandfather was there when I did it. There are two bottles of that 1962 Chateau Lafitte Rothschild left. An excellent choice," he continued, fingering a large key on his heavy chain, as he backed away before doing an about-face in military style.

"Tell me, what brings a charming and lovely lady like yourself to Jamaica on holiday alone? I assume you are alone?" Gary asked, looking at her in the moonlight.

"I had a really rough winter. I needed a sunshine break in a bad way. I had heard about The Falls and decided to come," she said simply.

"Alone, I understand," said Gary.

"Alone," said Jacqui with a smile, looking up at Mr. James as he uncorked the bottle and ceremoniously poured a small amount for Gary to taste.

"I would say the lady has an adventurous streak," said Gary, sipping the first-growth wine. He rolled the rich bouquet in his mouth before swallowing. "Excellent, Mr. James."

"A tiny little adventurous streak," said Jacqui.

"I somehow don't get the feeling it's very tiny," said Gary.

"What do you do that allows you to keep a residence at this hotel?" asked Jacqui.

"I keep my polo ponies here," said Gary easily. "Robert Davids, an old friend of mine who runs the hotel, puts up with me and I do small errands like the one I did this morning. I run a pimento plantation down the coast called Spicey Hill Farms. I spend a lot of time there when I'm not looking after some of my family's interests on the island."

From the first sip of wine, to the perfectly done steaks, to the small drams of Tia Maria liqueur, the conversation flowed easily between them. A sweet breeze bathed them, scented with jasmine.

"Do you still travel abroad to play polo?" asked Jacqui.

"Rarely, if ever," said Gary. "I'll play in an international competition if it's staged here, but I'm officially retired."

"Why?" she asked. "You must be one of the best players in the world."

"Home," said Gary, in one simple word. "I wanted to be home. I was tired of being a guest in someone else's country. I have a stake in this land, a deep historical and emotional tie that I couldn't ignore any longer."

Jacqui listened, trying to understand what motivated him, what complex background made up a man like him. The striking difference between Gary and the other men she had known was that he seemed to know exactly who he was. More than that – he had direction and a sense of purpose.

"My grandfather, Winston Gordon, was a man ahead of his time as well as a unique character. He said you could tell the worth of a person from their eyes. Based on this philosophy, he once loaned a man named Chen enough money to rebuild his grocery store after it was destroyed by the earthquake of 1907. The Chen family ended up building the largest supermarket chain on the island.

"He lent him the money because he trusted his eyes. That started a friendship that lasted three generations," said Gary, lightly tracing the outline of her long manicured nails. "Am I reading your eyes?" He slowly brought her hand to his lips. "Can I trust what I think I see?"

"To meet and share dinner is one thing. Trust is a totally different matter," said Jacqui, amused, looking into his emerald eyes that were illuminated by the light of the flickering lantern. "Trust is a big word. With trust there isn't any room for illusion."

He stared at her intently, silently pressing for her to continue.

"I've always thought that trust is a subtle gift that is attained by a lucky few. When you trust, you lose the sensation that time is slipping away and suddenly feel as if you're being pulled upward by a magnet. But trust is very dangerous," said Jacqui, her eyebrows raised. "It listens to the often unheard little voice inside all of us that encourages us to be daring and spontaneous."

Gary watched her and felt he was being pulled into her through her eyes. He knew that he had walked on a corner of her soul, touching a very sensitive nerve. More than anything, he wanted to find out what made her so vulnerable.

"Anyway, my daddy told me if a man ever says 'trust me' I should run like hell," she said with a wink.

"We islanders are a very passionate people who grab each day's pleasure with the rising sun. We don't allow much time for thinking. I find myself in the company of a beautiful woman. I want the minutes I spend with you to be filled with spontaneity so each moment will become special on its own and every moment we share is precious," said Gary.

"Is that island philosophy?" she asked, suppressing her laughter.

"That's Gordon philosophy," he said with a smile. "Let's go see the show."

He led her through the garden to the large open-air entertainment area. Most of the hotel guests were assembled and Cool Runnings, a three-man band, was singing reggae and calypso songs. The performers wore shiny silver costumes and moved with lithe grace across the stage. Their beat was unmistakably Jamaican.

They made their way to the bar, several people greeting Gary along the way. The lead singer introduced a special song made famous by Harry Belafonte. Jacqui was immediately captivated by the melody and the words.

" 'Oh island in the sun, / Willed to me by my father's hand, / All my days I will sing in praise, / Of your forests, waters and shining sands.' "

The other singers joined in, rendering the melody like dancing palm leaves in the cool evening breeze.

"How do you like calypso?" he asked.

"I love it," she responded. "I want to get a copy of this so I can listen to it on a snowy night in New York and remember tonight." He smiled his response, grasping her hand for a moment.

At the end of the show Ruell the MC, a brown-skinned young man dressed in a black suit and bow tie, came to the microphone. He ran down the list of evening activities.

"For those of you who want to dance the night away, the disco is open with reggae music until you say so," he said, pointing at the audience. "There is also dancing under the stars right here with Cool Runnings until midnight.

"Tonight is jazz night in the Sunset Bar and Ivories Piano Bar is open until you say so. There is also crabbing on the western beach. For those of you who have signed up for the moonlight rafting, you should meet in the main lobby at 10:30. We hope you enjoyed the show. Have a wonderful evening," he concluded.

"Wow," commented Jacqui. "I came here on vacation. If I did everything on that schedule I think I would die of exhaustion."

"You probably would," agreed Gary. "But with all those activities you can exercise your right not to do anything."

They went dancing in Scandals disco, first to rock and roll and then to oldies. The way he moved and held her body excited Jacqui. When they were hot and sweaty, he took her hand and they walked slowly to the beach, kicking off their shoes. The sand was still warm from the hot sun.

"This feels so good," said Jacqui, digging her feet in the sand. "All winter long I thought my feet would never warm up."

Gary glanced at Jacqui, her face lit by the glow of the moon. He sensed something in her that touched him in a way he hadn't been touched for a long time. Her untapped smouldering sensuality seemed to beckon him.

"All the years I spent in boarding school and travelling, I used to dream about this beach," he said, picking up a stone and throwing it. It skipped twice on the surface before it fell into the water.

They walked along the beach with Gary pointing out the stars and constellations like the Seven Sisters and Cassiopeia. He rested his hand on her shoulder, slowly urging her close to him.

"I bet I know what you are going to do next?" she murmured as he put his other arm around her, pulling her to his chest.

"Let's see," he said, holding her face in his hands, lightly tracing the outline of her top lip and then the bottom. Jacqui involuntarily let out a sigh before he lowered his lips to hers.

His kiss was chaste at first, but when he ran his tongue over her lips, his kiss deepening, he awakened a desire that Jacqui had forced herself to forget. She was captive in his embrace at the edge of the dark water, illuminated by the moon.

They picked up their shoes, and walked slowly along the shore. Gary showed her a short cut to the dining room before they walked through the richly scented garden to her room. On reaching it, he put his hand out for her room key, opening the door.

"Thanks for a lovely evening," she said.

"It's not over yet," said Gary suggestively.

"It is for me," she said politely but firmly, smiling at him.

"There is always tomorrow," he said. "I enjoyed the evening." He stroked her cheek with his thumb before placing a gentle kiss on her parted lips.

Jacqui watched him walk down the corridor before she closed the door quietly. Lost in thought, she automatically began taking off her clothes and hanging them up. Touching her cheek, she felt a tide of emotions that brought a rush of sweet pleasure mingled with confusion.

Gary was pleased with himself as he walked through the property, savouring the stillness, confident in the knowledge that by tomorrow night Jacqui would be as open to his affection as a dewsoaked flower. He spent the better part of his walk trying to figure out whether the chase or the conquest was better. "It's like marlin fishing," he eventually decided. "After fighting a fish for so long, it's almost a letdown to finally pull it on the boat, the fight over."

Chapter 6

Jacqui heard a bell ringing in her sleep. She grabbed the extra feather pillow, burrowing her head underneath. She was savouring the last glimmer of her sweet dream as she pushed her hand out, groping for the phone.

"Huh," she said groggily into the phone.

"To the stables, my beauty," boomed Gary's voice in her ear. "It's a beautiful morning for a ride."

"What time is it?" she asked in a raspy voice, as she pushed the pillow from her face, still seeing darkness.

"Just before six. Are you getting out of bed?" he asked.

"It's not even five-thirty, you creep," she cried out in frustration, glancing at the illuminated dial of her alarm clock. "Call me in an hour and I might be more agreeable."

"Sit up, fling off the sheets that are covering your beautiful body and plant your feet firmly on the floor," said Gary. "If you don't do that I will come and get you," he threatened.

"I'm out of bed, but I'm not thrilled," said Jacqui, doing exactly what he said.

"See you in fifteen minutes," he said, and grinned as he heard Jacqui throw the phone on the floor before clattering it down on the receiver.

With her hat in hand, Jacqui walked on the dewsoaked lawn to the stables in the cool grey morning, watching the sun slowly begin to warm the island.

"Good morning. How are you?" she asked the stable boy, when she slipped through the side door of the stable.

"Not as good as you, miss," he responded, looking up from tightening the bridle of a chestnut mare.

Approaching the mare slowly, she stroked her behind her ears as she talked in a low soothing voice. A pair of hands spanned her waist and slowly turned her around.

"Good morning," Gary said pleasantly. His hair was still damp from his morning shower. "How are you this fine West Indian morning?" He smiled at her, making her feel as if she was the most special person in the world.

"I'm fine, but I like gentle wakeups," she said breathlessly, all too aware of the devastating effect of his electric presence.

"I'll remember that," he said. He turned his attention to the mare. "She was a beauty of a runner in her day. She's part Arabian, which accounts for her speed. Her name is Maid Marion. I sold El Maestro, her son, to Chukka Cove last year."

Lester, the stable boy, helped Jacqui to mount Maid Marion while Gary mounted a stallion, Island Jack, with practised ease. They trotted slowly along the trail, following a stream to the beach. The gentle slope was covered in a sea of green leaves. Maid Marion picked up Island Jack's restlessness and was throwing up her front legs as they neared the last shallow crossing before the beach.

"We'll give them their head when we get on the sand," called Gary.

As soon as Island Jack's hoofs hit the sand, he broke into a canter, with Maid Marion quick to follow his example. Jacqui was prepared for the sudden change and gripped her seat firmly, admiring Gary's almost regal posture and broad shoulders. He rode as if he and the horse spoke their own language. Looking relaxed and in control, he galloped along the water's edge.

When they reached the end of the wide expanse, he applied pressure with his thighs, pulling back the reins with smooth confidence.

"Let the horse cool down for a bit," said Gary. Holding the reins in his hand, he gracefully dismounted in one sweeping motion. Then he draped the rein over Island Jack's head. He looked to see if Jacqui needed any assistance, but she was already on the sand.

"The creep you hung up on this morning is going to kiss you good morning," he whispered sensually, moving his arms around her, slowly lowering his lips to hers in a deep searing kiss. The first rays of the morning sun burst through, warming Jacqui as much as the kiss as she allowed her body to lean on Gary.

She felt her knees buckle as she put her hands on his shoulders, easing into him. They kissed on the sunlit beach, the sand marked only by two sets of horse prints.

"Is that a more gentle wakeup?" he asked her when they parted, watching her redden slightly, enjoying her sultry innocence. "I think I like being called a creep."

* * *

After their ride, Gary returned to his villa, changing into a pair of cut-off shorts and a t-shirt, the clothes he felt most comfortable in. He looked around the house for signs of Trina. "Where the hell is that girl," he muttered, walking down the path from the villa.

He had arranged to meet Jacqui for breakfast. His mouth was watering for a hearty Jamaican meal like mackerel rundown, liver and onions or ackee and saltfish. He cut through the service path and was almost at the end when he saw Trina walking towards him, her eyes downcast.

"Where the hell were you last night?" he asked.

"Where the hell were you?" retorted Trina.

"Trina, we can't continue like this," said Gary. "I'm warning you not to pull another stunt like this again."

"Stunt, you say," she said menacingly. "What do you plan to do – send me off to some obscure spot so I don't inconvenience you by being in the way?"

Jacqui, walking down the path towards breakfast, stopped short when she saw Trina and Gary. She took in the exchange with growing dread, tasting bitter jealousy as she observed the exotic woman who had a firm and mysterious hold on Gary. She was the kind of woman every man must fantasize about taking to bed. Her provocative sensuality was like a shining beacon to a shipwrecked sailor.

Unnoticed by both of them, Jacqui watched Trina shake off Gary's hand before turning abruptly and flouncing off in the opposite direction. She took several deep breaths before she joined Gary.

* * *

Gary led Jacqui to the dock after breakfast and motioned for her to climb into a beautiful Welcraft. He took his time moving along the coast. The pristine white sand beaches were dazzling, reflecting the bright morning sun as the boat passed over clear patches of sand surrounded by sea grass. Gradually Jacqui's tension eased, and she saw that Gary, preoccupied throughout breakfast, was also relaxing.

When they reached Dunn's River Falls, cascading down the mountain like a fan, Gary dropped the anchor. They swam the short distance to the mouth of the river and the base of the falls.

Holding hands, they negotiated the slippery falls amid the bellows of the local guides assisting scantily clad climbers. When they reached the top, the boat anchored offshore seemed like a toy surrounded by aqua water. The grey clouds were a blanket rolling in behind the Epworth mountains. They immersed themselves in the cold water.

Later they climbed back down the falls, and swam back

to the boat. Pulling up the anchor, Gary started up the engine and glanced at Jacqui. Droplets of water were glistening on her already brown skin.

Gary hugged the reef before he directed the boat towards another cove. Jacqui had to catch her breath. She thought she had seen every beach from Montserrat to Morocco, but the splendour that stretched before her eyes was by far the most exotic and beautiful she had ever seen.

"What is this place?" she asked.

"Laughing Waters," said Gary. "The first James Bond movie, *Doctor No*, was filmed here."

A babbling stream, surrounded by a beautiful green lawn, wound its way down the hillside, falling first into a pond before cascading into a waterfall that formed a natural pool at the bottom. A freshwater stream etched its way in the powder-white sand to the expansive stretch of the sea lined by coconut trees.

Handing Jacqui a snorkel mask, Gary dove into the water, surfacing ten feet from the boat. Diving in behind him, she adjusted the snorkel mask and they made a lazy circle in the water that was three colours of blue. Schools of tiny fish flitted around them as they swam to the shore. They flopped on the beach, their breath coming in short bursts.

"This is too beautiful," she said, running her fingers through her hair and lying back on the sand.

"It's prettier at night," he said, sitting beside her.

"Impossible," said Jacqui, taking in the broad expanse of splendour as she dug her heels in the sand, and scooped up a handful of grains. They were quiet for a moment, absorbing the beauty. Jacqui's mind ran back to the encounter she had witnessed that morning.

"Gary, I know we just met so this question may be none of my business and premature, but I'm going to ask you anyway," she said, watching him. "Who is Trina Doyan?"

"She's in guest relations," said Gary easily, playing with

a coconut leaf.

"Are you involved with her?" asked Jacqui, glancing away.

"Not in the way you think," he responded, touching her shoulder.

"That was two questions. Now do I get to ask you some questions?" he asked.

Jacqui was about to respond when she felt a raindrop on her lip. The sun was obliterated by an encroaching mass of clouds. Within moments, a few drops had turned into large stinging bullets, pounding their bodies. They jumped up and ran into the water, swimming quickly back to the boat.

"It's going to rain all afternoon," said Gary as the rain pelted them on their way back to the hotel. "The bars at The Falls will be doing a booming business."

* * *

It did rain all afternoon. Heavy warm raindrops tumbled from a dark sky. Most of the guests had taken refuge in the bar or the games room.

Jacqui was stretched in a hammock, her body wrapped in a towel, in a thatched hut on the beach. She let the churning seas and rain cleanse her. It was late afternoon when the sun finally came out, drying up the puddles as it made its languorous journey across the sky. She watched its path, grateful for the time at The Falls before she would eventually have to confront Geoff. The humiliation of the King affair cropped up in her mind and an unexpected tear welled up. Closing her eyes, she felt the tear roll down her face.

"Now, now, none of that," said Gary, coming into the hut. He slipped his hand under her damp hair and wiped away the glistening teardrop with his thumb. He allowed his hand to linger, catching a glimpse of sadness emanating from Jacqui's eyes.

"This is a place where we lock all our troubles away. Now I came to find you to tell you to go and get dressed," he said, slowly massaging her neck, instantly feeling the tension in her. "I've managed to worm us a reservation at Mahogany Hall."

"Why are you doing this?" she asked, wanting to trust him, afraid.

"I told you last night. I like your eyes."

* * *

Ainsley was waved through the gate into Jamaica House, the prime minister's office. He drove his Jaguar down the drive, lined with yellow and red lilies. Along the front of the two-storeyed white modern structure were "No Parking" signs. Despite this, cars with ministerial and diplomatic licence plates blocked the driveway.

"Damn foolishness," thought Ainsley, wondering how these high-placed people could run a country if they couldn't obey a simple traffic sign.

He walked into the building, past the portrait of Sir George Michaels and up the winding staircase to the office of Derrick Bloomfield, one of the most respected members of the prime minister's staff. He gave the secretary his name, knowing Derrick would keep him waiting in a show of power. Taking out his *Gleaner*, he read PJ's column with a grin. After waiting half an hour, the secretary finally motioned him in.

"Good afternoon, Derrick," said Ainsley as he walked in. "Please don't get up." Derrick looked like King Farouk sitting in an enormous chair especially configured for his massive weight. No two men could have been more physically different. Ainsley was a tall, extremely handsome man with striking almond colouring and clean-cut good looks. Derrick was pasty-pale and so obese he could have joined a circus as the fatman.

"Sorry to have kept you waiting, but you know, these affairs of the state," said Derrick pompously.

"I'm sure," answered Ainsley, noticing that Derrick's tie was stained and crusted over with food.

"I just asked you here to congratulate you, old boy. Commander of the United Nations Task Force on narcotics. Well done."

"Thank you," said Ainsley, wondering when Derrick would get to the point. The phone rang. Derrick was on the line for over five minutes, a one-sided, longwinded conversation. He took the time to glance around the room, noticing the catalogues for electronic security and communication equipment. There were two recent copies of an English magazine that specialized in analyzing new military equipment.

"The prime minister felt I should talk to you about the demarcation of authority," said Derrick, slightly winded from his conversation.

"I've already received my orders from the prime minister who has the cabinet responsibility for the Ministry of Defence. I'm here so we can talk about how we are going to coordinate our information and get those animals," said Ainsley tersely, his patience wearing thin.

"We will," said Derrick reassuringly. "Right now, though, I think your major concern is to have your troops trained and ready for when they are needed. I want them to be the best. We're after these men in a big way."

"I would like to put a team out at the Kingston docks for surveillance," said Ainsley, gauging Derrick's reaction.

"That's all under control. I have looked after that personally," said Derrick. "Now that we have this all squared away, how about a drink? The Windies are licking the English in the third test series."

* * *

Gary watched Jacqui enter the lobby wearing an off-the-shoulder white dress that clung suggestively to her body. Her hair was in a French knot and a few tendrils trailed over her neck. He pinched a rose from the flower arrangement on the front desk and walked over to greet her.

She saw his approach from across the room, his white dinner jacket earning appreciative looks from the female guests.

"Good evening, Jacqui," he said, taking her arm. "I've got something special planned for you tonight." In the circular driveway, illuminated by the cascading fountains, a horse and buggy stood waiting.

"Good evening, Egbert," said Gary to the carriage master, who was dressed in black trousers and a shirt made of the red and black bandana plaid that was a popular island print. Gary assisted Jacqui into the buggy. She was laughing with delight.

"Oh, Gary, this is wonderful," she said as he handed her the white rose. Clicking his whip, Egbert urged the horse along as they crossed the main road, before passing through the canefield across from the hotel.

The full moon in the electric blue sky cast shadows against the sugar canefields that surrounded Mahogany Hall. Built as the plantation owner's residence, the Georgian great house was nestled in a bend on the Roaring River.

Mr. Boxer, the maître d', welcomed them warmly, assisting Jacqui out of the buggy before escorting them through the house that had been turned into a four-star restaurant. He gave Jacqui time to look at the antique maps of Jamaica that were framed on the wall leading into the lounge.

He seated them at a secluded table on a stone patio, lit by a lantern. They enjoyed cocktails, serenaded by the roaring river as they studied the menu in the dim light.

Jacqui was so entranced by the sound of the river that she was reluctant to follow the waiter, dressed in a stiff tuxedo, to their table in the formal dining room decorated in heavy Victorian furniture with red velvet upholstery.

"Would you like wine with dinner?" asked Gary.

"I would love some," said Jacqui as Gary was handed the leatherbound wine list.

"Pick a number between one and sixty-nine," he said, looking down the wine list.

"Thirty-six," she replied.

"Excellent choice," said Gary, closing the menu, indicating number thirty-six to the waiter. "You chose fine champagne," he said.

They ordered the hot and cold antipasto and the mixed seafood grill for two. Every single bite melted in her mouth, washed down with the intoxicating Moët Chandon champagne.

After dinner, they were led to a fragrantly scented garden for dessert. There a calypso band played softly in an ivy-covered gazebo. Sipping expressos, they watched a masterful preparation of *bananes flambées*.

The waiter melted butter in a large skillet, carefully browning the sugar before adding a drop of lime. With a practised eye, he poured in a blend of liqueurs, heating the mixture over an open flame until it was hot and bubbly. Adding slices of fresh bananas to the sweet fragrant liquid, he let it simmer until the bananas were tender. With great ceremony, he set the bananas upon heated plates, doused them with brandy and then set them alight.

Jacqui's eyes widened like a child watching fireworks, when her plate was set before her. "The bananas with all that liqueur is bad enough, but dousing it all with brandy and igniting it is just plain sinful," she said in between mouthfuls.

"What do you say about the vanilla ice cream," he teased as he leaned back, watching her polish off her portion with ease.

"The vanilla ice cream is immoral," she said, laughing. "My father's favourite pastime is to watch me eat. When we used to go flying, he would radio ahead to the kitchen to make sure they had plenty of pie."

"You fly?" he asked, looking at her curiously.

"I could fly before I could drive. My father is a colonel in the air force. He holds a Purple Heart from Korea and a Bronze Star from Vietnam. He taught me how to fly," said Jacqui proudly. "I think he set a few records that have yet to be broken."

"What did your mother have to say to all this?" asked Gary.

"My mother died in a car accident when I was ten. We were stationed in Hawaii at the time," she said, looking at Gary. "Please don't say you're sorry."

"I won't. My father passed away less than two years ago and it still feels as if he is with me every day," said Gary. "So it's you and the colonel."

"That's right. It's just me and the colonel," said Jacqui. "You see, with Dad in the service, we lived all over the world. I was too young to remember the Philippines and Germany but I have vivid memories of Spain. After Mom died, Dad got posted stateside to my mom's and his hometown, Dayton, Ohio. He wanted me to have a stable environment growing up.

"My mom was Jace's childhood sweetheart and the love of his life. I don't think he's ever really recovered. Flying was the way we both got over our grief," said Jacqui. "All I have to do is to close my eyes and the memories of those crisp spring mornings come back to me. We would fly over golden wheatfields and endless plains that were intersected by meandering rivers. The world became a mixture of space and land and I was respectful of its dimensions. We would fly to Kentucky for a bluegrass festival or to Indianapolis for the races."

"It must have given you a unique perspective of the world," said Gary.

"Very," said Jacqui, laughing. "For years I thought Southern Comfort was a soft drink. I earned a few hundred pops by naming the planes in the field and identifying their engines."

"Do you still fly?" he asked.

"I've kept up with my hours of air time, but not much else," she said, almost sadly.

"What do you miss the most?" he asked, studying her face, animated with pleasure.

"I don't know," she said, nibbling at his unfinished dessert. "Do you mind?" she asked, taking the plate. "Strange as it may sound – I guess I miss the comforting roar of the engines. When I'm stuck on the subway or locked away in four square walls in New York during the winter, I dream about the freedom up high above the clouds."

The calypso band was still playing in the background and Gary put his hand out for Jacqui's, leading her onto the dance floor. He held her close, running his hand down her back as he moved his body to the music, drawing her into the hypnotic beat. There were a few other couples on the dance floor, but as far as she cared she was dancing alone with Gary.

The music stopped playing but they remained in each other's arms. A cool breeze rustled, scented by the nearby frangipani tree, as Jacqui shivered, moving ever closer to Gary. His arm tightened around her and he placed a seductive kiss on her bare shoulder.

"I want to take you to a place that will replace the roar of the engine as your most comforting sound," he whispered in her ear.

He signed for the bill, and slipped Jacqui's shawl over her shoulders as they walked through the lounge. In the former ballroom of the great house, there was a reception thronged with guests. The air was filled with tantalizing scents and the uniformed waiters were busy serving drinks.

"Good to see you, GG," called a huge fat man that Jacqui recognized from the Yacht Club. "I heard it was a great polo match on Saturday," he said, his speech littered with gasps as he struggled for air under the bulk of his enormous frame.

"How are you, Derrick?" said Gary, putting a protective arm around Jacqui's waist.

"Who is this gorgeous woman you have with you? I could well understand if you didn't want to introduce her to me," he said, extending his sweaty hand. "Gary likes to keep the best things for himself."

"Jacqui, this is Derrick Bloomfield. He's on the prime minister's staff. Derrick, this is Miss Jacqui Devron. What's going on here?"

"A state reception for the visiting President of Venezuela. Your name is on the guest list, so you must at least join us for a drink. There are lots of people who would be delighted to see you and meet Miss Devron," said Derrick.

"Thanks, Derrick," Gary replied, leading Jacqui into the party. They were stopped frequently as he exchanged greetings with friends.

"Gary, good to see you," said a ruddy, short, blond man with blazing red cheeks.

"Harrison. How are you?" Gary shook his hand warmly. "I've heard great things about your place in Negril."

"Thanks," he said, smiling, his tobacco-stained teeth

playing with his lower lip. "We've got the largest swimming pool in the Caribbean. We've been using it for windsurfing lessons." Gary introduced him to Jacqui as Harrison Blake, owner of the popular Ecstasy Resorts for hedonistic pleasure-seekers.

"They have a pyjama disco every night at two a.m. and you must wear your pyjamas or nothing at all," whispered Gary, winking at her.

Across the room, Jacqui recognized the Countess standing on the terrace. She looked dazzling in her emeralds and diamonds. Gary spied her at the same instant and they walked in step to greet her.

"Good evening, Gary," she said as he bent down to kiss her cheek.

"Good evening yourself," he said, looking at her with concern. "How do you feel?"

"I'm feeling very well," she said, patting his hand as she turned to Jacqui. "I'm so glad Gary brought you. I knew our paths would cross again." Julia clasped Jacqui's hand and they exchanged a warm look as Gary looked on quizzically. "This is my polo partner from Saturday's game," explained the Countess. "We had a marvellous time. Gary, have you been to Portland lately?" she asked.

"It's been a few months. I could do with a little taste of Paradise Cottage," said Gary, watching a tall man with salt and pepper hair cross the room, followed by several people.

"Excuse me, would you please," he said, throwing a meaningful glance at them as he headed over to the tall man.

"I think I saw a piece of your work," said Jacqui to the Countess.

"The painting in Ivories at The Falls," guessed Julia correctly. "I did that years ago, long before there had been any development in Ocho Rios. The Falls held a tiny beach cottage with outdoor conveniences back then."

Jacqui listened with interest, but her eyes were on Gary who was across the terrace in deep discussion with the man. When he looked up, and saw Jacqui looking at him, a smile flashed across his lips. With a nod of his head, he signalled Jacqui discreetly and she moved gracefully across the room.

"Sir, when do you think it will be decided on?" asked Gary.

"Within the month," responded Sir George Michaels. "It's on the agenda for Cabinet, but I have to check with my permanent secretary to see the exact status. Parliament might not meet for another two weeks. You know Parliament doesn't sit during the cricket test matches," he added with a smile, looking at Jacqui.

"Sir, I would like you to meet Miss Jacqui Devron of New York. She is visiting our island. Jacqui, this is the Right Honourable Sir George Michaels, Prime Minister of Jamaica."

"It is a pleasure to meet you," she said, putting out her hand, momentarily stunned to think she was talking to the head of state. But within an instant, she felt at ease, as he inquired how she was enjoying her stay.

He was called away a moment later to attend to official duties. "You know the prime minister?" she asked Gary, incredulously.

"You forget this is a small country. He and my father were schoolmates. I've known him since I was knee-high," said Gary. "Now if you don't have any other questions, let's say our good nights to the Countess and leave. I don't like cocktail parties in general and I have something much more fun in mind," he said, lightly running his finger along her shoulder and down her arm in a butterfly touch that made her shiver. He looked at her with an open lust that was noticed by Derrick Bloomfield, the Countess and the prime minister.

Jacqui found herself welcoming Gary's protective arm on

the buggy ride home. The glorious star-studded sky stretched over the swaying fields of sugar cane. "Yu haffi meet me at de dock. Me have very special tour for de lady," he said, in raucous patois, making Jacqui break out in hysterical laughter. "Special price," he announced.

"What is the special price?" asked Jacqui, wriggling out of his arms as they reached the hotel.

"Come to de dock fe see. Me nah tek no fe an ansah."

Excited about this unknown adventure, she nevertheless felt the warning signals going off, once alone in her room, as she quickly slipped off the white gown and changed into her low-cut one-piece bathing suit and a pair of cotton shorts and long-sleeved t-shirt.

As she neared the boat, she saw that Gary's strong rugged gestures were softened in the lantern light, giving him an impression of youth and vulnerability. He helped her into the canoe. The motor broke the stillness of the night and they skimmed 'over the water's surface, tiny waves lapping at the side of the boat in harmony with the tree frogs that chimed from the shore.

"It's the perfect time to go to Laughing Waters. After the rain, the sea is at her best, the tide is low and the moon is glowing," Gary said, pulling Jacqui close to his body.

He coasted right up to the beach, cutting the engine and pulling it up with a practised touch, just in time to jump out and guide the canoe to the beach. Climbing out, Jacqui almost lost her balance and fell against Gary, as an unexpected wave rocked the boat. His hand grazed her chest as he steadied her, sending shock waves up and down her body. Taking a bag from the canoe, he walked along the beach to a spot he seemed to know well. Gary spread a blanket that was in his bag and began to gather up sticks and dried coconut leaves to light a fire.

"There's something I want to show you," he said, peeling off his shirt, his muscles rippling in the soft moonlight, when the fire was crackling. "It's a waterfall that I have always called Little Falls. It's not visible from the beach." He reached out for her hand, admiring the way her suit moulded her supple body.

Jacqui marvelled at the peace and unspoiled beauty of Laughing Waters at night. Hand in hand, they slipped into the satin embrace of the freshwater pool, the soft silky sand sinking under their weight.

The water was a perfect temperature, as Jacqui slipped under its surface, only to be enfolded by Gary's strong legs. Wrapping his fingers in her hair, he bent towards her as she closed her eyes, allowing the sensations to overwhelm her. He moved his mouth over her cheek down to her chin as she slid her arms around his neck, drawing him to her. Pulling her head back, he let his mouth slowly caress her before he lowered his lips to hers in excruciating sensual slowness.

The perpetual hum of the water eventually drew them to the cascading falls and they stood under the flowing spring water. Thigh to thigh, chest to chest, cheek to cheek, their breathing became one, and Jacqui could feel herself becoming moist, in tune with the flowing water.

They waded back to the pool, Jacqui's skin tingling from the rush of the water and his touch. Every inch of her was aware of Gary, as he gazed at her, holding her face lovingly in his hands before he kissed her again, enveloping her mouth with his passionate demand.

Jacqui's teeth were chattering by the time they got back to the blanket, more from anticipation than cold. He took one of the towels and draped it over her body, rubbing her sensually until her chattering stopped. Settling her on the blanket, he reached into his bag and pulled out a bottle of brandy and one snifter. He poured a liberal amount in the snifter and passed it to Jacqui.

"This will warm you up," he said, settling down on the

blanket, his chest to her back. The stars blanketed them, bathing them in their magic glow.

"Tomorrow will be a perfect day for sailors," remarked Jacqui, the brandy, hot and burning, leaving a glow in her throat. "Red sky in the morning, sailor's warning. Red sky at night, sailor's delight."

"That it will," he responded, moving the towel away so he could feel her bare back against his chest. Lowering his hand, he let his mouth linger on her neck. She turned and found herself pulled into his arms, his body pressing her down into the soft sand beneath the blanket, which took on their shape. The fire crackled but she was barely aware of it, so swept away by the power of his touch, despite the voice inside her screaming caution.

He kissed her brow, studying her face before he took possession of her mouth, almost gentle and wooing. A small part of her wanted him hungry for her, brutally demanding, so she could have an excuse to put an end to the lovemaking before it progressed too far.

But then her consciousness, her entire being concentrated on the unhurried movement of his hand as he pulled away the strap of her bathing suit. His hands caressed her hot flesh, her body suddenly convulsing in one agonizing grip of desire. He stroked her lightly but sensually, her body responding to his caresses in a potent and exotic way. He lowered his head to take the tip of her breast into his mouth, and she found herself aching to feel the touch of him everywhere. Shuddering against him, she looked at his head nestled at her breast in the moonlight.

He looked up at her, his body tense as a whipcord as he saw her half-closed eyes, filled with desire, slowly melting like ice cubes. It was all he needed to see.

"Mr. Gary, Mr. Gary," a voice called out in the darkness. "Tippy here, sir. Mr. Robert sent me to find yuh. Him sey it's an emergency."

"Shit," said Gary, burying his head in Jacqui's shoulder. He looked at her. The effects of their lovemaking were still etched on her face. "Tell him I'll be there shortly," called Gary, sighing. "Robert wouldn't have sent out a search party if he didn't need some help."

Helping Jacqui sit up, he replaced her bathing suit and rolled up the blanket. They put out the fire, and were back on the sea in less than five minutes.

The ride back was washed with silence, as Gary held Jacqui closely in the crook of his arm and pushed the canoe to its fullest.

"I'm sorry about this," he said when they were back on the dock. "I'll take a rain check for tonight." He pulled her in his arms, holding her tightly against his body, letting her feel the full extent of his arousal. The embrace sent a shaft of desire piercing her very being, so intense that she let a low moan escape from her lips, as she strained against him.

With a final kiss, he disappeared off the dock, running to the hotel as she walked dejectedly along the beach to her room, feeling totally frustrated and confused. Despite all the danger signs, she had almost made love to a man she barely knew and was sorry that she hadn't. Her body burned with the need for release that his passion had aroused in her.

She slipped into the shower, soaping her body, trying to remove not only the sand but the scent of desire that oozed from her every pore. Dousing herself with cold water, she emerged from the shower flushed and starry-eyed, not recognizing the expression in her face.

Towelling her hair vigorously, she replayed the events of the evening over in her mind. Nothing was making much sense. "Who is Gary Gordon?" she wondered as she turned in bed, his eyes, lit by the point of moonbeams, haunting her dreams.

* * *

84

"What the hell can be so important that you sent someone to Laughing Waters?" fumed Gary when he approached Robert at the front desk.

"I'm sorry," said Robert, shrugging his shoulders at his friend's rage. "I was told to give you this immediately," he said, handing Gary an envelope.

Gary grunted an unintelligible reply as he tore open the envelope. He skimmed the contents quickly, then headed to his Land-Rover parked in the hotel lot. The gears crunched under his hand and he swung out of the gate, forcing the guard to run. He headed down the main road towards town and stopped at a small rum bar with a thatched roof that was frequented by many local politicians and their girlfriends.

He walked into the bar, not meeting anyone's eyes. He ordered a drink at the bar. A sullen young woman plopped down a plastic dish of ice, a shot of rum and a bottle of warm Pepsi. He left his money on the bar and when she returned with the change she whispered his message.

Gary went through the back door and the acrid smell of animal faeces and urine filled his nostrils. He walked in the dark past the chicken coop to a small wooden gingerbread house, built at the turn of the century, that had withstood several hurricanes. Gary knocked on the door and then gently pushed it in.

"Did I interrupt anything important?" asked Ainsley, sitting at the huge table that dominated the tiny room. There was a huge smile plastered on his face as he watched a touch of pink creep over Gary's countenance.

"Don't be an ass," said Gary. "What's up?"

"I wouldn't have interrupted so delicate an encounter if I didn't desperately need your help again."

"Not again, Ainsley. I don't have the stomach for undercover work," Gary groaned.

"I need you to find Natty," said Ainsley.

"Why don't you go and find Natty yourself?" said Gary.

"He won't talk to me, you know that," said Ainsley. "I know that he'll talk to you. Crime has spread it all over that you're a ganja man now. Natty is bound to have heard and he'll see you. I just want to find out what he knows."

"How the hell am I supposed to find a guy who has managed to hide from the police for the past four years?" asked Gary. "Never mind, don't even answer that. I'll find River Baby."

Chapter 7

The hot afternoon sun was finally moving across the cloudless blue sky when Jacqui returned to The Falls. She had spent the day touring the north coast, stopping at the hotels and attractions. She had loved the Plantation Inn with its sunwashed pale pink decor and the Jamaica Inn with its famous Winston Churchill suite. The Dunn's River Falls Hotel, Footprints and Sandals Resorts had all been magnificent, but what really took her breath away was Noel Coward's Firefly in Port Maria. It was a simple cottage with a spectacular view of Cabarita Island and the ever-changing coastline. There was no doubt that it had been his inspiration for the song, " A Room with a View."

She sauntered through the lobby, past the rushing miniature falls, pushing away the memory of making love with Gary at Laughing Waters. Settling in a plush chair on the tea terrace, she appreciated the laid-back serenity of The Falls in comparison to some of the glitzy overdone resorts she had visited.

Trina was walking past the pool, reminding guests of the street carnival that evening. She was wearing a skimpy bikini that moulded her beautiful body like a piece of wax. She passed Jacqui, her eyes raking over her, taking in her wrinkled beige linen shorts and blouse. A smirk settled on her face as she met Jacqui's eyes.

"Hello, Trina," said Jacqui.

"Were you speaking to me?" said Trina coldly.

"I beg your pardon," said Jacqui, her smile evaporating. "I was just trying to be polite."

"Listen, Janet," started Trina.

"The name is Jacqui. For someone in guest relations, you seem to have a real problem dealing with people," she said, matching Trina's hard glare.

"Whatever your name is, I have a little piece of advice for you. You might think you're someone special, but you're not. Gary has a different girl like you each week. The hair colour changes and so do the accents, but you're all the same. I think that even you are smart enough to understand that," said Trina, smiling sweetly.

Jacqui's mouth went dry as Trina walked away with the stealthy grace of a Persian cat. She joined a very handsome man who was the colour of the finest Swiss milk chocolate and had a physique that showed every one of his finely toned muscles. Trina sat down next to him and despite her turmoil Jacqui was struck by how beautiful they both looked as she watched Trina trace a long red manicured nail down his well-muscled back to his tapered waist.

* * *

The sun was setting in a burst of tangerine, amber and rose. The reggae band was playing in the garden. The entire outdoor area had been turned into a large street festival and every employee, from the chambermaids and gardeners to the general manager, was dressed in costume.

"Welcome to the streets of Ocho Rios," called Brian Foster, the resident manager. He was dressed as a pocomania dancer, a member of a religious cult that was prevalent in the rural parts of the island. He wore a white sheet like a toga, a turban and a garland of flowers around his neck. The tables had been laid out in square formations to represent the streets of Ocho Rios with authentic-looking street signs placed at strategic intersections. 'Please do not piss here' read one of the signs over a Red Stripe bottle with a candle. Carnival music played in the background as the spicy smell of barbecued chicken and beef kebabs mingled with the jasmine-scented breeze.

A large wooden sky juice cart with the word 'Jah' painted on it, meaning God in the Rastafarian language, pulled alongside her. Disguised behind dark glasses, the vendor expertly scraped the ice with a paint scraper from huge blocks into a small plastic bag. Adding two squirts of sugary red liquid and one of green syrup, he popped a straw into the bag and presented it to Jacqui with a flourish.

"One love, boss," he said, flashing a smile that showed two rubies embedded in his front teeth.

She saw Nikko and Al by a Rastafarian who was peeling pineapples, and went over to them. Gary joined them, resting his hand familiarly on her waist and allowing his fingers to trail down her back as he greeted Al and Nikko. Wearing all white and his riding boots, he explained that he was portraying a plantation owner in the carnival.

"Where were you all day?" he whispered as they were blessed by a country preacher. "I missed you."

"Out shopping in town," she said lightly as a peanut cart with steam whistling from its spout was pushed through the crowd by a vendor named Nutsy who was calling out to people, and dispensing packets of roasted peanuts to the guests.

They ate under a sign that read, 'NO TRESPASSING. The next goat that passes here will be curried goat.' They filled themselves with shrimp kebabs, dripping with garlic and butter, and roasted potatoes.

After dinner, Robert Davids, dressed as Henry Morgan in a resplendent cape with high boots and dark pantaloons, swirled his cape and clutched the butt of his sword as he took his place in front of one of the microphones.

"We wanted to bring you a taste of Jamaica," began Robert. "We hope that you will fall in love with The Falls and come back again and again. I just wanted to take this opportunity to wish one of our guests a very happy birthday. *Otan Joobi Omedetou,*" he said in Japanese, the spotlight hitting Nikko as the band started playing.

Nikko put her hands to her face, totally taken by surprise. She looked around in amazement, watching two men carry in a huge cake that was lit with candles.

"She is surprised," said Al, beaming. "That mean I get baby." He hugged Nikko and then Gary as they brought the cake over and everyone sang.

The live reggae band started playing again as everyone milled around, sampling the street market fare. An ice cream vendor pedalled up on his bicycle, the wheels strung with red, green and pink Christmas lights. A standard bicycle had been transformed into a mobile ice cream disco stand. On the handlebars was a cassette player and a speaker and in the back basket, a second speaker hooked up to a car battery. He fixed them each a grapenut cone and told them to "stay cool" before he pedalled away.

Gary led Jacqui toward a booth that had been set up as a street corner gambling game. The booth was run by Adelai, a local street gambler who was missing more teeth than he possessed and had the fastest-talking mouth Jacqui had ever heard.

Jacqui saw a crude board with five objects painted on it: a heart, a crown, an anchor, a bee's wing and a diamond. There were three dice in a cup, representing the symbols.

Adelai called out in a loud voice for everyone to place their bets and Gary promptly put down his money. "Do you want to play?" he asked, handing her some cash. "I love this game. It's called Crown and Anchor. I used to sneak out of school with the boys to play. I have a system that is unbeatable."

He put his money on the crown and anchor. Adelai took two other bets and threw the dice, revealing two crowns and a diamond. He paid Gary off, clearing the board, calling for another round. Gary won another round, but lost the next three rounds he played.

"I thought you had an unbeatable system," she teased, placing a bet on the table. "You may think this is some unique English gambling game, but the guys who used to fix the planes taught me a version of this game before I could hold a throttle," she said, throwing him a glance as she won. Then she split her bet and doubled her winnings. A dumbfounded look settled on Gary's face as she won again, causing Adelai to curse as he dipped his hand into his money pouch to pay Jacqui off.

Afterwards they strolled aimlessly through the booths, with Jacqui looking at the wood carvings and t-shirts. "I thought you went shopping today," he said.

"I did, but I always like to look," replied Jacqui, flashing him a brilliant smile.

"So you're a gambler, eh?" he said, looking at her, sounding pleased.

"It just depends on the game," she replied, licking her ice cream cone. "How do you know Japanese?"

"Another list of questions from the inquiring mind," said Gary. "I had a bit of a rebellious period in my younger days. My father wanted me to become a lawyer and return to the island to enjoy a sparkling legal career. I made it through the first year – I read all the briefs, attended the lectures and went through the motions. Although I loved the theory of law I knew I didn't want to spend my life practising it. I was on my way back to Jamaica and was waiting in Heathrow for my flight when insanity overtook me. I cashed in my ticket and got on a plane to Japan and ended up staying there for two years."

"Your father must have had a fit," said Jacqui.

"That is the understatement of the year. He ranted and raved and threatened me with every conceivable form of blackmail. My grandfather was a bit more understanding. It seems that he had gone off to Africa when he was about my age. I think he understood what I did better than I did at the time," said Gary.

"Those years were a gift," said Jacqui.

"A gift," repeated Gary, pulling a banana off a hanging bunch. "That's a good way of looking at it." For a moment they both watched Trina parade around in her silver maillot in her role as the Jamaican beauty queen.

"I'm sorry about last night," he said tentatively.

"So was I," said Jacqui, wondering what game he was playing.

"I have an appointment that I have to go to, but I'll be back later. Can I stop by your room?" he asked, running two fingers across the slender column of her neck, slowly moving them down towards her chest.

"I see," said Jacqui, with a smile that she didn't feel. "Is that how you operate?"

"Jacqui, there is nothing I would rather do than drag you back to my place and spend the night with you," he said.

"I'll bet you say that to all the girls," said Jacqui, shaking her head.

"I don't," he said, matching her gaze. "I have to find an old friend in the bush. Believe me, it's not very glamorous."

"How could I refuse such a gracious invitation," said Jacqui, linking her arm in his firmly as she accompanied him into the parking lot.

Wondering how on earth he had got himself into this situation, Gary unlocked the door of his weatherbeaten Land-Rover.

"This is what you drive?" she asked incredulously as she tried to close the door that creaked but wouldn't properly latch. The engine sputtered, sounding like the heart of the tinman as Gary pulled out.

"This British-built lady may be older than the hills, but

don't let her sensible good looks fool you. She can get through a flooded river or a rocky road far better than these modern vehicles. The only problem is that when it rains you tend to get wetter inside than outside because the inside is riveted," explained Gary as they drove to the White River.

They turned off the main road, driving along the bank under the bridge. At a small clearing, he parked the van, leading Jacqui to a bar by the river bank.

Three young boys, wearing cut-off trousers that were falling off their youthful bodies, were standing in the river holding soda bottles filled with kerosene with rags stuffed into the mouths. They held the flaming bottles aloft, letting the rags burn off in the wind, their machetes poised in mid-air.

"What are they doing?" Jacqui asked.

"Tell her, nuh," Gary said to one of the boys.

"We a ketch fish," responded one boy, his machete flying through the water as he axed a fish.

They moved closer until they reached the muddy bank of the water, watching as another boy tried to catch a fish, but missed, landing in the water.

"I'm going to try my hand at this," Gary said, rolling up his pants and walking into the slightly murky water.

Jacqui laughed a deep throaty laugh, watching Gary hunched over in the water, trying to catch a tiny fish with a big machete. He cheered when he caught one, while she furiously slapped at the mosquitoes that had begun to attack her ankles.

His frivolity ceased when he heard the sound of a motor, and made out its silhouette. "Sorry me late, boss," called a deep voice. Gary thanked the boys and assisted Jacqui into the boat, introducing her to River Baby.

"How did you get that name?" Jacqui asked the short, stocky man as they moved along the eerie river, under the tropical foliage that extended from each bank, almost touching in the middle, blocking the stars from view.

"When me was a baby, dem say eight weeks old, dem throw me in the Swift River. Me nevah drown. Me swim up to de top. Since den, dem call me River Baby," he said, moving his head. The swish of his soft long locks mingled with the sound of water splashing against the side of the boat.

"Where we going?" asked Gary.

"Free Eyes. Dem sey yuh should check dere," said River Baby. The boat moved up the river in total darkness. In the distance a light became barely distinguishable, and the music grew louder as they neared the thatch-roofed club which was on a steep muddy embankment.

The club was lit with red and green lights. The licorice smell of white rum mingled with the screen of cigarette smoke. An assortment of characters sat perched at the circular bamboo bar and a domino game was in progress at a corner table.

The sound of grunts and curses rang out occasionally, mingled with the sound of slamming domino tiles on a scratched wood table. Jacqui felt as if every pair of eyes was staring at her. Gary motioned her to a seat at the bar, ordering rum and Pepsi for them. The ice came in huge chunks in a dirty yellow plastic bowl with an ice pick to break the large blocks so they could fit in the glasses.

A dreadlocks joined them at the bar, glaring at Jacqui before he spoke in a low voice to Gary. He looked the Jamaican version of a Star Wars creature, his long frame dressed in a t-shirt in red, green and gold, with a handful of gold chains wrapped around his neck.

"Have you seen Natty?" asked Gary.

"Last me 'ear, him up in de hills," said the man, accepting Gary's offer of a drink.

"Me 'ear different," said Gary.

"Me nuh know what yuh a 'ear, but me sey him up in de

hills," said the slender man.

"Come nah, man. Me jus' wan' fe see him and Pearly. Cha, me know Natty longer dan yuh, boss."

"Ah true?" asked the Rastaman, disbelievingly.

"Yah man, ah true. Natty been smokin' ganja and makin' baby modders since me was a bwoy. Soon dem mek him a national hero, if him not one already," said Gary, getting a good laugh from the bar patrons as he signalled for another round. "Dem call me de green-eyed devil."

"All right, Busha, me a go tell yuh," said the man, pulling Gary closer to give his instructions.

"T'anks, skip," said Gary. "Me nuh a forget yuh."

He turned to Jacqui. "We have to go somewhere else. It is a bit of a walk. You can stay here or come with me," he said, depositing some bills on the bar.

"I'm coming with you," said Jacqui instantly, glancing around once again, seeing only shadows in the haze of the smoke and inadequate lighting.

Following him outside, she expected to return to the river, but was led away from the bank toward an almost non-existent path that seemed to lead nowhere. She could not see more than a foot ahead of her in the dark, so she clutched Gary's hand. The thicket had overgrown, scratching her as she passed. Rocks and brambles strewn along the way made walking difficult.

"I have to see a friend I haven't seen in a while," Gary offered, saving her the trouble of asking.

Presently, a tiny glow became visible in the hill a hundred yards in front of them. For a moment, Jacqui thought it was the light of a fire, but it was steady and kept getting brighter as they got closer. Gary led her toward the light before stopping at a rough pathway that snaked its way up a hill where Jacqui could see the outline of a shack.

Whistling twice, he waited and then whistled again. "Natty, it's Gary Gordon," he called out.

The door of the shack creaked open, sending a thin shaft of light down the hillside.

"Irie, man. Long time me nuh see yuh," a dreadlocks responded, motioning him along. "Yuh not alone?" he asked suspiciously, seeing Jacqui's figure emerge.

"She cool, brethren. Yu no haffi worry," responded Gary.

When they entered the zinc-roofed shack, the smell of fresh ganja assaulted Jacqui's senses. A kerosene lamp illuminated the contents of the shack. There was a camp bed with a worn coverlet, a white rum calendar with a nude girl and a goat and a crude wooden table with two uneven chairs.

Sitting on one of the chairs was an ebony-skinned woman, whose breasts hung to her waist like ripe cantaloupes. She was diligently at work cutting up the ganja, not even glancing up when Gary introduced her as Pearly.

"How long yuh been away this time?" asked Gary, as he eyed the bales resting on the plastic tarpaulin on the dirt floor.

"Me been up in de hills for ninety days straight. Ninety days and fe what. Me nah even go mek a likkle money on dis crop. Me tell yu fe true. De news na good. Me vexed to raas at what me hear," said Natty as he continued to cut off branches, passing them to Pearly.

Working with a sharp kitchen knife, she cut up the ganja with the precision of a diamond cutter and packed it into the plastic strips that had already been cut.

"What's the news?" asked Gary.

"Yuh ask me wha' de news. Me 'ear yuh is de news," said Natty. "So yuh finally come into de business."

"In some sort of way," he replied. "Come nah, Natty. Wha' 'appen? Me asking yuh as a friend."

"All types of guns," replied the Rastafarian. "Me 'ear dat de Storm and Thunder posse soon get some. Very soon, but me t'ink yuh already know dat."

"Why yuh t'ink so?" asked Gary, oblivious of Jacqui's shocked expression.

"Yuh t'ink me a fool," said Natty, laughing softly. "I gonna tell yuh one t'ing. Soon de posses a call a big war. Me a tell yuh dis – your friend – dat prime minister dat sit pretty inna Jamaica House and drive him criss car, him nevah give one raas 'bout de people dat voted him in. Me a vote fe him once, but nevah again. "When dem wan' fe ketch him – dat man will nevah know what 'it 'im." Natty watched Gary pace around the dirt floor. "What yuh gonna do?"

"Me nuh know, but somet'ing," said Gary. He watched Pearly sort through the ganja. He picked up a large bud with a vein of purple running through the tiny leaves. Fingering the bud, he sniffed it.

"Good stuff?"

"Da best. Some sensimillia," said Natty.

"How yuh stay?" asked Gary, playfully pinching Pearly's cheek. She reached over to slap him.

"How come yuh nuh check me?" she asked, revealing several missing teeth that came from sucking on sugar cane from before she could talk.

"Yuh wan' Natty fe kill me?" asked Gary, patting her arm. "How de pickney stay?"

"Dem stay alright. De oldest want fe be a doctor. Me haffi do plenty wuk if him fe go a school."

"Stay cool," said Natty, putting out his hand. "Yuh must know dem have it out fe yuh. "

"Thanks for the warning," said Gary, taking his hand. "Too long since me see yuh, brodder."

"Long time me nevah see yuh, and de next time me nah wan' it fe be at de set-up fe yuh funeral."

Jacqui was filled with fear and fury as they made their way over the dark bramble-strewn path to the bank of the White River.

"How it go, man?" asked River Baby.

"Fine," said Gary. "T'anks, man. Me really appreciate it."

"Me know," said River Baby, his soft laughter filling the air as the sound of the fading reggae music resonated over the water.

The return trip back to the hotel was made in silence. Jacqui couldn't look at Gary and concentrated on the passing scenery that held no interest for her. Gary pulled into a parking spot and hadn't even pulled up the emergency brake when Jacqui was out of the vehicle. In one fluid movement, he followed her.

"What is the matter?" he asked, reaching for her.

"Why did you go out there?" she asked.

"I told you that I had to meet a friend," he said.

"Some friend. Is he your local distributor of ganja in your territory?' she asked.

"It's not like that," said Gary.

"I'm so naive," she said, throwing her hands up in the air. Her mind was reeling as she thought about the ramifications of his occupation. "I never would have guessed you were a drug dealer."

"Jacqui, it's not what you think. I went out in the hills to find out what was going on. You see, here in Jamaica, there are two types of communication. There are the formal lines and then there is the bush telegraph, which is usually more reliable and accurate. I have an interest in this area. I need to know what's going on," said Gary.

"You are nothing but a drug dealer," she said, running her hands through her hair and down to the nape of her neck.

"Jacqui, ganja is part of the life in Jamaica. It's woven into the fibre of the country. It's been used for hundreds of years as a medicinal remedy. Natty and the little bit of ganja you saw tonight isn't the problem. It's the drug barons who pay guys like Natty barely enough money to keep food on his table. They are the problem and the ones who are ruining this country.

"You yourself heard Natty say someone is bringing guns onto the island. That concerns me a lot more than a little ganja. Ganja is a problem in America, but not here."

"Gary, please don't pretend anymore," she said. "I see it all. You have the perfect cover as an international playboy with impeccable contacts. You are even on intimate terms with the prime minister. I'm not surprised you are concerned about the guns. It may affect your drug shipments."

"You've been watching too much *Miami Vice*," said Gary, feeling his patience snap.

"Don't be so condescending. With all your noble talk about your country, you are just a hypocrite. You are so righteously defending people who break the law," said Jacqui.

"You know, Jacqui, you sound like a narrow-minded American who thinks that sugar grows in boxes and the ganja you secretly smoked in college miraculously came pre-rolled," said Gary coldly.

His words slowly registered, her fury apparent in her tight lips and clenched teeth. The air around them was filled with tension.

"That was unfair," she said angrily.

"Not half as unfair as what you are doing," he retorted, matching her glare. "You are making judgements about things you don't understand."

"I thought you were different," she said, too hurt to say anything else.

"I thought *you* were different," he said, putting his hands in his pockets, not looking at her.

"I'm so glad last night never happened," she said frostily, turning and walking away without a backward glance.

He watched her walk away, shaking with anger. He couldn't remember when he had been so riled. He had been wasting his time. Passing Ivories, he stopped in to have a drink to cool his rage, but all he could think of was Jacqui's flashing eyes. The marlin had played with the teaser but got away.

Chapter 8

Jacqui stood at the summit of the hill astride Maid Marion. She had ridden over the cloud-covered ridge and she could see the sun peeping through the light cover, sending a shaft of light into the turquoise water that crashed against the shore.

She felt a little foolish that she might have jumped to a hasty conclusion about Gary. She allowed her eyes to scan the horizon, noting the pleasing layout of the hotel, the partially finished equestrian centre and the cove at Whispering Waters. Slowly she made her descent.

Hidden behind the foliage on a bend on the hillside was a magnificent villa with a large deck and a beautifully landscaped pool. Jacqui nudged the horse forward.

The loud voices reached her ears before she saw the movement of the two figures on the porch. She was riveted by what she saw. Gary walked out wearing his jodhpurs and riding boots, his polo shirt in his hand. Trina was two steps behind him, her silky kimono outlining her sensuous figure. Her hair was wild and tousled, emphasizing her gleaming dark eyes, narrowed in fury.

"Listen, Gary, I don't want to live like this anymore. I feel like an animal in a cage," Jacqui heard her yell.

"It's a hell of a lot better than a shack in Trench Town," he retorted. "Trina, please let's just drop this," he added, holding his head in his hands. "I don't want to say anything we might be sorry about later."

"Why?" she challenged him. "What will you do? Send

me back to Trench Town or bundle me off to Canada where I'll be safe and you can continue your little games?"

"Trina," said Gary helplessly.

"Don't Trina me," she said vehemently. "I told you I want to get out of here. Don't think you're doing me a favour by letting me stay here. I know you're doing it for your own good." She turned to walk away, but apparently thought better of it as she swung around again, her hair bouncing off her shoulders. "Do me a little favour. Stay away from me when you can't hold your liquor. I abhor drunk men and you were disgustingly drunk last night." The slam of the door was heard through the hillside.

Gary watched as Trina walked away. He slipped on his shirt and Jacqui slapped the horse into service, quickly returning to the path. With each passing moment, Gary was turning out to be more dangerous and devious.

* * *

The sun was burning hot as Jacqui, Al and Nikko walked around the Carinosa Gardens, stopping at the bird aviary filled with golden pheasants, screaming cockatoos and white doves. Al made funny noises and weird faces, furiously snapping photographs. The waterfalls and streams were surrounded by exotic flowers, and giant royal coconut palms accentuated the tropical beauty.

Under the shade of the lignum vitae tree, Nikko began talking in a melodious flow of sounds, her eyes shining as Al began to translate the story of their courtship.

"Al and I were in school together. I was number one student even though I was woman. He was number two student. I never raise hand in class. Al always raise hand. I always know right answer." Al scowled at her at that point, but continued translating.

"When we go to university in Tokyo, my honourable

husband could not pass calculus. To save himself and his family great embarrassment, he came to me for assistance. After much work, he pass exam," said Nikko through the voice of Al.

"At end of course, I discover I miss her. I knew I need smart woman to help me in life. So I marry her," said Al. Nikko started talking very quickly and Al covered his ears.

"Okay, okay, she said to tell you she is sure I did not tell you that I stood on her doorstep for one month with orchid flower, very rare and precious in Japan."

Later on, Jacqui took a walk, taking refuge from the scorching heat by the flowing freshwater stream. Slipping off her sandals, she leaned back and closed her eyes for a moment, only to have her repose interrupted by a little boy.

"Hey lady, beg yu some lunch money," he implored, his large brown eyes tugging at Jacqui's heart. There was a washrag hanging from the back pocket of his frayed pants and his feet were bare. Digging into her purse, she pulled out all the change she had and handed it to him.

"T'anks," he said, smiling shyly, and Jacqui had a sudden urge to give him a hug. "Me name Howard. Me a businessman," he said, putting out his hand. "What yuh name?"

"Jacqui. What kind of businessman are you?"

"Me is a guide. Me can be yuh guide fe today. Me tek care of everyt'ing," he said, patting himself on the chest.

"That's really sweet, but not today, thanks," said Jacqui in amusement. Howard retreated, looking dejected.

Al and Nikko joined her, announcing that they were going to climb Dunn's River Falls, and inviting Jacqui to join them.

"I think I will go into town," said Jacqui. "Enjoy the falls and I'll meet you back at the hotel."

"Don't forget tonight is the island party," said Al, taking Nikko by the hand as they walked.

* * *

Ambling along the main street of Ocho Rios, Jacqui could not resist stopping at Casa de Oro, an exclusive duty-free store with a vast selection of perfumes. She had to pull herself away from an exquisite Cartier watch, which she knew she couldn't afford after her three months' suspension.

She wandered into the large open-air craft market. It was a maze of tiny bamboo and wood stalls, each stocking the same repetitious assortment of wood carvings, straw baskets, t-shirts and clothes.

"Hey, lady. Come look in my stall. See it here. Just tek a look, no charge. Me have de best price," cried each and every vendor, in the same high-pitched wailing chant, anxious for patronage.

Looking at a "No Problem" t-shirt that made an irresistible gift for Josh, she overheard an American couple talking. "Sweetheart, do you think all these people are crazy?" asked the woman in a broad southern accent.

"I don't know, honey, why do you ask?" he said, adjusting his big hat.

"With all these straw baskets around, I just thought everyone must be crazy. Isn't that what they do in the insane asylum?" she said, causing Jacqui to walk away to contain her laughter.

Much to the distress of the vendors and racketeers, who plied everything from ganja to hair braiding, Jacqui left the market with only a few small purchases, walking along the main beach to a thatch-roofed bar. The *Caribbean Princess* was docked in the harbour, dwarfing all the hotels on Mallards Point. She ordered a beer, taking a seat at one of the low rickety tables in the sand. A number of newspapers had been left on the table. She picked up the *USA Today*. Glancing at the headlines, she read that King had bought out

104

The Cotillion in Atlantic City, making it another coup for his ever-expanding empire. Thumbing through the paper, she put it aside without reading another article. The problems in Eastern Europe, the crisis in the Middle East and the crime rate in New York were far away from the white sand and turquoise water that glistened in the bright tropical midday sun.

"Miss Jacqui, Miss Jacqui," called a familiar voice. Jacqui saw Howard, a huge smile plastered on his face, running up to her. "Me been looking fe yuh everywhere. Me have tour fe yuh."

"No thanks," said Jacqui, moving to pick up the paper.

"Me beg yuh some lunch money," he mumbled, looking down, scraping his feet.

"What happened to the money I gave you before?" she asked, amazed at the nerve of the child.

"Miss Jacqui, de money finish," he said innocently. "Me buy a bulla and a drink and de money gone."

"You want a drink?" she asked, feeling sorry for him.

"A Pepsi and a patty," he said, eyeing the glass heater filled with vegetable, meat and lobster patties. Sitting down without an invitation, he began looking at the *Gleaner*.

"Is me daddy boss dat," he said excitedly, pointing to a picture on the front page. "Me daddy wuk for dat man deh so."

Jacqui peered over to see the source of his elation. In slow motion, she picked up the paper, the hair on her arms standing on end. She blinked to banish the stars that clouded her vision. Drawing a deep breath, she read the headlines.

'Nominations for Jamaican of the Year: Frontrunners: Field Marshall Sticky the DJ, Poetess Miss Matty and Gary Gordon – Hotelier.' There was a picture of Gary, obviously taken a few years ago after a polo match.

'Gary Gordon, chairman of Tropical Properties, has been an example to emulate in the tourism industry, in his

105

community projects as well as in his efforts to expand pimento exports to Russia. His excellence in sports has continually brought his country honour,' read one of the testimonials.

Within the last twenty-four hours, all her nagging doubts and suspicions about Gary had been confirmed. He must have known who she was from the moment he stole her seat on the plane. Gary was the one who had written the letter to *Elegant Travel* threatening to sue the magazine if there wasn't a retraction. He had wooed her to ensure a good review for his hotel, even holding his mistress at bay. It certainly explained Trina's hostility towards her.

Despite his charm and his attentive manner, Gary was a manipulative, conniving hustler. She knew she had to ensure that there would be no doubt about the integrity of her review. Another scandal so soon after the King affair would totally ruin her career. No magazine would ever hire her after this.

Dertermined to finish her assignment and leave The Falls, she spent the afternoon checking her notes and confirming facts, reluctant to return to the hotel. As far as she was concerned, if she never saw Gary Gordon again, it would be too soon.

When she arrived back at the hotel in the late afternoon, she paused only for a moment in the lobby before catching a glimpse of Gary in deep discussion with Robert by the miniature falls. Seeing him made Jacqui remember a quote from *Islands In The Sun* by Alex Waugh. 'Visitors, pleasure seekers and yachtsmen come to the island for two things: to give and be given a good time.' The quote hit home as she realized that she was just a bit of new blood timed with the weekly arrival of tourists. She glanced around uncomfortably, suddenly feeling as if everyone knew who she was. So Josh's elaborate plan hadn't fooled anyone, especially Gary. He had probably planned to bump her off the flight. Without a second glance towards Gary, she hurried to the room.

* * *

"Katherine Charlotte Jameson," called the uniformed military officer as he stood in the doorway of her office in the US Customs building in Washington, DC.

"That's me," she said, turning around from her desktop computer.

"I've got a top-level security clearance package for you –" he said, stopping in mid-sentence when he saw her. She was beautiful, with a long mane of golden blonde hair, cornflower blue eyes and the face of an angel. She should have been a model instead of hiding herself away in a backwater hole of the federal government.

"I'll sign for it," she said, standing, revealing her nearly six-foot height without heels. Her plain black skirt, white blouse and modest jewellery could not hide the perfect proportions of her toned body.

She signed her given name, though everyone called her Casey, while the officer pretended to inspect her ID while sneaking frequent glances at her. Taking the package, Casey flashed him a smile with her straight even white teeth, one that would stay with him until he was old.

After closing the door she immediately slit through the security seals of the classified document. Her good friend, Pierre Monclure of Interpol, stationed in Lyon, France, had run a computer check for her. She studied the records and accessed her computer past the green and blue levels into the red level, the top-secret data.

Pierre's records showed dramatic changes in cash balances in any accounts over a twenty-four-hour period for any country. They were compiled using all central bank records and monitored the millions of electronic transfers through CHIPS, the Clearing House Inter-Bank Payment System. Casey isolated the records for the Cayman Islands, Nassau, Switzerland, Jersey and Guernsey Islands and New Caledonia in the South Pacific.

She entered the data from the Interpol records, merged it into her data bank and ran a cross-check. The computer hummed, running over thousands of bytes of information. She wandered over to the window while the computer worked. Picking up her cold cup of coffee she took a sip, absently watching the tour buses on the Mall near the Washington Monument that was surrounded by flowering cherry trees.

The computer bleeped a prompt message on the screen and she typed in Cayman Islands. A list was printed which she promptly tore off and took to her desk. There it was. Another eighty-million-dollar electronic transfer of funds. She turned back to the computer, querying it with every question she could think of while she compiled a striking dossier of transfers from Cayman into an unnumbered Swiss account.

After an hour, she pushed her chair back and stared in wonder, marvelling at the brilliance of the plan. She knew that someone very powerful must be behind it.

* * *

"By the way, I thought you would like to know I'm introducing a dance contest as a feature of the weekly island party. Trina is going to coordinate it," Robert said to Gary as they walked towards the beach.

"That sounds fine," said Gary, slightly distracted, wondering where Jacqui had been all day. He had tried to find her several times during the day, but the nomination announcement for the Jamaican of the Year had him on the phone most of the day.

"I can see that the chairman has other things on his mind," said Robert, chuckling, watching the waiters load trays of fresh lobsters and fish onto the boats for transport to the island party.

"Whoever thought up this island party anyway?" asked Gary.

"I can't believe that you would ask that. You can't be serious," said Robert, stopping.

"I am. Who thought it up?" he asked.

"We did, though I guess I shouldn't be surprised you don't remember. When we finished sixth form, we came up to your grandfather's cottage for a holiday."

"That's right," exclaimed Gary. "It was Ainsley, PJ, you and me. We had the place to ourselves."

"Glad to see your memory is still intact," said Robert. "We went out to the island with a few cases of rum, plenty of ice and four lovely virgins."

"Oh yeah," said Gary, smiling. "If I recall we were going to stay out there until the rum or the ice ran out, whichever was first. I think we stayed out there for two days."

"It was three, Gary. You passed out the last day and had to be carried off," reminded Robert, laughing as Gary looked at him sheepishly.

***

"Can I get my messages?" said Trina as she pushed her way to the front desk.

"One moment please, Miss Doyan," said Jennifer Parker, the front desk clerk, who was trying to return keys, take a payment and answer the phone all at once since her partner was on a break.

"Didn't you hear what I said?" hissed Trina, her dark eyes narrowing. "I said I wanted my messages and I want them now." She strummed her long cherry-red manicured nails on the counter as the girl hurried to comply with her demand.

Trina glanced at the message, her eyes growing huge with concern as she checked her watch. She was about to leave when Robert, who had watched the exchange with disapproval from the executive suite behind the front desk, joined her.

"Is there a problem, Trina?" asked Robert.

"None at all," said Trina, giving Robert a huge smile as she pocketed the message. "I'm just getting ready for the island party tonight. I've put together some new soca tapes from carnival. I think the guests are going to love the show that's planned for tonight." She gave a warm smile that nearly melted his heart and touched his hand briefly before hurrying away, taking the short cut behind the dining terrace to Gary's villa.

She slipped into the villa quietly, checking for signs of Gary. He seemed to have been out all day. She picked up her clothes for the island party and went to the supply cupboard outside the kitchen. She took out the lantern that she had left there and hung it on the terrace. With a final sweeping glance, she locked the door and returned to the staff quarters to dress for the party.

* * *

Jacqui paced around her room, feeling claustrophobic despite its large proportions and comfortable furnishings. Al and Nikko had stopped by to pick her up for the island party, dressed from head to toe in clothes they had purchased at the craft market. Despite their protests, she had declined to join them, but the cabin fever was making her crazy. She slipped into an old pair of shorts, a t-shirt and her old soft moccasins and left her room, roaming around the nearly deserted property.

She walked past the stables and glanced up the hill to where Gary's villa stood alone on the precipice. It was totally dark except for a blue light hanging from the deck. She somehow found the beacon comforting as she followed the path from the stable to Whispering Waters.

The moon reflected a white line across the water as Jacqui approached the beach, taken in with the beauty. At an opening in the dense foliage that surrounded the cove, she pushed her body through. She almost slipped down the dirt-encrusted face of the cliff but held her grip, jumping the last few feet onto soft white sand.

Whispering Waters lacked the exotic beauty of Laughing Waters, but it had a magic all its own. There was a mysterious silence that hung around the cove. She took a few steps forward, her toe hitting a fallen coconut as she muttered softly to herself.

She had a perfect view of the lights of the island party, and was admiring them when she saw a blue light flash. It flashed several times and then once before it stopped. Out of the corner of her eye, she saw a glow, like the bright light of a firefly. She saw it again, brightening before it moved away. The smell of the burning cigarette reached her nostrils as she heard the rustle of leaves. Moments later, she saw two distinct silhouettes emerge from the bush by the stone wall of the cliff. For a second she thought she had imagined that the shadows had moved, but when a long arm flexed in the moonlight, Jacqui's heart stopped. The light had picked up the barrel of an Uzi submachine gun.

Jacqui watched, mesmerized, as the shadows on the beach began to move bales towards the water's edge.

One of the men pointed in her direction. Jacqui did not hesitate. She did an about-face instantly, grabbing onto the exposed roots of the hillside, pulling herself up the dirt-encrusted cliff with a strength she didn't know she had.

A cold sweat broke out on her forehead as she started to

run, the breath choking in her lungs. Checking behind her to see if she was being followed, she saw a light move at the entrance to the cove, revealing the outline of a boat navigating through the slim mouth of the treacherous reef.

Shaking and frightened, she realized what a risky thing she had just done. She ran straight back to her room, slamming the door and locking it. She checked the window and drew the curtains, trying to regularize her breathing.

With shaky hands, Jacqui packed her bags. There was no doubt in her mind that The Falls was a first-class property, but how could she as a credible journalist write a glowing review about a hotel that was a cover for drug smuggling. The thought frightened her more than she cared to admit, all the while thinking that Elizabeth Hartley's review may have touched on something.

Too keyed up to sleep, she wondered what Josh would have to say to the turn of events. She was more convinced than ever that Gary's attention was purely business. He was a dangerous man and she would be glad to get away from him and his hotel.

***

Sputo was moving towards the boat when he saw the slender figure of a white woman half-hidden in the foliage at the bottom of the cliff. He put his maimed hand on Bigga to restrain him, applying slight pressure to Bigga's arm. They both turned to look at her, sending the intruder scurrying up the hill.

"Who dat?" asked Bigga.

"Doan know, but I goin' find out," said Sputo.

Foolish Pleasure pulled in as close as it could. Whiskey threw out the anchor and Bigga and Sputo assisted in loading the heavily laden bags into the boat. Jack jumped into the water as Whiskey handed him a crate which he

112

effortlessly carried on his back to the beach.

The boat pulled out with the same ease with which it had entered Whispering Waters. Bigga and Sputo struggled to hoist the heavy crate of semi-automatic weapons up the face of the cliff. They moved quickly to where Bigga had stashed a 1971 Chevrolet that was rotting in more places than it was whole. They hoisted the crate onto the back seat and covered it with a ragged blanket in case of any unexpected road blocks with policemen who had not been paid off already.

Few words were exchanged as they drove for several miles along the main road, turning off near Oracabessa. The old road through the canefields was dark and had potholes that could swallow a car. At an abandoned sugar warehouse, they whistled twice before handing over the crate to Crime, one of the trusted members of the Storm and Thunder posse.

Leaving Bigga behind, Sputo returned to The Falls, parking in a wooden area on the other side of the road before taking up a post by the service entrance.

He glanced at the clear sky, remembering the days when he was Robert Unity, a young man with a dream. Now Robert Unity was dead in the eyes of God and the Registrar of Births and Deaths in Spanish Town, thanks to a powerful political connection. In the early sixties, Robert had earned the name the Lord of Trench Town for his heroic feat of robbing from the rich and sharing the spoils with his brethren in the downtown Kingston ghetto. There wasn't a week that went by when a bank wasn't robbed or a company's payroll removed with a minimum of fuss. As soon as Robert said he was the Lord of Trench Town, clerks would gladly hand over their cash, wishing him luck.

His luck turned sour one night when he was pulling a job at an appliance store to get stoves for the ghetto community. Lieutenant Reginald Anderson was waiting with the toughest squad of men from Hunt's Bay Police Station. In the struggle over Robert's gun, it went off, lodging a bullet in Anderson's spine, paralyzing him from the waist down. In his pain, he grabbed Robert's hand and shot his thumb off to make sure he would never be able to hold a gun again.

He escaped to the ghetto and was taken in by a young pregnant woman who nursed him back to health in gratitude for his assistance to her community. Sputo grew to love her and her child as if it was his own. It was during those long months of hiding that Robert Unity destroyed his past and became Sputo, one of the founding members of the Storm and Thunder posse.

Just before one in the morning, Sputo watched the tall lean figure of Trina approaching. He couldn't help but marvel at her elusive beauty and felt proud of her in ways he couldn't express. It was a privilege to be able to call her daughter. She was the light of his life.

"How it go?" she asked breathlessly, reaching his side. She took his maimed hand in hers with no thought of disgust.

"So and so," he replied. "Me see a white woman at de cove. She run 'way but me nuh sure what she see."

Trina pondered for a moment, running the guests over in her mind. Gary had been there for the dance contest, but she didn't remember seeing Jacqui.

"Me t'ink me know who dat. She name Jacqui Devron. She been carrying on wid Gary. Doan worry," said Trina. "Me goin' tek care of her."

Chapter 9

At seven a.m., Jacqui slipped onto the tour bus bound for Kingston and took the back seat. She pulled her Yankees baseball cap over her head and put on her sunglasses, wishing she could melt into the upholstery.

They left late, running on typical Jamaica time, and drove through Fern Gully, the tropical rain forest, before climbing into the hills where the gentle rolling green meadows were bathed in the early morning mist.

They had just passed through the town of Moneague, a one-time resort frequented by the English whose grand hotel now served as a school, when the engine started to smoke. The driver pulled over quickly and popped the hood. A cloud of steam rose and one by one, they piled off the bus.

"What's going on here?" demanded a female tourist with a most obnoxious New Jersey accent. "I have to go to the bathroom." She repeated her complaint several times until her husband of less than a week held up his fist at her and she finally stopped yammering.

Jacqui walked a few feet down the road, swearing that she wasn't going to stand in the hot sun and wait for a replacement vehicle. She walked past the bus and put her thumb out at the speeding cars that whizzed past her. A huge open-backed army truck, courtesy of the British government, lumbered down the road, creating a vibration that could be mistaken for an earthquake. She frantically motioned to the truck and it slowed down and pulled over. Jacqui ran over to the driver.

"Sir, I was wondering if I could get a lift to Kingston?"

she asked, motioning to the broken-down bus. "I have to get back to town."

He looked Jacqui up and down for a moment. "If yuh brave enough to git in de back wid dem men, den g'wan. Doan sey me nevah warn yuh," said the sergeant.

Jacqui rushed back to the bus and grabbed her bag before running across the street again, nearly getting killed by a speeding Lada. She threw her suitcase into a bed of camouflage helmets and found that she was levitated into the back by several strong pairs of hands and deposited into a sea of soldiers.

She smiled self-consciously as she squeezed her body into the small space between two brawny men, feeling the force of twenty pairs of eyes upon her.

"Good morning. I'm Captain West," said the soldier next to her, putting out his hand. He was the blackest man she had ever seen and his perfect pearly white teeth picked up the sun. "This is Corporal Grange and Corporal Brown and the rest of the men of the United Nations Anti-Narcotics Task Force attached to the Jamaica Defence Force. The charming character you met in the front is Sergeant Hardcastle."

"I'm Jacqui Devron. I am pleased to meet all of you. Thanks for the ride."

"No problem," responded Captain West.

"You look like you've been up all night," said Jacqui sympathetically, taking in their muddied fatigues and boots.

"It's more like two," replied Captain West.

"Feel like t'ree," said Corporal Brown. "Next time, me hope we git de right place. Dem must a laugh at us sitting at Don Christopher's while dem ten miles down de..." Before he could get the last words out of his mouth the truck, careening around a corner, almost slammed into a Ford that had stopped in front of them. Jacqui landed in Captain West's lap.

116

A traffic jam had been created because two trucks could not pass each other on the narrow road and amidst the honking and shouting, neither one was willing to negotiate the treacherous Mount Diablo, with its blind curves, in reverse. The stranded drivers got out of their cars to see what was happening and higglers appeared from the bush selling naseberries and ripe mangoes. A crowd appeared as though by some preordained signal.

"Anybody dead? Any blood?" called out an elderly one-legged man who was running down the hill.

The rum bar opened, the pyjama-clad proprietor grateful for the unexpected flood of business. A political discussion was instantly underway, with participants blaming the government for not widening the road and then the British for building it. A pregnant woman walked up and down in front of the rum bar, pulling up her shirt to expose her swollen belly, screaming that she was in labour.

It took the better part of an hour for Captain West and his men to coordinate the slow process of moving fifty vehicles so the trucks could pass each other. Jacqui felt like a pig on a spit being roasted over an open fire. Every inch of her body was covered with sweat and her hair was as wet as if she had just walked out of the shower.

When the traffic finally moved, they stopped at Faith's Pen, a roadside truck stop perched precariously on the side of a cliff featuring shacks with names like Uncle Bill's Cow Cod Soup and Sweet Blossom's Juices. Jacqui greedily drank the ice cold cola she had been handed, thinking it was the most wonderful thing she had ever tasted. She let the sweet liquid roll down her tongue to her parched throat. New York seemed very far away at that moment.

* * *

Ainsley walked into his office, located in an old barracks

at the Jamaica Defence Force compound in Central Kingston. He swung his hat onto the rack and sat down at his desk, rifling through his messages. He knew it was too early to expect a cup of coffee. He wearily dropped his head into his hands and closed his eyes. A shuffle of steps and a cleared throat forced him to pull his head up.

"Sorry to disturb you, Ainsley," said Donald Francis, coming in.

"Donald, you're not disturbing anything," said Ainsley groggily, rubbing his eyes. "Come in, though I can't offer you coffee at this ungodly hour."

"I don't want coffee," said Donald. "I have some information that might be useful. A man of mine visits a lady of the evening who I understand is quite young and quite hot. It seems she gets regular visits from a well known Kingston businessman who told her about more guns for the posses. He intimated that connections for these gun shipments reach into the towers of Jamaica House."

"Did he give you any names?" Ainsley asked.

"Not yet, but he said he would meet me tonight and tell me. He begged me some money for Chini Brush so he could visit his girlfriend," said Donald, laughing.

"Poor fellow," said Ainsley, knowing Chini Brush was an aphrodisiac for men that prolonged their climaxes.

"I took your advice and hired another guard service. The docks have been relatively quiet but I'm waiting for the Storm and Thunder posse to bribe and bully their way back in. By the way, are you going to the soca fete tonight?"

"Can't," said Ainsley. "I've got too much work."

"I'll be there," said Donald with a smile.

"Be careful with your meeting tonight. You know you're a marked man. They won't hesitate to kill you if they think you're too close."

"Don't worry. If I could survive the seventies in Jamaica, I can survive anything."

* * *

Gary called Jacqui's room twice that morning and finally went over to knock on the door. It was half-open and the cleaning woman was making the bed. He saw no sign of Jacqui's belongings.

"Is this room occupied?" he asked.

"No, sir, the person checked out early this morning," she said, returning to her task.

Gary walked into the sunshine in a daze, wondering how she could have left without a word. He checked with Jennifer Parker at the front desk to confirm what the maid had said and wandered to the pool.

Trina was running the water volleyball and he sat down to watch her. She was really very good at what she did. There wasn't a guest who wasn't participating and having a good time.

"Hi Gary," she said, walking over to him, putting her arm around his shoulder. "How did you think the dance contest went last night?"

"It was great," he said without feeling.

"What's wrong?" she asked.

"Nothing," he said.

"Come on, Gary. I can see that something is bothering you," she insisted.

"It's nothing," he repeated, shaking himself. "There's a soca fete in town tonight. The theme is black and white. Would you like to go?"

"I would love to," she said, a huge smile lighting her face. "I have the perfect dress to wear." She planted a kiss on his cheek and walked away. Gary didn't watch her, his thoughts too troubled by Jacqui's sudden departure.

* * *

Skyline Drive was a winding road etched into the edge of Jack's Hill, with each hairpin turn bringing a breathtaking view of the lights of the city, stretched out like the hand of God.

Jacqui had called Trevor after she checked into the New Kingston Hotel and was promptly invited to a party at his house that evening, following his explicit instructions to wear black and white.

They pulled up a steep driveway to Sussex Lodge, a magnificent house perched on one of the highest ridges. The house itself was a mass of cement, small windows and endless wings, but the gardens were beautifully decorated with balloons and streamers and the kidney-shaped pool and cabana that overlooked the city were reminiscent of a Greek bath house.

Maxine welcomed them, accepting a chaste kiss from her husband as she greeted Jacqui warmly.

"Welcome to a Night in Black and White," said Maxine. "I'm so glad you could come. This is our annual event for a children's home in Kingston. I always get worried that something will go wrong."

"She does that all the time," said PJ, walking over to join them. "She worries that she'll run out of ice or beer, but the parties are always a success. Last year the party didn't start until after midnight and ended at lunchtime."

"It only ended then because we ran out of Red Stripe," said Maxine.

PJ offered to get them drinks and Maxine led Jacqui to the stone ledge in the fragrantly scented garden. The city lights twinkled like the jewels in a crown, silhouetting the immense harbour. A single ship made its way through the narrow channel opening. A cool breeze whistled across the ridge, scented with gardenia, orange blossom and pine.

"That's the undertaker breeze – the evening breeze that comes up from the sea and cools the hills. The daytime

120

breeze is called the doctor breeze. In December, when the crisp wind blows, we call it the Christmas breeze."

PJ brought them their drinks and led Jacqui through the striking assembly of people, of every shade of colour – brown, black, red and white. The men were dressed in jeans and caribas – open-necked shirts worn out of the pants – but the women were truly spectacular in elegant cocktail dresses and elaborate pants suits in black and white.

She was introduced to Caspar Chen, a short Chinese man with a permanent grin plastered on his face. His daughter Liz was the belle of the party with three men hanging on to her every word. She was a striking mixture of Indian, black and Chinese. She was delighted that Jacqui would be at Pimento Hill next week.

"I'm not a golfer but I'm going to the tournament to do the driving and keep an eye on him," said Liz, winking at Jacqui. "I was hoping for a touring partner while they sweat it out on the course. We can always catch up on the highlights at the cocktail parties. That's all they do anyway, talk about the day's play."

PJ introduced her to a couple who were in the middle of a friendly argument but called a truce to meet her.

"Delighted, Miss Devron," said Dick Robinson, a cinnamon-coloured man in his mid-fifties with a full head of dark hair with only a sprinkling of grey. His wife Sheila was a tall stately pale-skinned woman with kind eyes and a reserved elegance enhanced by her impeccable carriage.

"How was your sail down from Miami?" asked PJ. "Dick just bought an Australian Southern Cross."

"Perfect," said Dick. "*Sea Quest* is a masterpiece of engineering. We touched upon a storm in the Windward Pass, she held her own like a trooper." He spoke of his boat like a man did of a cherished mistress.

"We're breaking her in at the Port Antonio Calcutta week after next. If you are around, you must join us," invited

121

Dick. "We could always use extra crew."

"What's a Calcutta?" asked Jacqui.

"It's a one-day tournament that is held before the Blue Marlin tournament season," explained Sheila. "It gives the fishermen a chance to practise before the actual tournament season starts."

They moved en masse to the bar, laden with Myers and Appleton rums, Gilbey's gin, Smirnoff and Ostrov vodka, Red Stripe Beer, Guinness Stout, Johnnie Walker Black and a wide assortment of liqueurs like Rumona, Tia Maria and Sabena. Dick's and Caspar's voices grew louder, drawing amused side glances from guests.

"Dick and Caspar always behave badly at parties," said Sheila with a resigned sigh. "Believe it or not, they are the best of friends, and although Caspar golfs and Dick fishes they share each other's interests, as well as half of Kingston's. Their drinking escapades are legendary, and Dick assures me that they are still quoted in parts," she added. Her expression was totally serious, but Jacqui sensed her dour Scottish sense of humour.

"How long have you lived here?" asked Jacqui.

"Twenty-five years and counting," said Sheila. "Truth be told, I never expected to end up living in Jamaica."

"How did you?" asked Jacqui, smiling.

"When I was in my twenties, I was an air hostess – a stew as you say today. I had just literally walked from London to Kingston and had a well deserved three-day layover. When I got to town, I contacted an old school friend and we went out and painted the town red from the Glass Bucket Club to the Myrtle Bank Hotel. At a party, I saw Dick across the room chatting to a very stacked blonde. I was sternly warned to stay away from him," she said.

"Obviously you didn't," said Jacqui.

"Quite right. I went right up to him and asked him to dance. We had a beautiful time together and he managed to drop me off at the airport just in time for my flight."

"About a year later, I was back in Kingston on another layover. I was having lunch at the Myrtle Bank when I ran into Dick. He asked me to spend my holiday here, but I told him I was going to Australia to meet my fiancé. I ended up coming back for a month's holiday and we were married shortly after that," said Sheila.

Charles Whittingham arrived at the party. Jacqui and Sheila watched him move through the crowd, almost self-consciously, pausing from group to group to exchange greetings.

"Do you know Charles?" asked Sheila, noticing Jacqui watching him.

"I met him the night I arrived at the Yacht Club party," said Jacqui. "Is he a nice man?"

"Nice is not a word I would have ever used to describe Charles. He is a very frustrated man. He has wanted to build a hotel for so long and hasn't been able to find the right property. He had his heart set on a lovely piece of land on the north coast near Ocho Rios but the owner did not want to sell and no matter what tactics he used, the man wouldn't part with it. He can be pleasant, but there is something about him I have never warmed to."

She paused for a moment, looking at Jacqui before she continued speaking. "The most important lesson I learned when I first came to Jamaica is that you can't simply judge by appearances. You know, this country is truly colour blind. It's not the colour of the skin that matters here, it's the social class. And it's the same with love. I never expected to marry a brown-skinned man, and I don't think my parents ever recovered from the shock, but I've never regretted it."

Jacqui thought about what Sheila said. Then excitement rippled through the crowd as the Dragonnaires played the first bars of one of their current hits. There was a mad rush for the dance floor as bodies flowed in unison to the sultry rhythm. Hips swayed and muscles flexed as the dancers moved to the beat, their bodies quickly glistening with sweat.

Charles greeted Sheila and then touched Jacqui with a clammy hand, immediately putting her off.

"This is one of my favourite songs. Let's dance," he said, pulling her hand as he led her to the dance floor. Under the guise of sensual dancing, Charles pulled her very close to him, rubbing against her as he gyrated his hips in a manner that was anything but enticing.

When the next song started, Jacqui moved away from Charles, finding his sweet cologne so overpowering that she felt as if she would choke. He followed her off the dance floor, taking her hand in his sweaty palm.

"Will you be at Pimento Hill next week?" he asked.

"I think so," said Jacqui noncommittally.

"I hope so," gushed Charles. "I think that when I met you last I told you that I have a villa there called Dreamscape. There is always an interesting group of house guests and I always host a dinner. It's the social highlight of the week," he added arrogantly. "I hope you will come. It may give you a chance to renew old acquaintances."

She was bewildered by his last remark as he moved away, feeling as if he knew more about her than she would care to have him know. Spotting PJ at the bar with Dick, she began to pick her way through the crowd. She felt a large hand on her shoulder.

"Not so fast, little girl," said a low raspy voice.

"Donald, how nice to see you," Jacqui exclaimed, genuinely happy to see him again.

"How about a dance with a confirmed old bachelor?" he asked, putting out his arm as he rubbed his whiskers.

"My pleasure," she replied, taking his arm.

"I've been thinking about you since I met you," he said.

"How sweet," she said. "How is your yacht?"

"*Ali Baba* is doing just fine. She's ship-shape and ready

for a trip to the cays this weekend," said Donald, moving his bulky frame with surprising grace.

"Sounds great. I'll be in Kingston for the weekend before I'm off to the north coast again," said Jacqui.

"I wish you could stay here for a while," said Donald, his eyes glistening.

"You're something else, Donald," Jacqui laughed.

Donald was filled with such life. He was dancing, talking and at the same time greeting every woman in sight without making her feel uncomfortable.

As Donald turned her, Jacqui spied Trina at the edge of the crowd. Her cutwork-embroidered dress was open to the waist in the back, emphasizing her fabulous figure and colouring to perfection.

Gary was standing next to Trina, looking devastatingly handsome in black linen trousers and a crisp white shirt. He was talking to Derrick Bloomfield, who was so huge he looked like an oversized balloon, threatening to explode at any second.

Jacqui let Donald's frame shield her as she studied Gary with a new eye. Here was the Chairman of Tropical Properties and the man who was suing *Elegant Travel*. How could she have missed the aura of power that clung to him like a second skin.

* * *

Allistair Brody, attorney-at-law, Queen's Counsel, joined the party. He was wearing a short black bolero jacket with tight matching trousers. He saw the beautiful young woman standing beside Gary. Flicking his eyes over her fabulous body, he felt a flash of heat surge in him. He watched her turn away in panic, her eyes cold with fear. He flashed her an ominous grin as he wove his way through the crowd to greet Charles.

"Allistair, I'm glad to see you could make it. How have you been?" asked Charles.

"Busy. Very busy. That's why I haven't gotten back to you on that bank matter," said Allistair. "As a matter of fact, I don't think the practice has ever done this well."

They took a long look at the women at the party, commenting on their physical attributes and counting the number of women they had slept with, both grossly exaggerating their scores. Nodding his head toward Trina, Allistair said, "Do you see that luscious creature next to Gary?"

"That's Trina Doyan," said Charles. "You must remember her. I think I introduced you to her in the club several years ago."

"That's her," said Allistair incredulously. "What a gorgeous girl. She's even better looking now. I had a night with her I will never forget. She was sweet sixteen and the nicest piece I'd had in a long time. She was a real tiger," he laughed.

Charles glared at his friend, startled by his admission. The idea that he had possessed Trina filled him with envy.

* * *

The band finished their first set and Donald led Jacqui off the dance floor. She was glistening with sweat and dying for a cold drink. She gulped the ice water greedily as she wiped the perspiration off her forehead with a bar napkin. The DJ had taken over and was playing a set of slow songs.

"Hey, Gary, congratulations on the nomination," said Donald as Gary approached them at the bar. Jacqui could feel her heart beating in her ears.

"Thanks, Donald. I really appreciate that, especially coming from a former Jamaican of the Year," said Gary, shaking Donald's hand. "Good to see you. It's been ages."

He turned to look at Jacqui, his face expressionless. "Hello, Jacqui," he said evenly.

"Hello, Gary," said Jacqui, taking a side step, instinctively pulling away from his compelling presence.

"Would you excuse Jacqui?" asked Gary. "I was hoping she would have a dance with me."

"Thanks anyway, but I'd rather not," she said, absently moving her hand toward Donald's arm.

"Go ahead," said Donald, urging her on. "I have your company all day tomorrow, so I can share you tonight."

Gary gently directed her to the dance floor and she felt totally helpless as she was pulled into his arms. Despite everything she knew about him, it still felt so good to be held by him.

"Why did you leave? I thought you would have at least said goodbye," he said, lifting her chin with his finger, their eyes meeting.

"I just had to leave," she said lamely, watching his expression that demanded an answer.

"Jacqui, I didn't mean what I said about you being close-minded. I'm sorry if I hurt your feelings," he said, pulling her closer.

"Why didn't you tell me you were the chairman of Tropical Properties?" asked Jacqui.

"I thought you knew," he said. "What difference does it make what I do?"

"I'm sorry, Gary, but it matters. It matters a great deal," said Jacqui.

"Why?" he demanded. "What does it matter what I do? The time we spent together was very special."

"Just like the time you spend with your girlfriend," said Jacqui.

"What the raas are you talking about," said Gary, grasping her arms as he stopped dancing, forcing her to stop as well.

"I saw you with Trina," she said, shaking her head. "That's the least of it. I don't know which is worse – you being a drug dealer or the chairman of Tropical Properties."

"Jacqui, don't say that again," said Gary angrily, his grip tightening on her. "It's an unfair accusation and I'm not amused by it. Once and for all, I am not a drug dealer and I do not have a girlfriend."

His patronizing tone and controlling manner infuriated Jacqui. "I thought a lot of things about you – but I never thought you were a liar." She shrugged his hands off her in a fury, leaving him on the dance floor in the middle of an Anita Baker love song. Counting backwards to restore her temper, she moved towards the bar to get a drink.

Gary stood in the middle of the dance floor, his arms still in mid-air after Jacqui walked away. His pulse was throbbing with anger. Realizing he was standing alone and looking like a fool, he moved off the dance floor, picking his way through the throng of people that was still growing. He made his way to the bar where PJ stood with Maxine.

"Gary, you made it," she said, hugging him. "I'm so glad you could. Thanks for your gate prize. That free weekend at The Falls really helped ticket sales."

"Anytime for you and your kids. You've done wonders with the children's home. Hey, PJ," said Gary, turning to him. "How goes it?"

"Not too bad, though I hate to start a week losing to you in polo. How was your week with the press? Did *Elegant Travel* give you a glowing review or did they trash your property again?" he asked.

"*Elegant Travel*? There wasn't any press at the hotel last week," said Gary, looking at PJ strangely.

"You have definitely slowed down since our days at Munro College, my dear friend," said PJ, an innocent grin spreading on his face. He looked around the room and saw Jacqui in a nearby corner. "Hey, Jacqui, come here a minute!" he called. Somewhat reluctantly, she came over. "Now, Gary, there is no way you can convince me that you didn't meet Jacqui Devron, Associate Editor of *Elegant Travel* Magazine."

Gary's expression froze in shock before a pained look flashed in his eyes, changing the bright emerald to a deep jade of anger. The slight droop of his shoulders and the momentary unsteadiness of his hand cut through her. "He couldn't be that good an actor," thought Jacqui, desperately wanting to believe that he really didn't know who she was.

"We weren't formally introduced as such, but I understand a lot of things now," he said coldly. His face had turned to stone.

"Gary, I had no idea you were connected with the hotel until I read it in the newspaper yesterday," said Jacqui.

"Sure," said Gary angrily. "A lovely lady miraculously arrives at The Falls alone, within a day after receiving my letter, and very cunningly does some in-depth research."

PJ and Maxine glanced at each other and then back to Jacqui and Gary. PJ didn't want to move, but Maxine forced him away. She knew from experience that Jacqui would have to be a strong woman to hold her own against Gary. She didn't need any gawking observers.

"Gary, I thought you were a polo player and a farmer. That's what you told me," she pleaded.

"Please," said Gary, holding up his hand. "You will never convince me that Fiona Geller didn't respond to my letter. There you are claiming to be so upset that I'm the chairman of Tropical Properties, as if you didn't know. So they sent you down incognito. At least this time your magazine is improving their track record. You actually did interview me in an underhanded sort of way. Is that your usual modus operandi?" he asked coldly.

"What's the matter. Do you have something to hide?" she snapped.

"Listen, Miss Devron. I have an excellent resort concept and a beautifully run property. See if you can't write an accurate assessment of The Falls, not some fictional fabrication you writers think up," said Gary, letting his anger show through his jade eyes.

"For your information, it was felt that it would be in the best interest of the magazine, your hotel and our reading public that another review be conducted without management knowledge. That was done in order to get the most honest and accurate assessment of the property. It is a common practice that I am sure you are aware of," she said calmly, though her anger at his accusation was taking root.

"Just a little warning. Stick to the facts when you write your story. I wouldn't want your personal feelings to compromise the review."

"You really have a nerve," she said, clenching her fists to keep from slapping him. "How dare you threaten me. I wouldn't be surprised if you tried to use our encounter as a bargaining chip. Is there nothing you won't do to get your way?" she asked, walking away, shaking with anger.

She was so furious that she kept on walking through the party toward the pool house, not trusting herself to talk to anyone. Gary had the ability to get under her skin and make her lose control more than anyone she had ever met in her life.

The undertaker breeze rustled under the heavily laden mango tree. The moon was only a shiny glow beneath the wispy clouds. Leaning back against the tree, she took a sip of her drink, forcing herself to breathe evenly and calm down. Voices drifted over from the far corner of the pool, near the cabana.

"Just stay away from me," said a shrill female voice that echoed with a familiar twang.

"Don't pull that on me. You just keep doing what you're doing. Don't forget – I know where all your skeletons are buried." The clouds above moved in the night air, sending a shaft of moonlight toward the darkened corner, picking up the white of Trina's dress.

"That's what you think, Charles," said Trina, backing away from him. "I'm getting sick and tired of you."

Gary approached them, his face etched in fury. Jacqui pulled back into the shadow of the mango tree, not wanting to be seen.

"Leave her alone, Charles. I don't want to have to tell you again," said Gary.

"Gordon, you may own a few dozen companies, but you don't own me and you can't tell me who I can talk to," he said, hatred pouring out of his eyes.

"Stop harassing Trina. I don't want to tell you again," said Gary.

"You think you own her. You're just like your father," said Charles vehemently.

"Don't push me anymore," said Gary, taking Trina's arm. "This isn't the time or the place."

"Just walk away, you big coward. You will never take me on man to man," he said, with a sinister laugh.

Jacqui stayed in the shadow of the tree, watching as Charles walked to where she stood. Holding her breath, she stood absolutely still as he stood just in front of her to straighten his shirt and spray some breath freshener in his mouth. Even without seeing his face, she could smell his cologne wafting over her as the breeze blew north. She waited a decent interval before she followed their path back to the party. With a sweeping glance, she saw Gary talking to PJ and Caspar by the bar. Jacqui knew he saw her because his eyes narrowed, but he didn't break the tempo of his conversation.

Charles left almost immediately. Jacqui was uncomfortable. She felt as if Trina was watching her every move. Meanwhile, she noticed Trevor watching PJ and

Maxine. Caspar kept a hawk's eye on Liz, his daughter, who was being charmed by three men. Derrick Bloomfield stood at the bar, furiously sweating despite the cool breeze, his eyes darting around since moving his head seemed to be such an effort. Sheila kept a watchful eye on Dick as he chatted up two young girls. She had never seen anything quite like it – everyone watching everyone else.

"Great party, isn't it?" asked Trevor, approaching her.

"Just wonderful," said Jacqui, hoping she didn't sound too sarcastic.

"I heard what happened with you and Gary," said Trevor sympathetically.

"News seems to travel fast here. I guess it's just your reliable bush network."

"PJ did it innocently. I asked Maxine," said Trevor.

"I'm sure he did," said Jacqui, not wanting to talk about it.

"Jacqui, you pulled a fast one on Gary, with me as your accomplice. He has every right to be mad. As soon as I got Josh's call, I could have predicted that this would have happened. He was bound to find out sooner or later," he said, putting his arm around her, trying to comfort her.

"West Indians are quick to express their anger, but just as quick to forgive and forget. Take a walk through any market and you can hear a string of Jamaican bad words that would make even the most hearty sailor blush. You can almost see the nearby bottle begging to be smashed in a fight. Now return to that spot an hour later. You will see the same two men sharing a warm beer."

"Is that supposed to make me feel better?" asked Jacqui, flashing Trevor a smile nevertheless.

"I hope so," he said. "There is nothing you can do about Gary except let him cool off. He is not the kind of man who likes to have the wool pulled over his eyes. Be happy, my girl. Our friend Josh would never forgive me if

132

you didn't have the time of your life." Trevor took her hand to lead her to the dance floor. On the way, they were stopped by Donald Francis.

"Jacqui, I'll be by for you at eight o'clock sharp tomorrow morning," said Donald. He glanced at his watch. "Or should I say this morning. We'll be going to Maiden Cay."

"I'll be ready and waiting," promised Jacqui.

"Do you need a lift back to your hotel?" he asked.

"Donald, that's out of your way. I'll make sure that Jacqui gets home safely," said Trevor.

She kissed him on the cheek, accepting a hug from him before he left. "What a lovely man," said Jacqui.

"He is one of the nicest people I know," said Trevor.

* * *

Donald Francis left the party in a jovial mood. He was on his way to the docks to meet the cousin of one of his workers. All he had been told was that the man's name was Clock and he would be able to recognize him because one arm was shorter than the other.

Warmed by the rum and the night of dancing, Donald took his time negotiating the turns of Jack's Hill. He had to keep his appointment and finally confirm who was behind the drug smuggling on his ships. As he made the final wide turn down the hill, the last soca song still ringing in his head, a car pulled out from a side road and roared in front of him, pulling a hard left and abruptly stopping.

"What de raas is wrong wid yuh?" shouted Donald, braking hard. "Are you a fucking madman?"

The car door opened slowly and a man's feet touched the pavement. Donald's adrenaline started to pump as he slowly raised his eyes. The figure took two steps forward and Donald picked up the glint of the Desert Eagle in the moonlight.

Donald knew who his killer was even before he caught the cold hard glare of his eyes. He knew then that he had been right from the start about who was behind the drugs and guns. He hadn't needed Clock to confirm what he already knew.

He expected the fear to rise in him, but instead his last thought was one of disappointment that he wouldn't have a chance to tell Ainsley who was responsible. He heard the click of the gun and felt a momentary searing of pain as the bullet entered his throat and the warmth invaded his body. He was already dead when the second bullet lodged in his head.

* * *

Charles drove like a madman to the foot of Jack's Hill, pulling onto the main road without a cautionary glance. He pushed his expensive Mercedes sedan to the fullest, avoiding the potholes as he took a series of alleyways. He rested one hand on the butt of his gun, trying to control a rage that was burning out of control. He increased the car's speed, trying to erase the thought of Allistair in possession of Trina's body.

His member was so hard that he could barely drive as he pulled down a road off Maxfield Avenue, a rundown part of Kingston that had once been a nice residential section. He parked and set the alarm before glancing around and walking to the front door of a small house.

"Me nevah expect yuh tonight," said Shereen, the madam of the house. She was a buxom woman with charcoal skin and a huge cleavage outlined by the tight-fitting dress she wore. "Wat yuh want?" she asked warily, moving towards the door as if her massive bulk could keep him out. She knew his peculiar taste only too well, having taken care of it enough times in the past.

"Where Greater Sally?" he asked, one foot closer to the bottom of the wooden steps that led upstairs to the three tiny 'working rooms'.

"She restin'. She nah entertain no more tonight..." But she cut off her words when Charles handed her two bills. He took the stairs two at a time, his heart racing.

He was breathless when he opened the door. She was lying on the rumpled bed, her long lean black body glistening in the faint light. Her sheer nylon apricot robe showed her perfect breasts, the size of champagne glasses, her slim waist and her triangular mound.

Greater Sally looked at him and closed her eyes. She had the body of a young girl but her eyes were those of an old woman. She was tired and her supple body ached. The Canadian Navy was docked in Kingston Harbour for training and she had been busy for the past twelve hours.

"Greater Sally," panted Charles, fumbling with his belt buckle. He started to unbutton his shirt and in his haste, ripped it off, buttons flying in the air. Sally smiled to herself, enjoying the power that the sight of her body could elicit. He kicked off his shoes and dropped his pants, his erect member throbbing for release.

"So, Daddy," cooed Greater Sally. "You have come back for more of my sweet stuff. Sorry, but yuh mek a mistake. Me nuh want yuh."

"Yes you do," he said savagely, kneeling down in front of her. He would beg her if he had to, but there was no way she was going to refuse him.

"Me tired," she said, getting up and pulling her transparent robe around her perfect young body, outlining the gentle curve of her protruding buttocks.

Charles handed two bills to her and she threw them back at him.

"Dat nuttin, Daddy," she said. He handed her another

two bills and put another one for good measure. Her eyes flashed momentarily before she grabbed the notes and slipped them into the fake satin bag with the rest of her money. This was one trick whose money she wouldn't have to share with Shereen.

He placed a few slobbering kisses on her mouth, pushing his coarse tongue over her swollen lips before trailing his mouth down to her breasts. He sucked and tugged on her nipples like a newborn baby as Greater Sally sighed with boredom.

He instructed her to lie on her back on the bed with her feet touching the floor. He lowered his thick lips to her triangular mound, taking a deep breath of her perfumed crotch, sucking her juices. The movement of his tongue in her flowing wetness brought his erect member to a near-explosive climax.

Sally faked an orgasm, hoping he would leave since he usually wasn't able to complete the act, but suspecting that on this particular night she wouldn't be that lucky. When he finished, he pushed her body back on the bed, making her face the wall. Slipping onto the soiled sheet behind her, he pawed and squeezed her supple breasts with such pressure that she almost gasped. She bit her lip, thinking about the new shoes and bag she had seen last week at Lee's New Kingston, the fashionable department store in town.

He held his erect member against her back, letting her feel his power before he spread her cheeks roughly, pushing his engorged head into her with brutal force. He was no better than a wild animal, moving in and out of her with paralyzing strength. Her body was coated in sweat and within seconds, he jerked violently, his hot sticky liquid flowing down her thighs.

"Trina, Trina," he called out hoarsely before collapsing against Greater Sally who hadn't reached her sixteenth birthday.

Chapter 10

The gently rolling hills of Hanover danced on the horizon, the colours of gold and yellow shimmering like waves in the sun. Jacqui stood on the terrace of the great house at Pimento Hill Golf and Yacht Club, surveying the scene. The sea was totally flat, reflecting the sun like a sheet of glass, almost blinding to the naked eye.

The spectacular villas, manicured fairways and immaculate greens were sprawled out before her, highlighted with blooming flowers along the paths and in the villa gardens. Golfers were lining up their tee shots as a sailboat was docking at the yacht club, just a short walk from the beach bar. Seeing the boat brought Donald Francis to mind. The perfection of the scenery lost its vibrancy when she thought of him.

It was hard for her to believe that someone as vibrant as Donald, with such warmth and charm in his ruffled manner, could suddenly be dead. Accepting death was something she had gotten used to at a young age, but Donald's brutal murder made her feel uneasy about Jamaica. Beneath the sultry days there was an evil lurking that made her very uncomfortable.

Donald's funeral had been a sober event held at the St. Andrew Parish Church on Half Way Tree Road. The service was scheduled to start at two but there was a colossal traffic jam from the Clock Tower to Cross Roads as the employees of SHIP JA, Donald's company, and hundreds of dock workers crowded into the church and poured onto the streets.

Jacqui had watched Gary and the Countess exchanging a look as he put his hand over hers comfortingly. Seated next to them was a very handsome man whose chiselled features were twisted in sorrow. Charles Whittingham was seated in the second to last pew next to Allistair Brody who looked immaculate in his English morning suit.

The church was stifling and the overhead fans were dropping spitballs of hot air instead of whispers of breezes. Derrick Bloomfield had lumbered up to the podium to deliver an emotional eulogy. Now, just at the memory of his words, Jacqui found herself wiping away a tear that trickled down her cheek.

* * *

She walked along the magnificent course to the press booth to register. Picking up her press packet, she greeted several journalists with whom she had a passing acquaintance.

"Hello, Jacqui. So nice to see you again," said a familiar voice. Jacqui took a deep breath before turning around to confront her nemesis.

"Geoff," said Jacqui, her eyes meeting his. His good looks were as manicured as ever and a cold feeling passed over her.

"I'm glad to see you're back in the saddle," he said. "It's been a while. Let me buy you a drink." Jacqui was more repulsed by him than she could have ever imagined.

"It hasn't been long enough," said Jacqui, taking two steps away from him. She was not ready to deal with Geoff or his lines.

"That's not how you used to feel," he said suggestively, blocking her path. He let his eyes roam down her body, giving her a knowing look.

"That's how I feel right now. Will you get out of my

way," she said, pushing past him.

She entered the formal stateroom where the opening cocktail party was being held. There was an impressive array of professional golfers and celebrities. She spotted Congressman Ogilvy in a corner talking to the senator from Indiana and a popular daytime television actress whose wedding on the show had broken every single rating.

She saw Caspar on the terrace, waving his hands wildly, deep in conversation. Charles Whittingham walked up to Geoff Roth, greeting him like an old friend, and she suddenly remembered that this wasn't Geoff's first trip to Jamaica. Moving slowly, she watched them greet the Congressman, who gave both men hugs. She was so shocked that she took a step backwards, and felt a splash of cold liquid on her arm.

"I'm so sorry," said Jacqui, turning around, finding herself face to face with Jack Palmer, one of the great golf players. "I'm terribly sorry. It was my fault. I wasn't watching where I was going."

"Don't worry about it," he said easily. "It's just vodka which doesn't stain. I hope you didn't get your Moroccan blouse wet."

"No, not at all," said Jacqui. "You've been to Morocco?"

"Just a few months ago. I had always wanted to go, but thought it was too far and too dangerous. Then we read this article and decided to give it a try," said Jack. "I loved it."

"Do you recall the magazine?" asked Jacqui curiously.

"*Elegant Travel*. We carried the issue around with us. It had a great survival guide with a page of commonly used phrases."

"I'm glad you enjoyed it. It was an experience to put it together," she said, feeling immensely pleased as she noted his surprised expression when she introduced herself.

"I am pleased to meet you," said Jack, shaking her

hand. "Are you on assignment?"

"I am working on the magazine's cover story for September. Pimento Hill is one of the properties we are featuring," she said.

"Wonderful. This happens to be one of my favourite courses. I'm playing in the Pro-Am tomorrow and if my partner doesn't show up by then, I may just have to rope you in as my celebrity player. I do hope you play," he said, laughing.

"I'm sure your partner will show up," said Jacqui, praying she wouldn't have to embarrass herself in front of hundreds of people. Her golf game was rusty at best.

Manuel Espito, one of the top golfers, stopped to talk to Jack. Jacqui thought he was terribly charming with his accented speech as he explained about the fund he had started to assist the children of caddies.

Out of the corner of her eye, she saw Charles break away from the Congressman just as Trevor walked in with a gorgeous brown-skinned young woman with legs that went on forever. Jacqui wondered where Maxine was – and whether PJ was with her.

It was time for the official proceedings to start. The Honourable Barbara Green, the tourism minister, was a striking woman with the most beautiful black velvet skin that Jacqui had ever seen. She welcomed everyone to the Jamaica Open and Pro-Am.

"Not only does this promise to be one of the most exciting golf tournaments ever held in Jamaica, but it is also being held on one of the most beautiful courses in the world. The Pimento Hill facilities should keep our non-golfers occupied, and for those of you who like more hedonistic pursuits, Negril is just around the coast with its seven miles of white-sand beaches."

The minister then introduced BG Ellis, the tournament director, who looked gruff but spoke so quickly and concisely that even non-golfers understood him.

Jacqui saw that Charles was still talking to Congressman Ogilvy. Geoff joined them again, looking very neat in a white linen blazer that was perfectly pressed. He was sipping his scotch and tapping his foot in a gesture that was all too familiar to her. Finding the whole party oppressive, she took refuge in her room with its view of the sea and the western edge of the property.

* * *

The tropical sun rose over the mountain, burning away the clouds that drifted lazily over the island. The sun caressed the tops of the palm trees as it bathed the fairway in its golden rays.

Over twenty Pro-Am teams assembled by the club house, listening to BG Ellis explain the rules for the two-ball, best-ball eighteen-hole competition. There were mixed teams of professionals and celebrity amateurs, playing for a variety of local charities. The famous Nancy Nichols had been partnered with Caspar Chen while Manuel Espito was playing with Charles Whittingham. Much to Jacqui's surprise, Gary had arrived and was playing with Jack Palmer.

Her heartbeat quickened as she watched him walk towards the first tee, the wind lifting the collar of his golf shirt. He looked as if he was in such control that Jacqui felt slightly unnerved. She could still taste the lingering bitterness of their fight. She found Liz near the third tee and they followed the tournament under the blazing hot sun that was making Jacqui feel as if she would wilt. The major networks, sports channels and magazine correspondents watched along with fans as the golfers confidently took their strokes, lined up their drives and sank their putts. It was a test of skill on the challenging course of Pimento Hill. At the nine-hole bar, Jacqui gratefully gulped a cold drink before Liz led her to the fifteenth hole.

"This is the most difficult hole on the course," said Liz. "It's a par five with water on both sides and a strong sea breeze that blows across the tee." Jacqui could see that the tee shot had to pass by the stone windmill, over a pond and remain on the fairway.

Charles knocked his ball out of bounds, and his cursing was picked up on the live radio commentary. Gary hit a double bogey. Then Liz watched her father sink a hole in one, much to the crowd's astonishment.

"I can't bear to watch the rest. I'm sure we'll hear about it tonight. Let's go wait in the bar," suggested Liz. "We can watch BG tabulate the results as if he was counting the returns from the national election."

They ordered drinks and waited until Caspar came in, his arm draped around Nancy, a grin spreading across his face. "Liz, I've never played such good golf. Never, never," he called out.

There was a low rumbling in the air. Jacqui's ears perked as she listened to the sound of the approaching jet. Golfers and spectators were gathered on the lawn by the pool near the eighteenth green. Jacqui moved outside, watching the Concorde streak across the sky, the full sound only reaching her ears when it was close to the horizon. Within seconds, there was only a thin white wispy trail in the sky to bear witness that the Concorde had ever flown past.

From a distance, Gary watched Jacqui's face soften in childlike rapture when the Concorde was overhead. He remembered their conversation in the moonlit garden when she had told him about her father and learning how to fly. Now, her hair curled at her shoulders and was gently lifted by the breeze. He had never seen her smile like that and wished he was the one who had made her smile that way. His eye caught hers and she looked away. He felt a rush of anger.

How could she have carried on the charade about what she was doing at his hotel. He should have trusted his instinct when he thought she wasn't the average tourist. She was nothing more than an over-ambitious New York career woman who would go to any lengths to get what she wanted. He turned away, unable to push away the thought of how she felt in his arms and the way her lips felt under his. Despite what she had done to him, she excited him more than any woman had in a long time.

Jacqui felt her cheeks flush under Gary's scrutiny. Knowing he was the chairman of Tropical Properties and probably a major drug dealer as well as a two-timing liar could not erase the memory of how his ragged breath felt against her bare skin as the gentle breeze bathed them. She watched him, his green eyes softening with laughter as he talked to one of the golfers. With everything she knew, she still felt compelled by his magnetic presence and the passion he had elicited from her.

"Before I announce this morning's results, I want to say that today's Pro-Am was the finest golf I've seen played in a long time. A fine round to everyone," said BG. There was a round of applause.

"This year's winners of the Jamaica Open and Pro-Am are Nancy Nichols and Caspar Chen playing for the Heart Association," he announced.

Caspar had been pacing up and down near the bar, avoiding the jibes and taunts from his friends. Now he froze in his steps. "Repeat that," he yelled, his eyes widening.

"Don't make me repeat it," said BG. "You won."

"Yes, yes, yes," screamed Caspar, his arms outstretched, his hands clenched in a victory fist. He ran up to BG and grabbed Nancy, enveloping her in a bear hug before he started jumping up and down, calling for champagne.

"Let's get out of here," suggested Liz. "He'll be like this all afternoon."

"Gladly," agreed Jacqui.

They went to Round Hill, going up its stately drive past elegant villas. At the beach, Liz introduced her to Franz Josephs, the general manager. He insisted on taking them on a tour of the magnificent property and took great pride in showing off the newly decorated villas. They were so perfect that Jacqui thought she would be afraid to sleep there in case she messed up the bed.

"Girls, I want you to enjoy the beach," said Franz, in his polished Viennese accent. "Just drink to your hearts' content. I have some champagne on ice."

They spent the afternoon lying on cushioned chaises longues. Their only activity was getting up to slip into the silky water to cool their parched skin.

"What's on for tonight?" asked Jacqui, lazily opening one eye as she took a sip of her Suffering Bastard, made with dark and light rum, lime juice and Mai Tai mix, garnished with a strip of cucumber rind and served in a large old-fashioned glass.

"There is Sir Harry's party at his estate next to Pimento Hill, called Rat Hall," said Liz sleepily as she turned on her back.

"I know a few guys who could call that home," murmured Jacqui, letting the sun's rays lull her.

* * *

Rat Hall was set on a hillside overlooking the golf course and the sea. It was built to resemble an English country hall from the days of Ivanhoe, but loving touches of the Caribbean had been added, including a large open breezeway, a huge terrace and a well loved garden filled with exotic flowers and fruit trees.

Sir Harry, dressed in a black smoking jacket and ascot, was greeting his guests, welcoming them to his home.

"Good evening, Caspar," he said. "And to you, Miss Liz. You grow prettier by the day. Congratulations on your stunning victory, Caspar."

"Thank you, Sir Harry," replied Caspar, beaming. He was in a jovial mood and still drunk from his afternoon's escapades.

"Welcome to Rat Hall," said Sir Harry to Jacqui, putting out his hand.

"Thank you. I'm Jacqui Devron," she said, taking his hand.

"Ah, yes. Miss Devron from *Elegant Travel*. I hope you are enjoying your stay and that everything is to your satisfaction."

"Yes, thank you," she said. "I was wondering if you could tell me how a pimento plantation became a golf course."

"That's an excellent question with quite a simple answer," said Sir Harry. "The Duke of Windsor cancelled his holiday at Round Hill because there was no golf course nearby. We couldn't let that happen again, so a group of us got together and built the first villas and started Pimento Hill in the early fifties."

Sir Harry circulated to greet his other guests as Jacqui wandered into the party. Trevor and Gwendolyn, his long-legged girlfriend, were comfortably ensconced at a secluded table.

"Good evening, Jacqui," said Charles, resting his hand on her forearm. "I see we meet again. How are you?"

"I'm fine, thank you, Charles," said Jacqui, gently moving her arm away from his sticky fingers. "Sorry about the Pro-Am."

"I really messed up that shot. I could have given that stupid reporter who kept following me around a kick in the mouth," he said as his eyes narrowed slightly. "I'm glad that's over so I have the rest of the week to relax and enjoy my guests. Did you enjoy the party in town the other night?"

"The party was fine, but Donald Francis's death really shook me up," she said, looking at him. The confrontation between Gary and Charles about Trina by the cabana at Sussex Lodge ran through her mind.

"Yes, that was terrible," he said sympathetically. "I hope it hasn't affected your opinion of Jamaica. The island can be a bit violent at times, but then again Donald was involved in some pretty unsavoury things."

Jacqui didn't respond, trying to picture Donald involved in something underhanded. Somehow the description didn't fit the man she had met. Charles saw her expression harden.

"How was your week on the north coast?" he asked, changing the subject. "Where did you stay?"

"It was a lovely week. I spent most of my time at The Falls but I managed to get out and see quite a few places," said Jacqui.

"The Falls," said Charles, his eyes widening in dismay. "I know the place. I hope it wasn't too dreadful."

"Not at all. It is really a lovely property," said Jacqui.

"I've heard terrible reviews about the place. As I recall, *Elegant Travel* gave them a horrible review for management and service. I guess that Gary Gordon hasn't been able to put that one together too well. It can't compare to Pimento Hill which is one of the finest properties on the island. If Pimento Hill is a Roll Royce, then The Falls is a sixty-five Volkswagen," said Charles, laughing at his own poor joke.

"You really don't like Gary, do you?" she asked.

"Like him," spat Charles. "I hate his guts and his rotten family, starting with his sainted grandfather Winston and his lying cheating father Neville. The Gordons pretend they are

146

so lily-white and pure with their fancy airs and legacies, but I know they are as dirty and common as they come."

"What do you mean?" she asked, surprised at the vehemence of his statement. "What did Gary ever do to you?"

"It's not just what he did to me. It's what his family did to my family," said Charles. "You see, my father was a man of the people. He was a founding member of a trade union to make sure the poor agricultural workers received their fair share of pay from the sugar plantations. Neville, Gary's father, didn't want that to happen. He was too shortsighted to realize that if his workers were well cared for then he would get better work. He refused to give even the smallest pay raise to the men who had made him the rich bastard that he was.

"Neville framed my father by saying he had started a fire at one of his plantations. He lost his post with the union and couldn't find another job. He was a proud man and having to beg money for food to put on the table broke his spirit and he died shortly after that," said Charles bitterly.

"I'm so sorry," said Jacqui, shocked at his story.

"That wasn't enough, though," said Charles disgustedly. "Neville couldn't keep his hands off my mother. So if you ask me if I don't like Gary, the answer is I hate him and with very good reason.

"I'm not telling you this to get any sympathy," he continued. "He is out to destroy anything that stands in his way and right now I'm standing in his way. Don't let Gordon's pretty manners take you in. He's not what he appears to be."

Jacqui's mouth was dry when Charles took her arm and began to introduce her around. She met a number of famous golf players before he introduced her to Congressman Ogilvy and his wife Alice. The Congressman took his pipe out of his mouth to shake her hand. His nose was already bright red and peeling.

Geoff joined the group, flirting with Alice Ogilvy who looked like a cream puff in a white and beige cocktail dress that had too many buttons and ribbons. He eyed Jacqui with a smug look, letting his eyes roam up and down her body, taking in her sleeveless red mini dress that set off her tan.

Unable to bear being in such close proximity to Geoff, she took her leave. "It was a pleasure meeting you, Congressman and Mrs. Ogilvy. I'm sure we will run into each other again," she said pleasantly.

"I am sure we will," said Geoff.

She moved away, watching Geoff from the corner of her eye. She saw Charles signal Geoff and he tapped the Congressman on his arm, impatiently waiting for him to finish his conversation. The three men walked out into the garden.

Something is up, Jacqui thought. Geoff and Charles together gave her a very queasy feeling.

* * *

Rat Hall's garden held every fruit tree grown on the island and was scented with the spicy fragrance of pimento. James Ogilvy paused to light his pipe.

"Charles, I must tell you I always enjoy my little jaunts to Jamaica, especially the congressional junkets," he said. "However, due to the increase of media attention on Jamaica and other issues, I feel I should limit my involvement. I am up for re-election this fall."

"I can understand your sentiment," said Geoff, ignoring the deadly look that Charles flashed him. "Your successful political career means a great deal to all of us, but I feel very strongly that we have to finish with the obligations that we have undertaken. The consequences if we don't might be more than any of us are prepared to deal with."

148

"I'm not sure," said the Congressman. "The House Ethics Committee has been making discreet inquiries into my activities, and so has the opposition in my congressional district."

"I have made all the necessary arrangements in Cayman. You really aren't involved in any way," said Geoff reassuringly.

"Why don't we take a ride into town," suggested Charles. "Lord Nigel's Reggae Saloon is still a great club. We can finish discussing this later."

The Congressman's face broke into a wide grin as he remembered what a wild time he had there the year before. There wasn't a club like Lord Nigel's in all of Washington. The girls were free and easy, the rum flowed and the back room had more pleasure per square inch than Times Square in New York. Running his hand through his thinning hair, he followed them back inside. He would have to tell his wife that pressing matters required his immediate attention elsewhere.

Chapter 11

Three fishing boats were coming towards the shore as the sun glistened on the water, bathing the world in an amber glow. A doctor bird, with its black and red streamers, alighted on the balcony, just inches away from Jacqui. For the past hour, she had been trying to get through to New York to speak to Josh. She needed some reassurance from a friendly voice.

"Jacqui, how are you?" asked Pat, her voice echoing on the telephone. "Are you having wonderful weather? It's raining and miserable here."

"It's eighty-eight and balmy," replied Jacqui. "Is Josh in?"

"No, he's not. He's in Venezuela and will be back on Monday."

"Pat, I need to find Elizabeth Hartley," said Jacqui. "There's something about her last review I need to talk to her about."

"Hold on and I'll look," said Pat. "She hasn't done much work for us lately. Here it is. I have a number for her in Miami."

"You're a doll," said Jacqui, jotting down the number. "Lunch at the Palm when I get back."

"I am looking forward to it. Have you met any gorgeous aristocratic millionaires who want to take you away from it all?" asked Pat, laughing.

"Several, but I just can't make up my mind," said Jacqui lightly. "I'll keep in touch. Please give my best to Josh."

She tried unsuccessfully to reach Elizabeth at the number Pat had given her. She left a message on her machine and went to the dining room to have breakfast.

Afterwards she walked to the course, catching Manuel Espito at the sixth hole. He made an impossible shot from a sand trap to the green that had the crowd clapping appreciatively. The press booth was busy when Jacqui walked in. She immediately caught sight of Geoff, flirting with one of the models for the annual swimsuit layout for *Sports Illustrated* that was being photographed at Pimento Hill. Walking to the beach, Jacqui wondered what she had ever seen in him. She caught up with Liz at the beach bar and was firmly led away by the hand towards the parking lot.

"Where are we going?" asked Jacqui as Liz opened the door of Caspar's new Mercedes Benz.

"On a saloon tour," said Liz mysteriously, with a big smile on her honey-coloured face.

Moments later they were speeding along one of the most beautiful stretches of coastline in the world where beaches and coves washed right up against the road. The water rippled, changing colour in waves of aquamarine and sapphire as it rolled out against the horizon.

Liz navigated her way through Montego Bay, where the square was crowded with people. A bronze statue of national hero Sam Sharpe, who had led a slave rebellion in 1831, stood in the centre. Nearby was a donkey, with baskets of flowers, whose owner was glad to have his picture taken – for a price.

They stopped at Doctor's Cave Beach, one of the oldest properties in the city. It had a beautiful bar with gleaming brass railings and green leather booths. They moved to the Sea Palace with its rustic atmosphere and then to Sunset Lodge which featured swings at the bar overlooking the sea.

They had lunch at the Royal Caribbean, enjoying the delicious fresh lobster salad, before going to Rose Hall, a beautiful stone great house that was hauntingly perched on a summit with a commanding view of the sea.

"Legend had it that Annie Palmer, the White Witch of Rose Hall, murdered her husband and abused her slaves," said Liz. "She was eventually killed in a slave uprising. The history books say she was mad, but I see her as a young English girl who came out to the colonies to get married and was overwhelmed by the slavery and class differences, not to mention the behaviour of the men."

"I think that would have been enough to drive anyone mad," said Jacqui.

They stopped at the beautiful Half Moon Club for tea, enjoying the mento band that was playing on the Sea Grape Terrace. Despite the lushness, Jacqui was painfully aware of the squalor amid the splendour. Along the route, there were squatter towns with crude zinc fences and wooden shacks sandwiched on every inch of available land. She watched barefoot children with swollen bellies playing with goats by the side of the marl road. She couldn't shake the nagging feeling that even though Jamaica was blessed with natural resources, it was doomed to an endless cycle of poverty.

The sky was turning into a fire-burst of coral, tangerine and fuchsia when Jacqui returned to her room. She tried Elizabeth Hartley's number and a high southern voice answered the phone on the third ring.

"You don't have to tell me who you are," said Elizabeth. "I always read your work."

"I was hoping you could help me out," began Jacqui.

"What can I do for you?" asked Elizabeth.

"When you covered The Falls at Ocho Rios, what happened that warranted the negative review?" asked Jacqui, explaining that she had just visited the resort.

"That awful place. I've just about stopped having nightmares. If you really want to hear the story, I will tell you, but I warn you it is not pretty." Jacqui stretched her legs out on the table in front of the couch and propped the phone under her ear, ready to take notes.

"I had a reservation at The Falls which was confirmed by the office in New York," began Elizabeth. "When I checked in I was told there was no room for me but they would give me a smaller room in the meantime.

"Well, Jacqui, it was the size of a broom closet where the maids change. I was given a key and when I came back from dinner I found that my bags had been picked. My passport and radio were gone. When I went out to the desk to complain, Gary Gordon, the owner, said I had to go report this to the police. Before I knew it, I was put in a rickety old car with a driver and sent off to the police station," said Elizabeth.

"He didn't take you?" asked Jacqui.

"Are you kidding me?" exclaimed Elizabeth. "I was taken on a ride on a dark winding country road, in a car that broke down twice and was driven by a man who had a thumb missing from one hand. The police station was a converted bus," said Elizabeth.

"What did the police do?" asked Jacqui.

"They kept me waiting for an hour. Then this officer agreed to take my report even though he wasn't on duty. He straightened everything on his desk, asked for a cup of tea and then painstakingly creased the long white paper while he took my report in longhand.

"Jacqui, I thought I would die by the time he wrote down my statement. I had to repeat each word at least three times. All the while one of the men was entertaining three women, leaving with each of them at separate times. The movie Casablanca was playing on a five-inch black and white set in the corner."

"Didn't Gary..." said Jacqui, trying to interject a question, but Elizabeth was determined to tell her story.

"The bathroom was a hole in the ground outside, next to

the chicken coop. Don't dream of the luxury of toilet paper," said Elizabeth.

"Didn't Gary know you were with *Elegant Travel?*" asked Jacqui, pushing in a question.

"He certainly did. He returned my passport the next morning and warned me that this is what happens to careless journalists. I got so mad that I picked up a drink and flung it in his face. I don't think I ever acted so unladylike in my life," said Elizabeth.

"Do you remember when this was?" asked Jacqui.

"It was late last January because I was working on the cruise supplement for *Elegant Travel*," said Elizabeth. "I'm positive of that."

They talked for a moment longer before Jacqui hung up, promising to keep in touch. She tossed her pad away in dumbfounded horror. It simply didn't sound like Gary. Despite his faults, Gary was a very gracious man. He wouldn't do that to a guest, much less a reporter.

She was just stepping out of the shower when the phone rang. Quickly wrapping her dripping hair in a towel, she grabbed the phone.

"Jacqui. It's Charles. I hope you haven't forgotten about my dinner party this evening," he said.

"No, I haven't," said Jacqui, towelling her hair. "Thanks for calling."

"I am looking forward to your company," said Charles.

* * *

Gary was sitting in the far corner of the lounge having a quiet drink with Jack Palmer. He had spent the day at Spicey Hill, his pimento plantation, and his face and his hands were tinged with red. He watched Jacqui stroll in, oblivious to the stares from the patrons at the bar. Her elegant long lean lines were emphasized in her black sleeveless jumpsuit that was open in the back.

"Quite an attractive lady," commented Jack. "I am a great admirer of her work."

"Is she that good?" asked Gary, sipping his drink without taking his eyes off Jacqui. His anger at discovering her association with *Elegant Travel* had cooled slightly, but for the first time in his life, he felt used.

"I think so," said Jack. "You're lucky if she visited The Falls and liked it." Gary didn't respond, but watched Jacqui as she ordered a white wine, absorbed in her thoughts. Excusing himself, he picked up his drink and slowly moved across to the bar, coming up behind Jacqui. He stared at her in the smoky glass mirror until she looked up, their eyes meeting in the glass.

"Hello, Jacqui," said Gary. "Are you working as the aggressive editor from *Elegant Travel* or incognito as the sweet buckeye from Ohio?"

Jacqui glanced at him, taking in his face as she picked up her glass of wine. "I am on assignment at Pimento Hill," she said, taking a sip. "I should ask you if you're working. Taking time off from your little forays up the White River?"

"Touché," said Gary, smiling as he leaned his hip on the empty stool next to her. "Can we start over again?" he asked. Jacqui looked at him expectantly. "How would you like to tek a bwoy home wid yuh tonight?" There was a mischievous smile on his face.

"I wouldn't," she responded sweetly. "I prefer to take a man home with me."

Gary shook his head, his eyes alight with laughter as a warm look crept over his face. "You know, Jacqui, from the first moment I saw you I knew things were going to happen between us fast."

"I'm so glad you think so, but I prefer my men to be slow and sensual," said Jacqui, taking another sip of her wine.

"True, true, sweetheart, but never mind. I'm going to make you see stars," said Gary in a mock lecherous tone.

"If I wanted to see stars, I would bend my head back and gaze at the sky. When I'm with a man, a real man, I like to see fireworks."

"You're too much for me," Gary laughed. "How about if we get out of here and go to Negril. I know a little restaurant on the cliffs that serves the best pan-fried snapper you will ever eat – accompanied by the sound of waves crashing against the cliffs under a blanket of stars."

Jacqui appraised Gary and realized, ironically, that despite all that she had learned about him, she was ready to go wherever he wanted to take her.

Geoff Roth sauntered into the bar and spotted Jacqui talking to Gary. He made his way over to her side, putting a hand on her shoulder. Gary watched as she instinctively pulled away, her hand instantly clenching into a tight fist.

"Hi, Jacqui. I hope you are ready. Charles is waiting for us. I'm Geoff Roth of GRI Advertising," he said to Gary, putting out his hand. Gary was not at all surprised by his limp handshake.

"I've heard some great things about your property – especially from Marty King," said Geoff.

"Thanks. How is Marty?" said Gary.

"I'm keeping him pretty busy. I'm sure you know I handle all his advertising. We've had a great year. I think I can do the same for you. Perhaps we can talk," said Geoff smoothly.

"Perhaps we can," said Gary, instantly taking a dislike to Geoff, wondering why his old friend Marty King would do business with a man like him.

"Sorry to cut your conversation short with Jacqui, who can talk your ear off, but we have a previous engagement. See you around," said Geoff.

Jacqui glared at Geoff, then turned to Gary and said,

"Thanks for your invitation. I have some business to tie off. Perhaps some other time."

"No problem," Gary responded easily. He watched Jacqui walk out of the lounge, stunned that she would rather spend the evening with that North American pansy than with him. He joined Jack, who signalled the bartender, ordering a twelve-year old rum.

"What's this for?" asked Gary.

"Your double bogey," said Jack, trying not to laugh. "At least I did mine on the course."

* * *

The moment they were outside, Geoff called to Jacqui. "Stop for a second. What's your hurry?"

Jacqui turned on him with a vehemence she had been suppressing. "Don't you dare come one step closer to me," she hissed.

"Hey, baby. I'm sorry. Did I just break in on one of your new love interests? I'm glad to see you've gotten over your aversion to men," said Geoff.

"Not men, just boys. I seem to be encountering nothing but boys lately," said Jacqui. "You know, you are just a two-bit untalented hustler who knows how to climb on the backs of people to get what you want."

"I treated you really good. We had something that just fizzled out. You couldn't ask me to pretend about things I didn't feel," said Geoff.

"Fizzled my ass, you cold-hearted contemptuous bastard. It fizzled right after I got you an introduction to the Desert Palm and an entree to the King Casino organization. Then you turned the tables and left me in a mess that I'm still trying to clean up."

"That's where you are wrong," said Geoff. "I didn't manipulate you or the situation. Check again and see who did. Now I want you to get a hold of yourself and stop going over these unimportant details of what happened. We have bigger fish to fry tonight."

Jacqui took two steps forward and grabbed the lapels of his silk jacket, crushing the delicate fabric as her body shook with anger.

"Don't do that," he whined. "I just got this jacket back from the pressers."

"Shut up and listen, you little worm," she said in a low husky voice that Geoff had to strain to hear. "Get a hold of myself, you say. I'm warning you for the last time. Stay away from me and my magazine. Don't go and try to put the blame elsewhere when you were the one behind the King Casino story. I'll bet you just laughed when you heard I was suspended. If you tamper with one of my stories again, I swear I'll make you the sorriest excuse of a man that there ever was." She released his lapels, shoving him away before walking to the waiting golf cart, directing the driver to Dreamscape in a shaky voice.

"Jacqui, wait. That's my golf cart," called Geoff, but Jacqui was already halfway down the hill, oblivious of his calls.

* * *

Jacqui was overwhelmed by the sheer size of Dreamscape as Charles's manservant ushered her through the house to the gazebo by the pool. Congressman Ogilvy and his wife Alice were there as well as other celebrities and professional golfers. The drinks were refilled effortlessly and the smoked marlin and oyster appetizers lay temptingly within arm's reach.

Geoff arrived after Jacqui was settled comfortably next to an Englishman who had been in Jamaica since the early fifties. He threw Jacqui a dirty look, settling in the empty chair next to Alice Ogilvy who smiled seductively at him. She was wearing a peach organza dress with lots of ruffles and frills.

The conversation was lively, peppered with stories about golf, when the dinner bell chimed. Jacqui found herself seated next to Manuel Espito and across from BG Ellis. The table was set with the finest Lennox china, sterling silver and Waterford crystal, softly illuminated by long tapered white candles. The beef with Béarnaise sauce was tender and juicy, accompanied by ackee quiche and roasted Irish potatoes.

Jacqui felt Charles staring at her, making her feel uncomfortable. Geoff was talking to one of the swimsuit models. Her shimmering evening gown fitted her as if she had been dipped into it like wax. It was transparent and his eyes stayed glued to her breasts. She couldn't stand being in the same room with him. Just looking at him made her feel as if she needed a bath.

Charles tapped his fork lightly on his crystal water glass, inviting everyone into the living room for coffee. Happy to get away from the table, Jacqui went to the powder room, but found that it was in use. Instead of waiting, she walked upstairs to find a bathroom. She took a cautious peek in the master bedroom. Its dull beige tone and nondescript furnishing lacked warmth. She felt as if Charles had bought the house exactly as it was, down to the silk flowers in the tiny white bud vases.

She walked down the hall to the bathroom, passing a guest room. The glow from the lamp on the table illuminated a set of monogrammed toiletry cases that she had given Geoff on his birthday. She took one step into the room, not having realized until that moment that Geoff was Charles's house guest. On the table, there was an ashtray full of ashes and matches, but no cigarette butts. She glanced over her shoulder cautiously, before looking around again. She noticed a crumbled-up book of matches, picked it up, and unfolded it. It was from the Congressional Country Club.

Jacqui's eyes trailed over the piles of papers neatly arranged on the table. There was an open file for a company called FPL registered in the Cayman Islands. Clipped to the file was a ledger of bank transfers to a Cayman account. She suddenly gasped, a wave of nausea welling up in her.

Her name was in bold print on a list with her New York bank account number and a fifty-thousand transfer order to the FPL account in Cayman. Her vision was blurred and her next breath came in one gasp as she saw Josh Travers's name alongside hers on the ledger.

She leafed through the file, picking up a photograph that was stuck inside. It was a picture of a Princess boat called *Foolish Pleasure.*

She was so caught up in the papers that she didn't hear the noise in the hall until it was almost too late. In a split second, she slipped behind the door, still clutching the papers and the photograph. Her heart was pounding so hard that she could barely hear the footsteps walking down the hall. She held her breath, her hands moist with sweat as the picture almost slipped from her grasp.

The steps came closer. Jacqui watched Charles walk past her from the crack in the door. He glanced in the room for a moment before he walked down the back stairs. He stopped halfway down the stairs, before continuing.

Jacqui waited a moment, her breath coming in short spurts. She was about to move cautiously into the hall, when she heard the clink of china cups on a tray and the crack of the swinging kitchen door. She froze, rooted in her spot. Charles's manservant walked halfway up the stairs to meet him. He looked over his shoulder.

"Me jus' git de word," said the manservant. "Me a go Treasure Beach tomorrow fe pick up de new load."

160

"Good," said Charles, as Jacqui watched the back of his head nodding.

"Me gonna tek Niney wid me. Him know de area best. Him all set up," said the manservant. "Me nuh want no mistakes dis time."

"Me neider," said Charles emphatically as he went down the back stairs.

Jacqui waited until she heard the kitchen door creak before she cautiously moved from behind the door. The papers were still in her hand and she slipped them into the evening bag with shaky fingers. Smoothing her hair, she descended the main stairs to the party.

Cocktails and liqueurs were being served and the guests were milling around the garden, talking in small groups. Charles glanced at her suspiciously when she walked in, immediately walking towards her. She took a seat next to Andrea Walters who was a playing editor for *Golf Digest* as well as a tournament player. ,

"What do you do when you're not playing golf?" asked Jacqui.

"I have a part-time job as a waitress at the Cream Puff Bakery in Phoenix," said Andrea.

"Why a waitress?" asked Jacqui, laughing.

"Because the pressure of getting an order right is greater than sinking a putt," she said. "Isn't that right, Manuel?"

"It certainly is," Manuel agreed with her as the grandfather clock chimed. As if by preordained signal, the players began to look at their watches.

"I hate to say this, but I have a tournament to win tomorrow," said Andrea. "Charles, thank you for a lovely evening, but I'm afraid I will have to say good night."

"I'll say good night as well," said Jacqui, standing up to join Andrea.

"Jacqui, you're not playing in a tournament tomorrow," said Charles, walking up to link his arm with Jacqui's. "You have no excuse for running to your bed."

"Thanks for the invitation, but I'm not feeling a hundred percent," she said. Her discovery in Geoff's room had actually made her feel ill.

Andrea and Jacqui shared a golf cart driven by Charles's manservant, on the short ride back to the great house. The night air under the star-studded sky was smooth and crisp as the moon illuminated the long fairways – a serene peaceful view from the top of the hill. When they reached the hotel, the manservant assisted Andrea out first.

"Thanks a lot. I always look forward to Mr. Whittingham's dinners," said Andrea.

"Thank you, Miss Andrea. Good luck tomorrow," said the manservant, showing a rare smile.

As Jacqui took his hand to say good night, she was aware of something odd in his grasp. Her hand almost slipped from his because there was no resistance to her grip. Her instinct to recoil her hand and her understanding came simultaneously. Covering her embarrassment, she thanked him, moving hurriedly through the entrance. He was missing his thumb.

Chapter 12

Geoff woke up with a slight hangover and immediately called downstairs for coffee. He lit a cigarette, the nicotine helping him gain his equilibrium. Shuffling around the room, he began to look over the papers he had brought down for discussions with Charles and the Congressman.

He picked up one file and put it in his briefcase, feeling as if the papers weren't as he had placed them. He picked up two more files and put them away, looking for the FPL file. It felt very light the instant he picked it up and when he opened it, his heart started to pound. The entire ledger of bank transfers was missing.

"Charles," he roared, waiting for him to come. "Charles," he screamed hysterically.

"What the hell is your problem, man. You want to wake up someone in New York?" said Charles, pulling the cord of his robe around his stout middle.

"It's gone. All of it," cried Geoff.

"What the hell are you talking about?" asked Charles, bewildered.

"It's gone. The records for FPL. It's all gone. Who the hell was here?" he demanded, a tiny drop of saliva rolling out of the corner of his mouth, his eyes glazed over in shock.

"Sputo!" called Charles. "Sputo, get up here!"

A moment later Sputo appeared upstairs, ready to leave for his trip to the south coast.

"What 'appen?" he asked.

"Did you see anyone up here last night?" asked Charles.

Sputo thought for a moment. "Dat one. Me a see her," he said finally, his eyes narrowing.

"Which one?" asked Charles and Geoff in unison.

"De one from de Falls," said Sputo.

"Jacqui," said Charles with his lips pressed together.

"Oh, shit. We're really in trouble now," said Geoff. "I'm leaving today."

* * *

The subtle knock at the door turned to loud pounding. Jacqui glanced at her alarm clock. The dial was reading just minutes after six in the morning. She closed her eyes again, but the banging continued. Reluctantly, she got up.

"Sh, sh," she said softly at the door. "Who is it?"

"Room service," said Gary's familiar voice. "Please open up," he pleaded.

Jacqui was too tired to work out which hat the man on the other side of the door was wearing. Was he the pimento ambassador, the chairman of Tropical Properties, the charming polo player or the secretive drug baron?

"Go away," she said.

"Not until you open the door," he retorted. Jacqui paused for a moment, then reluctantly opened the door, finding Gary standing there in a pair of jeans and a t-shirt. He gave her a cursory glance as he walked into the room, his presence dwarfing her.

"If you don't mind, may I ask what you are doing here at this ungodly hour?"

"I can see that you weren't expecting company," he said, taking in her skimpy t-shirt. "I'm really here to get you out of bed and into the fresh air, unless you have plans with your Mr. Roth."

"He's not my Mr. Roth," said Jacqui vehemently. Her

164

cheeks had flushed to a high pink colour, her hair was a jumbled mass of curls on her head. He had to control the urge to take her in his arms and run his fingers through her hair.

"I want you to get dressed and grab your bathing suit. Forget about makeup or anything fancy," said Gary.

"I'm not up for one of your adventures," Jacqui groaned, only wanting to get back into bed.

"Nonsense," he said, trying a new tack. "You certainly aren't the typical tourist. It'll be a nice addition for your article. I promise you won't be disappointed."

The challenge was all she needed to hear. Jacqui got ready faster than any female he had ever known and within minutes they were in the deserted parking lot, climbing into Gary's convertible BMW. As soon as they left the property, she brightened up and responded to his playful mood. They drove along a road that was carved through the middle of a canefield, the cattle just rising from their sleep as the egrets, long-necked white birds, sat amongst them.

"I'm glad to see you have another mode of transport except for the Land-Rover," said Jacqui, enjoying the plush feel of the car's leather seats.

"I told you that the British-built lady can take on flood water and keep moving. I hope you don't experience that while you're here," said Gary.

In a tiny village nestled in a rocky cove, a white chapel on the roadside was reflecting the sun as a group of women of every shade of black and brown walked along the side of the road, bearing baskets of colourful fruits and green bananas. The woven baskets were balanced precariously on their heads as they walked with practised diligence to the market to sell their wares.

Jacqui was charmed by the scene. It helped to erase the image of her name on the ledger that kept flashing before her eyes. Just for today, she wanted to put it away until she could deal with it.

At a turn in the road marked by two rum bars named Tootsi's and Topsies, one on either corner, Gary followed a rough marl track that was barely a road for several miles. At a curve stood another rum bar and a postal agency bearing the sign 'Spicey Hill.' A crooked orange signpost, its black paint so faded that it was barely legible, indicated four miles to Jericho, three to Bethlehem and one to Spicey Hill farm.

They followed the sign to Spicey Hill along the marl road, taking the ruts slowly until they reached the gate post.

Gary called out a greeting and the gate was opened. Parking the car by a shipping container that Gary explained had been turned into an office, he led her towards a dirt trail etched in the hillside.

As far as the eye could see there were rows and rows of grey-barked trees planted on the sloping hillside and the air was scented with the sweet smell of pimento. Gary touched her arm, pointing out the villages of Jericho and Bethlehem, tiny little jewels carved out in the jutting mountainside.

As Jacqui followed Gary up the path to the barbecue pits, he picked up some drying berries, fingering them gingerly. "As early as the 1770s pimento has been shipped from Spicey Hill Farm to England. Pimento is also known as allspice and it is aptly named because of its many uses. People tend to confuse pimiento the spice with the Spanish garnish called pimiento. If you want a description, pimento is a cross between nutmeg and ginger."

"Outside of a spice, what are the other uses for pimento?" asked Jacqui, totally intrigued with the new facet of Gary's character. This seemed to be the one thing that could control him – nature, the elements of the sun, rain and wind. He seemed to possess infinite patience for his land.

"After the fully matured dark green berries are sun-dried for about ten days, the ripe berries can do amazing things. They are the basis for pimento liqueur. I made quite a good batch last summer. Pimento forms the base for many men's colognes and the dried berries are used for roasting meats."

"Is that what gives the jerk chicken such a great flavour?" asked Jacqui.

"That's right. The jerkers prefer pimento wood – they say it gives the special flavour. With its popularity, we'll have to be careful not to destroy too many trees," said Gary, as a man whose hair grew in the shape of a bird cage came up.

"Good morning, boss," said the man as he dumped the bucket filled with ripe berries.

"Good morning, Monster," said Gary. "This is Miss Jacqui."

"Howdy do," he said, tipping his head, a broad grin settling on his face.

"Who do you sell your pimento to?" she asked, fascinated with the spice business.

"Well, Jamaica is one of the world's largest producers. Most of the crop is sold to Russia. I have been on several trade missions there and am scheduled to go again in the late summer," said Gary. "I remember last January when I was in Moscow, it was thirty-five degrees below zero, and that was without the wind chill factor. It was the lowest temperature in forty-five years. I couldn't walk from the hotel to the car without feeling as if my skin was being peeled off layer by layer. All I could think about was that it was eighty-eight degrees in Jamaica."

Jacqui's eyes widened as she remembered that Elizabeth Hartley said she had been in Jamaica late last January when she met Gary·Gordon.

"How long were you there?" she asked casually.

"Oh, I was in Moscow for only a week. I should have been there longer but it was too cold! So I retreated to London which in comparison seemed tropical, and ended up staying there till early February – my attempt to finalize my negotiations with Moscow by long distance cost me three

167

extra weeks!" Gary laughed ruefully. "And believe me, at the end of it London seemed as cold as Moscow."

"Poor island boy. The cold got to you," she laughed, teasing him. "So far you drink pimento, use it to spice your food and wear it as a cologne. Is there anything else?"

"I heard something very interesting when I was in Moscow. During World War II when the Russian soldiers were freezing to death in Siberia, they used to put pimento in their socks. Apparently pimento exudes heat and kept their feet from freezing," said Gary as he led her down another trail to the sorting station for the ripe berries.

There were several women sitting under a roof made of zinc sheets performing the monotonous task. They all brightened when they saw Gary. To the left, there was an open fire in a crudely built stone barbecue with a delicious smell wafting out into the air, mingling with the pimento.

"Mr. G, how you do," called a woman. She had a wide forehead and broad cheekbones that indicated Maroon blood, as Gary told Jacqui later. "You and the lady mus' hungry. Me have some nice roasted breadfruit, saltfish an' some boiled green banana."

"Got any pear, Doreen?" asked Gary.

"Some nice fresh pear," said Doreen, producing two avocados which Jacqui realized were being called pears.

They sat by the fire, enjoying the breakfast. Jacqui ate well for the first time in days. The food tasted better than Charles's fancy dinner. The men began to drift in for their morning snack, all of them eyeing Jacqui surreptitiously. Only when Monster arrived did she find out why.

"Boss, in all me born days, me nevah t'ink ya bring a woman up here," said Monster.

"Me haffi agree wid wha' him sey," called Doreen who was serving portions of green banana. As everyone joined in the laughter, Gary turned away and Jacqui could see he was actually blushing.

168

"I get no respect around here," he murmured, picking up the lighthearted banter as he teased Monster about having as many as a dozen children with as many baby mothers.

"Me cyaan help it if me services are in high demand," Monster said, grunting with laughter as the rest of the workers joined in.

After breakfast, they left the sorting area, walking up to the higher ridge where the dense branches allowed tiny rays of the sun to peep through. Gary urged Jacqui to stop under a huge pimento tree. The view of the tree-topped hillside and the grand expanse of the sea was breathtaking.

"I love this place," he said, putting his hands on her shoulders, gently letting his fingertips rest at the base of her neck. "I can hear the echo of time. At one time you could ride across the island and never leave Gordon property. I know that Todd Gordon, my illustrious ancestor, walked these hills. This land is a part of me – of my heritage, but it's more than that. It's the future," he said. "I'm just safeguarding a trust that was passed on to me and that I will pass down."

"How did the trust get started?" asked Jacqui.

"Todd Gordon came to Jamaica from a town called Gordon in Scotland, on a leaky schooner as an indentured worker, bound into service for seven years. Though the journey and the tropics were enough to break most men, Todd Gordon thrived. Within a year of his arrival he was the overseer on one of the sugar plantations," said Gary.

"I'll bet he was handsome," said Jacqui.

"So I've been told. Bessie, whose great-grandmother was a slave, told me her grandmother used to talk about Todd Gordon. One night Todd learned from a man who had just arrived from Haiti that the French were planning to attack the island. He sent a runner to Port Royal and rounded up a group of men and set up an ambush. Needless to say, the first and last attack on the island by the French was unsuccessful.

"In reward for his service to His Majesty's government, Todd was released from his contract and received twenty-two square miles of crown land," said Gary, enjoying the feel of her body close to his. "Before he died he created a trust to protect the original crown lands for the family, along with a series of stipulations. The Gordon crest is a commitment to an ideal. It's a legacy of honour," he said. Jacqui looked at the pinky ring on his left hand bearing the crest of a horse's head with two swords crossed above it. It was the only piece of jewellery he wore except for his Rado watch.

"Do you hold the crest now?" she asked, gently easing away from his side, wondering how the glowing history she had just heard compared to Charles's version of the Gordons.

"My father entrusted it to me when he died and I shall give it to my children," said Gary as a gentle breeze scented with pimento bathed them.

"It must have been hard for you to know your destiny at such a young age," she said.

"I just accepted it," said Gary. "I was groomed from a young age by my parents and grandfather as well as a few others."

Not wishing to break the peaceful mood, Jacqui let a comfortable silence pass before she spoke. "Gary, I think there were extenuating circumstances when The Falls was reviewed last year," she said. "I don't think the reporter had a good experience."

"Jacqui, I didn't mean to insinuate that you wouldn't write a credible review using your best professional judgement," said Gary. "Do you think we could forget – just for today – who we are, and enjoy each other and the gift of this beautiful day?" Looking at her with unmasked longing,

170

he touched one of Jacqui's stray curls and tucked it behind her ear.

"Okay, I'd like that," she said, somewhat relieved. She didn't want to spoil the day.

They returned to the car, walking next to each other without touching. Once back on the main road, they followed the road that hugged the sea until they came upon a golden meadow set against a turquoise bay. Gary stopped the car and they watched the wind rustle the silky golden grass like the waves of the sea, creating a tapestry of rolling waves in blue and gold. Without a word, they walked through the meadow, the grass coming up to their waists.

Jacqui stretched her hands above her head, giggling with delight as she skipped through the grass. Gary watched her face alive with joy, her eyes playful as she frolicked through the meadow. The grass swirled around her long bronze legs as the bright sun pierced her light cotton dress, silhouetting her body, making him ache with desire.

"If I weren't so afraid of ticks, I would roll down the hill," said Jacqui, feeling as if she had been reborn. "I used to roll down hills like this when I was a kid. See if you can catch me." Jacqui took off through the field as Gary chased her.

They were both breathless when Gary caught up with her. Their breath coming in short spurts, Jacqui looked up at him, her eyes full of longing as the sun in the golden meadow fuelled the warmth between them.

He took another step towards her, tentatively reaching out to touch her cheek. She closed her eyes, leaning her head towards his hand as she swayed towards him. He touched her hair, tracing his finger slowly down her profile until he touched her lips. He opened his arms, drawing her into his tender embrace. She felt as if she had come home as a wave of contentment passed over her like the tide in the turquoise bay. He held her lovingly, caressing her back with his open palms. The electricity between them touched a

171

piece of Jacqui's heart she never before knew she had.

They walked slowly back to the car, barely touching with their fingertips, a subtle change in both of them. The masks had been stripped away. They drove silently along the picturesque coastline until they stopped at a small coconut stand to have water coconuts.

"Oh my God. A fire," said Jacqui suddenly, first noticing the black smoke and then the red and orange raging fire that was spreading quickly through the adjacent field, contrasting with the aqua sea.

"They're burning cane," said Gary, coming up to her side, chuckling. "Cane is burned before it is cut and has to be gathered before it rains."

The cane cutters stood a good distance back, watching the fire to ensure it was contained. Sweat oozed from their dusty mahogany bodies as their machetes glistened in the firelight.

Awed by the sight of a burning field, Jacqui sat quietly as they continued along the wide, well paved road that gently curved as they rounded the northwestern point of the island. The area looked different from the other parts of the island that she had seen. Much of it remained untouched. Its untamed spirit took hold of her, making her wish she could hold onto the moment.

They passed the north end of Negril beach, with beautiful ultra-luxurious villas perched at Rutland Point. There were tourists on bicycles and Rastas on motorbikes, their hair bundled in red, gold and green caps. The atmosphere was very rustic with cottages and bungalows hidden behind the natural tropical foliage.

Gary stopped at a little inn on the beach called Country. Grabbing a bag out of the back, he led Jacqui past the thatched huts and comfortable cottages featuring verandahs with hammocks until they reached the warm sandy beach. Jacqui stared at the continuous expanse of shimmering sand set against Jamaica's diamond-white water that turned to shades of turquoise and lapis lazuli as it melted into the sky.

"I have an old friend I want you to meet," he said, breaking her out of her trance as he motioned her to the bar. Jacqui looked around as Gary tried to yell over the loud music. A slight brown man with an electric smile moved languorously to the reggae rhythm. She didn't know how Gary could call it a bar, even though it served drinks. It had everything a corner drugstore would have plus more. There was toothpaste, suntan oil, newspapers, beach chairs that came in bags and a sign for a bureau de change.

"Blood, I want you to meet my friend Jacqui," said Gary when Blood finally lowered the music and came out from behind the bar.

"My queen. Welcome. My house is your house," he said with an easy manner and a deep seductive voice. He motioned for them to take a seat at the table under the shady umbrella while he signalled for Red Stripe Beer.

"So good to see you, Gary," said Blood. His movements were those of a young man, but Jacqui guessed he was in his sixties.

"You too, Blood. It's been a long time," said Gary.

Blood explained to Jacqui that he was a follower of the Rastafarian religion that believed in the natural way of life called 'livity'. He said he was a Rastaman even though he didn't wear locks, but that just because a 'brethren' wore dreadlocks, it did not make him a Rasta.

"Rastafarians eat only natural foods. We believe in a simple life, close to nature. Dat's all me ever want," said Blood, going to the bar to take out a rusty old cookie tin, the blue chipped paint giving few clues to its origin.

He opened the old tin and the sweet pungent odour of fresh ganja buds rose from the tin. Reaching in, Blood took out a handful, placing them on the lid. He picked out the seeds, throwing them on the sand as he crushed the buds with his fingers into fine flakes. He took out a piece of Rizzla rolling paper, and creased it at an angle, laying the ganja out piece by piece as he slowly built his spliff, his movements fluid and practised.

Blood explained that the Rastafarians worshipped the Ethiopian Emperor Haille Selassie. "Before he assumed the throne to become the King of Kings, Selassie's name was Rastafari. Dat is why we are called Rastafarians."

Jacqui changed into her suit, meeting Gary at the water's edge. The sand was the finest white powder. She ran into the water, taking a dive as the silky water washed over her skin. She swam out in one tremendous spurt, the untouched sandy bottom rolling in unblemished continuous splendour.

She swam back in to the beach, to where Gary sat on the sand in his well fitting trunks, outlining his lean slender hips. He handed her a cold beer as she lay at the water's edge, watching a parade of dreadlocks amble along the beach, dance-hall style music blaring from their huge ghetto blasters. Several white female tourists hung conspicuously onto their arms, their skin colours contrasting in the brilliant sun.

"So Miss Editor, how did you ever get started in writing?" Gary asked, seeming genuinely interested.

"It's a really long story," said Jacqui, revelling in the aquamarine water that was as warm as a bath.

"I have all afternoon," he said, stretching out next to her, taking in the way her bikini top moulded her supple body, now golden brown. "I've even read some of your stuff."

"Oh, really?" said Jacqui, a shy smile playing on her lips.

He watched her hesitate, wanting her to open up and reveal something of herself. Robert had forwarded her piece on Texas as well as her in-depth story on Morocco. He had been very impressed. With both stories he had come away with an insight into the charms of the places as unique travel destinations.

"I was studying journalism at Boston University – a fresh Ohio girl unused to the big city life," she said with a smile as she took a long sip of beer. "I was broke by Thanksgiving so I applied for a job in a hotel. I thought the hours would be good and it was better than waitressing.

"I ended up working at the Boston Copley for four years. I worked in every department from the front desk to marketing, from food and beverage to security. My nickname was 'I'll do it' because I would. I loved the hotel," said Jacqui.

"After I graduated, my roommate Suzanne and I moved out to the Cape. She worked as a waitress at one of the big nightclubs and I worked in a hotel running the front desk. The editor of the local newspaper was a regular at the restaurant and he asked me to write an article for the Sunday magazine of the *Cape Codder*.

"It was a guide to sizzling summer fun and the article ran nationwide with my byline and a picture of Suzanne, in all of her blonde voluptuous beauty, lying on a sand dune, wearing a bright yellow string bikini and slathered in oil with her golden hair flying in the wind," said Jacqui, laughing, as she played with a handful of sand, picking up a tiny white shell with pink trim.

"So how did you hook up with *Elegant Travel?*" asked Gary.

"Around the same time my article ran, *Elegant Travel* published a review about Cape Cod. There were some glaring errors which I found, so I wrote to the magazine and enclosed my article. A week later I got a phone call from a Josh Travers, telling me he had enjoyed my article and there was a ticket waiting for me at Logan Airport to go to Bermuda to cover the Newport-Bermuda Yacht Races. I was in Newport that afternoon and on my way to Bermuda the next day."

Gary watched her tell the story, her face glowing with pleasure. She had pulled her hair back in a tight braid, showing off her sensual features. His eyes slowly moved down her body, taking in the swell before her long legs and her beautifully manicured toes.

"Was it a good story?" he asked.

"The yacht race wasn't that exciting, but I was staying at this wonderful guesthouse and I got to talking with the landlady. She showed me her great-grandfather's diary which listed accounts of aiding the Confederates during the union blockade of the South in the Civil War," said Jacqui. "I thought it was such a great angle that I added it in, and sent my story to Josh.

"I flew back to New York and when I cleared customs there was a driver waiting for me. Poor Freddy," said Jacqui with a smile. "He had a devil of a time getting me into his car. I demanded his wife's phone number and wrote it on the bottom of my heel, in case they had to trace my corpse. He's never forgiven me for that. He left me off at the Citicorp building and told me to go to the twenty-seventh floor.

"I was whisked into this office and there was Josh, sitting at his desk, his shoes off, his tie in the file basket, his sleeves rolled up and his shirt unbuttoned. He was smiling like a Cheshire cat and I raved like a lunatic. When I finally let him get a word in edgewise, he asked me how my trip was and told me he was very pleased with my work. He just handed me my business cards and told me I was officially hired. He warned me not to complain about the high rents in New York, not to expect a raise and to be ready to go anywhere in the world at an hour's notice. That was seven years ago and in that time Josh has sent me to some pretty far-off places, always pushing me to bring back a story with depth."

"Are you friends or colleagues?" he asked.

"Friends," said Jacqui, shaking her head thoughtfully.

176

"We're good friends. He's always been there when the cart tips to pick up the apples before they hit the sidewalk."

A group of higglers moved en masse along the beach, calling out to anyone who would listen to their offers of aloe massages, reggae tapes, ganja tea and hair braiding. They made such a big deal about Jacqui's lack of interest in braiding her hair tourist-style that Gary had to shout at them to move away.

They went back to Blood's bar to get another drink and sample some of the barbecued shrimp and curried conch. A domino game was starting under the thatch hut by the bar and Blood urged Gary to join him.

He took his seat while Jacqui stood to the side, trying to get the hang of the game. After they picked up tiles, Gary's eyes glittered as he slammed down the opening domino with a loud yell. He had been transformed into a professional gambler who would have been right at home at the crap tables in Las Vegas or playing fan-tan in Macau. It showed Jacqui an important side of his character. He wanted to win in everything.

When Gary surrendered his seat to a waiting player, they bid Blood goodbye, then drove along the main road into town. It was hardly a town, with a main street that held a supermarket, disco and two rum bars. They continued to follow the sea along Lighthouse Road. There were bamboo huts serving as craft shops with bright t-shirts displayed on clotheslines amidst native wood carvings and coral jewellery. They passed enchanting secluded hideaways behind stone walls with names like Aweemaway, Pee Wees, Cool Runnings, Higher Heights, and House of Dread.

Gary pulled into Rock Café, a beautiful hideaway on the lava cliffs featuring tree houses and outdoor showers. They passed the pool surrounded by a carpet of grass to the bar overlooking the sea. Tossing off their t-shirts, they dove off the cliff into the crystal-clear water that was forty feet deep.

"Gary, this is so beautiful," said Jacqui, emerging in the water which was the colour of a natural sapphire. They swam into the natural cave. The tide swelled in and out, almost throwing Jacqui against the rocks, but Gary grabbed her, pulling her close as they swam out of the cave together.

Pointing to a railing embedded in the rock, Gary pushed Jacqui up. It was a ledge complete with a cushion for private sunbathing. They sat side by side, dripping wet, watching the horizon. Gary moved his hand to her neck, slowly kneading her muscles. Jacqui let out a low sigh, feeling the warmth of his fingers.

He gently eased her back onto the cushion, undoing her braid, spreading out her wet hair. His fingertips left a hot trail as he took time to learn each subtle nuance and curve of her body. Placing a velvet kiss in her hot cleavage, he unclasped her bikini top in a single unhurried motion, exposing her pale breasts to the sun as he sharply took in his breath.

He moved his palms slowly down her belly, their calloused hardness bringing her sweet pleasure. She was beginning to smoulder, but it wasn't enough for Gary. He wanted her panting and hungry for him.

"It feels so good to hold you again. I haven't been able to get you out of my mind," he moaned in her ear as he leaned over her, blocking the sun from her eyes.

"You've been filling my thoughts," she sighed.

He stroked her face, relishing the feel of her body against his. He lowered his lips to hers, teasing her until Jacqui strained against him, clutching his taut muscular shoulders. The taste of salt mingled in their mouths as Gary invaded her mouth with bold sensual strokes, his hands moving with unhurried caresses that turned her body fluid.

She moved her fingers through his hair, pulling him closer, her mind blank except for the sensations he was creating. His name escaped from her lips, burning his ears with desire.

"I haven't stopped fantasizing about you," he murmured, "how you feel in my arms." He spread a trail of smooth kisses down her neck, until his hot and demanding mouth found her breast. He felt a wonderful rush of pleasure while she writhed in his arms. He moved his hand down to her bikini bottom, rubbing her sensually, allowing his fingers to linger over her softness before he ran his hands over the inside of her thigh.

Gary felt Jacqui tense slightly, touching his hand that lingered. He reached up to touch her face. "I'm not going to make love to you now, baby," he whispered hoarsely. "But tomorrow morning I want to wake up and find you in my arms."

"Your bed or mine," said Jacqui, returning his kisses with a passion that left them both breathless.

Presently they climbed back into the water, their heated bodies welcoming the coolness. He pulled Jacqui towards him, their bodies melting into each other as she held onto his shoulders. He felt her wetness, mingled with the silkiness of the sea, as he quelled his desire to make love to her right there.

They went up to the bar and ordered Tropical Sins, watching the sun begin its eventual descent into the sea. The bar was deserted; most of the guests were away at Rick's Café watching the exact same sunset.

"That's why I live here. It's days like this – moments stolen from time that make life so special," said Gary as he put his arm around her. A peaceful feeling enveloped them both. Jacqui started to say something, but Gary put his finger to her mouth, rubbing her lower lip with a butterfly touch before he kissed her very slowly and tenderly, holding her face in his hands.

"It's been a beautiful day. Thank you for sharing it with

me," he said.

"Oh, Gary, it's been so special. I loved Spicey Hill and I love Negril," she said before he silenced her with another long languorous kiss, leaving her breathless, craving for more. His arms settled around her as they continued to watch the sunset.

Gary spied a tiny purple wild flower growing in a crevice in the stone wall. He picked it up, rubbing its soft petal across her cheek.

" 'Flower in a crannied wall, I pluck you out of the crannies. I hold you here root and all in my hand,' " recited Gary, looking at her. " 'Little flower, if I could understand what you are root and all, all in all, I would understand what God and man is.' "

"That's beautiful. Where is that from?" she asked.

"I love the way you're so sure I didn't write it," said Gary with an easy smile. "It was written by Lord Alfred Tennyson. He wrote a poem for each day of the year and that is his poem for April the first." He kissed her forehead and he rubbed his chin along her hair.

Jacqui turned to Gary, her eyes filled with love as she stroked his hair, her hand settling on his bare chest, relishing its warmth. "I wish we could just stay here. I don't want to have to go back to Pimento Hill," she said.

"Why?" he asked, tilting her head so he could see her eyes.

"I'm afraid we'll lose the magic we've found today," she said wistfully.

"You can never lose what you've already found," Gary responded, settling her against the broad expanse of his chest. "What is fe yu, cyaan be un fe yu. It's an old Jamaican proverb – what is yours is yours, what is not for you cannot be yours. This is ours. We won't ever lose that."

The last brilliant crimson bursts faded from the sky, leaving a farewell glow over the lovers on the cliff.

Chapter 13

Gary was dressing for the Buccaneer Beach Ball, his hair still damp from his shower. The drive back to Pimento Hill had been one of the loveliest that he could ever remember. The moon was a gleaming beacon in the sky. At Sandy Bay, he had pulled the car onto the shoulder so they could watch the glistening city of Montego Bay for a moment. Remembering how she had looked in the dusky moonlight as he brought her hand to his lips brought him an unexpected rush of longing. He was trying to sort out his feelings when the phone rang.

On being told to wait while the call was put through, his mind returned to Jacqui, her laughter in the meadow echoing in the wind and the silkiness of her body next to his in the water, open and loving... The way he had kissed her when they parted in Pimento Hill's lobby drew curious looks and puzzled stares from guests. He had surprised himself more than he had surprised Jacqui.

"Hello, Gary, how are you?" echoed a voice.

"Commander, so good to hear from you. Where are you?"

"Never mind that," he responded. "Tell me what's happening."

"Well," began Gary...

* * *

Casey shook her blonde hair and coiled it around her

fingers in a distracted motion. The computer printouts were piled high on her desk, the floor and almost every inch of available space. No matter how hard she tried, there didn't seem to be an end to the paper that flowed.

"Casey, are you coming with us?" asked William, one of the customs officers who worked down the hall.

"Coming where?" she asked, glancing up at William with a smile. He was the ultimate preppie, always beautifully dressed with his shirts perfectly creased, even at the end of a long day.

"The Dubliner. It's two for one tonight. The guys from Justice, FBI and DEA are all coming," said William, looking at Casey with unabashed admiration. He wondered if she knew that he was in love with her.

"Maybe later," said Casey distractedly, moving a stack of papers.

"Oh, come on, Casey. All you have been doing is work lately. You need a break and everyone wants to see you."

"Maybe I will stop by later. I just want to get through one more pile."

William left, discouraged, and the halls of government emptied out on the early spring evening in Washington. Casey was pouring over another printout when her private phone rang, startling her.

"Casey, how are you?" asked Pierre Monclure, her counterpart from Interpol.

"Pierre, I'm fine. What are you doing calling me so late? It must be nearly two in Lyon," said Casey.

"I've just received a lead that you may find interesting. Start checking the wire transfers from the Tortuga Bank in Grand Cayman to the Jersey Islands. You may find what you are looking for," said Pierre.

"Thanks, I'll start on it right now," said Casey, jotting down some notes.

"Do it tomorrow," suggested Pierre. "Your pretty

blonde head needs to be clear when you try to untangle the maze."

* * *

The reggae music got louder and louder as Jacqui walked onto the beach. The area was filled with every imaginable buccaneer, cutthroat, pirate, seafaring rascal and wench. On the far end of the beach a huge pit had been dug where jerk pork and chicken were being grilled, the tantalizing smells blending with the sea air. Another table had been laid with salads, breads, festival and bammy.

The bar, originally the hull of a ship, had been set up on the crowded beach. Walking barefoot on the still warm sand, Jacqui greeted Liz and Caspar.

"How was the tournament?" asked Jacqui.

"Manuel Espito finished seven under par, winning the PGA. The real competition was between the ladies," said Liz.

"Hey, foreign girl," burst in Caspar. "Where yu been. You missed great golf today. By the way, so did Gary," he added, the realization slowly dawning on him as a smile crept on his face.

"Who won?" asked Jacqui, avoiding Caspar's scrutiny.

"When the round was finished, Nancy Nichols and Andrea Walters had both scored six under par," Liz reported. "In his most sanctimonious voice, BG Ellis announced a sudden death playoff. Nancy teed off first, and drove a well placed shot two hundred and forty yards down the fairway. Andrea had come into form late in the day, but had birdied three out of her four last holes."

"Nancy birdied the hole," broke in Caspar. "She sank a nine-foot putt. Andrea birdied the hole and sank a ten-foot putt. It looked perfect, but a sudden breeze veered the ball ever so slightly, missing the hole by just a centimetre."

"Are you talking about my shot?" asked Andrea, walking up.

"'I'm so sorry," said Caspar.

"Don't worry about it. That's the break of the game," said Andrea lightheartedly. "Some years you win, others you lose. Keep in touch," she said to Jacqui, before going over to the bar, followed by Caspar and Liz.

Jacqui felt a clammy hand on her bare shoulder. She instinctively stiffened and turned to face Charles.

"Hello, Jacqui," said Charles, leering at her. A drop of saliva glistened on his lower lip as he took in her off-the-shoulder blouse and the kanga that was seductively wrapped around her waist. "I've been looking for you. Your old friend Geoff Roth wanted to say goodbye."

"How sweet," said Jacqui sarcastically. "So sorry I missed him."

"I bet you were," said Charles. "Did you have a fun day with your lover, Gary Gordon? I thought you were smarter than that."

Jacqui reddened slightly at his remark and matched his glare. "You know, Charles, your association with Geoff doesn't do much for you in terms of a character reference."

"Geoff did say you were a little prude. I am sure that can be changed," he said maliciously. "I do hope that you enjoyed visiting my home. When you were enjoying my hospitality, I believe you picked up something that didn't belong to you. Where is it?"

"I don't know what you're talking about," she said coolly.

"Oh yes you do, you little bitch," he said harshly. "I want back that ledger and photo. Don't think I won't get them."

"Sure, Charles," said Jacqui sweetly when she saw Gary walk onto the beach.

"Don't think you won't pay for this," he said when he

saw her inattention and Gary's arrival at the party.

"Don't think you won't," she said, walking over to Gary.

He was a magnificent pirate, looking every inch the part in a red and white striped muscle t-shirt that moulded his broad tanned shoulders and showed off his rippling muscles that were honed to perfection. His white drawstring pants were rolled up to his knees and a hoop earring, black eye patch and pointed three-cornered black hat completed his outfit.

Charles watched them for a moment, his expression sour. He went over to the bar and ordered a double rum, glancing at the couple. It was impossible not to sense the smouldering sensual electricity between Jacqui and Gary.

The torches had been lit and Gary led Jacqui along the still warm sand to where several couples were dancing. The lights flickered on the beach, their flames licking the air as the sea lapped rhythmically against the shore.

He gripped her hips with his hands, their bodies moulding perfectly together. Knee to knee, chest to chest, they matched each other's sensual movements, oblivious of what was happening around them. They were in their own little dream world.

The band called Chalice came onstage to a resounding cheer from the crowd. Their opening song set the crowd wild. When they sang their chorus, the audience joined in. "'It's never too late for an island boy, / Born in the sun and the rain, / The will to be free is stronger / Than the wind of a hurricane.'"

The crowd started dancing when they performed their Pocomania Revival song, as the handsome back-up singer came down into the crowd. Gary went off to get cold beers. Jacqui was clapping her hands with the rest of the crowd, when Trevor came up to her side. When the band took a break, he walked her a few feet away.

"You have barely said a word to me since we got to

Pimento Hill. Is there anything wrong?" asked Trevor.

Jacqui didn't answer, not knowing how to respond. Trevor's flaunting of his extramarital relationship had disturbed her. She knew that the lifestyle was different in the West Indies, but the almost jovial disregard for any morals regarding relations made her wonder.

"I think I know what is bothering you," he said, reading her thoughts. "There is an old expression in Jamaica. What the eye don't see, the heart don't feel."

"You must have a lot of blind people in Jamaica," said Jacqui.

Trevor laughed for a moment and then became serious. "If you are going to understand anything about Jamaica, you will have to learn that there is a different code of ethics here, though you wouldn't know it by the packed churches on Sunday. This is the land where Bob Marley grew up and preached "One Love.""

"Fidelity is not a well practised sport, I gather," said Jacqui.

"What is fidelity?" he asked. "I have friends who fill needs that I have that my wife can't. I am sure the same applies to her. Blame it on slavery or economics, many men have relations outside their marriages under the guise of third-world living. We are a drama-loving society and we enjoy living on the edge. And basically, men are just scared about growing old, and being in a society that encourages such freedoms helps us maintain the illusion of our youth."

"So West Indian men are searching for immortality?" asked Jacqui dryly.

"It's not immortality as much as it's wanting to have their cake and eat it too," Trevor laughed.

"What about Gary?" she asked.

"I was afraid you might ask me," said Trevor. "Gary is our own local international playboy. He has a black book of names and numbers by geographic areas that is so extensive he could open up a worldwide dating service. I once went to Rome and he set me up in one phone call."

"What's Gary looking for?" she asked.

"Hundreds of women have tried to figure that one out," said Trevor ruefully. "Gary is simple. He's been afraid of commitment because he spent too many years looking unsuccessfully for absolute perfection in one woman while most men look for one perfect characteristic in each woman. But in the past few years, he's changed in some ways," said Trevor.

"How so?" asked Jacqui.

"He's not the brash, wild, impetuous young man he used to be. Since his father died, he has become much more realistic and seems more willing to accept the world as it is, not as he wants it to be. He is also more serious and has developed a hard outer shell. Superficially he may act the same, but there's a subtle difference."

Jacqui listened, trying to get a better insight into Gary and who he was. She still felt there was an important piece missing.

Gary came over to her side and they went to the buffet, sharing a plate of grilled chicken, roasted breadfruit and fried festival. They both picked at their food, wondering if it was too early to leave the party.

A horn blasted in the distance as *Grand Slam*, a fifty-two-foot Hatteras, followed by *Sea Quest*, Dick Robinson's prized Southern Cross, pulled towards the pier at the yacht club, their sound systems blasting music.

"Leave it to Dick Robinson and Jerry Thomas to put a little life into this party," said Gary with a smile. They walked hand in hand to the pier, greeting Sheila and Dick who were on deck passing out rum punches.

A Jimmy Cliff song was played and the crowd voiced their approval. Gary took Jacqui in his arms and whispered the words to "Come Into My Life" under the velvet blue sky filled with brilliant stars.

"You know what I wish," she said, looking at him, feeling that who he was or what he did didn't matter.

"What?" he asked, nuzzling her neck.

"I wish I had met you away from The Falls, without the cloud of the review. Then we would know how we really feel about each other. "

"It wouldn't have mattered where I met you," he said. "I think we have something rare – kindred spirits. I want to hold onto that – be it only for a moment or for eternity."

Their eyes locked and it was if they had embarked on a long journey together in their souls. Every single movement and word exchanged brought them closer to the moment when they would relinquish their pretence in the exquisite expression of trust. Their breath became one and Gary was afraid to let her go at the end of the music and lose the essence of the moment.

* * *

Trina walked along the beach towards the yacht club at Pimento Hill. It was her first night off in weeks and she was anxious for some fun. Being cooped up at the hotel with Robert Davids as her watchdog was driving her crazy.

A cold clammy hand grasped her shoulder, spinning her around. She gasped, her hand flying to strike out.

"Charles, what the raas do you want?" she asked angrily.

"I just want to talk to you. Gary is on the yacht with Jacqui. You don't have to worry that he will see us together."

"I'm not worried," she said. " I saw you leave the party early on Friday night. Then they discover Donald Francis's body. I would be more worried about that if I were you."

"Shut up with your foolishness," he said, jerking her arm

hard. "Don't *ever* repeat anything like that again. Now listen to me. She knows about *Foolish Pleasure*."

"Who?" asked Trina.

"Jacqui, your sweet little Gary's new playmate," said Charles.

"What do you want me to do about it?" she asked.

"Be sweet to Gary for a change and keep him busy while I deal with her," he said, pushing her towards the pier. "By the time I'm finished with her, she'll be too scared to open her mouth and say boo."

* * *

Gary and Jacqui attempted to leave the party, but were waylaid by Caspar who insisted on having a 'roadster' with them. Jacqui could sense Gary's impatience as he quickly finished his drink. Then they were joined by Liz Chen who emphatically declared that they had to have a nightcap before they could leave.

Jacqui volunteered to get the drinks, but first climbed the stairs to the cabin below to use the bathroom. When she emerged, she found Charles waiting in the stateroom, sweating alcohol from every pore.

He took in her body hungrily as he swayed towards her in a menacing manner. She sensed his intention a split second too late and was unprepared for his violent assault. He grabbed her hair and pulled at her kanga.

"Now, it's our time," he said savagely, jerking her roughly.

"Get the hell away from me, Charles," said Jacqui.

"I am going to show you what happens if you mess with me," he sneered, breathing down on her. She turned her head away in disgust, making him tighten his grip on her arms. "You are a foolish stupid bitch who is sticking her nose where it doesn't belong. Where are the papers?" he

189

demanded.

Jacqui tried to break away from his painful grip, but his strength, aided by alcohol, was too much for her. Using his body weight, he pushed her towards the bed and threw her down forcefully, his body falling on top of her.

He pinned her arms to her sides and kissed her roughly, biting her lips as he forced his rough tongue into her mouth. She gasped for air, fighting against him. She was so revolted by him that the bile rose in her throat and she thought she would retch all over him.

"I know you want it," he raged when he released her. Jacqui let out a sob, turning her head away as he slavered over her throat, leaving a trail of sticky saliva on her neck. "Go ahead and scream," he hissed. "No one will hear you over the music."

"I don't want you. I want Gary," she sobbed. "You just want everything you think he has."

When he heard those words, Charles went into a rage. Letting go her arms, he yanked down her blouse, grabbing her breast roughly as he lowered his head. Jacqui hit him as hard as she could, punching at him and kicking him wildly over and over. Taken unawares by her attack, he backed away a bit and Jacqui raked her nails in his face.

"I see how you like it," he said with an evil laugh, taking a lunge at her. Every muscle in her body was tight as she kicked him with both feet, with all her might, sending him flying across the room. It was enough time for her to roll over, grab her kanga and stand on her feet.

"You contemptuous bastard," she rasped, her face red and tears shimmering in her eyes.

Charles laughed and in two steps was near her, trying to grab her hair. With her adrenaline pumping, she dodged under his arm and turned, raising her right knee. She planted an excruciating blow to his groin. He let out a yell, his knees bent in pain as his hands moved quickly down to clutch himself.

There was a knock on the door. "Hurry up in there. We have to use the bathroom," called out two voices. Jacqui was breathing heavily when she tied her kanga and unlocked the door. The two women outside met Charles's bent figure with amusement.

"Ah, Charles. Obviously the lady said no," said one, laughing.

"Don't think you've scared me," said Jacqui in a shaky voice. "I'll get you and that's a promise."

She walked out into the narrow hallway and climbed the stairs, her legs unsteady with each step. She greedily gulped the fresh air when she reached the deck.

Sheila saw Jacqui return to the deck, her hair a mess and her kanga tied awkwardly. She walked over to her, wondering if she had had too much to drink.

"Are you all right, Jacqui?" she asked.

"I've been better," she said, breathing deeply to calm herself. "Where's Gary?"

"On the top deck," she said, pointing to the upper deck.

Gary was standing next to Trina, their heads close together, his arm resting comfortably on her waist. Trina turned to look at him, flashing him a smile that could have had a shipload of navy men howling on their knees. It was a very intimate looking scene. Jacqui turned her head in disgust, feeling betrayed and sickened.

"They look wonderful together, don't they?" asked Sheila. "I feel so good when I see them together."

"Sheila, I'm going back," she said, her hands trembling and her face pale.

"I do hope you're not ill. Take two aspirins before you get into bed. Have a good night's rest and I'll see you in Port Antonio," called Sheila as Jacqui negotiated her way to the pier. With a backward glance, she saw that Gary was too engrossed in his conversation with Trina to notice her retreat.

Once off the beach, Jacqui ran up the long driveway to the great house hotel, wanting nothing more than the sanctuary of her room with its pale yellow walls. She slowed down only when her legs couldn't move anymore, her lungs burned and her breath tasted like fire.

She dropped to her knees, the tears burning her face as she choked for air. Huge sobs racked her body as she thought of Charles's attack. He wasn't going to get away with it. Wiping her face, Jacqui tried to pull herself together. Underneath the anger and rage, she knew it was the sight of Gary with Trina that had crushed her. She couldn't bear to think their day together had been nothing but an illusion.

Chapter 14

The Wag Water River, partially shaded by flanking sugar loaf mountains carpeted in a silky green moss, reflected the late morning sun. Each treacherous curve of the Junction road brought a splendour of beauty that couldn't be captured in a picture. Blood-red poinciana trees shaded the road and the steep sloping hillsides were planted with coffee. Village women were washing their clothes in the river, spreading the cloths on large grey boulders, creating a collage of brilliant colours against the landscape.

Maxine was driving at a reckless speed, taking the curves and passing the many trucks with ease. Jacqui was relieved when the road finally descended to the north coast plain and straightened out. They went through Aqualta Vale, where the valley was filled with hundreds of coconut palms planted in precise rows. The road met the sea as they passed by fishing beaches crowded with returning fishermen. The villages of Buff Bay, St. Margaret's Bay and Hope Bay flew by.

Jacqui fumbled with the radio, getting a weak signal. Maxine took over and found "Jamaica Today," an interview show that was just starting. "This is usually a good programme," she said as she skillfully passed a slow-moving truck filled with sugar cane.

"Good afternoon. I'm Heather Henley and welcome to Jamaica Today. Today we'll be meeting with this year's nominees for the Jamaican of the Year Award. Field Marshall Sticky, the radio DJ personality, Miss Matty the poetess and Mr. Gary Gordon of Tropical Properties."

Jacqui moved to adjust the dial but Maxine put her hand out. "I really want to hear this, if it's all right with you," she said.

"Sure," said Jacqui.

"Our first guest is the chairman of a large hotel, a local pimento farmer as well as the government spokesperson on pimento and Jamaica's finest polo player. Welcome to Jamaica Today, Gary Gordon."

His voice hit her like a bomb. It sounded eerie to hear him talking over the radio. It made her feel anonymous to hear his disembodied voice.

Gary talked about his polo playing days briefly and touched upon the history of The Falls.

"I understand that Tropical Properties has plans for Port Antonio. Can you tell us what these plans are?" asked the interviewer in a smooth voice.

"We are seriously considering a project that will be a very exciting development on the tourist scene," said Gary, avoiding the question totally.

"Trevor told me what you've been going through with Gary," said Maxine when Jacqui stole a look at her. "It's a burden to love a man like him. You always have to be at your best because they operate on a higher level and demand perfection."

"He's confusing and confused and I don't need a man like him in my life," said Jacqui. "He's not trustworthy."

"Gary may not be many things, but one thing he is and that's trustworthy," said Maxine. Jacqui was shamed into silence for speaking ill of Maxine's friend.

They entered Port Antonio, with its wide streets lined with coconut palms that were jutting out into the road. A faded blackboard stood near the banana pier in Boundbrook, listing the sailing schedule and the price per pound of each variety. Jacqui felt the words to Harry Belafante's song "Day O" come to life.

Well maintained Victorian and gingerbread houses lined the street, which was crowded with people, livestock and motorcycles. Outside the market, two country buses, one called 'Miami Romance', and the other called 'Miss Thatcher', were unloading yams, soursops and melons.

Maxine wedged the car into a tiny parking space. Several young men offered to watch the car for a fee as the two women cautiously crossed the street to the market.

The sights and sounds of the market were at their height. They walked past heaps of deep red tomatoes and pearl-white onions, bundles of escallion whose smell permeated the air and Irish potatoes in light brown skins lying side by side with bright juicy Bombay mangoes, oranges and green avocados.

Trade was carried out by higglers who called them "sweetie" and "darling" enticingly, inviting them to look. Maxine bought two sugar-loaf pineapples and the woman reached into her voluminous bosom to take out her change purse. The hum of patois echoed through the arcade that had been built when Queen Victoria was in her reign.

They hurried past the meat section, holding their breath. Carcasses of fresh goat, beef and pork hung on meat hooks, covered with flies. The back section was a bazaar with everything including shoes, material, clothes, household appliances spread out on brightly coloured plastic tarpaulins, baskets, wood carvings and straw hats. They walked out to the square that boasted six rum bars, a nineteenth century brick and wood courthouse and a clock tower where each of the four clocks told a different, and incorrect, time.

Once back in the car, they drove past Richmond Hill where Maxine stopped for Jacqui to take a picture of an old Anglican church complete with a bell tower and six john crows perched motionlessly on the roof, as if waiting for their picture to be taken. The graveyard held crooked tombstones, their inscriptions weathered by the wind.

They drove along a picturesque coastline that held the most exquisite variety of unruly sapphire seas crashing upon white-sand beaches. Each swell of the sea and curve of the mountains brought boundless beauty.

At Dolphin Bay, a Bavarian fortress called The Castle perched on black lava cliffs looked out of place in the tropical setting. The water changed to five distinct shades of blue in the narrow channel between San San Beach and Monkey Island, which was a tiny clump of land with trees.

They had lunch at Frenchman's Cove, where the surf roared in on whitecaps onto a magnificent half-moon beach. Maxine took her to the Blue Marlin Inn later in the afternoon.

"I can't thank you enough for the ride and the beautiful day," said Jacqui.

"My pleasure. I wouldn't let things with Gary get you down. You are in a very mystical and magical part of the island. I have always found that things get resolved here. Just don't let a little rain trouble you. It rains every day here."

The Blue Marlin Inn reminded Jacqui of an older woman who was wearing an old but well mended Chanel suit. It was still in fashion and she carried it off with such grace that it compensated for the slight fraying – in this case, the overgrown ivy on the main building and the weeds that grew in abundance everywhere.

A young man named John who acted as the guard, front desk manager and general handyman helped Jacqui lug her suitcase up the stone path that was overgrown with lilies and philodendrons. He stopped at a cliff-side cottage called Heaven and pulled out some weeds at the entrance before pushing open the door with his finger.

The cottage was cute, quaint, rustic and charming. It was cute because it was small, quaint because it was old, rustic because things didn't work and charming because there was no other word to describe its strange layout.

The living room was long and narrow with roughened stone walls and natural wood floors that were rotting in several places. The couch and mismatching Queen Anne chairs were worn and faded. One of the chair legs was broken and it was supported by a cement block and a brick. The loft with the bed was dark and a damp smell lingered everywhere.

Taking out only a few things, Jacqui changed into her suit, then followed the footpath down to the beach. Alongside the path, a clear stream flowed into a natural whirlpool of emerald water that ran into a sapphire sea. The beach was a slice of paradise set between two cliffs. Jacqui swam in the sea, feeling a strong undertow as she tried to swim back to the beach. The top layer of water was colder than the bottom as the fresh water mixed with the salt water. She plunged into the chilling river, the mineral water washing over her skin, reviving her before she went back to her cottage.

The shower had no hot water and in the middle of her shampoo, with lather streaming down her back, the shower head fell off onto her foot, sending a stream of water towards the ceiling as she let out a yelp of pain. She tried to turn the water off but the faucet came off in her hand.

When she finally overcame the challenges of the shower, Jacqui was greeted by a croaking lizard that sat on her one bath towel that was the texture of sandpaper and the size of a kitchen towel. Walking across the room to her bag, she made the mistake of looking at the soles of her feet. They were black with dust. Sitting on the bed in frustration, she wondered where Gary was and what he was doing.

Shaking off the thought, she dressed quickly and stumbled down the unlit, rocky, overgrown path to the beach for the barbecue. Dick and Sheila were already there, and greeted her warmly. The moon touched the treetops as the calypso band played softly on the beach, its beat matching the tempo of the surf against the shore. The rhumba box, bass, tambourine and guitar sounds mingled with the tree frogs. The dozen guests were having drinks.

Dick introduced Bruce Chatsworth of the Sir Henry Morgan Angling Association who joined them for a drink. "This Calcutta should be the best we've had in years. The conditions are perfect."

"I gather that the Calcutta is really a practice run for local anglers for the Blue Martin Tournament?" asked Jacqui.

"Yes, it's the unofficial kickoff for the season. First there's the Montego Bay Tournament, followed by Ocho Rios and then Port Antonio," explained Bruce.

"There's more to it than that," interjected Dick. "The anglers from Florida have the most up-to-date boats and high-tech angling equipment. But any good angler knows that a lot of it is instinct."

"They also put a cash prize together to sweeten the pot and the instinct," said Sheila dryly.

"Does the type of craft really matter that much?" asked Jacqui.

"Very much so," replied Bruce. "Marlins are deep feeders. There is no reason for them to be on the surface. They're very crafty, those devils. A marlin can weigh one thousand pounds, swim seventy miles per hour, jump five stones high, skim the surface and then sound straight down. The way the boat sits in the water as well as how it trolls are critical factors."

"A marlin can do a few other things too," said Dick. "It can attack your boat, stick its bill in your hull and if you bring it on board alive, it can gore you to death. Marlins tend to feed where the rivers meet the sea and there is a dramatic drop in the depth. That's why marlin fishing is so good off Rio Bueno, the Rio Grande and the Great River."

198

The band moved amongst them, with all the members, wearing tropical shirts and straw hats, asking for requests. Dick requested the "Big Bamboo" which prompted Sheila to punch him playfully in his arm.

"I want to play a lovely song for you," said the rhumba player after complying with Dick's request. "It's the song of a lovesick sailor who left his love in Jamaica." The bittersweet melody of 'Jamaica Farewell' reminded Jacqui that this was her last stop before the assignment ended.

They were ushered to the barbecue, which was filled with grilled lobsters, pork and chicken.

"Old girl, tomorrow we are going to bring in a beauty of a marlin. It is a sight you must see," said Dick, sipping his coffee after taking a deep draw of his cigarette.

"To *Sea Quest*," said Jacqui, raising her glass.

"And Quack Quack," said Dick. "My mascot. I bring a live duck painted in Rasta colours of red, green and gold."

Walking back to her cottage, Jacqui felt content, lulled by the good food and excellent company. There was a stillness to the lush surroundings which seemed to echo in her mind. She had managed to forget Gary for the entire evening.

But she had trouble sleeping with the persistent crash of the waves against the cliff and the dive-bomber tactics of the mosquitoes. She had never slept on such a lumpy pillow or a butter-soft mattress. She wished she could turn the ocean off as she tossed and turned, her mind filled with the image of Gary with his arms around Trina.

* * *

In the still of the cool night when the sea air blanketed the coast, there was a damp chill in the air. By the light of the crescent moon low on the horizon, two men pulled up anchor of a Bertram called *Foolish Pleasure* and its powerful engine broke the silence.

Niney navigated the boat away from the island's south coast towards the Pedro Banks where the deep waters swallowed thousands of souls.

"Are we going to stop to fish?" asked Denzil, a tall light brown fisherman who knew the waters like the back of his hand.

"No man, we have to go out further," said Niney.

"I nevah fish so far out," said Denzil, who by nature was a gentle man, wanting only to fish for his family and drink his rum. "Why we haffi go out so far?"

"I already tell yuh. Doan ask too many questions. We have somet'ing fe pick up, dat's all," said Niney as he pushed the boat past the strong current of the cays.

Through the dark of the night, they travelled through the black waters towards St. Andreas. As they approached the north side of the cay, Niney signalled and was answered.

Two boats met in the churning waters off St. Andreas and ten huge bales were loaded onto *Foolish Pleasure*. Within moments, Niney turned the boat around and headed back towards the Pedro Cays and Jamaica's south coast.

"Wat's all dis?" asked Denzil, having watched the transaction with a growing wonder as to what his longtime companion was doing.

"The white woman," said Niney with a laugh. "It beat going fishing and it worth one hundred times de money."

The early morning dawn was just touching the sky with hues of pink when Niney pulled into Calabash Bay. Denzil jumped into the water and was pulling the boat towards the shore, when he saw two men waiting for them by the beach. Several yards away was a waiting truck with a familiar logo on the side panel.

"Hurry up," called one of the men. "What de raas took yuh so long?"

200

"Rough current off St. Andreas," said Niney. "We got it all."

Denzil took a look at the man who was waiting on the beach and felt his heart stop beating for a second. He was staring at a duppy – a ghost who had been dead for twenty years and there he was standing there living and breathing. He started running down the beach without turning back despite Niney's call. He wanted to run as far away as he could from the Lord of Trench Town.

* * *

In the early morning light with the sea in shades of emerald and azure, the yacht club was in a frenzy of activity as the boats prepared for the Port Antonio Calcutta.

Shouts between *Island Madness* and *No Problem* were heard, littered with plenty of unique Jamaican curse words. Bruce Chatsworth was busy seeing to the final registration of vessels for the Twenty-First Port Antonio Calcutta run by the Sir Henry Morgan Angling Association.

Leading his group to *Sea Quest*, Dick bellowed his good mornings to Kapo, the captain, and Brown Man, the crew. He introduced Jacqui to everyone around.

Breakfast was waiting for them in the galley. Brown Man had pan-fried dolphin, left over from yesterday's catch. The aroma of tarragon and onions filled the air. "Don't worry, Jacqui, this isn't Flipper. It's a popular game fish," said Dick. They all sat down at the large galley table to consume the dolphin, known as mahee mahee in Hawaii. It was complemented with ortanique juice and harddough bread.

They were all on deck at precisely seven to watch for the signal that the Calcutta was to start. Pushing a button, Kapo raised the anchor and Brown Man released the side line, guiding the rope from the power winch into the locker.

Following Dick up to the flybridge, Jacqui stood with him as they passed through the channel by Navy Island.

"Errol Flynn used to own the island. It has about twenty acres. I met him once when I was younger. He's been dead half as long as I've been alive and every time I come here, I learn a new tale of his exploits," remarked Dick. "There are some old men who hang out in a rum bar in town. They used to bring Flynn supplies when he held his weeklong parties. Man, do they have stories to tell you! Have you heard about the headless corpse? It was a famous trial that took place here in the early fifties."

"What happened?" asked Jacqui.

"A butcher named Devries supposedly murdered his wife, cut her up and dropped her limbs at points along the sea. It all eventually washed up, except for her head. He was hanged. but he never spoke from the day he was arrested. There were always those who believed that he didn't do it. There were allegations that Errol Flynn was involved."

Brown Man, a slim part-Indian man with sharp brown eyes, lowered the outrigger, as he started to make preparations for the day's fishing. He began by setting the rods in the holders along the transom, attaching coloured lures. The shortest lure was in the ninth wave behind the boat. Attaching the bait – a longjaw, indigenous to Jamaica – he cast off.

Observing Kapo as he handled the boat, Jacqui marvelled at the ship's high-tech communication system. All the modern radio directional finders, VHF and SSB (ship-to-shore communication), were there. They moved at a speed of about six knots until they were almost four miles out to sea. The shore was clear as a bell, but dark clouds were moving from the east. Tied to the flybridge was Quack Quack, the mascot. The live duck was indeed painted in green, yellow and red to match the lures.

"It's moderate seas, about two to three feet, I should

think," called Dick, squinting his eyes as he bit down on his cigar. Walking alongside the transom, he inspected the Penny International fishing rods and thirty-pound test lines as if he were a general preparing for the battle of his life. Tossing the teaser overboard, he explained that it was actually five artificial squid tied together. Its function was to create a flutter in the water, attracting the fish to bite. "I've seen a marlin play with a teaser and then go for the lure," he remarked, gazing out to sea.

At his signal, Kapo increased his trolling speed to seven knots. Standing on the flybridge, Jacqui could see the underwater shelf as it dramatically dropped off. The clouds were rolling in. She lazily stretched out on a cushioned seat and was soon dozing lightly, rocked by the sea.

They had been trolling for nearly two hours, when she roused herself. She joined Dick on the deck for a drink.

The seas had grown noticeably higher and the sky was filled with rolling masses of dark clouds. A swell washed over the bow, pitching Jacqui forward, drenching her.

"Are you okay?" Dick asked. "It's a bit rough, I know – a tropical wave is expected to hit the island sometime tonight. But we have lots of time. And I feel it in my bones that we are going to land one today. It must happen," he asserted optimistically.

"*Island Madness* just landed a marlin," called Kapo from the controls.

"Damn! We can't let them win!" shouted Dick. "We *must* catch a marlin today. We're only going in if the weather gets much worse. Rods up is at four. We stay out until four – fish or no fish!" he ordered.

Dick explained to Jacqui that they had to have a fish on the hook, though not necessarily landed on the boat, by then. After that, they had just one hour to get back to the yacht club for the official weigh-in. Missing the deadline by more than a second meant being disqualified from the competition.

"Mister Dick, tropical depression reported on de radio. It's now about two hundred miles east of de Morant. Cays, travelling at ten miles an hour. *Island Madness* is returning to port," called Kapo, from his position by the radio.

"Hear me – hear what me a say," mouthed Dick. "We not going in until I say so. I'm going to land a raas marlin today!"

"What's the difference between a wave and a depression?" Jacqui asked.

"It's just a matter of intensity – but don't worry, a hurricane is the only thing you would need to concern yourself about, and that's not going to happen, it's too early in the year for one," Dick reassured her.

Admiring his will and determination, but a bit nervous nevertheless, Jacqui silently prayed that the rain wouldn't pound the deck too hard as the waves continued to rise above the bow. The sky was dove-grey darkening to charcoal in areas.

Almost an hour of sheer torture passed with Jacqui beginning to feel seasick from being tossed about. Being inside the cabin was worse. Claustrophobia drove her back onto the deck to ride out the storm as water pounded them from all sides.

"Boss, another tropical depression warning issued," called Kapo. "I know you doan wan' give up, but you doan think we should turn back?"

"No! I know these storms. She'll let up in a bit and stay that way until tonight. Then she'll unleash herself. Until then, we will just ride this out," instructed Dick. He glanced at Jacqui hanging by the rail. She had paled considerably.

"For God's sake, foreign girl, don't you dare get sick on me! That's the last thing I need," implored Dick.

An hour later, the rain let up as the storm abated and the sky turned into a patchy blue. They were passing the cove where the Blue Marlin Inn was just a few green copper roofs on the cliffs, when Dick spied man-o'-war birds soaring above. He instructed Kapo to follow the birds. Brown Man readjusted the lures as they began to pick up speed. Glancing at her watch, Jacqui saw that it was twenty minutes to four. Dick studied the rods, then glanced at the birds. It was difficult for him to face defeat.

"We'll leave the rods in until the last possible minute," he stated, eyeing the coastline. Shouting loudly, Dick told Kapo to speed up. The man-o'-war birds were now darting toward the surface of the sea.

Watching one of the rods, Jacqui noticed an almost imperceptible strain before it suddenly flew.

"Green and yellow lure!" cried Brown Man excitedly. "Outrigger flying!"

Kapo accelerated the boat, firmly settling the hook into the fish's mouth. Dick grabbed the rod which was peeling off the line, slamming his body into the fighting chair, hurriedly adjusting the fighting jacket on his shoulders.

"We have to land this raas fish! We'll pull her into the channel if we have to. Call the port. Tell them we're fighting a fish," Dick cried triumphantly, struggling to adjust his jacket.

Pandemonium broke out as Brown Man and Jacqui furiously wound in the other lines as fast as they could, to avoid tangling with the green and yellow line.

The amazing brute of the deep leapt out of the sea, causing Jacqui to take a step back in awe and fright. The mighty marlin threw its head from side to side, dancing on its tail in a most spectacular fashion.

Without warning, the giant fish suddenly dove. The battle – the challenge between man and beast – was on. Leaving his control deck on the flybridge, with the boat steady at three knots, Kapo assumed a position on the stern deck.

"Lean forward with your rod and pump back. You have

to have slack on dat line," Kapo cautioned, sharing his many years of experience, even though Dick was an acknowledged expert.

The seconds hung in the air, as Dick and Kapo negotiated the delicate balance of speed needed to tire the marlin out. If they pushed too hard, the line could snap and the entire battle would be lost.

The hours of pitching seas and frustration were wiped away as Dick fought the marlin. As they passed Dolphin Bay, where the Castle was majestically perched on the cliffs in glistening white, Jacqui clutched her ribs in awe as the fish reappeared suddenly, one hundred feet from the boat. Moving the boat forward slowly, Dick kept pumping and winding the rod. With excruciating slowness, he pulled the fish along the transom.

Meanwhile, Brown Man had readied the fighting gaff. Tying the rope to the port side, Kapo instructed him on how to bring the fish in with the current to that side of the boat.

Dick put on a pair of thick gloves and leaned over the side. Grabbing the bill of the fish, he looked for the green and yellow lure. Holding the trace, he pulled the bill out of the water. Brown Man, three feet further down the gunnel, sank the stainless steel gaff into the body of the fish.

With supreme effort they all heaved together, lifting the fish out of the water into the boat. It dropped on the deck with a thud.

"What a beauty! She must be over two hundred pounds!" exclaimed Dick, shedding his fighting jacket. "Full speed ahead! We have only eleven minutes to get to port!" Shouting excitedly, he grabbed the radio to send out "quack quack" messages.

In the meantime, Brown Man tied the rope securely to the tail of the marlin as Kapo taxed the engine to its fullest. Whatever frustration or boredom that Jacqui had experienced during the day had been quickly obliterated by the thrilling conquest of the brute of the deep sea. She couldn't believe how excited and exhilarated she felt.

As they rounded Folly Point Lighthouse, they entered the narrow channel marker for the Port Antonio Harbour and Navy Island. A large crowd had gathered on the pier. With only three minutes to the deadline, the race was being cut to the final second. Kapo cut his speed, slowing down the boat. Dick screamed unintelligibly at him to speed up, but Kapo as a wise captain knew he could be disqualified if his boat created too much of a wake. Precious seconds were ticking by.

"Move the raas boat!" roared Dick with the rope in his hand. The crowd on the dock was clapping, cheering them on. When they were about ten feet away from the slip, Dick tossed the rope to waiting hands on the dock, shouting out orders to his crew. They all massed a supreme effort as they struggled to throw the fish out of the boat into the water.

With only thirty-two seconds left before the deadline, five men struggled valiantly to pull the fish out of the water. Attaching the rope to the pulley, they heaved together, hoisting the marlin onto the scale.

With just twelve seconds left for the Twenty-First Calcutta, Dick Robinson had landed the last fish of the day, weighing two hundred and twenty-one pounds. Leaping onto the pier, where Sheila was waiting for him, he grabbed her in a bear hug, and let out a howl that resembled a lion after a kill.

Everyone was congratulating Dick as they headed to the yacht club with Dick quacking all the way, offering to buy the first round of drinks.

After the first round, Jacqui wandered back out to the dock, watching with interest as the marlin was cut open and the stomach inspected by a scientist from the University of the West Indies. Brown Man, assisted by several others, cut away the head and tail, sectioning off the rest to be carted away for smoking.

Jerry Thomas of *Island Madness* joined her, asking how she had enjoyed her day, before telling her that he had to go to his boat to begin the battening-down procedure for the inevitable tropical depression.

"We were all a bit worried about you out there with Dick," he laughed. "Someone should have warned you that even if you were dying out there Dick would not have come in until four o'clock. A hurricane could have blown straight his way, but he still would have had his eyes peeled to the sea."

Breaking away from the revelry, Dick went out to the *Sea Quest* to ensure that she was properly hatched down and secure. Jacqui tagged along. While she coiled some rope, he paused from his activities time and again to look at the pieces of marlin with pride.

"I may be a bit crazy, but not nearly half as much as I was when I was younger. Then, I would drink a quart of rum a day and think nothing of it. I knew we wouldn't get in trouble out there today, Kapo is too good a captain," remarked Dick. "Jamaica has had twenty-two hurricanes in its history. During Gilbert, boats berthed here ended up across the street in trees. I wouldn't risk *Sea Quest*," he continued earnestly.

After his careful preparations, Dick ushered everyone back to their quarters, wanting to return to the inn. Several very drunk anglers were still at the bar. "See you at the prizegiving later," they called.

"Absolutely! I wouldn't miss it for the world," Dick cried back.

* * *

Gary walked out of the meeting with his bankers, feeling

tension in every muscle in his body. Where else could a twenty-minute meeting run five hours, he thought. He wanted to rip off his suit and tie and plunge his body into the warm sea, but one look at the billowing clouds that covered Kingston killed the idea. He thought about Jacqui for the tenth time that day, still confused as to why she had suddenly run off at Pimento Hill.

He borrowed the secretary's phone, first to call his mother to make arrangements for dinner at the Blue Mountain Inn. He needed to talk to her and maybe she could help him understand women's behaviour. His second call was to Robert Davids at The Falls.

After greeting Robert and receiving an update on hotel business, Gary turned the conversation to personal matters. "Where is Trina?" he asked.

"She took two days off," said Robert.

"You let her go?" he asked incredulously.

"Of course," said Robert, preparing himself for Gary's onslaught. "She is entitled to her days off like everyone else on staff."

"Where the hell did she go?" he fumed.

"Gary, don't put me in the middle. First of all, if I did know I wouldn't tell you and second of all she has every right to go where she chooses."

"Where is she?" he asked, but he was met with silence on the other end. "You were always so fucking honourable."

"That's right and don't expect me to be any different," said Robert.

"I never would," said Gary.

* * *

Jacqui met everyone at the gate of the Blue Marlin Inn and they drove along a road that felt like one huge pothole. A light mist had settled in the air, giving everything a damp feeling.

"The Blue Lagoon is a natural partly fresh lagoon and they say it's bottomless, but it's about two hundred and seventy feet deep," explained Sheila as they drove on a narrow bumpy road lined with beautiful homes painted in white. "It's one of my most treasured spots on the island."

The lagoon, surrounded by lush, exotic trees, emerged in the shade of the deepest emerald. The drop at the edge from shallow to infinite was more dramatic than the drop at the sea shelf. The sun was setting as they joined the party under the thatch-roofed restaurant and disco.

As the darkness settled, the lagoon took on an eerie glow, so breathtaking that it made her melancholy. But she was quickly jostled out of it by Dick and his jubilance.

Dinner was a choice of snapper or lobster which hung live in a trap in the lagoon. Picking her lobster, Jacqui was offered the choice of having it curried, grilled or steamed and finally opted for grilled. After an hour of drinking and laughing, she found herself sitting by the water's edge in between Jerry Thomas and Bruce Chatsworth, eating the most succulent lobster that she had ever had.

The good-natured banter among the anglers was kept up all throughout dinner. Strategies and plans for the upcoming Blue Marlin Tournament were in the air. It was the largest fishing tournament in the Caribbean with entrants from the USA, Canada and even as far as West Africa.

Bruce Chatsworth approached the microphone that had been set up. He tried for several minutes to get their attention, but the free-flowing liquor had loosened everyone's tongue. Cutting his conversation short, Dick quickly ordered everyone to quiet down.

"It's my pleasure to preside over the presentation of

trophies for the Twenty-First Calcutta," began Bruce. "I cannot recall a time when it was such an exciting one.

"For the first fish of the day, weighing in at one hundred and fifty-four pounds, caught by *Island Madness* – Jerry Thomas, the angler," announced Bruce ceremoniously as he handed Jerry his trophy, to loud applause.

After the audience quietened down, Bruce tried to continue but a ruckus started in the bar, forcing him to stop for a long moment until the noise subsided.

"I know this is the announcement you have all been waiting for, so quiet down just for a bit longer," said Bruce. "For the last fish of the day, the trophy goes to *Sea Quest* and Dick Robinson, angler." There was a cacophony of whistling and handclapping as Bruce continued. "Dick also brought in the biggest, weighing two hundred and twenty-one pounds. I'm pleased to present this very well deserved cheque to my good friend Dick Robinson."

The crowd applauded even more vigorously as Dick ran up to the bar, slowing down only to slap Jerry Thomas on the back. Shaking Bruce's hand as he accepted the trophy, he turned to the crowd.

"Quack quack!" he cried, holding his trophy high as he turned to collect his cash prize. "Just wait until the tournament!" roared Dick.

Champagne corks started popping. The crowd was caught up in his victory. Soca music blared as the dancing got underway in the thatch hut over the shimmering waters of the Blue Lagoon.

Jacqui kept glancing out to sea, noticing that the sky was again getting cloudy very quickly. The stars that had been out were now totally extinguished. She could almost smell approaching rain and was happy to follow Sheila back to the car.

"How will Dick get back?" she asked.

"Dick is like a good house pet. He always manages to

find his own way home," said Sheila, pulling away as it began to mist lightly again.

"Is this going to be a bad storm?" asked Jacqui, looking with some concern at the sky.

"It shouldn't be too bad. You never know how quickly it's going to develop or how bad it's going to be, but if I know my husband, he will have organized a poker game to begin in our cottage just after breakfast. We're pretty well stocked for a few days. Dick doesn't like to take chances, especially after Hurricane Gilbert. He's always prepared for these eventualities."

They passed a battered-looking Land-Rover at San San that seemed familiar to Jacqui, but then again, all Land-Rovers looked the same when they were so old. It was drizzling by the time they returned to the inn.

Lying in bed, listening to the sea, Jacqui wished Gary wasn't dominating her thoughts. She pushed him out of her mind in disgust. Picking up a paperback, she tried to get sleepy. The rain started slowly at first, like staccato notes on the roof, but its beat quickly picked up into a steady downpour. It was soothing, cleansing rain. Putting her book aside, Jacqui snuggled into her sheets, allowing the falling rain and the crash of the sea to lull her into deep sleep.

Chapter 15

It rained steadily through the night. The dawn brought only a glimmer of light to the cloud-covered dull grey sky. A cool wind whistled through the cottage when Jacqui got up. The power had been turned off and there was hardly any water in the pipes.

The sea was angrily crashing against the cliffs, the spray reaching up to pound the verandah. Pulling on a pair of cotton pants and a long-sleeved cotton sweatshirt then grabbing her raincoat, Jacqui ventured outside. The rain felt like sticky jelly on her face as she made her way to Dick and Sheila's villa.

Just as Sheila had predicted, a poker game was in full swing with anglers from *Island Madness* and *Rum King*. The stakes were growing higher with each hand. The weather reports on the radio droned on in the background. Tropical depression warnings had been issued, urging all residents in low-lying flood-prone areas to evacuate.

"Have you heard anything about the investigation into Donald Francis's death?" asked Jerry Thomas. Jacqui's ears instantly perked up. "More than anything Donald loved fishing and I really missed his loud mouth yesterday."

"True, true, Donald did love a good fete. I have not heard a thing," Dick answered, throwing out a card. "I do hope they catch the son of a bitch soon. This is going to be a hell of a storm," he added, chomping on his Winston Churchill cigar. "I don't think we will be able to move until tomorrow. We've got enough food and liquor to last for two days. Relax, girl," he said to Jacqui. "Have a drink. It's the only way to enjoy a storm."

Jacqui played a few hands by the kerosene lantern, unable to swallow the stiff drink that Dick had prepared. The sky darkened and the rain intensified. Feeling restless, she left shortly before lunch, despite the protests of Dick and Sheila, who insisted that she join them for dinner. She was walking along the path to her room in the pouring rain when she spied the hotel car. She ran until she was close enough to bang on the trunk of the car to make it stop.

"John, can you take me to The Castle?" she asked, knowing she could not bear to go back to her dark cottage.

"Ah doan know," he said. "Folly soon flood, if it's not already. Me 'fraid to cross in dis rain. Me have a wife and chile at home fe look after."

"All you have to do is get me there," she said resolutely. I'll worry about getting back."

She wondered at her optimism as they drove the few miles down the road. The damage from the morning's rain was evident. There were a few fallen trees and leaves littering the road, making the drive dangerously slippery. Folly River was surging over its banks and the waves in Dolphin Bay were crashing violently. The sky was growing darker by the minute.

John left her by the steps at The Castle. The moat was raging and the fruit trees were sagging under the weight of the voluminous quantities of water. Dashing to safety past the glaring glass eyes of the stone crocodiles, she had not reached the door when a massive clap of thunder broke and the sky opened up, hitting her skin like cold hard pellets of lead.

She clutched the railing to avoid slipping down the stone steps, wondering why she hadn't stayed in the security of Dick and Sheila's villa. On reaching the pub, she ordered lunch, watching the sea swell amid the deafening sound of the relentlessly pouring rain. The kidney-shaped pool was overflowing into the sea and the outdoor garden was submerged in water, up to the tops of the large potted plants.

An attractive man came into the pub, introducing himself as Claude Maier, the general manager, and offered her a cup of tea.

"How was the Calcutta?" he asked in an indistinguishable European accent.

Jacqui concealed her surprise at his knowledge of her participation in the tournament. "It was fantastic, even with the rough seas," she replied. "I was on *Sea* Quest with Dick Robinson when he caught a two-twenty-one pound marlin. Did you have a chance to see it?"

"No I didn't. In this business, blue marlins are at the end of a long queue of things that just have to wait," he said, as a flash of lightning made them both turn towards the window. "But I'm sure you know about the demands of the hospitality trade, Miss Devron. I must say I particularly liked your piece on Texas. I grew up in the Swiss Alps, and I have always wanted to see what those wide open spaces look like."

Jacqui looked stunned for a second. "I'm not being fair, am I?" he smiled. "Robert Davids called me to let me know I might expect you to pop in for tea." He had the diplomatic aplomb of a consummate hotelier who knew how to get his point across, whilst putting people at ease.

"Did he now," said Jacqui, looking at Claude with an impish smile. "Word certainly does get around on this island."

"How about a cognac?" he asked, signalling for the bartender, who was wearing black trousers, a white shirt, a bright red jacket and white gloves. "The hotel industry is pretty well organized and we have good relations with Tropical Properties."

"I heard on the radio that Tropical Properties has

exciting plans for Port Antonio. "Do they involve The Castle?" Jacqui asked.

"I am not at liberty to divulge any of the details, but it will be a wonderful development for the area," said Claude.

Jacqui was filled with a thousand questions, none of which she got to ask as the concierge burst into the lounge in a state of breathless agitation.

"Landslide," he barely choked out.

"Take it easy, Mr. Lawrence," said Claude to the elderly man. "Try to tell me what happened."

"Landslide at Richmond Hill. It's bad. The entire hill is gone. It just happened."

"Oh dear God," said Claude as they both jumped to their feet. Jacqui grabbed her raincoat and followed Claude. Immediately he started giving orders to the staff. "Put together all the canned goods, blankets and candles that you can. There are at least fifteen families that live on Richmond Hill. We will have to be prepared to offer them aid and shelter."

"I'm coming with you," declared Jacqui.

"Good," said Claude. "We can probably use all the help we can get."

Driving was treacherous in the pouring rain. Mud and water had filled the potholes, making it impossible to judge where or how deep they were. At one spot, the water rushed above the tyres, swirling around them, some of it seeping into the vehicle.

Nothing could have prepared Jacqui for the destruction and devastation that awaited them at the foot of what was left of Richmond Hill. It was as if a giant had taken a big bite out of the hill, spewing its contents across the road. Zinc shacks were covered with mud and fragments of greenery. Trees that had been in the ground for two hundred years had been cruelly uprooted. Power poles and transformers lay in what had been the roadway, their wires twisted beyond

216

recognition. Shaken survivors gathered at the Anglican church at the side of the road, the only solid structure in sight.

For a moment, they gazed in horror at the chaos which lay before them. Then the wail of children above the noise of the relentless rain galvanized them into action.

They moved as quickly as they could to the bottom of the landslide, their progress hampered by the mud. A little girl wearing only a pair of torn muddy underpants was standing in the midst of the rain, crying loudly, bleeding from her head and arm.

The rain seemed to slacken off slightly and they could make out two figures, a man and a woman, on the ridge assisting people. The man was carrying an elderly woman, completely covered in mud, down the slippery slope, his progress marred by uprooted tree trunks. Following some distance behind him, Jacqui could discern a young woman carrying a baby. Her body was totally covered with mud and her hair was plastered to her head. The woman handed Claude the baby and did an about-face, struggling to climb back up the muddy hill.

"Get Mrs. Bryce and the baby inside," the man shouted above the rain. "There are at least two people trapped in a house on the other side. It's going to topple over any second. They're as good as dead if there's a second landslide. I'm going back up."

Jacqui supported Mrs. Bryce and followed Claude, who had taken the baby, into the church. Nearly twenty people had gathered, devastation written all over their faces. One woman was crying hysterically that she didn't have any insurance. Homes that had taken a lifetime to build had been washed away in a flash. The sobs of adults mingled with the cries of children. One man was lying on a pew, moaning in pain, his leg swollen and twisted. Jacqui saw a little boy with a deep head gash and a profusion of cuts and bruises.

She plunged back outside to see three people struggling down the hill, led by the man: One of them pitched forward as a low rumble was felt and the top of the hill began to disintegrate. Huge pieces of water-soaked soil flaked off its face. The survivors started running. As they neared the church, the mountain heaved forward, shifting soil and rock that formed a flowing river of trees and debris, taking everything in its path.

A Jamaica Defence Force truck had pulled up as close as possible to the bottom of the mudslide and a team of soldiers joined in the rescue.

Mrs. Bryce joined them outside when she heard the noise. "Mi t'ings dem gone. De pickney an' 'im grandfather sure dead. What me a go do now?" she wailed. Two soldiers moved towards her. "Yuh haffi help me."

"What is it?" asked one of the soldiers.

"Me tek care of de pickney in me neighbour house. De modder wuk fe dem rich folk in San San. De baby was in de house wid him grandfather when de mountain fall like de walls of Jericho," she cried, pointing to the flat mound that was once the house. Only a corner of the zinc roof was evident.

The soldier urged Mrs. Bryce back into the church and started up the hill, followed by two other soldiers, Claude and Jacqui, all steering clear of the river of mud which was making an irregular path down the mountain. One of the soldiers motioned them. They tried peeling off a section of the zinc roof with anything they could lay their hands on.

Unseen by the group, a Land-Rover pulled up next to the army truck. A clap of thunder illuminated the sky like a firecracker as Gary stepped out. His clothes instantly drenched and clinging to his body like a second skin, he saw the rescue attempt and immediately started up the hill, his progress hampered by the unstable top layer. He moved slowly over the muddy ravine, sinking past his knees in places, grabbing onto uprooted trees and pieces of debris for support.

Meanwhile the young woman Jacqui had first seen joined them. The rain had washed off most of the mud and Jacqui could clearly see her face. She did a double take.

"Trina," she said, in shock. Trina looked at her without any visible signs of recognition.

Finally the team managed to prise off a part of the roof. They were able to see an old man cowering down in the hole of what was once his home. A rope was handed down to him. The rain beat relentlessly on the lonely dark ridge, and it seemed like an eternity before the elderly man was hoisted up from his tomb.

"Praise the Lord," he cried. He was totally covered in mud. "A baby leave down dere in a next room. In a basket. Me push de door as far as me can. De opening too small."

They all moved cautiously around the roof, listening for the wail of a frightened child amid the clapping thunder. They could hear nothing. The mud was weighing heavily on the zinc.

"How many down there?" asked Gary, as he struggled to join them, pulling himself up.

Jacqui turned around sharply. "A baby," she said, stunned to see him. Gary barely acknowledged her presence.

Two new figures appeared. Dick Robinson and Jerry Thomas had heard about the mudslide on an emergency radio bulletin and pushed their car through Folly River before struggling to pull themselves up the ridge.

Suddenly they heard the faint cry of a baby.

"I can't get in there," said a soldier, peering down the hole that they had made in the roof to see how wide the door had been opened. "I don't think any of us can fit. It's really a narrow slit. We'll have to try to push open the door some more – but we're running out of time."

"I'll go," volunteered Trina.

"You will not," said Gary emphatically. "It's too dangerous."

"I'm the smallest one here." said Trina. They listened as the wails of the child grew fainter. "You can't tell me what to do just because you're my father."

Jacqui gasped. Was she hearing things?

"I can't let you do this," said Gary. "I don't want you hurt."

"She'll have a rope on so we can pull her out," said the soldier.

Jacqui had to close her eyes to stop seeing stars. How could she have not seen the resemblance between Gary and Trina. She nearly lost her footing, but grabbed on to a large branch of a breadfruit tree and focussed her attention back to the rescue.

A large flashlight was shone in the hole as Trina was lowered. She stumbled in the darkness, squeezing through the door slit then pushing her way through the mud, following the sounds of whimpering. The infant was frightened and drenched when she found him in a basket. She waded through the mud, holding the baby above her head.

They threw a sling down for her to put the baby in and then a soldier lay across the roof and leaned over the hole to pull her up. The roof was creaking and splitting under the weight of the rescuers and mud.

"Let's get out of here," shouted one of the soldiers. They moved carefully off the roof. The mud reached their thighs as they crossed the ridge. Gary carried the infant above his head and the group made slow progress to the church.

The church roof was leaking in six different spots, but offered a truly heavenly respite to the survivors.

"Trina, are you all right?" asked Gary, holding up her

arm. It was dripping with blood.

"I didn't even know I cut myself," she said as she glanced down, looking surprised when she saw the deep gash in her forearm.

"What the hell are you doing here?" he asked.

"I took two days off and Warren was in the area so I came to see him," she said defiantly.

"I told you how I feel about him," said Gary.

"And I told you how I feel about him," Trina retorted. "I know you think he's after my money, but look at what he's doing," she said, pointing to him as he tended a wounded man. "He's a doctor."

"Does he know the truth about you?" asked Gary.

"He loves me and accepts me for who I am. Can you say that?" she asked accusingly.

The doctor come over to the group. Jacqui now recognized him as the same man she had seen with Trina at The Falls.

"Mr. Gordon, I'm Warren Bailey. It is a pleasure to finally meet you. Let me see your arm, Trina," he said gently, looking at the wound.

Jacqui watched them together, still trying to digest the revelation that Trina was Gary's daughter. The courage she had displayed was admirable. Jacqui had seen a new unexpected dimension to the girl that obliged her to make a reassessment. But still she couldn't shake the feeling that there was a cold hard edge to Trina that weighed each word and calculated each action. She could not erase the unpleasant memories of Trina at The Falls.

Gary turned abruptly from the young couple. As he passed Jacqui, he gave her a cold look before walking back out into the rain with Dick. They returned a few moments later with Claude and spoke to the soldiers.

"There are still three people unaccounted for," said one of the soldiers.

"Can we still keep digging in this rain?" asked Gary.

"Not possible," said the soldier, with Dick nodding his head in agreement. "The ridge is just too soaked with water for us to even move on it.'

"I don't think we will be able to see three feet in front of us in the next hour," added Jerry Thomas. "If we all don't get out of here soon, we will be stuck here for the night."

Dick, Gary and Claude went outside, and Claude came back in a moment later.

"Jacqui, I've arranged a ride for you back to the hotel. I don't promise it will be luxurious, but you'll be in good hands. You were a tremendous help. God bless you," he said.

"No, Claude, I want to stay and help," said Jacqui.

"Please listen to me. I think it would be best if you went back. I will be there as soon as I can. You've done all you can," he said, hustling her out of the church into the pouring rain.

She saw the waiting vehicle, its engine running and the back door open, and she made a mad dash, leaving the scene of devastation and destruction behind.

Chapter 16

The inside of the vehicle was dark as Jacqui plunged into the rear seat. Preoccupied with Gary's coldness, she stared unseeingly out the window as she rang the muddy water from her hair. Dirty water trickled down her neck. She looked at her hands and clothes. She had never been so filthy in her life. The only thing she wanted was a hot shower, but she would have settled for a bucket of water.

Pellets of rain tapped insistently on the roof, mingled with the static-laced radio reception.

"This is a special announcement from the Jamaica Broadcasting Corporation. There has been a landslide at Richmond Hill." Jolted back to reality, Jacqui leaned forward, straining to hear the sketchy report. "Two people have been confirmed dead and three reported missing with sixty people homeless," the report continued. "All power to the eastern section of the island has been cut. Folly River has overflowed its banks. Meanwhile, the tropical depression has also caused major floods and road blockages in Kingston and Spanish Town. Sections of Portmore have been evacuated and the Flat Bridge is impassable. We repeat. There has been a major landslide at Richmond Hill in Port Antonio. This has been a special announcement by the Jamaica Broadcasting Corporation."

A flash of lightning a few feet in front of the vehicle ignited the scenery for a split second, illuminating the driver's profile. Jacqui gasped when she saw who it was.

"Gary?" she said in disbelief.

"Miss Devron," he said coolly.

"You really are a devious man. Where the hell are we going?" she asked.

"Certainly not the Blue Marlin Inn. You just heard yourself that Folly River has overflowed," said Gary as the Land-Rover hit an invisible pothole in the raging water that covered the road.

A small yelp escaped from Jacqui's lips. She heard him chuckle and wanted to lean over and punch him out.

"Where are we going?" she asked, fuming at his amusement over her discomfort.

"Somewhere safe where we can talk. We seem to have this terrible habit of not being able to stay in the same place long enough to have an intelligent discussion."

"How dare you?" she said, a razor-sharp edge catching in her voice. "Who do you think you are that you can control my plans?"

"I don't control your plans, Jacqui. You are very much your own woman, but we are going to talk. That's all," he said as a huge boulder bounded down the mountain five feet in front of them, crashing into the ravine. Her stomach did a somersault, and another when they hit a triple bend called "Come See Me No More" and Gary skidded on the wet windy narrow road.

Jacqui felt herself sink into submission as she huddled in the corner of the Land-Rover. She felt totally powerless. The landslide with its destruction had left her emotionally drained and the treacherous ride had nearly shattered her nerves. She heaved a sigh of relief when Gary pulled into a small driveway and stopped in front of a quaint Georgian cottage.

"This is where we will be spending the night," he said, turning to look at her for the first time. Mud was matted in his hair and a streak had hardened on his face.

"I have no intention of spending the night with you," she said frostily, wrapping her mudded raincoat around her.

"Suit yourself," he said easily, getting out of the car. He walked around the back and opened the door, removing a canvas bag.

Jacqui leaned forward and saw he had left the keys in the ignition. She pursed her lips together, wondering if she could remember the roads Gary had taken.

"I'll take these," he said casually, pushing his head back in the front and grabbing his keys. He tossed them up in the air, pocketed them and whistled while he walked up the landscaped path to the house.

Jacqui sat there for a moment, seething with anger. She listened to the rain pound on the roof. She had never before been in a situation where she felt so totally trapped. She sat there for as long as she could, but her damp clothes and the mud from her ears to her toes were becoming unbearable.

With many misgivings, she opened the door of the Land-Rover. At that precise second, the sky opened up, dropping hard bullets of rain. She started running, but her left foot sank into a puddle that was fifteen inches deep with cold water. She plunged face forward into the soggy grass, scraping her knees.

Cursing inwards, she walked into the house, trailing a stream of muddy water in her wake. Gary was walking down the wood steps, a towel draped around his waist after his shower. She took one cautious step into the low-beamed dining room. Just the sight of him brought her fury to a peak.

"Welcome to Paradise Cottage," he said.

"Charming," she said sarcastically, trying not to look at his lean muscular torso.

"Can I offer you a drink?" he asked, going over to the breakfront.

"Cocktails. You colonials are so civilized," she said sweetly. "Must be all that British influence."

"Quite right," he said arrogantly. He poured two

brandies and handed her one.

"Why don't you shower before dinner?" he suggested. "You'll feel a lot better when you wash the mud off. Everything you need is upstairs."

"You feed your hostages," she said with an astonished expression. "How very thoughtful."

"It's a rainwater shower, rural style, so don't expect it to be hot," he warned.

Jacqui didn't make a movement, but continued to stare at him with daggers of fury.

"Come nah, woman. Me hungry. The way yuh look mek me head hurt," said Gary.

Jacqui tasted the mud in her mouth. Without another word she fled past the study up the stairs into the living room. A lantern illuminated the high-beamed room furnished with a comfortable couch, two mismatched easy chairs, a mahogany coffee table and large down cushions with bright patterns on the floor. There was an antique roll-top desk in the corner and ink sketches of Portland from the days of the banana trade adorning the walls.

The roof sloped dramatically in the tiny second bedroom off the living room. Gary had opened the window a crack and a strong rush of wind torpedoed through the room.

The master bedroom had gleaming white walls. The baseboard was trimmed in Caribbean blue, which set off the antique canopied brass bed dressed with a soft white spread. In a corner was a white highboy trimmed in blue and trellised window boxes. She found a sweatshirt and a pair of shorts neatly folded on the bed. Gary had left a lighted candle in the bathroom.

Without a moment's hesitation, she stripped off her muddy clothes, leaving them in a pile, and turned the shower on full blast. A tiny trickle of tepid water came out. She stood underneath it, watching the dark water flow down the drain with a gurgling sound. She heard some movement in the bedroom, but she didn't care. She was too anxious to get the mud out of her hair and ears.

She heard the banging of pots when she stepped out of the shower. Her teeth were chattering and, spying Gary's navy blue terry bathrobe on a peg, she grabbed it. Tightening the belt, she rubbed the collar against her cheek, her senses filled with his spicy smell.

When she finally stopped shivering, she reluctantly discarded the robe and put on the clothes that Gary had left for her. She walked downstairs barefooted and Gary came out of the kitchen at the same time, wearing an old sweat-shirt and a pair of clean worn jeans. He was whistling when he went over to the breakfront to pour Jacqui a glass of wine from the breathing bottle. He handed it to her and she grabbed the glass, backing away.

"This kidnapping may get you more than you bargained for," she said.

"Kidnapping?" he said, sounding surprised. "I thought I was helping a lady in distress by offering her shelter."

"Oh, sure. Where am I sleeping?"

"Wherever you want," he said.

"Where are you sleeping?" she asked.

"In my bed. You once said your bed or mine, if I can recall rightly. Truthfully, I am very glad you are so interested in the sleeping arrangements. "

"Don't be so cute. You are too egotistical if you think you can share the credit of my seduction with a tropical depression," she retorted.

"All I want to do is talk to you," he said.

"Then talk," she said. "Aren't you just the sweet paragon of virtue with a black book the size of the New York City yellow pages."

He met her intense glare with a smug look and Jacqui had to resist the temptation to walk over and crown him over the head with the wine bottle.

"Why didn't you tell me about Trina?" she asked.

"How could I explain to you that I have an illegitimate daughter. I don't know how to explain it to myself sometimes," he said. "I thought I would tell you when I got to know you better, but I realize I was wrong. I asked you to give me your trust and I didn't give you mine. I was going to tell you that day in Negril, but I didn't want to ruin the magic of the day. I had planned to tell you that night after the party, but you disappeared."

"Hah," she said. "How am I supposed to believe you. You had plenty of chances. Who are you anyway? Which hat are you wearing today? The pimento farmer, the chairman of Tropical Properties or the local drug baron?"

"For the last time, I am not a drug dealer," said Gary patiently. "I don't need the money or the cheap thrills. I'm going to tell you this because I trust you. My friend Ainsley is the Commander of the United Nations Anti-Narcotics Task Force. I've been working undercover to help him find out who is behind the influx of guns onto the island. Donald Francis was murdered because of that."

"Donald Francis," said Jacqui, her eyes flashing. "Do you know who? Do you have any clues?"

"Nothing really concrete, but we're working on it." They looked at each other for a moment, his arrogance and her anger slowly melting. "Why did you leave me at Pimento Hill without a word?" he asked.

"Charles roughed me up, and when I escaped and went looking for you, I saw you with Trina. I jumped to conclusions and thought the worst," she said.

"Oh my God," said Gary, visibly moved as he took a step closer to her. "Did he hurt you?" he asked softly.

"He just shook me up pretty good," she said with a small smile, wanting to reassure him. She was deeply touched by his show of concern.

He made a movement to touch a wet curl that clung to

her neck but pulled back. He knew she would balk if he touched her now. They still had too many things to resolve.

"Why don't you look around the cottage while I get something for us to eat. You must be starved," he said.

She wandered into the study. Standing in the middle room, she took a deep breath. She suddenly felt very relaxed – as if she had all the time in the world. She was caught up in the charm of Paradise Cottage. The old wood and stone floors reeked of history and lingering spirits.

There was a warmth and intimacy to the room with its two comfortable upholstered chairs, large old-fashioned writing table and an entire wall crammed with books. She approached the desk, glancing at its several photographs, then picking up the small one in the silver frame. It was a photograph of a young Gary in a tuxedo being presented to the Queen. Next to them was a man in a top hat and tails. Goose bumps rose on her arms and the hair on the back of her neck stood up. Gary was the spitting image of his grandfather, Winston. There was also a fabulous picture of Gary and Bob Marley holding their hands aloft at the first Peace Concert.

She browsed through the well stocked bookshelf, picking out a used, crumbling copy of *Treasure Island* by Robert Louis Stevenson. The inside cover was marked with a childish scrawl: "Gary Gordon, Third Form." One entire shelf was devoted to first editions of all the James Bond spy novels by Ian Fleming. She picked up *Doctor No* and read a touching inscription to Gary from Uncle Ian.

Gary came in to refill her wine glass and sat in one of the chairs, his long legs stretched out in front of him on the small rug. He watched her for a while, then put out his hand for her, leading her back into the dining room where the fire had been lit.

Dinner was a feast of cock soup, smoked oysters, paté,

smoked marlin and capers. They ate slowly by the fire. Although he didn't touch her at all, the tone of his voice, the way he looked at her was like a caress. By the firelight of their picnic dinner, he made love to her with his eyes.

"Did you know Ian Fleming well?" asked Jacqui, interrupting his transparent lustful thoughts.

"Ian was a very special friend to a young boy," he said with a gentle smile on his face. "I grew up with James Bond as my imaginary playmate. Did you know, Ian got the name for his super-spy from an ornithologist by the same name who wrote a book called *The Birds of the West Indies*."

Listening to him, Jacqui realized why Spicey Hill Farms and Paradise Cottage were so important to him. They were his link to his past and his lifeline to the future.

Gary made coffee and carried it upstairs and they settled on the couch. The storm was more evident upstairs as the rain continued its relentless pounding and the wind picked up, sending an eerie howling sound like that of a crying cat through the house.

"Are you sure Charles didn't hurt you?" asked Gary, taking a sip of his coffee.

"He didn't hurt me but he got me really mad," said Jacqui. She wanted to change the subject. She wasn't ready yet to tell Gary about the reason for his attack. "Gary, about the last review that *Elegant Travel* did of The Falls. I spoke to Elizabeth Hartley, the previous reporter. She said she met you at The Falls late last January."

"I never met her. I wasn't even here. I was away for most of the month," said Gary.

"I know that now," said Jacqui. "But someone who claimed to be you treated her terribly. She also told me about a one-thumbed man who she said worked for you, and there is a one-thumbed man who works for Charles. I saw him at Dreamscape." She paused before continuing. "It's not much to go on, but Charles told me he has a big resentment against your family."

"There is bad blood between the Gordons and the Whittinghams," admitted Gary. "Charles has always been in competition with me. For the past several years, he has been trying to buy Whispering Waters from me but I can't and won't sell. The land is part of the crown trust which I have no right to sell. That is the only legacy my father left Trina, though I will never understand why. He violated the terms of the trust which I am obliged to honour. Charles has his heart set on that land.

"And I must be honest and admit that I don't want him as a neighbouring hotelier," said Gary. "Charles's father, Bruce Whittingham, was an immoral man. He wanted political power. He was organizing a union on my family's estate. In order to build his power base he started trouble. There was a rash of unexplained fires and then the work stoppages. One night there was a huge fire in the fields and the next day they found the machines had been tampered with.

"My father knew it was Bruce behind it. He asked him to the house to talk about it. Bruce threatened him with more damage if they didn't let him unionize. My father was not one to take the threat lightly and he swore he would expose him publicly and bring him down, which is exactly what he did," said Gary. "Charles has spent his life defending his martyred father, knowing it's a lie, unless he's managed to brainwash himself."

"Charles said your father had something to do with his mother," said Jacqui.

"I don't believe it," said Gary. "My parents had one of the few love marriages I have ever seen. I know my father and he would never have taken up with the likes of Gloria Whittingham. What an overbearing domineering woman. It was her push for power that was Bruce's downfall. The tragic thing was that two days after the scandal broke in the newspaper, Bruce Whittingham jumped off the Causeway Bridge."

Gary walked over to the roll-top desk where he took out a bottle of pimento dram. He poured two glasses of the liqueur, the colour of rubies, and offered a glass to Jacqui. Their fingertips touched as she grasped the glass, sending an electric jolt through her body. She took a sip of the spicy nectar that instantly warmed her throat.

"Who is Trina's mother?" asked Jacqui, a tinge of jealousy seeping into her.

"Trina's mother was the helper at our house in Cherry Gardens. She was a young girl, with sweet country manners and an obliging smile. I was a real cad. I was dating a lovely Jamaican girl who was too well brought up to indulge in my ungentlemanly desires. One weekend, I found myself alone with the helper and seduced her. I went off to boarding school in England the next week, never knowing she was pregnant. When I returned home on holiday, she was gone and I never gave it a second thought," said Gary.

"When did you find out about her?" she asked.

"At the reading of my father's will two years ago. She was brought up in the ghetto and would have remained there if Winston hadn't left the land at Whispering Waters, part of the original crown trust, to her. I couldn't let her stay down there and I didn't know what to do so I brought her to The Falls."

"So where is her mother?" asked Jacqui, struggling to maintain her composure.

"I have no idea, she migrated years ago. Trina was basically raised on the streets and looked after by the community," said Gary.

"This must have scandalized Jamaican society," said Jacqui.

"Not really," said Gary. "It happens all the time. Trina is a result of a tradition where the household helper has a sexual relationship with her master or is the person who gives the master's young son his sexual initiation. It has its roots in slavery. The helper may not be averse to getting pregnant because it gives her a chance to elevate her economic status. It may be a social elevation if the father is white or nearly white because the baby will be mixed which is a status symbol for the mother. The reality has been that a lighter skin means a better chance of advancement. I'm not proud of my relationship with Trina's baby mother. I'm not proud to have neglected Trina most of her life." Gary stared unseeingly at the wall.

"Baby mother," said Jacqui, confused. "What does that mean?"

"Baby mothers are unmarried women who have children," Gary replied, "and often for married men."

"So, white upper-class men and black baby mothers," said Jacqui. "How prevalent are they here?"

"These baby mothers are as much a part of Jamaica as the burning sun or the patois that rings in your ears. It's our tropical sin. Their very existence and survival is woven into the social and economic fabric of this country."

"Why didn't you think you could tell me?" asked Jacqui. "I would have understood. I wasn't an air force brat for nothing. I've seen a few of my father's friends suddenly find out they had a half-Vietnamese child."

"I thought you wouldn't understand our double standards. It is difficult if you haven't grown up here. Morality and immorality go hand in hand. Love and fidelity mean two totally different things. My grandfather once said that the island is like a beautiful high-class call girl wearing an elegant gown, but when she takes off the gown she is wearing torn underwear."

"How do you feel about it?" asked Jacqui.

"I guess I was a wild young man with a healthy curiosity who tried just about everything. I used to think I would die if

I didn't know what was beyond the hill and then over the next one. The world was waiting for me just to come and see it. Now I'm tired. I'm tired of running over the hills and chasing moonbeams. I just want to cherish and be cherished. I don't think there's much else in life worth fighting for."

Jacqui was quiet when Gary finished talking, deeply affected by his revelations. His emerald eyes were unfocussed and he was lost in his own thoughts. She reached over to touch his hand and he held it for a moment and brought it to his lips. With an intimate squeeze, he went over to the roll-top desk to help himself to another dram. He took a sip before facing her.

"Who was Geoff Roth to you?" he asked.

"He's someone I dated in New York," said Jacqui.

"Are you still in love with him?" he asked, staring at her.

"I never was," said Jacqui, her heart beating.

"Who is he?" asked Gary.

"Geoff Roth is a very manipulative and calculating man who doesn't do anything without it being part of his grand master plan. From the socks he wears to the restaurants he eats in, it is all part of a contrived image. I was taken in with his style and it didn't take me too long to realize there was no substance there, but by that time the damage was done."

Jacqui took a deep breath before continuing. "I did a story on the King Casino in Atlantic City and was accused of taking a fifty-thousand-dollar bribe to write a favourable review. I denied any wrongdoing but there was a record of money in my account. Marty King threatened to pull all his advertising if I was still associated with the magazine, so I was suspended for three months and farmed out to write a teen lovelorn column until my suspension was over."

"So my questioning your professional integrity hit a sensitive nerve," said Gary.

234

"A very sensitive one," said Jacqui, shaking her head. "I couldn't allow one ounce of scandal to touch my review, especially since a lawsuit was threatened. Josh warned me that if anything happened in Jamaica, I wouldn't be given a second chance. I know I could pound the pavement but I wouldn't find another job with a decent publisher."

"I didn't know," said Gary. "I'm sorry you were put through hell again." He started moving towards her. Suddenly, there was a terrific crash and the sound of splintering wood.

"What was that?" she asked, bolting upright.

"Sounds like the pear tree has just fallen. Let me go check it out and make sure it didn't hit the house. Be back in a second," he said, dashing down the stairs.

The kerosene burned low in one of the lanterns, dimming the room. Jacqui lay back on the cushions, listening to the pounding rain. She heard the back door creak. The tension was slowly ebbing out of her. She closed her eyes for a moment, thinking she would just rest. Within seconds she had drifted off to sleep.

Gary inspected the fallen tree and hinged a banging shutter. He came back upstairs and stopped on the top step when he saw Jacqui's sleeping form on the couch. Her hair was a cascading mass framing her face. He walked over to her side, fingering a curl. He picked her up and she sighed deeply, nestling against him. He carried her to the canopied bed and covered her with the quilt, quelling the desire to take her in her sleepy state. He bent down and kissed her brow. As much as he wanted her, he didn't want her drowsy and passive. He wanted Jacqui burning hot and aching for him.

Jacqui woke an hour later. The cool wind rustled through the eaves, and the dim kerosene lantern flickered, casting dancing shadows. She got out of bed and opened the door to the porch, feeling the cool wind rush across her face. She watched the lightning flash brilliantly as the thunder rumbled seconds later.

Gary came up behind her, slipping his strong arms around her waist, pulling her body against his. She relaxed in the warmth of his bare chest, feeling his breath against her skin as he nuzzled her ear, relishing each curve of her body. He tilted her head back and a flash of lightning electrified their eyes, whispering what their hearts had known from the start.

Their love was as powerful as a tropical storm and they were explorers caught in the middle. Their course was completely uncharted. It was as if they had fallen into a chasm, as wide as the raging hurricane and steadily increasing in intensity. Born out of the forces of the wind and the sea, combined with the strength of the storm, was their passion – a raging tempest that was completely out of control.

"I've waited a lifetime for you," he whispered, guiding her back to the bed.

"I'm here now," she murmured.

He held her as if they were the only two people left on earth, kissing the bare softness of her neck, slowly caressing her body with silken strokes. He lowered her onto the bed and lifted her shirt off with ease. He held her face in his hands, lowering his lips to hers in a slow sensual kiss that instantly turned hot and devouring. He left a trail of hot molten kisses over her neck and then kissed the hollow between her breasts, breathing in her scent. He took possession of one rose-tipped nipple, first with his long sensitive fingers then with his mouth.

"I've thought about having you with me like this a thousand times," he whispered as Jacqui ran her hands along his smooth muscled back, aching to get closer to him.

With every touch and caress, he willed Jacqui to respond. She had never felt so vibrant, so filled with burning passion as he slowly made a study of her body with his hands and mouth. Gently, he pulled down her shorts. When he spread kisses down her thighs, tasting her sweet odour, Jacqui felt a rush of pleasure so poignant that she writhed with delight. She pulled him toward her, her entire body shaking.

"Let me love you," he whispered sensually in her ear as he held both her hands above her head. They stared into each other's eyes, filled with love, reading each other's expressions.

She kissed him fervently, her body moving against his in exquisite intimacy, in a rhythm that was time-old. She felt his movement in response, and her breath caught in her throat as she felt his subtle penetration of her deepest being. As in everything, he was unhurried and when his possession was total, he wrapped his arms around her, and stayed still for a moment, giving her time to savour the sensation of his body in hers.

Every move he made, each way he touched her and filled her senses, branded her as his. He wouldn't satisfy himself until he felt her tense, watching her face soften in rapture. She whispered his name with a shaky breath and clung desperately to him. Only then did he allow the intense spasm of delight to overtake him.

The storm had subsided and a calm filled the air with the stillness of the eye of a hurricane. There was a magical silence that brought the sound of a heartbeat to a level of great power. It was as if they had both harnessed the strength of the tropical storm – broken and trained it like a wild horse. They were riding together on the crest of the tempest.

Chapter 17

Charles Whittingham left his house in Red Hills, paying little attention to the storm that raged. He started his Isuzu Trooper and drove towards downtown Kingston. His windshield wipers were on the highest speed and his bright lights were on. Few cars had ventured out onto the road in the terrible conditions and even the dogs had taken shelter from the rain. He passed through Allman Town, Tivoli Gardens and Rema before he pulled into Port Kingston. He took a lane and then turned into an alley that wasn't on any road map and parked. He dashed out into the pouring rain and went into a crudely built cement building.

"Open up," called Charles.

"Who dat?" called Sputo.

"Whittingham," Charles shouted above the rain.

Sputo opened the door, holding his maimed hand that always throbbed in the rain. "Wha' 'appen. Me nevah expect fe see yuh."

"Yuh all set for tomorrow?" Charles asked. "I have a feeling we have to be extra careful."

"All set," said Sputo.

"The code is Blue Champagne," said Charles. "Make sure it's passed on."

"I got it," said Sputo. "What else?"

"One other thing. Do you remember dat white bitch?"

"Me know de one," said Sputo.

"I hear she's in Port Antonio," said Charles. "See if you can't find her and take care of her for good."

"No problem," said Sputo, a sick smile showing on his face.

* * *

The heavy rains let up around dawn and a grey mist enveloped the John Crow Mountains. A cool wind filtered through the eaves of the bedroom as Gary cradled her body to his. His usually taut muscles were relaxed, gently uncoiled in the aftermath of their intense love. There was no illusion or fantasy to the level of intensity they had reached the night before. Jacqui sensed the warm presence next to her before she felt his butterfly touch.

"I remember you like gentle wakeups," he whispered, kissing her neck.

"Mm. Very gentle," she murmured. "It's better than being forced awake at some ungodly hour by a creep."

"I love when you call me that," he said, pulling her into his arms, enjoying the feel of her body against his.

"I'm starving. What's for breakfast?" she asked.

"Plenty of pear. We lost the tree last night," he said.

They took a rainwater shower that was filled with long wet kisses and intimate caresses. Anyone passing the little house in the hills would have heard the laughter. Gary wrapped a towel around his waist and slipped the robe around Jacqui, planting a kiss on her nose. In the bedroom, he put on a pair of shorts and a t-shirt.

"What am I going to wear?" she asked, rummaging through the highboy.

"How about this shirt," he said, handing her a smelly t-shirt that was covered with paint.

"Don't be ridiculous. Even in these extreme conditions, I wouldn't be caught dead in that," she teased.

He passed her a man's blue Oxford shirt that had survived from his school days and a pair of shorts with a

239

drawstring that adjusted to her slim waist.

They went down to the kitchen, which was small but organized with maximum efficiency in mind. Hanging brass pots gleamed against the stark white wooden interior. Gary went outside to pick some oranges and pears and Jacqui checked the canned goods which consisted of mackerel, sardines and onions.

Within minutes, Gary had made a fresh pitcher of ortanique juice, had sardines and onions frying on the stove and was slicing pears.

"I'm very impressed that you could make this meal out of nothing," said Jacqui. There was a heightened glow to her skin and her eyes, tinged in yellow, were radiant.

"I had to learn to cook at the tender age of fourteen when I got kitchen privileges at Munro," said Gary, carefully measuring the coffee into an old stove-top percolator.

"Why? What did you do?" she asked, laughing.

"Kidnapped the class," answered Gary. "I wasn't totally responsible. I had Ainsley, Robert and PJ as willing accomplices who disclaimed responsibility."

"I figured I wasn't the first person you'd kidnapped! How did you kidnap the entire class?" asked Jacqui.

"It was easy," said Gary. "I told the headmaster that my grandfather was deathly ill and I had to go to Kingston to see him. Once off school grounds, I hired a truck and arranged for it to be outside the gates after prayers on Friday. PJ and Ainsley had the class waiting and Robert convinced the headmaster that the class was going to do a charitable project. What a brilliant day we had. We drank beer and swam in the surf at Bluefields and snuck back into the school without a hitch."

"How did you get caught?" she asked, trying to contain her giggles.

"It seems while we were enjoying our rites of young manhood, my ailing grandfather Winston had stopped off to visit on his way to Round Hill. He showed up in his chauffeur-driven Bentley, wearing his golf clothes and smoking his enormous Macundo cigar."

"How did you get out of that one?" asked Jacqui.

"I think my grandfather was in league with the headmaster, but he eloquently pleaded my case and instead of expulsion, I got kitchen privileges for the rest of the term. Truthfully, I don't know why they call it privileges," he said, serving breakfast on ceramic plates, accompanied by huge steamy mugs of coffee.

"This is delicious coffee," said Jacqui as she felt the caffeine enter her bloodstream. The rich brew had the aroma of perfume.

"What you are drinking is Paradise Cottage coffee – the best in the world, I might add," said Gary, looking pleased. "The freshest Blue Mountain coffee beans that are sun-dried in the crisp mountain air, combined with rain water and the old method of perking. This house was originally Winston's cottage. He used it during the summer to go bird shooting."

After breakfast they took a walk to Black Rock, the nearest village. The road was littered with branches and a fallen tree blocked the way. At a curve in the road, the Rio Grande Valley spread out before them, its meandering river making progress towards the sea. Raindrops clung to the leaves of the spathodia trees, whose dark green leaves were accented with bright red flowers.

They walked past a herd of goats at the entrance to Black Rock, marked by a small circle of flowers planted by the local youth club. Opposite the flowers stood a wooden stall with a piece of zinc for a roof, held down by four rocks. On a crude wooden shelf were a few bruised bananas, a piece of pumpkin and white yam, and an open packet of Craven A's, the foil removed and the tobacco side showing.

Black Rock consisted of a square. Tacked onto the door of the Black Rock Postal Agency was a rusty, nearly illegible sign for Cafenol tablets. To her amazement, Jacqui counted no less than four churches in the square – Seventh Day Adventist, Anglican, Evangelical and Church of Christ.

Activity was slowly returning to the village, encouraged by the opening of the rum bar at the far side of the town square. The Twice As Nice Lounge had peeling paint and a zinc roof that hadn't survived the storm. Gary led her past the shop that held a small assortment of groceries: the ever-present 'bully beef' which was canned corned beef, sardines, washing powder and McEwans Strong Ale.

Separated from the shop by a wire partition was the rum bar. It boasted a large bar with stools, three wooden tables that sat precariously on the uneven floor and a huge sound system consisting of four sets of six-foot speakers that looked like they could blow the roof off. Crates of empty Red Stripe beer bottles were stacked haphazardly against one wall and peeling Jamaica Tourist Board posters decorated the joint.

"Good day to you, Mr. Gary," said a light-brown-skinned man who was smiling broadly, showing that all his front teeth were missing.

"Good day to you, Rocky. We came to see how you fared during the rains," said Gary, his hand settling comfortably on Jacqui's waist.

"Not too bad," said Rocky. "Some flooding in de valley but everyt'ing alright. Me hear dem have a whole heap of trouble down at Richmond Hill."

"A whole heap," responded Gary. "Jacqui, I would like you to meet Rocky. He is the most notorious scoundrel and womanizer in Portland. Don't trust him an inch."

"Yuh too bad, boss. Yuh jus' 'fraid dat dis pretty woman favah me instead of yuh. Howdy do, Miss Jacqui," he said, flashing her a beguiling smile as he handed Gary two cold beers.

They took seats at one of the rickety tables, watching

Rocky deal with an endless stream of ladies calling for his attention. Despite his lack of teeth, Rocky had a charm and vibrancy that oozed pure sensuality.

Beckie and Archer, the village domino champions, challenged Gary to a game, which he accepted without a thought. Rocky pulled her aside and gave her some pointers, explaining that dominoes was a game of strategy, involving twenty-eight tiles from double blanks to double sixes.

The game was accompanied by a serious of loud thuds on the worn-out table, frequent cursing and cheers from an audience of villagers who were watching the game. When Gary tossed the final tile, winning the match, the shouts of approval echoed through the bar.

There was an intimacy and warmth to the Twice As Nice Lounge that couldn't be matched anywhere else. Jacqui sipped a Ting, the local grapefruit soft drink, watching Gary joke with Beckie. From the prime minister to the village drunk, Gary had the unique ability to make everyone feel important.

Gary bought drinks for everyone and after the flurry of activity died down, Rocky left the bar and joined them at their table.

"Praise de Lord in the name of sweet Jesus. Him really ansah me prayers."

"What 'appen, Rocky," said Gary. Rocky gave Jacqui a side glance. "She cool, boss. Yuh ken talk wid her."

"Yuh know dat me born and growed in Portland, but me have family down at Farraquehers Point on de south coast. De other night, me cousin Denzil come up here in de middle of de night. Me nevah expect him so I was out visiting. Me wife nearly ketch me wid me baby modder.

"Boss, Denzil is a big man, but him so 'fraid, him start fe cry when him see me," said Rocky.

"What happened?" asked Gary.

"What happened was dis. Him friend Niney ask him fe

help him wid him boat. Him promise him a heap a cash. Dem go out to sea fe fish in Niney's boat. Dem go out past de Pedro Banks and Denzil get 'fraid. Him want fe know why dem go out so far. Off St. Andreas dem meet a man and collect a bale of white woman," said Rocky in a low voice.

Jacqui looked at Gary questioningly. "Cocaine," said Gary.

"Dem come back in and dem land de boat at Calabash Bay. While dem was unloading, Denzil see him."

"Who?" asked Gary.

"De duppy, him sey," said Rocky. "Denzil sey him dead twenty years, but him see him."

"Who?" repeated Gary.

"The Lord of Trench Town," said Rocky, his eyes widening.

"Robert Unity. I thought he was dead," said Gary.

"So did Denzil, but him see him hand an' him missing him thumb. Him remembah how him los' him thumb."

Jacqui gasped, catching Gary's eye. He grabbed her hand, signalling her to be quiet.

"Him sey dem load de bale of white woman into an Island Builders truck and him hear dem tek it to Ocho Rios," Rocky continued.

"Where is Denzil now?" asked Gary.

"Him wid me. Him 'fraid fe go back," said Rocky.

"Tell Denzil to stay out of sight for a few days," said Gary, his brow knotted with worry. "Thanks for telling me this."

"No problem, boss." Rocky left to take care of the patrons at the bar.

"I've known about the transshipments, but I had no idea how it was being done," said Gary.

"I've heard the name Niney before," mused Jacqui, her brow wrinkled in concentration. "When I was at Charles's house for dinner, I heard him tell his manservant to take Niney with him."

"Let's go," he said, getting up abruptly.

"What are you going to do?" she asked as Gary settled the bill and they walked out into the village. The sun was finally breaking through in a few blue patches amidst the grey cirrus clouds.

"I'm going to call Ainsley and get over to The Falls," he replied as he picked out a fresh sugarloaf pineapple at the fruit stand, ordering for it to be cut. He devoured a thick juicy chunk in one bite.

They walked back to Paradise Cottage and closed up the house to return to town. The ride down the hill was treacherous, with water covering the deep potholes.

"Let's stop at The Castle," suggested Gary as they pulled onto the main road that wasn't in much better shape than the parochial road. "I want to find out what happened on the rescue."

"Speaking of The Castle, what are Tropical Properties' plans?" she asked, slipping her arm around him.

"Am I finally being interviewed by *Elegant Travel* Magazine?" he teased.

"You could say that," she responded easily.

"Is this on the record?" asked Gary.

"Do you want it to be?" she asked, looking at him.

"No, because the plans aren't finalized."

"Then it's off the record," said Jacqui.

"I'm awaiting approval from Cabinet to open The Casino at The Castle. I've been working on the approval for the past five years. It will be the first casino on the island."

"Congratulations," said Jacqui, excited by his announcement. "Do you promise *Elegant Travel* an exclusive interview? I'd love to scoop *Travel and Leisure*."

"It depends who covers the story," he said with a smile.

They pulled over the raging moat of The Castle and Mr.

Lawrence greeted them, escorting them out to the terrace for tea. They were served huge plates of cheese and cucumber sandwiches and an orange cake that melted in Jacqui's mouth. Claude joined them with a progress report on Richmond Hill.

"They found another body early this morning. Poor guy must not have known what hit him," said Claude. "Most of the families are staying in the church and the community centre. I've put two families up in the staff quarters. The Salvation Army arrived this morning and set up a soup kitchen in the old government stores building."

"What about the road and power?" asked Gary.

"We are running off generator power. They don't expect to have the electricity restored before the end of the week. I think we'll be lucky if it's by the end of the month. The road was just opened an hour ago."

"Did The Castle suffer any damage?" asked Gary.

"None to speak of. Two villas were flooded but the furniture had been removed. I have two crews cleaning up the damage."

"Do you think we will be able to open the casino on time?" asked Gary.

"I do," said Claude, looking at Jacqui. He was surprised that Gary was talking openly about the casino since it was a project that he had held very close to his chest. "I do hope that you can spend some time here and enjoy our facilities," he said to her.

"I've seen enough to know that this is one of the loveliest hotels on the island," Jacqui assured him.

Gary excused himself and went into Claude's office to use the phone. He waited several moments for a dial tone and tried six times, each time receiving a recording. On the seventh time, he got through.

"United Nations Field Command. Corporal Kelly speaking."

"Is Commander Gunther in? This is Gary Gordon."

"Sorry, sir, the commander is on field duty. Can I relay a message?"

"Do you know where he is?" asked Gary.

"I am not at liberty to say, sir," said the corporal.

"Tell him to contact me at The Falls," said Gary.

"Very good, sir."

He returned to find Jacqui and Claude in an animated conversation. He was struck at how vibrant she looked. She looked up at him and smiled, and her blazing sensuality washed over him like a brilliant ray of sunshine.

"Claude, thanks for tea," he said, putting his hand out for hers.

"My pleasure, Gary. Good luck with the Jamaican of the Year Award tomorrow. I'm sorry I won't be able to make it into town for it. Best of luck to you, Jacqui," he said, kissing both her cheeks.

The sun had finally come out as they passed over Folly River, which was still flooded. Gary had to jump out of the vehicle and haul a fallen coconut palm out of the way before they could reach the Blue Marlin Inn.

Once they were inside Jacqui's cottage, Gary pulled her into his arms, his lips devouring hers in a feverish kiss. He wanted to take each piece of clothing off her body and watch her face as they made love with the waves crashing in the distance.

"I have to go to The Falls," said Gary reluctantly.

"I want to come with you," she said.

"I wish you could, but I don't know what's going on. It might be dangerous. I can't shake this feeling that what Rocky told us has to do with the Falls."

"Gary, last night is not something I indulge in lightly. I don't want to be another listing in your black book. I want to help you. Don't you know that?" she asked, feeling an unfamiliar tightening in her chest.

They arrived at Jacqui's hotel room. Gary fumbled with the door key. A feast of lights greeted them as they entered, with a view of the mountains and the enchanting harbour.

Jacqui ordered Gary into a hot shower, noticing how the strain of the past few days was showing. She gently bathed his face in ice, wincing at the size of his cuts.

"Is that better, sweetheart?" she asked, rinsing out the cool cloth. "How do you feel?"

"You'll have to come a little closer to ask me that," he said, pulling at the strap of Jacqui's dress.

"Garfield Winston Gordon. Aren't you the least bit tired?" she asked.

"I'm never too tired for you," he whispered, pulling her into his embrace with an urgency that left them both breathless.

Gary felt as if he was lost in the swell of the ocean, a tide of emotions overwhelming him as each of his senses were filled with her. The all-consuming fiery release left them both trembling and they lay entwined in the afterglow of their love, each breath and touch magnified a thousand times.

"Go to sleep," he whispered, nuzzling her neck.

"I just want to hold on to this for as long as I can," she whispered, turning to kiss him. Gary buried his face in her sweetly scented hair, knowing exactly how she felt.

* * *

The sun was streaming into the room as Jacqui slowly woke up, feeling as boneless as a kitten. Without opening her eyes, she savoured the presence next to her, slowly moving her hand to caress Gary's warm smooth skin.

A smile played on her lips even before she opened her eyes to find Gary, propped on his side, gazing at her. Touching her cheek, he slid the sheet off, exposing her body to the sunlight.

"May I please speak to Mr. Jameson," asked Ainsley when he finally got through the international lines to Washington DC. After several frantic phone calls to contacts at the FBI and Interpol, he had been given Jameson's name at the United States Department of Customs.

"There is no Mr. Jameson here at US Customs unless you are looking for my father in Massachusetts," a woman said with a laugh, accustomed to having people ask for Mr. Jameson. "I'm Katherine Charlotte Jameson, known as Casey."

"I'm so sorry. I was expecting a man. I'm Commander Ainsley Gunther of the United Nations Anti-Narcotics Task Force in Jamaica. I was told you might be of some assistance to me."

"Yes, Pierre Monclure, my counterpart, called and told me I could expect to hear from you. How can I help you?" she asked.

"Were you able to trace the payments made into those Cayman accounts?" asked Ainsley.

"I think I have the information that you are looking for," said Casey. Ainsley tried to understand the fragments of information and how they related to the cocaine and guns in Jamaica.

"I hope I get a chance to meet you one day," he said when she had finished, wondering what this woman who had the voice of an angel looked like.

"You never know if you'll get lucky. Let me know how things go in Jamaica," she said.

* * *

Jacqui was lost in thought on the late dusky afternoon drive back to Kingston. She paid little attention to the banter between Sheila and Dick. The mountains, rolling endlessly on the horizon, were silhouetted by a blue halo. The sea crashed noisily along the coast, demonstrating the full backlash of the storm.

After they passed Annotto Bay, a small town with a stinking river running through it, Dick slowed the car as they came upon a long, slow-moving line of traffic.

"What's wrong?" asked Sheila.

"It may be an accident," said Dick, as they inched forward. Eventually they saw that several large boulders had been placed in the road. There was a group of men at the blockade, dressed in sloppy clothing, holding a kitchen assortment of weapons.

"What the hell is going on here?" asked Dick. "I don't see one set of stripes."

"Maybe it's a roadblock because the government hasn't fixed their water," said Sheila.

A man with an M-16 moved toward the car. Jacqui glanced past him to the man who was walking behind him, peering into each car. Seeing his face made her draw her breath. She quickly looked down to his hands, and saw that his right hand was missing a thumb.

"Dick, this isn't a roadblock," Jacqui whispered hoarsely. "It's a trap for me. That man is known as the Lord of Trench Town. They think I know something. I can't let them get me!"

"I'll stall them," Dick said immediately. "Can you get out of here?"

"Where will you go?" Sheila asked, her eyes wide with concern.

"I'll get to The Falls somehow," said Jacqui, crouching down, watching Sputo's progress along the line of cars.

When the first man approached the car, Dick opened his door suddenly, catching the man in his legs. As he staggered backwards, Dick stuck out his leg and tripped him. He fell to the ground, his M-16 clattering uselessly at his side.

Jacqui was out of the car before he hit the ground. She

slithered behind the car before sprinting across the road.

"Stop. Wait," she heard as she started running, afraid to look back. The sound of an approaching motorcycle was coming closer. She turned around to see Sputo running towards her, a gun in his good hand. The motorcycle was about to pass him.

"Miss Jacqui!"

The motorcycle was nipping her heels when she turned around again. It was Natty, the Rastafarian whom she had met with Gary that night at White River. His locks and his medallion were flapping in the wind.

"Get on," he hissed. Jacqui jumped on the back and grabbed onto Natty. With one final backward glance, she saw Sputo fade in the distance, his shouts dimming as they moved away with electrifying speed.

Chapter 18

The guard raised the barrier when Gary approached the entrance to The Falls. There was no evidence of the storm as he pulled into the parking lot and slammed the door, heading towards the lobby. He had to navigate his way through a group of tourists who were playing hide and seek around the property.

"Excuse me," said Gary, walking past two dazed-looking women who had obviously spent the entire afternoon at the bar.

"Hi, Gary," called Trina, walking over to greet him.

"Hi," he said, looking at his daughter. The way she smiled at him was so like his father's, he was always momentarily taken aback.

"Is everything all right in Portland?" she asked.

"They opened the road and hope to have power by the end of the week," he said.

"We have to talk," said Trina. "About Warren."

"So we do," said Gary, taking her arm and leading her to a pair of Queen Anne chairs in the corner of the lobby.

"Do you love him?" he asked, feeling a tinge of jealousy.

"Very much. I know you think I'm young, but he's what I want. I'll be able to build a life with Warren."

"I'm sorry," said Gary. "About everything. I know I haven't been much of a father, but in the time I've known about your existence, I've tried. I really have."

"I know," she said.

"We'll work things out," he said, giving her a reassuring

hug.

"That's just what your mother said when I spoke to her this evening," said Trina. She looked around and saw Jennifer Parker, the front desk clerk, signalling her. "Sorry, Dad. I'm running the dance contest at the island party and I'm waiting to hear from the band. See you later." She leaned over to kiss his cheek affectionately before running over to the front desk.

Gary sat there for a moment, the emotion welling up inside him. It was the first time she had ever called him 'Dad'. Unleashed feelings of tenderness and pride overwhelmed him as he watched her stride elegantly across the lobby.

Gary went to the front desk to check his messages. To his disappointment, Ainsley hadn't called. Greeting a few staff members, he entered the executive suite and paused at Robert's closed door. He knocked and waited for Robert's grunt before he opened the door.

"I thought I told everyone I didn't want to be disturbed," said Robert, his eyes glued to Patrick, an elderly hotel worker. He glanced up to see Gary. "I'm sorry. I didn't know it was you. Sit down. You might want to hear this. Please start again, Patrick."

"Well, sir. Two days ago me see an Island Builders truck come to de building site. Dem unload bags and dem bring dem down to de cove. Whispering Waters," he added.

"How many men?" asked Gary.

"Dat day it was two, but today, me see t'ree men walk to de cove," said Patrick. "Dem do de same t'ing de odder day. "

"When?" asked Gary, knowing 'the other day' in Jamaica could mean last year.

"De first time dem do a dance party," said Patrick.

"Two weeks ago," said Robert. Patrick left quietly as they digested the news.

"I would like to know what the hell is going on," said Robert.

"I have an idea," said Gary calmly. "Have you heard from Ainsley?"

"No, I haven't and I would feel a lot better if we did. I would like you to settle this mess immediately," he demanded. "I am overbooked and have fifty obnoxious travel agents for tonight's island party. I'm going on vacation to New York. It's more peaceful there."

"You always say that," said Gary with a laugh. "I'm going to the villa and then out to the island. Let me know if you hear from Ainsley."

"Will do," said Robert, picking up his phone. He watched his boyhood friend leave, wondering what was going on.

* * *

Jacqui felt every muscle in her body shaking as they bounced along the gnarled road. Natty was covering the miles of dangerous curves at intense speeds, mindless of the treachery of passing cars and cattle.

At a rum bar next to a deserted marina near Oracabessa, ten miles from The Falls, Natty finally stopped. It was early evening. The smell of barbecued chicken rose in the yard, mingled with the stench of rotting garbage.

"We jus' goin' stop here for a minute while me tek care of some business."

"No problem, Natty," said Jacqui as she lifted herself off the seat, her knees nearly buckling as she stood. "I don't know what I would have done if you hadn't come around."

"Yuh nah have fe t'ank me. Yuh is a friend of Gary's. Anudder t'ing – me nuh too happy with dem idiots."

"Which idiots?" she asked.

"Dat Storm and Thunder posse. Dem t'ink dem rule

t'ings. Dem nuh rule bumboklaat. "

A woman came out to talk to Natty. He took a piece of newspaper out of his large tam and unrolled the ganja he had secreted inside. The woman picked up a bud and sniffed it. Natty rolled a spliff, lit it and took a long draw before passing it to the woman. Then he turned to Jacqui. "Come, gal, I wan' show you some'ting," he said, motioning her to the dock.

They saw a pleasure boat, almost hidden by shadows, in the nearly deserted marina. As they moved closer to the boat, they could see two men on the dock. Jacqui inadvertently stepped on a rotting plank. The groan of splintering wood shattered the silence. They froze in their steps, slipping down to the dock, moulding their bodies to the shadows.

"What was dat?" asked a tall brawny man. He stopped working and peered into the darkness.

"What was what?" asked the other, his hand on his gun as he took one step forward.

"Me nuh know. Me t'ink me 'ear somet'ing," said the first as he took two cautious steps forward and peered into the darkness. The water beside the boat rippled as a school of flying fish passed.

"Is nutting, man," he said eventually.

"Yuh sure, Whiskey?" asked the other. "Me nuh wan' fe mess up. Is a big t'ing tonight."

"It all cool. Hurry up, nuh, Jack. We haffi mek time."

They stayed in their positions until Natty was sure they were pulling away. Cautiously raising her head, Jacqui glanced at the name illuminated by the rising moon. She wasn't surprised when she saw *Foolish Pleasure* painted on its bough.

"Tell Gary," whispered Natty as they cautiously returned to his bike. "Dem headed fe de Falls. Me no wan' nutting bad fe happen to me friend."

* * *

Gary showered and dressed in a pair of dark khaki pants and a dark green polo shirt that picked up the flecks of colour from his worried eyes. He tried to reach Ainsley again, but was given the same message by Corporal Kelly. He then tried to reach Jacqui. The phone rang without an answer at Ainsley's apartment. Glancing at his watch, Gary knew she should have arrived. He held the phone to his ear, just listening to the continual ringing, trying to reassure himself that there was nothing to worry about. He kept hoping against hope that if he hung on long enough she would walk in and pick it up.

He walked through the property, stopping at the front desk before going to the Sunset Lounge. Preoccupied, he sat down at the bar.

Ainsley was sitting on one of the love seats, attentively listening as a new arrival, obviously enamoured with his good looks, divulged her life story. He was casually dressed in a dark linen shirt and trousers and his boots were handmade. His deportment was impeccable and the air of a debonair rascal clung subtly to him like a mountain mist.

He spotted Gary and graciously made his excuses, walking over to the bar.

"Good to see you, GG," he said, putting out his hand. "The hotel looks lovely."

Gary looked up at him in surprise. "Where have you been? Did you get my message?"

"What message?" asked Ainsley, taken aback.

"I have been in touch with your office twice today," said Gary. "I left a message with Corporal Kelly."

"One of Bloomfield's men," said Ainsley. He gestured towards the deserted swimming pool, motioning with his eyes for Gary to follow.

256

"The United Nations Anti-Narcotics Task Force and the prime minister's office have a bit of a communication problem or a demarcation of authority as Derrick calls it," he continued once they were out of earshot. "Anyway, there are a few more pressing matters. The information that Natty gave you about the guns was right."

"You found them?" asked Gary.

"In an abandoned sugar warehouse. A case of Desert Eagles from Israel Military Industries with the serial numbers rubbed off. By the time we got there, several guns were missing. The configurations of the bullets match those that were taken out of Donald," said Ainsley, directing Gary towards the beach.

"It's all related to the Storm and Thunder posse who are operating in over a dozen cities in the United States. They have been using Whispering Waters as their base for transshipping narcotics. They were pretty smart to know that you would never be raided, but tonight will be different. We have it from an excellent source that they will be moving a major shipment out of Whispering Waters tonight."

"Take a look at this," said Gary, pulling out the picture of *Foolish Pleasure* that Jacqui had given him. "I believe this boat may be involved. Do you know anything about it?"

"Where did you get this?" Ainsley asked, staring at the photograph. "This boat is now under surveillance."

"Jacqui found it at Whittingham's house in a guest room," said Gary.

"Ah, yes, the mysterious Jacqui," said Ainsley, smiling. "I hear she is quite lovely."

"And quite taken," returned Gary. Ainsley looked at his friend in surprise. He had known Gary most of his life. They had caroused and hell-raised in the far-off ports of the world, but he had never known Gary to allow a woman to get under his skin.

"Robert reports that an Island Builders truck delivered

257

packages here two days ago and three men slipped onto the property this afternoon, heading towards Whispering Waters," said Gary.

"I have a surveillance team set up at Whispering Waters and another team deployed around the hotel. The cove is wired with microphones and video cameras. There is a Coast Guard PT boat patrolling to the west, one police marine boat standing by and the helicopter is over the first hill, awaiting my signal."

"Ainsley, I have three hundred guests here tonight. You can't just run a military operation. Robert will kill both of us," said Gary.

"Every precaution will be taken. My men are very well trained. Between them, they have trained in Israel, Canada, Britain, India, Namibia and America. I think they can handle this. We'll just contain the guests on the island and keep the danger to a minimum."

* * *

Trina hung the blue lantern on the porch of Gary's villa. Then she went inside and put the finishing touches on her makeup before slipping into a billowing skirt and a slinky tube top. She checked over her music tapes for the dance contest and looked at her watch for the fifth time. She slipped the flashlight with a blue bulb in her pocket. She set the blue light on the porch, making sure it was blazing brightly. As soon as the guests were dancing to Sparrow's latest calypso, she would give the signal.

* * *

"Sorry, you can't go in there. It's for hotel guests only," said the security guard at the entrance to The Falls, taking in Jacqui's unkempt appearance and the retreating dreadlocks with one sweeping disdainful glance.

"I'm here to see Mr. Gary Gordon," she said, trying to straighten out Gary's wrinkled drawstring shorts and shirt.

"He's not here. If you would like to leave your name, I will let him know you stopped by," said the guard.

"Please," said Jacqui, with mounting irritation. "I see his car in the parking lot. Let me just leave a message at the desk," she begged.

The guard finally relented to her pleading and a sense of relief flooded her once she was inside the property. At least she could warn Gary.

She walked past the Sunset Lounge towards the pool and passed the beach bar, her eyes peeled for Gary. The guests, wearing straw hats and brightly printed shirts, were lining up at the dock to take the canoes to the island party.

"Is Mr. Gordon on the island?" asked Jacqui to one of the recreation coordinators standing on the dock.

"I've been here since early evening and I haven't seen him," said the young man.

She walked across the beach, moving towards the stables. An eerie silence had settled as she neared the stable. She heard the familiar neigh of Island Jack as she walked along the trail to Gary's cliffside villa.

She increased her pace as she got close to the villa, seeing the blue light hanging from the porch like a welcome lantern. Dashing up the verandah steps, she was disappointed to find the door locked and the house deserted. The big bay-glass window showed a two-storeyed cathedral ceiling and the living room was decorated in white and blue with plants in every corner.

Jacqui turned, and surveyed the scene. The island party was in full swing, the lights blaring like the Christmas tree in Rockefeller Centre. She reluctantly walked down the stairs and made her way back to the trail. Halfway down, her foot caught a rock and she stumbled, almost falling. There was a rustle of leaves behind her and as she turned, she was grabbed by the throat from behind. The blow to her head brought a cloudburst in front of her eyes. Her body crumpled like a falling domino and she twitched for a moment before she lay perfectly still.

* * *

Gary and Ainsley were crouched under a Flame in the Forest tree, on the eastern cliff overlooking Whispering Waters. It was perfectly still except for the lulling sound of the tide and the tree frogs.

"*Foolish Pleasure* is two miles away and moving in," whispered Ainsley, passing the night vision to Gary. Looking into the night vision was like looking at a black and white television screen except the black was replaced by green. There was a dull burst of light on the far side of the cove, where the steep cliff met the sea.

"What's that in the corner?" asked Gary, returning the night vision to Ainsley.

"One of the chaps guarding the stash is smoking a cigarette," said Ainsley, pausing for a moment as he listened to a radio communication from his ear phone. "Do you know it wasn't until this afternoon that I remembered when you and I explored that cave. We couldn't have been more than six," said Ainsley.

"You were so scared that we had discovered the road to China," said Gary, smiling at the memory while recognizing that Ainsley was trying to relax him.

"I know we could pick up the stash, but some fancy lawyer would have this thrown out of court," whispered Ainsley. "We need the videotaped proof of the act." He took out his weapon of choice, a .44 Magnum. He checked it and placed it on the ground next to him, then reached into his knapsack. He took out a 9mm pistol and handed it to

Gary.

"Just in case," he said. "You do remember how to use it?"

"It's been a while," Gary said, picking up the weapon, checking its weight in his hand.

"Come in Alpha One, Come in Alpha One," came over the radio. "Subject half mile off the reef in a Princess," said the voice.

"Beta, do you read?" asked Ainsley.

"Roger," replied Beta. "Party is in full swing. All guests at hotel are accounted for. Suspect keeps checking watch. Wait, she is flashing a light."

"Charlie and Delta units, stand by for approach," said Ainsley. They both watched the blue light flash on the island. The light flashed once, then twice, and after a ten-second interval, one more short flash.

Gary watched in horrified fascination as *Foolish Pleasure* slipped effortlessly through the treacherous reef. A huge brawny man was silhouetted on the bough as the boat turned off one engine and he threw off the anchor, securing it before the motor was cut.

Gary and Ainsley watched two members of the Storm and Thunder posse emerge from the cave and, with the assistance of the two men from the boat, methodically load the vessel with cement bags filled with cocaine.

"How much stuff do you think it is?" asked Gary.

"I estimate it must be about four thousand pounds of cocaine with a street value of at least one hundred and eighty million dollars," whispered Ainsley.

"Alpha One, this is Charlie. Stand by for a man approaching the beach."

"Roger," said Ainsley as they watched a movement across the cove that gripped their attention.

* * *

Sputo stared at the limp figure that was sprawled on the ground before him. Kicking her body over, he reassured himself that it was Jacqui. He had missed her at the roadblock but she wasn't going to get away this time. She had caused too many problems to be allowed to live through the night.

Pulling a piece of cord from his pocket, he put the gun under his arm, turning Jacqui over again so that she was lying face down. He awkwardly tied her hands together, having trouble pulling the knot without his thumb. Satisfied with his effort, he dragged Jacqui's body a few feet before hoisting her effortlessly on his shoulder and walking towards the cove.

The loading was temporarily halted.

"Who dat?" called Whiskey as Jack and Bigga pulled out their guns.

"Is me," Sputo said as he neared the boat. "Me ketch de raas gal." He approached the group and dropped Jacqui's body on the sand like a sack of potatoes, kicking her once.

"Who is she, Sputo?" asked Whiskey.

"She is a spy. DEA, CIA, FBI. Me nuh know, but it no matter. She bad and she know too much," said Sputo, walking over to kick her body again.

* * *

"It's Jacqui," said Gary, choking for breath as he instantly recognized the shirt as the one he had given her that morning. "They have Jacqui," he croaked.

"Code Daisy, Code Daisy," said Ainsley into the radio as he put a restraining arm on Gary.

"Move in now," grunted Gary, shaking off Ainsley's arm, oblivious of everything else. In less than a second he had watched his whole world start to fall apart. He had never felt more threatened or vulnerable in his life.

"Let them finish loading. If we storm in, they'll kill her," Ainsley said, not wanting to add that she might already be dead.

Gary looked at Jacqui, lying face down on the beach. She was so still, so limp, that he felt that his very being was ripped from him. He took several deep breaths, collecting himself, becoming more concentrated and driven than he had ever been in his life.

"Ainsley, we have to move in now," he said tersely.

"We will," said Ainsley calmly, holding up his hand as the posse resumed loading. His breathing was steady, but inside he was filled with dread. He knew the Storm and Thunder posse were ruthless killers who believed dead men tell no tales.

* * *

The minutes ticked by with excruciating slowness while the final bags were loaded. Whiskey received his payment from Sputo. The boat engine started, the sound harshly breaking the quiet.

"What yu gonna do wid her?" asked Whiskey. "Yuh wan' us fe tek care of her?"

"Watch what me a do," said Sputo. He picked Jacqui up at the waist with one hand and dragged her inert body into the water. "Yu haffi see what t'ree days in de sea do to a body. She soon look like a blowfish," he said, his sinister laugh bouncing off the walls of the cove.

"Surrender immediately," barked a voice as a blaring light blew up in their faces, blinding them.

Sputo dropped Jacqui's body and reached for his gun, struggling out of the water. Whiskey drew his gun, shooting into the bush twenty feet from where Gary and Ainsley were crouched.

Gary jumped up. "I'll cover you," said Ainsley as Gary hurtled himself down the craggy face of the cliff. He had to get to Jacqui. She was dying and he was helpless.

A shot rang out from *Foolish Pleasure*, missing Gary by an inch. His eyes locked on Sputo who was steadying his gun on him. Gary watched him about to fire, knowing the bullet would not miss its mark. He prepared himself for the impact. Then, just above his ear, he felt the heat from the high-speed bullet fired with expert precision from Ainsley's .44 Magnum.

It lodged in Sputo's heart and Gary watched his eyes widen as the bullet burrowed itself deep within his chest cavity, piercing his lung and severing his blood supply, instantly paralyzing him. In the glare of the searchlight Gary watched the realization of death pass across his eyes.

"Trina," muttered Sputo, his eyes glassy as he expelled his last breath. His body shuddered and then was still.

Whiskey fired a round, wounding an agent. The bark of his gun was silenced by a round of fire from an automatic M-16 that pulverized his body into a piece of swiss cheese.

Gary hit the ground, flying head first into the sand as the back-up agents moved in. Crawling on all fours, he reached the water's edge.

Gary dashed into the water where Sputo had thrown Jacqui. She had been underwater nearly a minute. Half-walking, half-swimming, he thrashed around, diving continually as he looked for her. Despair gripped him and he held back the tears of frustration that rose in his eyes. She couldn't be gone. He had only just found her.

* * *

Roused into consciousness by the black water that rushed around her head, Jacqui sputtered for breath. Slowly regaining her senses, she slipped one hand out of the poorly tied knot, swimming underwater as far as she could before cautiously surfacing for air. The ringing in her head was as jarring as the gunfire on the beach.

Taking a deep breath, she willed one arm over the other, her body moving mechanically, her hand outstretched to avoid crashing into the coral reef. By the time her hand slammed down onto the rough mass, she heard the gunfire stop. Her head was throbbing hard as she used the last ounce of her strength to pull herself onto the sharp coral wall. It was only then that she let the misty darkness overtake her as she collapsed in exhaustion.

* * *

Ainsley was supervising the final stages of the operation, ensuring that there were at least two copies of the videotapes. He watched Gary, who was half out of his mind with grief searching for Jacqui. Instructing four coast guard drivers to assist him, he shook his head in regret, not holding much hope that Jacqui was still alive.

He walked over to where Sputo's body lay. Sergeant Hardcastle was searching the body. "Commander, I think I have something here," he said, handing Ainsley a slim diary.

Ainsley turned the pages thoughtfully. "Good work, Sergeant, I think you just found the missing key. I want you to get four of your best men and send them out on *Foolish Pleasure*. I don't want anyone to find out about this until we've met with the appropriate parties."

"Anything else, sir?" the sergeant asked.

"Yes. I want you to go to the island and find Trina Doyan and bring her back to me," he said tersely. "Don't let her stall you."

"What is the next plan of action?" asked Captain West.

"Well, according to this log, it seems the transfers and payoffs are due tomorrow. Robert Unity, also known as

Sputo, and his boss Charles Whittingham, were the local link. It seems Whittingham is working with someone in the government who is very powerful. It is all beginning to make sense," said Ainsley, more to himself than to Captain West.

"How so, Commander?" the captain asked.

"The South American drug cartels will do anything to get their cocaine to the United States markets. About six months ago, we received reports that they were using the cays south of the Pedro banks. Baja Nuevo and the Roncador Cay, which belong to Colombia, are being used as rendezvous points for the Jamaican fishermen and their South American counterparts. They pick up the cocaine and return to Jamaica, their boats filled with it."

"Where do they land?" asked Captain West. "Our JDF men are supposed to be patrolling the waters."

"There are so many hidden coves on the south coast, especially around .Farraquehers Point and Treasure Beach, that it is impossible for our limited sea power to cover the waters. They land at some remote spot and use legitimate vehicles to transport their cocaine to places on the north coast like Whispering Waters, which is very safe from the police, and then they wait until they are ready to ship out."

"And a little always remains on the island," said Captain West grimly.

"Absolutely," said Ainsley. "It fuels the drug problem in the ghetto. With an operation this size, they must have some very powerful, well placed US contacts who have the ability to move large amounts of cash and arms."

The posse members were being handcuffed and readied for transport to Spanish Town Penitentiary. Jack saw Sputo's and Whiskey's bodies lying on the beach in pools of blood. The whites of his eyes began to show.

"Yuh kill me brethren. Me a go lick yuh down. Me a go come and me a beat yuh, me a go t'ump yuh an' den me a go kill yuh. Me have de guns. Me have de power. Storm and

Thunder posse, a we rule t'ings," he cried.

"I suggest you contain yourself," said Ainsley quietly, with such a voice of authority that Jack shut up. "The only thing you will rule is how many pages of the Bible you will read per day. Get them out of here."

* * *

Trina was dragged reluctantly away from the island party by Sergeant Hardcastle. Her apprehension grew as he forced her down the rocky-faced cliff of the cove. When she saw the activity, her heart beat faster.

"What's going on here?" she asked.

"I was going to ask you the same question," said Ainsley.

"Did the guests from the island party take the kayaks here and have a nude campfire?" she asked.

"Good try," said Ainsley.

Gary, knee-deep in water and filled with desperation in his fruitless search for Jacqui, saw Trina being brought onto the beach. Leaving the four divers, he hurried out of the water.

"What's going on here?" asked Gary. "Why is she here?"

"I'm sorry to be the one to tell you this, but Trina has been helping her friends in the Storm and Thunder posse use The Falls as a base to ship cocaine out of Jamaica."

"That's a damn lie," she said vehemently.

"Is that so?" Ainsley asked. "Would you mind telling us why the code word of blue champagne which is written in this book is the same message you got this evening? Please don't try to deny it. I spoke to Jennifer Parker. You were seen signalling the boat with a blue light. It's still in your pocket, isn't it?"

Gary felt his last traces of control flitter away. His face

was taut with fury and the veins on his neck popped out. "Why," he whispered hoarsely.

"I don't know what he's talking about," said Trina, her eyes roaming the beach. Suddenly, she saw a familiar figure lying in the sand. "Sputo," she screamed, breaking away from the group and running to him, a sob catching in her throat as she dropped to her knees by his side.

"You killed him," she shouted at Gary. "You killed the one person that loved me."

"He's a dangerous man who tried to kill Gary," said Ainsley, trying not to see the devastation on Gary's face.

"He was my father," Trina wept, holding Sputo's limp hand. "He looked after me all my life. He loved me!"

"I never knew," Gary said quietly.

"You were never interested in finding out. You never cared," she sobbed.

"You sold your birthright," said Gary, feeling like a failure for the first time in his life.

"My birthright was that your father had a pang of conscience about his son's bastard daughter. You never considered me a legitimate member of the great Gordon family. I knew that you would figure out a way to take it all away from me," she cried.

"Why did you do it?" he asked, his throat tight, unable to bear his daughter's betrayal and losing Jacqui in one night.

"You don't know what it's like to grow up as a high-coloured girl in the ghetto," she said. Her expression grew cold and blank. "You don't know what it's like to live in a one-room tenement with a bathroom for eighteen people and the constant sound of gunfire and mad dogs. Ever since I was a little girl, there have been men leering at me from corners, offering me money for five minutes behind a zinc shack that reeked of urine.

"Where were you then, my high and mighty father?"

said Trina accusingly. "Were you there to protect me as the men ran after me and gang-raped me? Were you there to provide me with food and give me Christmas presents? You were too busy playing polo around the world and having your picture taken with beautiful women on your arm. When did you ever care?" she asked, as her voice broke again and she buried her face in Sputo's shoulder, her body racked with sobs.

Gary walked away heavyhearted, knowing he was responsible for what had happened. A sense of hopelessness was beginning to overwhelm him as he joined the divers again.

The powerful white light kept on sweeping the beach. Gary, waist deep in the black water, peered out into the darkness.

"We may have to wait until tomorrow to find her body," said one of the divers.

Suddenly the light from the helicopter picked up a form on the reef. "I see something!" Gary yelled.

Ainsley radioed the helicopter to move in. Within a minute, the rescue team dropped one man down.

Gary was watching from the water, almost afraid to hope that Jacqui was alive. He watched as they dropped a sling and strapped her into the carrier. The helicopter moved carefully across the cove, and deposited her on the beach.

He was standing at the water's edge, his arms outstretched to grab the rope and help to settle her on the sand. He cradled her head to his chest, gingerly feeling for her pulse.

"Get a doctor," he called out hoarsely as Ainsley joined him.

Jacqui opened her eyes slowly, trying to adjust her focus. She thought she was dreaming that she was safe in Gary's arms. Something harsh and stinging invaded her nostrils, causing her to see stars. She gripped his arms. When she felt the pain in her body, she knew she was alive.

For a brief moment, she focussed on Gary's face, trying to smile wanly, but even that movement brought excruciating pain. There was a second face next to Gary's that looked vaguely familiar, but then the mistiness overtook her.

She was vaguely aware of being carried into Gary's bedroom at his villa, and of Gary's hand by her side. She was barely coherent when the doctor examined her.

Afterwards Gary brought a pitcher of cold coconut water upstairs. He had been amazed when the doctor told him that, except for some cuts and bruises and a huge bump on the head, she was fine. He found Jacqui lying inert on the bed. He stripped off her wet clothes. Her back was a series of bruises that were already turning yellow and purple. Tenderly, he wiped down her body with a soft rag. Wrapping her in his warm robe, he patted her hair with a thick towel, gently letting his fingertips roam over her tangled curls, with a whisperlike touch, until he felt the bump on her head that was the size of a robin's egg. He saw her grimace and suppress a moan of pain.

"I know it hurts, sweetheart. I'm going to get you an ice pack."

Gary ran downstairs to fix the ice pack and returned to find her trying to sit up. She cried out in pain.

"Gary, they were after me at the roadblock," she said. She was trying to communicate urgently but the words were coming out disjointed.

"Hush, love. Everything's all right now. Lie back down." He applied the topical medicine to her hands. She didn't make a sound, but the sting brought tears to her eyes that Gary kissed away. Pulling her up and supporting her shoulders, he handed her two pills and a glass of cool coconut water.

"I couldn't find you," she mumbled, the room spinning

out of control.

"I'm here now."

"Stay with me," she whispered, unable to keep her eyes open.

"Hush and go to sleep. I'll be right by your side," he whispered, turning the light off and pulling the soft cotton blanket up around her. He kissed her cheek, stroking her hair as he waited for her breathing to become steady and regular before pulling the rocking chair to the edge of the bed.

From her troubled sleep, Jacqui felt as if someone was strangling her. No matter how hard she tried to move her arms to push the hands away, she couldn't. A small whimper escaped her lips as she struggled with the demons that played havoc in her mind.

Gary was at her side in a second, holding her as he whispered soothingly. "Shh, wake up, Jacqui. It's just a bad dream. You're safe." He pulled her up into a sitting position, holding her cheek against his until her shaking stopped.

"That's better," he whispered, slipping her back against the down pillows as he pushed her wet hair off her damp face.

"Don't leave me," she whispered.

"I'll be here for you." It was a simple statement, and he didn't know how much he meant it until he heard his own voice. His heart was frayed with the intensity of his feelings. He sat by her side all night, not allowing the delicious escape of sleep to overtake him in case she needed him. He had almost lost her and he sat there wondering what his life would be like if she wasn't there to fill the open chasm in his soul.

Chapter 19

Jacqui woke up and found that every muscle of her body was racked with pain. She tried to raise her head off the pillow but dropped it again as a blinding spasm left her gasping for air. She moved very slowly to the bathroom, noting her pale and drained reflection in the mirror. She gratefully rested her head against the white marble tiles, relishing their coolness.

Gary came in shortly afterwards. He immediately came to her. She didn't say a word, but held out her arms to him.

He took solace in her embrace, holding her for a long time.

"Trina was in on it," he eventually said, the hurt raw in his voice.

"I'm sorry," she said, holding him, wishing she could take away his pain.

"How do you feel?" he asked gently, running his finger over her dark circles.

"I feel as if there are one hundred little red rum devils having an all-night soca fete in my head," she said with a wan smile.

"You know, I almost went crazy when I thought I lost you," he said, looking into her now familiar eyes.

"You couldn't get rid of me that easily," said Jacqui.

"I am going to keep an eye on you from now on," he said. "We're going back to town. Do you think you're up to the trip?"

"No problem," she said, leaning back against the pillow,

trying to suppress a grimace.

* * *

The entrance to King's House, home of the governor general, the queen's representative on the island, was guarded by a huge stone gate. The soldiers on duty recognized Ainsley's Jaguar and waved it on along the road that was lined with pink and white lilies.

"What are we doing here?" asked Gary, shifting uncomfortably. "I thought we were going to see the prime minister."

"Sir Oliver Cameron is a man of great integrity and he will be able to help us," Ainsley responded as they reached the roundabout in front of the wooden colonial great house.

"The governor general is a ceremonial figurehead who doesn't hold any real power. I think we should go see the prime minister and tell him everything."

"Gary, we can't do that. The guilty party was the biggest contributor to his last political campaign. Do you really think he'd do anything that would destabilize his position or create any problems in his party?"

"What makes you think the governor general will listen to us?" Gary asked.

"He will listen to us out of courtesy," said Ainsley. "He is the only one who can handle this situation with decorum and diplomacy without destabilizing the government. If we bring it to Jamaica House they will be looking for scapegoats like a witch hunt in Salem. Stop procrastinating or we'll be late."

"We have to agree on something before I go in with you," said Gary. Ainsley looked at him quizzically, knowing Gary rarely offered conditions.

"You can't bring up Trina's involvement at all. I will deal with Whittingham. Sputo is the only other one who really knew and he's dead. She is young and stupid, but she's still my daughter," he said.

* * *

An hour later Ainsley headed over to the command post of the task force. He parked his Jaguar under an almond tree and walked inside, looking at the puddles of water on the floor from the leaking roof, compliments of the tropical depression.

"Commander, good afternoon," said Corporal Kelly.

"Good afternoon, corporal," said Ainsley pleasantly. "Please ask Captain West and Sergeant Hardcastle to join me in my office immediately."

Ainsley went down the hall into his office. The walls were filled with commendations and trophies, including those for his service in the Sinai, Namibia and Sri Lanka. He buzzed for his secretary, desperately needing a bracing cup of Blue Mountain coffee.

"Commander, you wanted to see us?" asked Captain West, walking into his office, followed by the sergeant. The look of success was written across their faces.

"Gentlemen, that was an excellent piece of work last night," began Ainsley. "My compliments to you and your men."

"Thank you, sir," they said in unison, pleased with his compliment. They knew that their commander was short on praise, but when he gave some, it was usually well deserved.

"First thing I want you to do is send Corporal Kelly off on a very long errand to some place like Mocho. That should keep him busy. Then I want you to assemble all the men for a debriefing. Our next mission begins in three minutes. We are going to catch a murderer," he said, looking at them. "Any questions?"

"No, sir," they responded.

274

"Then get going. You only have two minutes and fifty seconds left."

* * *

Later that afternoon, the team was set up behind a house in Norbrook, a fashionable neighbourhood in the St. Andrew hills above Kingston. There were two cars on the street when Ainsley arrived.

"What's the status?" he asked.

"According to that notebook we found on Unity, he should be leaving to pick up his payoff within the hour," said Captain West.

"Let's wait and see. I hope you're right," said Ainsley as he prepared to wait. "If not, we're going in."

An hour later, his back was beginning to burn with tension and his neck ached from a lack of sleep. They watched the driver bring the specially configured car around to the front of the house. Several moments passed before the front door opened.

"Let's go," said Ainsley, followed by Captain West and Sergeant Hardcastle, joined by the highest ranking police superintendent in the service.

"Good evening, Derrick," said Ainsley as Derrick Bloomfield laboriously made his way down the three steps to the driveway.

"Ainsley," said Derrick in surprise, looking at the law enforcement officers. "I'm just on my way out. I have a pressing appointment. Come see me in the morning."

"Your payment won't be arriving today or any other day," said Ainsley. "You've imported your last load of guns and collected money for the safe passage of narcotics for the last time."

"How dare you speak to me like that!" Derrick sputtered. "I am a highly esteemed member of Parliament for Port Kingston. I don't appreciate your comments and I'm sure the prime minister won't take kindly to your accusations." Derrick's brow was slick with sweat. "Now if you will excuse me, I must be going."

"You did a nice job murdering Donald Francis," said Ainsley, walking over and eyeing him. "Real clean. An Israeli Desert Eagle fired at close range. You couldn't miss, could you?" he asked.

"I don't know what you're talking about. I didn't murder Donald Francis. You know he was involved in drug trafficking. That's the very thing you and I are dedicated to eradicating, within the demarcation of our authority, of course," said Derrick, his eyes bulging out of his face as he surreptitiously eyed the officer behind Ainsley.

"You had a clean gun that couldn't be traced," said Ainsley. "When you heard that Donald was going to meet Clock that night, you had to act fast. You were too worried that Clock would reveal your identity. You didn't have time to arrange for Sputo or any of your Storm and Thunder henchmen to do your dirty work for you, so you had to do it yourself."

"You will never be able to prove that," said Derrick.

"Don't bet on it. Your old friend Sputo, the Lord of Trench Town, has," said Ainsley, watching him sweat. "You helped destroy his identity so he could operate freely again."

"You have it all wrong," said Derrick, his jacket stained with one huge spreading mass of perspiration. "My guidance and direction are needed. No one understands how things operate in the ghetto. If I wasn't there, it would be a chaotic war."

"You're in league with Charles Whittingham and the gunmen from Port Kingston to keep a tight rein on your political constituency. You are the one who is instigating the ghetto war."

"I'm preserving Jamaica. I'm saving it from itself," said

Derrick, taking a step backwards.

"Don't move, Derrick. I would really hate to have to shoot you, though I don't think a bullet would do you much damage. You are going to my version of hell," said Ainsley.

"I have a right to make a call. I am a duly elected member of parliament. You owe me at least that courtesy," said Derrick, his face ashen.

"Who are you going to call?" asked Ainsley. "Allistair Brody, your lawyer, or your connection in New York? Take him away and put him in isolation with water only."

"What are the charges?" asked the police superintendent, the handcuffs ready and waiting.

"Murder and crimes against the state," said Ainsley. "If that doesn't get you the end of a rope, Derrick, you'll at least have to look forward to thirty years in the government guest house with a lovely view of the harbour."

* * *

Charles paced anxiously around his office and accidentally bumped his hip on the heavy mahogany desk. Sputo was over an hour late and he hadn't heard from him since the afternoon before. He dialled Derrick's number, but was told he had just left.

He heard the vehicles approach the gate and on looking outside, recognized the unmarked police car assigned to the Anti-Narcotics Task Force. Grabbing his gun from his briefcase, he opened the safe, took out a wad of cash and stuffed it into his back pocket. He heard the knocking on the door as he unlocked the back gate and slipped through, climbing into his Trooper that he had parked there that afternoon.

He pulled out into rush-hour traffic, honking his horn and sliding in and out of the maze of cars. He had to go somewhere safe to think. The car seemed to automatically navigate to Maxfield Avenue.

"What yuh doing here?" asked Shereen, answering the door in a turquoise bra and black slip, her hair in multi-coloured curlers.

"Where's Sally?" he asked.

"She restin'. Every time yuh come, she nuh wuk fe two days," replied the madam. "She haffi wuk tonight."

"No, she doesn't," said Charles, handing her a bill that had her eyes shining like the lights of a Christmas tree. She slipped the money into her huge cleavage and motioned Charles upstairs.

Greater Sally heard the footsteps on the stairs and pulled the belt of her robe tighter. She knew it was Charles even before he burst into the room with a wild look in his eyes.

"So, big daddy," she said, her wine-coloured lips pouting. "Yuh gonna be nice to Greater Sally today?"

"Shut up and take your clothes off," he ordered, his member already hard from the sight of her.

"Tell me why me should," she said, getting up to walk over to the tiny table by the bed.

"Shut de raas up and tek off yuh clothes," said Charles, throwing the money on the bed.

Greater Sally looked at the money and quickly picked it up, tucking it away in her fake satin bag.

She slowly loosened the belt of her robe and dropped it halfway, hearing Charles's quick intake of breath and his pants unzipping. A small smile crossed her lips. With the money she had saved, she would be able to pay for her tuition at modelling school.

* * *

The cocktail party for the Jamaican of the Year was underway by the pool of the New Kingston Hotel. The eighty-foot palms swayed in the undertaker breeze that cooled the Liguanea Plains. Members of the diplomatic corps, the honourables, the ministers, doctors and barristers as well as every other important member of the community were there for the award. Jacqui joined the party and was greeted by Dick and Sheila Robinson and Caspar Chen.

"We've been so worried about you. We heard what happened. Where's Gary and is everything all right now?" asked Dick, noticing Jacqui's bandaged hand.

"I'm fine, and I think Gary should be arriving shortly," she said, giving them a brief account of her experience.

"How much longer are you staying?" asked Sheila.

"Just another day. I really have to be getting back. There's the story to finish and an issue to launch in New York."

"How exciting. I haven't been to New York in years," said Sheila. "The theatre, Chinatown and your wonderful Central Park. It's such an exciting place compared to Jamaica."

"How can you say that, Sheila," said PJ as he and Gary joined the group.

"Yes, Sheila, how can you say that?" asked Jacqui with amusement. "Since I've been here there has been an earthquake, a landslide and a tropical depression, not to mention the manmade disasters. But this island does have a way of reviving the spirit and soothing the soul," she added, looking at Gary who returned her smile.

Men in red uniforms trimmed in black ushered the guests into the ballroom which was decorated with exquisite arrangements of birds of paradise and anthuriums. The military band was playing a march, wearing velvet brocade jackets trimmed in gold rope and pale green pants. Their tasselled caps were perched precariously on their heads, moving with the tempo of the music.

Gary squeezed her hand before he went to join the processional, and Jacqui followed the Robinsons to the table where they were joined by Caspar, PJ, Trevor and Maxine. The master of ceremonies took his place at the podium, asking the guests to remain standing as the honour guard escorted the nominees into the ballroom.

"Field Marshall Sticky, DJ personality," he announced as a slim man wearing a silver-fringed tuxedo moved down the aisle as if he were dancing.

"Miss Matty, distinguished actress and poetess." A large round woman wearing a colourful head wrap walked down the aisle.

"Garfield Winston Gordon, farmer and businessman," announced the master of ceremonies. Gary walked into the ballroom, his eyes focussed ahead.

"Garfield," whispered Jacqui, her mouth open in shock.

"I know," said Maxine, laughing, as the audience clapped the nominees before they took their seats.

A withered old man who looked as if he needed help walking up to the podium was introduced as Sir Isaac Aarons, the founder of the largest group of companies on the island, knighted by Her Majesty, the Queen, a barrister by training, Jamaica's representative to the West Indian Union and the first recipient of the Jamaican of the Year award.

"Jamaica is at a crossroads," began Sir Isaac, whose frail frame belied a voice that was as strong and as clear as a bell. "Ever since I was a little boy, every speech I can ever remember started with those words. This occasion is no different.

"I can remember when the tram cars ran down King Street and races were held at Knutsford Park. I also remember with great pride that this tiny island sent hundreds of men to serve in the West India Regiment during those dark days of World War Two. It wasn't only the men who served, though. From bake sales to dances, the fine women of this country raised enough money to buy a plane," said

Sir Isaac, his eyes twinkling. "Mind you, in those days a plane was made of papier maché and wire.

"We are indeed at a crossroads again as Jamaica continues to struggle, but let me say how proud I am to see another Jamaican of the Year Award, which symbolizes the contribution an individual has made to the development of our nation," concluded Sir Isaac to thunderous applause. Jacqui was touched by his words and commanding presence.

The master of ceremonies then introduced the governor general. "The Jamaican of the Year award is chosen by the people to honour an individual who has made a substantial contribution to the nation," began Sir Oliver Cameron in a raspy voice.

"The man that the people have chosen has brought his country honours on polo fields across the world, has improved our trade relations with Russia and has been a driving force in our tourism industry. It gives me great pleasure to present this award to Mr. Gary Gordon." The applause was deafening as Gary came to the podium.

"I don't know if I should be standing here," began Gary. "Sir Isaac and the governor general are a hard act to follow. This is a wonderful honour, however it's far from exclusively mine. Each and every person who I've worked with shares this award because we are all committed to building a better Jamaica. Ladies and gentlemen, thank you for this honour."

It took Gary several moments to make his way from the podium and accept congratulations from well wishers. He stopped to kiss the Countess who looked splendid in a royal blue dress.

"Congratulations," said Jacqui, leaning over to kiss him when he reached the table.

"Thanks, but I expect a much greater reception when this is over," he said with a smile, his eyes raking her face, noting the dark circles under her eyes.

They were served dinner which was constantly

interrupted as Gary graciously accepted congratulations. As dessert was being served, one of the ushers came to their table.

"Miss Devron, I have an emergency overseas call for you from a Mr. Josh Travers in New York. Would you come with me?" he asked.

"Gary, I'll be back in a minute," she said, squeezing his hand before she followed the man to the front desk. What could Josh's call be about? She picked up the courtesy phone, but before she could utter a word, she felt someone grab her arm. The phone clattered to the floor.

"Don't move or say a word," said Charles menacingly.

"Get your hands off of me," she said, only to feel the metal chamber of Charles's gun in the small of her back.

"Where is the ledger? I want it now. No more games," he said.

"I don't know what you're talking about," she said hotly.

"Like hell you don't. Get moving," he said, wrenching her arm and pushing her towards the door to the courtyard.

* * *

Gary was bored as he listened distractedly to an elderly English woman while constantly watching the door for Jacqui to return. Ainsley appeared at the entrance to the ballroom and Gary quickly excused himself, moving through the crowd.

"What happened?" he asked.

"We got Derrick locked up in Hunt's Bay but we missed Charles. Where is Jacqui?" asked Ainsley.

"She went to get a phone call," said Gary. The realization suddenly dawned on him. "Oh God!"

Closely followed by Ainsley, Gary raced down into the lobby. There was no sign of Jacqui. They ran out into the deserted courtyard, just in time to see her being dragged by

Charles past the pool. She was fighting him every step of the way until he finally slapped her across the face and shoved the gun under her neck.

"Shut up, you stupid bitch. You've caused too much trouble. Where is the ledger?" he rasped.

"Let her go, Whittingham," shouted Gary as he and Ainsley ran through the courtyard.

"Fuck you, Gordon. Get away from me," he said, holding the gun menacingly.

"Aren't you just the big man with the gun," said Gary, taking one step closer to him. "It's me you really want to take on. Be a real man, Charles. Fight me. You've been dying to do it for years," he said, watching Jacqui's terrified eyes. He couldn't bear to see Charles's hands on her. He had to get her away from him.

"Don't take one step closer or I'll kill her," said Charles, his eyes bulging with anger as he wrenched Jacqui's arm behind her back.

"The game is over" said Gary, watching Jacqui's frightened eyes. "*Foolish Pleasure* was caught last night and Sputo is dead."

"You raasklaat," Charles said, pulling at Jacqui.

"Fight me, Charles," said Gary, praying he could divert Charles enough to leave Jacqui alone. He pulled off his tie and slipped off his jacket, tossing them to Ainsley. "Do it for the sainted memory of your old man, the Causeway jumper."

"I want to see you dead so I can spit on your grave," said Charles, pushing Jacqui to the ground as he took one menacing step towards Gary.

"You can kill me, Charles, but you will never beat me," said Gary.

Jacqui picked herself up. Instantly, Ainsley was at Gary's side, his hand on the butt of his gun, though he knew Gary could handle Charles.

"It was never enough for you that your father destroyed my family," said Charles, moving with the practice of a street fighter. He tucked his gun in his pants and threw a wild punch at Gary.

"My father never destroyed your father. He destroyed himself with his greed and corruption, just like you," said Gary.

"It's not greed. It's my birthright. Whispering Waters is as much mine as it is yours. Our father had no right to give it away," said Charles.

"Our father?" said Gary incredulously. "You really are totally mad. Neville is not your father."

"You know your father always had a thing for my mother. When Bruce found out how Neville had double-crossed him with the unions and had seduced my mother, he couldn't face himself. Your father killed him just as if he pushed him off the Causeway," said Charles.

"You think you're my half-brother," said Gary with a laugh. "You are so deluded to think that my father would even look at your mother."

"He did. I saw them at parties dancing together. He couldn't keep his hands off her. Do you think I want Neville to be my father? I don't, but he is and half of everything you own is mine. All I want is Whispering Waters."

"Whether he was right or wrong, my father gave Whispering Waters to Trina, my daughter. You are no more my brother than the devil," said Gary.

"Trina is your daughter?" Charles gasped.

"Yes, she is. Think about it, Charles. With your convoluted thinking that you're my half-brother, you now can think that you've been lusting after your own niece. But again, nothing that you think or do surprises me, knowing the kind of low-life, common, unscrupulous man that you are," said Gary.

"Just like our father," said Charles.

"Just like your father," said Gary.

Charles let out a right hook, hitting Gary on the jaw.

"You're finished," grunted Gary, landing a punch in Charles's gut.

"Never. Not to you," he rasped, lashing out at Gary. They fell to the ground, exchanging punches that would have left most men unconscious. For each of them, it was the fight of their existence.

"Ainsley, stop this," said Jacqui, gripping his arm.

"This is something they both have to do," said Ainsley.

Gary pounded Charles with his bloodied fists as they rolled dangerously towards the pool. Gary punched Charles in the face and they both fell into the pool. Charles gasped for air, not knowing how to swim.

"Leave a little for my men," called Ainsley. He reached in and pulled Charles out by the collar, draping his body over the side of the pool as he planted his boot at his neck. Charles gasped for air and lay there like a limp rag doll.

"Do be a good little chap and get up without too much fuss," warned Ainsley, lifting his gun from his belt. "We're going to take a nice drive and you can tell me all about your friend Sputo and your activities with Mr. Bloomfield in Port Kingston."

Oblivious of the crowd that had gathered, Gary stumbled towards Jacqui and took her in his arms, hearing her draw her first steady breath. "It's all over," he whispered in her ear, holding her tightly, unmindful of how wet he was.

"What's going on here?" demanded PJ.

"Our friend Gary is just taking care of business," said Ainsley with a smile.

"So I see," said PJ. "Is this your first official act as Jamaican of the Year?"

* * *

"Love, what happened between us was so special that it leaves me breathless. Don't ever doubt that," he said, taking her in his arms.

"I'll try not to," she said, gently disengaging herself.

"Where are you going?" he asked.

"There's something I want to show you," she said, going into the bedroom and bringing out her bag. She reached inside the zippered pocket and took out a small picture, handing it to him.

"When I was at The Falls, I took a walk to Whispering Waters during the island party. A boat was waiting by the reef and there were men at the cove. I saw a blue light on the island that flashed. Then the boat moved in. I swear I saw a gun.

"I found this picture of a boat which I think is called *Foolish Pleasure* among Geoff's papers at Dreamscape," she continued. "Charles knows I found it, that's why he was roughing me up. It must mean something."

"Sweetheart, I want you to listen to me," said Gary, paling considerably. "I'm not sure what's going down, but you are not safe. You know too much and what's more important – they think you know too much."

"This is as much my fight as it is yours," said Jacqui.

"Please listen to me, my love. These guys play for keeps. They think dead men tell no tales. The Robinsons are leaving this afternoon. I want you to go back to Ainsley's house in Kingston and lock yourself in," he said, taking her in his arms.

"Gary," she protested, but his lips lingered on hers, leaving her breathless.

"I beg you to do this. I'll call you there tonight. Reserve tomorrow night for us," he said.

* * *

Their intimacy was electric as he touched her behind her knee with his index finger, then slowly traced his finger up her thigh, along her belly to her breast.

Everything melted in a blur for her as she moved to take him in her velvet embrace. He gently held her hands down as he traced the moist lips of her sweetness. Jacqui was lost in the oblivion of the passion he had begun to create.

He spread her hair on the pillow like a fan, and gazed at her again, not touching her – almost not needing to. They were soulmates who had travelled different paths to reach the same fork in the road. Nothing else mattered.

Jacqui felt every fibre of her being respond as he kissed her lingeringly. She was drowning in the sea, engulfed in an ocean of pleasure that knew no bounds. Gary instinctively knew how to please her, playing her body like a master violinist completely at one with his music, as instinct, finesse and passion blended together in exquisite splendour.

She watched the flutter of his eyelids and the knit of his brow as she searched for his warmest part, wrapping it lovingly beneath her soft hands. Gasping with pleasure, he entwined one hand through her hair and placed the other across the small of her back, lifting her to him, drawing her out, willing her to respond. Their chests rose and fell at the same time.

His body, her spirit, their warmth drew them together in a precision that was more destiny than a twist of fate. She was totally lost, swept up on the cloud of passion he had created. Jacqui closed her eyes, her hands clasped with Gary's as she matched his tempo, until they both exploded on a crest as bright as the tropical sun.

* * *

Gary stumbled out of bed an hour later, not wanting to leave Jacqui's side, but overcome by a gnawing hunger. He went into the sitting room to call room service and when he turned around, he knocked Jacqui's bag off the table, sending its contents to the floor.

He had started to pick up her things when he saw her open notebook by the chair leg. He reached over to pick it up and Jacqui's bold handwriting flashed out to him. He was immediately caught up in her promotional idea for The Falls at Ocho Rios. It was a very simple but brilliant proposal. She had outlined the entire campaign involving *Elegant Travel*, The Falls and the media houses. He glanced at the sleeping figure on the bed with a smile.

This was not the woman to underestimate.

* * *

"Ainsley, what a pleasant surprise. I didn't expect to see you before I left," said Jacqui, opening the door of the hotel suite.

"I just came by to see if you were okay."

"I'm recovering from my adventures," Jacqui smiled.

"You'll be relieved to know that Charles is enjoying his stay at Hunt's Bay until we can expedite his trial. Derrick is crying from hunger – it seems that he doesn't like the food at the government guest house," said Ainsley with a smile that quickly faded. "Unfortunately, there is another piece to this puzzle that is not solved."

"What's that?" asked Jacqui.

"Charles and Derrick were just links in the cocaine, cash and arms triangle. There are huge amounts of money that move through the Cayman Islands and we haven't tracked who is behind it. We're working with US Customs to try to track these payments to the myriad of banks around the world but it is like trying to find a needle in a haystack. I've been racking my brains trying to come up with a profile of the monsters who know how to manipulate governments and systems. They must be power-hungry egomaniacs who are familiar with countries and have a very legitimate cover. Trying to make sense of the tiny fragments of information to find out who is really behind it has been one of the major challenges of my career," said Ainsley.

Jacqui was silent for a moment, then she went into her bag. She handed the ledger to Ainsley.

"This is what Charles was after last night. I think it may help you," she said.

He scanned the contents quickly, before looking up at her in surprise.

"I know my name is there," Jacqui said. "That's why I told Gary this fight is as much mine as it is his or yours. All I ask is that you keep me posted. I have a few of my own scores to settle."

"That's a promise," said Ainsley.

* * *

Jacqui looked out at the scenery and the luminescent sea that stretched along the Palisadoes Road. The view tore at a piece of her heart. Gary rested her hand on his thigh in such an intimate gesture that Jacqui had to hold back a tear.

"You know, I am really going to miss Jamaica. There is something enchanting and mesmerizing about this island," she said, listening to the sounds of the sea.

"Why don't you stay awhile," he suggested, for the tenth time that day.

"I can't stay now, you know that," she said. "I've got some things I have to settle." She shivered even though the night air was warm.

"So when will I see you again?" she asked unashamedly.

"When I take *Elegant Travel* to court," he laughed as they pulled up to the departure unloading area. "You'll hear from me soon, I promise," he added softly.

He got out of the car and gave the porter her bag. He walked over to her side and slipped his hand in hers, pulling her into his arms. He held her tightly, wishing he wouldn't have to face the empty void she was leaving in his soul.

"Jacqui, there is so much I want to tell you," he said.

"Some things are better left unsaid," she said, touching his lips gently, before kissing him.

"I hate saying goodbye," he said, pushing a wisp of hair away from her face and tucking it behind her ear. "Think of us down here in the tropics." His eyes glistened with tears.

"Every day," she promised.

"Walk good, my love," he whispered, breathing in her scent that he knew would haunt him in the weeks to come.

* * *

Jacqui felt empty and fragile as she automatically showed her documents at immigration and entered the departure lounge.

She found it hard to walk without feeling physical pain. Grace Jones's "My Jamaican Guy" was playing on the public address system and Jacqui could only sigh.

When the flight was called she walked down the long corridor filled with rum advertisements to the tarmac. Hostile-looking security guards were posted along every gate. She took several deep breaths of the salty Kingston air and a last look at the five peaks of the Blue Mountains silhouetted against the blue velvet sky.

She had just settled in her seat in first class when the stewardess approached her.

"Are you Miss Devron?" she asked.

"Yes," said Jacqui, hoping she wasn't going to be bumped off the flight.

She returned in a moment with a split of champagne and a single red rose. "Compliments of Mr. Gordon. Enjoy your flight."

The enormity of her loss struck her as the engines began warming up. She felt as if she had just lost a limb and had to learn to live without it. She slipped on her earphones to drown out the noise and the monotonous pre-flight instructions. Bob Marley's mournful song, "No Woman No Cry," invaded her ears, the words pricking at her soul. "Good friends we've had, good friends we've lost along the way." The melody echoed her feelings. Pushing her head back on the cushion, she let the tears fall freely, knowing she wouldn't have been able to stop crying even if she had tried.

The plane taxied down the runway. Holding the rose to her cheek, she watched the lights of Kingston fade from view as the island slipped into a veil of darkness surrounded by a black sea.

Chapter 20

Jacqui woke up with a start, her body drenched in sweat on that hot summer morning even though the air conditioner was humming at full blast. She kept her eyes closed. She had an overwhelming sensation that Gary was lying next to her. She could almost hear his steady breathing and feel the warmth of his body, so tangible was his presence. She reached over to the side of the bed and the familiar feeling of despondency washed over her when she felt the smooth sheet next to her. She wondered if she would ever stop waking up in the morning and having as her first thought a wish that Gary was beside her.

Her hands were uncharacteristically shaky as she tried to apply her makeup. The clock radio had switched on, the news filled with reports of sections of the city that were blocked off for the visit of the president of the Soviet Union. Jimmy Cliff's song, "Many Rivers to Cross," came on. It caught Jacqui by surprise, the words bringing a rush of memories that were so achingly familiar. The phone rang, startling Jacqui out of her reverie.

"Hello, kitten," said her father, Jace Devron.

"Hi, Daddy. How are you?" she asked, trying to sound buoyant.

"I'm fine. I'm just calling to find out how you are?" he asked.

"I think I'm all right," she said.

"I wanted to wish you luck today. I wish I could be there with you," said Jace.

"Thanks, Daddy. I really appreciate that. When the shit hits the fan, don't let the guys at the hangar tease you too much."

"Not a chance. I'm too proud of you," he said. "Come home soon. I miss you."

"I'll come home as soon as I can. I promise," said Jacqui, a catch in her voice.

"I'll have the Piper Cub gassed up and waiting for you," he said.

* * *

Half an hour later Jacqui was walking down Lexington Avenue. The city was already stifling hot and the pavement was oozing heat. She felt the soles of her shoes melting in the sidewalk. The streets were crowded with legions of men in republican blue and demure grey suits marching along like toy soldiers mass-manufactured in Taiwan.

"Extra! Extra! Read all about it. Soviet President Arrives In New York," shouted the newspaper hawker.

Jacqui handed him her change, flashing him a smile, and made her way down 53rd Street to the Third Avenue Coffee Shop. The air conditioner wasn't working properly and the café was hotter than outside. She pushed her way past four Boy George lookalikes and a group of Polish nationals to grab a seat at the counter. Gus moved down and poured her a cup of coffee. She took one sip and pushed it away.

"What did you do to the coffee this morning, Gus?" she asked. "It's terrible."

"It's the same Maxwell House coffee I've made every day for the past forty years. Ever since you came back from Jamaica, you've been complaining about my coffee," he said, taking away her cup, obviously hurt.

Jacqui closed her eyes and recalled every detail of Paradise Cottage and her time with Gary. The memories of the fragrance of the earth after a tropical rain and the black velvet sky studded with stars like diamonds grew more poignant with each passing day. It was a longing in her soul that would take a lifetime to overcome.

But from today on she was going to work on it. She couldn't understand how, after her first call to tell him that she had arrived safely, he had not called her back even once. She knew she hadn't imagined what had happened between them. It was very real. But it seemed to have faded on his side as quickly as the setting tropical sun.

* * *

Geoff Roth sat in the living room of his East Side coop with a view of the river. He had stubbed out his ninth cigarette for the morning and his lungs still craved nicotine. He was wearing his Calvin Klein underwear and paced between the couch and the desk, his hands slick with sweat as he tried to reach Congressman Ogilvy's office. After swearing and cursing at the secretary and the legislative assistant, he was finally put through.

"Geoff, I told you never to call me here," said James Ogilvy.

"I had to. I haven't heard from you. Have you seen today's *Times*?" asked Geoff.

"Yes, I have, and I really can't help you," said the Congressman. "I've been brought up on charges by the House Ethics Committee. I don't think we should talk again. Please don't contact me." The phone went dead.

Geoff lit another cigarette and read the special to the *New York Times* by Jacqui Devron. His stomach rolled over each line and then each word of "Tropical Sins – An Illusion of Paradise."

She had been so thorough that not one stone was left unturned. With the cooperation of the United Nations

Anti-Narcotics Task Force and other organizations, she had ferreted out Derrick Bloomfield's connection, exposed Charles's role and his involvement with the Storm and Thunder posse, traced the cash from Cayman and directly implicated Geoff.

The worst was the comment made by Marty King, vowing to never again associate himself or his organization with GRI Advertising. He stared at Jacqui's name under the headline. If she had been next to him, he would have taken his bare hands and strangled her. He dropped his head in his hands, wondering how he was going to get out of this mess. He would have to sue, of course. Surely she couldn't prove his involvement. There was a knock on the door.

He looked through the peephole to see a tall beautiful blonde.

"Mr. Roth? Mr. Geoff Roth?" asked the blonde. "Can you please let me in? I would love to talk to you."

Geoff opened the door a slit, too preoccupied to remember that he was wearing only his briefs. His eyes stared unseeingly at her.

"Yes?" he said.

"My name is Casey Jameson. I'm a special agent with the United States Customs Service. I need to ask you a couple of tiny questions regarding your Cayman Island bank account," she said with a brilliant smile.

"I don't know what you're talking about. Get the hell out of here," he said, trying to push the door closed.

"I wouldn't do that," she said, pulling her gun. "You see, Mr. Roth, I have a warrant for your arrest."

"My arrest," he said, a sinking feeling in his stomach.

"I'm sorry," she said sweetly. "I'll try to be very gentle with you when we take you downtown, but my friends won't be nearly as pleasant as I am." She entered the room, followed by two men.

"Allow me to introduce you to Special Agents Kirk and

Rodgers of the US Customs Service. They will become your very good friends."

"Casey, at least this time he's sort of dressed," said Agent Rodgers, smiling. "You're lucky, Mr. Roth. The last time Casey arrested someone, she pulled them out of the shower."

"I have the right to make a phone call," he said, moving towards the phone.

"Not until we take you to your new home," said Casey. "By the way, there is one other person I would like you to meet. This is Marion Walters of the Internal Revenue Service," she said courteously as a short fat woman wearing Ked sneakers waddled through the door carrying two shopping bags.

"Nice view," said Marion appreciatively. "I wonder how much it will go for on the auction."

"Marion doesn't believe in fancy trappings, but she has everything she needs to find out what you've been up to."

In her shopping bags were two calculators, pencils and accounting paper. "Baby, when I get finished with you, you won't know what hit you," said Marion Walters with a deep laugh, shaking her fat frame.

"Mr. Roth, I would take her word for it. She did my taxes for me," said Casey with a brilliant smile as she cuffed Geoff.

"Can't I at least dress?" pleaded Geoff.

"Sure. Pants only. By the way, thanks for making my job so easy. Good luck, boys, and I'll see you downtown later. Marion, go easy on Mr. Roth. I suspect he's had a rough morning."

* * *

Josh sat in his office, his tie in the file basket, his shirt-sleeves rolled up and his collar unbuttoned when Jacqui popped her head into his office.

"Jacqui. Come on in. Where the hell have you been?" he asked. "Do you realize that you still work here? You haven't been in the office for more than an hour in the past two weeks. The September issue is opening tonight at the Rainbow Room and Pat has had to take care of all the arrangements."

"I've been busy," said Jacqui.

"You know our policy about freelancing," said Josh sternly. "Who are you working for? Is it *Condé Nast*? They have been trying to hire Matthew for the past few months. If it's the salary, we'll try to match it."

"I'm not working for *Condé Nast*, Josh," said Jacqui. "I've been investigating the King Casino scandal which involved the magazine, you and me." She looked directly at him.

"I know it involves you, but not me," said Josh. "Someone has been feeding you a line."

"Josh, someone once asked me if we were friends. I said we were. I was wrong – so very wrong. Friends don't put their friends in jeopardy or use them," she said evenly.

"I don't know what you're getting at, but I would never dream of putting you in jeopardy," said Josh.

"Sure you did. You passed the money you received from the King Casino deal into my account. I know about you. You accept bribes in exchange for glowing reviews," said Jacqui.

"Don't be so naive. You should know after all this time how the business works. Your story on Morocco helped the government get a development loan for a new tourism project. All I got was a small commission. You were the one who was responsible for the new investment. A positive review means the difference between development money and starvation," said Josh.

"We're supposed to be credible journalists, not public

relations practitioners who go to the highest bidder," said Jacqui in disgust. "What you are doing is unethical. After all our years together, I think you owe me an explanation."

"I don't owe you anything. I gave you every break along the way. If it wasn't for me, you wouldn't be where you are today."

"Josh, I beg to differ with you and I think you do owe me an explanation. You see, I found a ledger that belongs to a company called FPL. It had my name on it," said Jacqui, as she tossed him a copy, watching his eyes for a reaction. "It also had your name on it. Obviously Geoff was a better bookkeeper than you thought. You passed the money you received from the King Casino deal into my account. The ledger detailed a number of bank transfers in your name through Cayman to a Swiss account, and there's a Jamaican connection, so like I said, I think you do owe me an explanation." She spoke calmly but her eyes were tinged with yellow in controlled fury.

Josh scanned the ledger and then shrugged. "You went to Jamaica on a glamour trip I planned for you. I lived there – with the people in the worst part of the ghetto. I worked with a man who was running for parliament in the area. We soon realized that in order to ever achieve anything, we had to divide and rule the opposing factions. We maintained the precious balance of power that was so critical. Without that, the area would have been in constant turmoil. You just visited the island. I lived there in the Third World with its backyard politics."

"Don't try to sweeten this. You laundered drug money with Geoff Roth to buy arms. You were Derrick Bloomfield's contact in the States. I finally understand why you spend more time up in the air than on the ground. What you are really doing is pedalling your influence and trading it for arms. That's how you've been able to live beyond your means all these years. I sometimes wondered about that,"

298

she said, looking directly at him. "So how did you get the money from the King Casino?"

"Geoff," he said. "I have access to all the reporters' and editors' bank records for payment purposes. I washed the money through your account and then had my bank in Switzerland telex that it had been deposited in the wrong account and arranged for a transfer of funds."

"Why me?" she asked.

"I just needed your account for twenty-four hours to escape Fiona's and the auditors' watchful eyes," said Josh.

"You sold me out," said Jacqui, shaking her head. "I would have expected it from anyone else but you."

"What are you complaining about. You're back on track. Australia is coming up and I'll give you the assignment. The little setback didn't hurt your career in the long run. Your story on Jamaica is going to be a smash. Wait till you see what has been lined up," said Josh, dismissing the conversation.

"I'm leaving *Elegant Travel*. I can't work with people I don't trust," said Jacqui.

"Jacqui, you can't just walk out on what we've built at the magazine because your ego has been bruised. Don't you see the influence we have?"

"I'll be at the launch tonight for Fiona's sake. Jamaica was my story. After that you won't be seeing me," said Jacqui firmly.

"What are you going to do?" he asked.

"Read today's *New York Times* for a start," she said, walking out without a backward glance.

* * *

The yellow checkered cab inched its way along 59th Street towards the West Side, trying to negotiate through the rerouted traffic. Gary sat back in the cab, taking in the sights and sounds of Manhattan, anxious to get to the Algonquin Hotel. The Armenian cab driver cursed the communists in five languages, using colourful expletives whose meaning Gary could easily guess at. His ears were burning by the time they reached Sixth Avenue. He pushed the money into the plastic holder and grabbed his royal blue carry-on before stepping into the street.

"Welcome back to the Algonquin," said Tony, the doorman who had been there since the end of World War II.

"It's nice to be back," said Gary, walking into the lobby that was permeated with history, with its oak panelling and Tiffany lamps.

"Good morning, Mr. Gordon," said Mr. Burns at the front desk. "It's good to have you back again. I've taken the liberty of putting you in the Somerset Maugham suite. Is there anything else you need?"

"Yes, as a matter of fact there is. I would like the September issue of *Elegant Travel* Magazine," said Gary.

"Yes, sir," said Mr. Burns. "I'll let Mr. Topkins, the concierge, know. No problem at all."

"Right. No problem," said Gary, smiling.

Gary started peeling off his clothes as soon as he walked into the suite. Ten days in Russia to sign the pimento contracts had made him crave some of the pleasures in life. The most sumptuous room in the best hotel in Moscow was illuminated by one bare light and had bath sheets the size of face towels. The noisy pipes had not allowed him one full night's sleep. He missed his home. He needed to smell the breeze gently scented with pimento and feel the rejuvenating rays of the tropical sun.

He stepped into the shower, enjoying the warm pressure of the warm water. The phone was ringing as he blasted himself with cold water. Grabbing a towel, he plodded into the bedroom.

"Gary, you finally arrived. How was Russia?" asked

Ainsley.

"Thank God, it was a little warmer than last time. Where are you calling from?" asked Gary.

"Let me just say I'm downtown. Is everything still set for tonight?"

"From my end. How about you?" asked Gary.

"It looks like everything is under control," said Ainsley. "Good luck with everything and I'll catch you later."

"Later," said Gary, hanging up the phone. He rubbed himself down vigorously, trying to rid his body of the effects of flying. He walked over to the window, looking out onto the Avenue of the Americas. He tried not to think of Jacqui, but her face, glowing in the morning sun, appeared before him. The vision was so clear he almost reached out to touch her. Normally a man of action, for the last two months he had wallowed in his own indecision and fear. Now he was ready to act.

* * *

"Mr. Gordon, I don't know how to tell you this," said Mr. Topkins, the concierge, when Gary emerged in the lobby an hour later. "I don't understand this, but there isn't a copy of *Elegant Travel* to be found. I personally checked every newsstand within a four-block radius. I don't believe the magazines were delivered."

"How can that be?" asked Gary, secretly amused. "It's a current magazine. I thought you could get anything in New York."

"I will get you a copy," said Mr. Topkins, ringing his hands. "I have to get you a copy. Just give me a little time."

Gary strolled to the cashier to change some money. Mr. Burns was busying himself at the front desk, trying to hide a snicker. "I think you have Topkins in a serious bind," said Mr. Burns.

"How so?" asked Gary.

"The concierges from the top hotels like the Plaza, Sherry Netherland, Essex House and the Waldorf have an ongoing competition that wagers that there isn't a reasonable request that can't be filled. They meet on a monthly basis and tell their most outrageous stories. I understand that they have quite a large betting pool and our Topkins was in the top of the running until you came by with your simple request," said Mr. Burns, enjoying the situation.

"I see," said Gary, highly amused.

"Anyway, I happen to have the general manager's copy which one of the secretaries borrowed and has asked that I give back when you're finished. Apparently it's the hottest item in New York today."

"I'll withdraw my request from Topkins. I wouldn't want to ruin his chances," said Gary, tucking the magazine under his arm. He sauntered into the lobby and settled on a rich green leather sofa. He ordered a drink and opened up the magazine, and looked for the full-page advertisement of The Falls. He turned his attention to Jacqui's article and became so engrossed that he neglected to drink his rum.

JAMAICA'S ELEGANT INNS - AN AUTUMN RETREAT

Come back, man Come back to the land of hot days, cool nights, temperate breezes and warm people.

Jamaica is more than long powder-white-sand beaches, azure seas and sultry nights. It's a rich, dynamic, multifaceted tropical island that has produced some of the word's finest rums, coffee, and cigars as well as singers and athletes.

In the land of Bob Marley, who almost singlehandedly brought reggae music to the international scene, the magical beauty of the island overwhelms you. How can it not with the chain of majestic Blue Mountains running down its spine, surrounded by sapphire seas, emerald hills, golden sands and violet sunsets. Many a tale and song have been written about the island that the writers of the Bible used, Errol Flynn claimed, as the source of their description of paradise.

There are two astounding records that should give you a good insight to the third largest Caribbean island. First, there are more miles of winding, bumpy, curvy roads per square mile than in any other country in the world. That's pretty impressive, but not as astounding as having more churches and bars per square mile than anywhere else in the world except New York City.

Jamaica is like an exotic and willful woman with a voluptuous and seductive past. Discovered by Columbus in 1494, she survived a dozen earthquakes, a score of hurricanes, slavery and colonial rule to attain self-government. Although independence was granted in 1962, the British influence is still felt in the parliamentary system, the deference to Her Majesty the Queen and the ritual of afternoon tea. In many ways, though, Jamaica is like a rebellious teenager, looking to see what she wants to be when she grows up, experimenting along the way.

Behind the glittering resorts and luxurious villas lies the contrast. The exotic mix of black, white, Indian, Chinese, Arab and Jew is startling. At first, you will think things seem to run without much rhyme or reason, but after a short time a method can be discerned in the madness. You cannot remain detached for very long. It lasts only until you feel yourself caught up in the rhythm and then you know you're hooked on cool runnings.

We've only brought you a small sampling from among the many beautiful resorts and attractions. There's The Falls at Ocho Rios, Pimento Hill Golf and Yacht Club near Montego Bay and the Blue Marlin Inn in Port Antonio.

We have just a few words of wisdom for our autumn travellers. "Soon come" could mean anything from a minute to an hour or a week. "No problem" – well, there's no problem that can't eventually be solved. Start saying "Good evening" after three in the afternoon and "Good night" after six in the evening. It's English driving, so look to your left – constantly.

For our more adventurous travellers, you can cruise around the island with stops in Boston, Quebec, Emerald Isle, Alexandria, Bombay and Java to name a few places. For those who are looking for points off the beaten track, there's Pretty Bottom, Pity Me Stomach and Me No Sen Yu No Come in the District of Look Behind in the Cockpit Country.

Beneath the surface, through the maze of lanes in downtown Kingston and the winding country roads, past the street vendors with luscious ripe Bombay mangoes, beats the heart and soul of a nation whose passion is life and whose life is passion. It doesn't matter if it's listening to a cricket game being played halfway around the world in the middle of the night, discussing local politics which dominates the bar talk, or dancing most of the night away to reggae and soca music. Jamaicans have a passion for living.

Come for a visit. Let the sun warm your body and your spirit as doctor birds and doctor breezes welcome you on your long-awaited autumn retreat.

Following this introduction was a detailed description and assessment of the resorts visited by Jacqui, including a glowing review of The Falls. Gary returned the magazine with thanks and strolled out of the hotel, past the famous Blue Bar and onto the street. His senses were assaulted by honking horns, garbage overflowing onto the sidewalks and several homeless people sitting in the alleyways with their shopping carts that held all their worldly possessions. He picked his way through the crowd on Fifth Avenue, the street one constant moving mass of motion that vibrated as a subway passed underneath. Gary stopped at every magazine stand he saw, asking for *Elegant Travel Magazine*. At the fourth stand, he finally questioned the man wearing the large apron with *Daily News* printed on it.

"I can't find *Elegant Travel* anywhere," said Gary to the short, fat, balding man. "What gives?"

"Vat gives?" asked the man in a broad Yiddish accent with a shrug. "I think they put something funny in the magazine. Try my brother's stand inside. He just got a shipment," he said, motioning to the building on the corner of 46th and Fifth Avenue.

Gary walked into the lobby of the building and stopped at the newsstand. A bundle of *Elegant Travel* magazines were still wrapped in their brown paper. The radio in the shop was tuned to WKNY.

"Phone lines are now open for the thirty-second caller in our Great Jamaica Escape," announced the DJ. "If you've read the latest issue of *Elegant Travel* carefully and have the right answer to this question, you could win an all-expenses paid vacation for two to The Falls at Ocho Rios in fabulous Jamaica."

Gary watched as six magazines sold in less than a minute. He paid for his two copies, lingering for a moment to hear a caller win a beach chair-in-bag as a consolation prize. He felt very pleased with himself as he walked up Fifth Avenue, clutching his precious copies under his arm.

* * *

Jacqui wandered the streets of Manhattan, feeling free for the first time in a long time. She relished the heat, bought an ice cream cone on the corner and watched a mime performance on the sidewalk. She spied a new dress shop that had opened on Madison Avenue. In the window was an exorbitantly priced, open-back, beaded black dress. She stared at it for a minute, her credit card sweating in her wallet. She walked inside to try it on and it fitted her like a glove.

"It's my party," she reasoned as she paid the store clerk.

On the radio she heard WKNY announce the Great Jamaica Escape. She listened breathlessly as a vacation to The Falls at Ocho Rios was given away, wondering who had stolen her idea.

* * *

Gary was pacing around Marty King's well appointed reception area, looking at photographs of the King Resorts and Casinos around the world. There was a flurry of people rushing in and out of the office.

"Mr. King will see you now," said the receptionist, motioning Gary inside.

"Gary, my boy. So nice to see you," said Marty, standing to his full six feet seven inches as he buttoned his jacket and extended his hand to Gary.

"It's great to see you," said Gary, looking around. "You've done quite well for yourself. This is quite an improvement over where we used to play cards."

"Funny you should mention that place. Even with all my casinos, I still go down to that club in the Bowery that moves every month or so for a good crap game," said Marty, laughing, as they both reminisced about the illegal gambling house in lower New York where they had met fifteen years before. "I was heading down there tonight for a session. Would you care to join me?"

"Not this evening," said Gary. "I have an engagement for The Falls this evening."

"I'm sorry to have kept you waiting, but the advertising agency I used to use was brought up on money laundering charges and my organization was implicated. I've been handling calls all day. If I ever get my hands on that little runt, he won't walk for a week. By the time I'm finished, there won't be any more GRI Advertising," said Marty, not noticing Gary's grin. "I gather you didn't come all the way to New York to see me without a good reason. What do you need?" he asked, offering Gary a cigar.

"I need your help," said Gary.

"Shoot," said Marty, lighting his cigar and blowing a big smoke ring.

"I have just received the licence to operate the first casino in Jamaica. I need the King Organization to manage it."

"You've known about the casino for over a week. I was just wondering what took you so long." Marty reached into a drawer in his massive desk and tossed a contract at Gary. "I had my lawyers draw it up when I heard the news."

"You're a crafty devil," said Gary, throwing his head back, his rich laughter filling the air.

"Let's shake on it now. We can leave all the legal bullshit to the lawyers. Heaven knows I pay them enough."

"No problem," said Gary, puffing away at his cigar.

"You remember my dad?" asked Marty.

"Sure," said Gary. "Who could ever forget him?"

"He just turned eighty-six and got his first pair of glasses. He's just in from Nassau with his new girlfriend. Let's go tell him that he will have a new King Casino to play in. He'll be so excited," said Marty, leading Gary out.

* * *

The Rainbow Room was a dazzling setting, suspended beneath the clouds and the stars, sixty-five hundred feet above the world. Jacqui entered the supper club late and saw all heads turned to the podium where Fiona Geller was welcoming the guests.

"To celebrate our issue on Jamaica, we couldn't think of

a more appropriate setting than the Rainbow Room where the Rockefellers and the Morgans danced and dined. The Rainbow Room enhances the spirit of New York and gives an added sense of confidence to all who pass through it. The experience is like a rite of passage, the memory of the visit a milestone in our minds."

Jacqui scanned the crowd and her eyes met Josh's. He looked at his watch and mouthed "You're late" before turning his attention back to Fiona.

"So is Jamaica, our tropical paradise featured this month by *Elegant Travel*. One visit there becomes a lingering memory, a milestone in our lives. This particular issue will have a special place in *Elegant Travel's* memory. We have received word that the magazine has been sold out all over New York and the Great Jamaica Escape campaign in conjunction with The Falls at Ocho Rios is a runaway success."

Jacqui felt a sense of accomplishment, but it was mixed with the disturbing feeling that she had been had. She again wondered who had stolen her idea. She looked up and her heart stopped: there was Gary, his eyes glowing. Beside him was the Countess, bedecked in emeralds.

"Hello, Jacqui. It was a wonderful article," he said, coming to her side. "You do remember my mother?"

"The Countess is your mother?" she said, shocked. "Of course I do," she added quickly, regaining her composure as Julia kissed her on both cheeks.

"Congratulations on your sold-out issue. You truly saw what was invisible to the eye," said the Countess, touching Jacqui's hand.

"Thank you, but I had very little to do with it. I think it was your son who made it happen," she said, meeting Gary's gaze briefly. "How is Trina?"

"Trina is much better," said the Countess. "Warren started his surgical training in Canada and Trina is going with him to study hotel management."

"I'm so glad," said Jacqui sincerely. Fiona Geller was working her way through the crowd.

"Hello, Jacqui. Mr. Gordon, we can't thank you enough for your assistance with our promotion. I don't think we've ever had such a successful issue."

"I'm glad I could be of some help. I do hope you will be covering the opening of The Casino at The Castle," said Gary.

"Of course we will," said Fiona, eyeing Jacqui. "I do hope this means that you've forgotten about the lawsuit."

"I did a long time ago," said Gary.

"Fiona, may I talk to you?" asked Jacqui, beckoning her two steps away from Gary and his mother. "I know this isn't the most opportune time to bring this up, but I'm leaving the magazine."

"Don't be ridiculous. You can't leave us. You're part of the family," Fiona exclaimed, loudly enough for Gary to hear. His surprise was evident.

"I've been asked to join the *Washington Post* as a foreign correspondent."

Fiona was quiet for a moment as she looked at Jacqui. "What can I say. I wish you all the luck in the world. You know that. Will you be available for freelance work?"

"I'll keep in touch and let you know," said Jacqui. She rejoined Gary and Julia.

"My dears, I'm gone. I'm meeting an old beau at The Carlyle," Julia said, winking at Jacqui. "Have a wonderful evening."

* * *

Josh walked to the Citicorp building in the hot summer night air, sorting through the plans he had put in motion that day. He now knew he had underestimated Jacqui, but he was still confident that she wouldn't turn him in. Even so, he had spent the greater part of the day opening up new accounts in the Jersey Islands and New Caledonia in the South Pacific.

He signed into the building and took the elevator to the twenty-seventh floor, enjoying the quiet. He unlocked his office door and turned on the small desk light and his computer. He waited while the machine warmed up and then checked if any deposit confirmations had come through. The transaction from Switzerland to the Jersey Islands was there as expected. He knew that the confirmations for the South Pacific transaction would take at least a day. He was reviewing the accounts when there was a knock on the door and a beautiful blonde walked in.

"Mr. Travers? Mr. Josh Travers?" asked Casey Jameson.

"Who are you and what are you doing here?" he asked.

"You could say I'm part of the security," said Casey. "I'm Special Agent Jameson with the United States Customs Service. We have a few questions regarding an eighty-million-dollar payment to a Cayman bank account in the name of FPL."

"I don't think I can be of help, Miss Jameson," said Josh.

"I'm so sorry to hear that. With all these illegal electronic transfers, we thought you might be able to clear up a misunderstanding that we had at the office."

"Look here, Miss Jameson. I'm the managing editor of one of the most prestigious travel magazines in the world. I don't know what you're talking about," said Josh.

"Neither did your friend Geoff Roth, but he was very gently persuaded to clear up some misunderstandings that we had," said Casey, a smile on her face. "I'm sorry you can't help us out, but there is someone who would very much like to meet you."

310

She walked to the door and let in Special Agents Kirk and Rodgers, followed by Commander Ainsley Gunther. "Mr. Travers, I just want you to know that I really believe you when you say that you don't know what I'm talking about. You must lead such an interesting life compared to the boring life we government workers lead. Isn't that right, boys?"

"It sure is, Casey," said Agent Kirk.

"Miss Jameson and gentlemen, I don't know how I can help you and I'm quite busy right now, so if you'll excuse me," said Josh, looking at Ainsley who looked vaguely familiar.

"Remember me, Josh?" asked Ainsley. "You should from your days in Port Kingston."

"I can't say that I do. Sorry I can't be of assistance. It was nice of you all to stop in unannounced, but I'm really quite tied up at the moment."

"You still think you can run the world, don't you?" said Ainsley.

"I don't know what you're talking about," said Josh, his patience ebbing.

"You run the world from your office in New York with your writers doing your dirty work for you," said Ainsley.

"I am the managing editor here. That's my job," said Josh.

"Is it your job to ensure that the posses get their guns?" Ainsley asked.

"I remember you now," said Josh. "You used to be on guard duty in Port Kingston. You should understand better than these Americans that I help developing countries reach their true potential. Our work allows them access to development money."

"You think the Third World needs a benevolent white godfather like you?" asked Ainsley. "You're trash – just like Derrick Bloomfield. Because of you children die of crack

311

overdoses in the streets and gun battles rip neighbourhoods and families apart. Guns that are bought with your embezzlement money."

"The balance is carefully monitored and there is stability," said Josh. "Isn't Jamaica thriving now?"

"Who are you to play God with people's lives?" asked Ainsley.

"I provide a necessary service for countries that need it. Without me, there would be chaos in the world," said Josh, looking at Ainsley as if he was the one who was crazy.

"I would like to tear you apart, but I'll wait until you're extradited to Kingston for your trial. I can promise you a room with a view next to your friend Derrick Bloomfield," said Ainsley, controlling his desire to kill Josh.

"Okay, boys, take him away," said Casey after reading him his rights. "I want you to copy every record off the hard disk. I don't want one detail to slip by us so the guys at Justice won't have any complaints." She looked at Ainsley who was watching her. "So, Commander, now that's complete, what's your pleasure?" she asked, her blue eyes meeting his.

"I beg your pardon," said Ainsley, not quite used to the self-assured style of American female law enforcement officers.

"What's your pleasure?" she repeated. "What are you drinking?"

"Rum. What are you drinking?" he asked.

"Tequila," she said with a smile. "Any preference as to where you would like to drink?"

"Commander, make sure you're close to home," called Special Agent Rodgers. "Casey can drink any man in the department under the table."

"Let's try the Algonquin," suggested Ainsley. "I haven't been thrown out of there in a while."

* * *

"Welcome to New York," said Jacqui coolly after Julia left. The big band at the Rainbow Room was playing a calypso tune.

"It's good to see you, Jacqui," said Gary.

"I don't think I've told you what a great promotional idea the radio contest was," she said. "How clever of you."

"I got it out of your notebook. It was all your idea. I didn't steal it, I just borrowed it," he said, moving closer to her and touching her waist, his fingers grazing the bare skin on her back. "I've missed you."

"Oh, really," she said, backing away. "Why haven't you called. It's been over two months. If you missed me so much, why didn't you call?"

"Jacqui, please don't make this any harder for me," he pleaded. "It is difficult for a man like me to admit I've fallen deeply in love with you and want to commit myself to you. It scared me how intensely I felt about you. I felt so vulnerable, I didn't know how to deal with it."

"I'm so glad you've made up your mind and decided to share it with me, but it's too late," said Jacqui, turning her back on him as he admired her open-back dress.

"You know, just looking at you from any angle still leaves me breathless," he said, placing a kiss on her shoulder that sent shivers down her spine.

"I'll call for an oxygen mask," said Jacqui sweetly.

"Hey girl, don't be feisty. I'm pouring my heart out to you. I have been half-alive without you. I've been haunted by your lingering presence each day. I want you to take a chance on us," he said, his eyes pleading with her.

"I don't like playing risky long shots," she said.

"It's a sure winner," said Gary.

"Gary, you just walk back into my life with your sweet

313

talk after weeks of silence and expect me to fall off my feet. I have feelings too, you know, I have insecurities. I'm not Cinderella and you can't ride up on your white charger and rescue me from evil. This isn't a game you're playing. This is reality – real life," she said.

"And I want to share it with you," he said.

"Gary, this whole experience in Jamaica has changed me," said Jacqui, looking out over the skyline, the Empire State Building looming in the distance. "I have had to question people I thought were my friends and the values I believed in. I'm not prepared to naively put all my trust in any one person again for a long time. I have to build myself back first. My life is taking a whole new direction. I'm going to be a foreign correspondent. Can you cope with that life?" She looked into his emerald eyes that were sparkling with hope.

"You don't have to give up anything to be with me, my love," said Gary, reaching out to tuck a stray curl behind her ear. "We'll work it out if we want to and I do want to."

"I guess we will," said Jacqui slowly, drawing a deep breath.

"So what's next?" he asked.

"Let's blow this joint," she said in a husky voice.

"What did you have in mind?" asked Gary.

"Eggs Benedict," said Jacqui.

"That's breakfast," he said.

"You can call it whatever you want," she said, looking at him with a smile that came from her heart.

"How about if we start with a bottle of champagne at the Algonquin?" suggested Gary.

THE END

ABOUT THE AUTHOR

Dana S. Cohen, a native of New York, holds a Bachelor's Degree in Economics from Russell Sage College, Troy, New York and a Master's in Business Administration from George Washington University, Washington, DC. Miss Cohen is a tourism professional and has travelled extensively, including the Caribbean. She has a special affinity for and unique understanding of Jamaica where she lived and worked for seven years. She currently divides her time between Miami, Florida and St. Maarten, Dutch West Indies, and is at work on her next novel.